Polquillick

Daphne Neville

ISBN: 978-1-291-89274-1

PublishNation
www.publishnation.co.uk

Also by Daphne Neville:

The Ringing Bells Inn
Sea, Sun, Cads and Scallywags
Grave Allegations
The Old Vicarage

CHAPTER ONE

1953

Stella Hargreaves hurriedly slipped from her bed, rushed across the room and opened wide the casement window. With a contented smile she stretched out her long arms and squealed with delight, for the July morning was fine. Above the twisted branches of the old apple tree at the foot of the garden, the sun shone brightly amidst a sea of vivid blue, its plainness broken only by a small gathering of fluffy, white clouds drifting idly by. Stella sighed; its manifestation reminded her strongly of the piece of Wedgwood adorning the sideboard in the dining room.

Leaving the window open, she reached for her dressing gown, put on her slippers and descended the staircase happy to be alive. In the hallway at the bottom, she peered into the large oval mirror hanging beside the coat rack, to check that no unsightly blemish had appeared on her face overnight. Satisfied that all was well, she slipped into the kitchen where her mother busily washed dishes in the sink.

"Stella," she gasped, pushing back one of the many curlers bulging beneath a red silk headscarf. "I didn't hear you come downstairs. You're up early. Would you like a cup of tea?"

Stella hugged her mother and kissed her flushed cheek.

"Yes, please, Mum. But just look at the morning. Isn't it perfect? I think I must be the luckiest girl in the whole wide world."

Mrs Hargreaves dried her hands. "It's no more than you deserve," she said, pouring tea into a bone china cup. "I've some toast under the grill, would you like a slice?"

Before Stella could answer, the back door opened and a tall, grey haired man crossed the threshold carrying a large galvanised watering can.

"Morning, Dad," beamed Stella, lifting her tea cup and saucer from the Formica top table. "Is the day really as gorgeous as it looked from my bedroom window?"

1

Dad filled the can from the cold tap overhanging the kitchen sink. "Yes, love. The wind's in the southeast so we should all enjoy a fine day of uninterrupted sunshine, just as I predicted. It'll have my tomatoes ripening quicker than we'll be able to eat them."

The telephone bell rang in the hallway.

Mary Hargreaves stopped buttering toast and groaned. "Oh dear, I do hope that's not someone ringing to say they're ill and won't be able to make the wedding."

Stella ran into the hallway and picked up the black, cumbersome receiver.

She laughed on hearing the familiar voice on the other end of the line. "Ned, I'm glad it's you, but don't you know it's really unlucky for a groom to see his bride on their wedding day?"

Ned laughed. "But I can't see you, can I?"

"Well, you know what I mean. I don't want anything to instigate even the tiniest little blip. I want everything to be just perfect."

"So do I, and that's why I'm ringing, just to make sure you and everything else is alright, and of course to say, please don't be late and give me heart failure, because I'll be a nervous wreck as it is."

"I won't be late, I promise. I'll be there on the dot, as the church clock strikes one because I love you to bits, Ned, and I can't wait to be your wife."

Six hours later, Ned Stanley stood nervously waiting at the chancel step, along with his best man, who was also his best friend, George Clarke. Both men, similar in height and build, one dark haired, the other a light shade of brown, chatted as the pews of the ancient village church filled up with family and friends of both bride and groom.

In the front pew, on the right hand side of the aisle, near to Ned and George, sat an elegantly dressed couple. They were Ned's mother Molly, and his new step-father, Major Benjamin Smith. Beside them, wearing clothes of the latest fashion, sat Ned's biological father, Michael Stanley and his young wife, Marilyn, formerly his secretary.

Ned grinned. It had been a long time since he had seen both his natural parents in such close proximity to each other, without arguing.

2

Stella's mother, dressed in pale blue, tripped up the aisle and took her seat at the front on the left-hand side of the church along with other family members. Ned caught her eye. "Is she here yet?"

Mary nodded and thought, not for the first time, how fortunate her daughter was to have met Ned. For without doubt, she was confident he would prove to be a steady and reliable husband.

The rector walked up the aisle, spoke to the two young men and then signalled to the organist to commence with the Bridal March. Ned gulped and swallowed hard, partly through nerves, partly through seeing his bride on the arm of her father as they emerged through the arched, church doorway, and partly through knowing his bachelor days would be over within the hour.

After the ceremony and the picture taking outside in front of the church in the glorious late July sunshine, the party went to a small, nearby hotel for the reception, where George, the best man, made a magnificent speech, which had the guests in fits of laughter.

Ned thought it a noble effort, and knew he was putting on a brave face having recently split up with his girlfriend, Elsie Glazebrook. Not that George was at all sorry to have put an end to their relationship. He was glad, deep down, to have escaped her clutches, her possessiveness and her endless hints of marriage. Ned grinned, recalling the final reason for the conclusion of their eighteen month courtship: Elsie had let it be known that once wed she wanted to return to her native Manchester and take up residence there. This idea had not appealed to George at all. He was a Southerner and had no desire whatsoever to move up North and be plagued by endless months of tiresome rain.

George danced with the chief bridesmaid. Ned tried to convince him they were a good match, but George would have none of it.

"I'm having a break from women," he said, loosening his tie. "I want to enjoy the summer as a carefree bachelor. I might even go away for a while to escape Elsie's endless telephone calls and letters. She still wants me back, you know. Not that I can blame her."

"Any chance of that happening?" Ned asked, knowing the answer would be in the negative.

George laughed. "Good God, no. I must admit I do miss her a bit, but not enough to patch things up and try again. Besides, she'll not be happy until she has a ring on her finger and is living a stone's throw away from her folks up North."

"Why don't you come with us to Cornwall?" asked Stella, sitting close by Ned's side.

George looked aghast. "What, on your honeymoon? Don't you think that would be taking the role of a gooseberry a bit too far?"

Stella blushed. "Well, I don't exactly mean you to be with us constantly. But we are going to be away for a whole month, and so if you were to come and join us for a while, in the village you and I have both heard such a lot about, then it would be nice for us to have your company, along with Ned's other chums already down there, that is."

Ned nodded his head vigorously. "I think that's an absolutely splendid idea, because I'd love nothing more than to introduce you both to the people I've got to know in Cornwall."

Stella and George were both familiar with Ned's first visit to Trengillion in Cornwall during February the previous year, where he had gone to convalesce after an illness, and whilst there had encountered the ghost of a young woman who had been murdered.

George frowned. "Okay, but where would I stay? I know you've a room booked in your spooky pub, but surely it's too late for me to make a reservation anywhere now, and I don't fancy sleeping in my leaky old tent."

Ned beckoned to his mother who was leaving the dance floor with her husband, Major Smith. "Mum, do you think there's a chance of the Ringing Bells Inn having any vacancies. Stella and I would love George to come with us to Cornwall and meet everyone, but of course he'll need somewhere to stay."

"What, on your honeymoon?" Molly said, panting as she tried to catch her breath, thinking she must have misheard.

"Oh, come on, Mum, don't you start. It will be a holiday as well as a honeymoon, and having George there will be no different to other people I know being around."

Molly grinned, much amused. "I suppose not. Would you like me to give Frank a ring and find out?"

"Would you? We'd be most grateful. I'd do it myself, but you're so much more familiar with the Inn's present set-up."

Molly returned shortly after with a smile on her face.

4

"Well, the Inn's full at present, but one room, your old room in fact, Ned, will be vacant on Wednesday. Frank had been saving it for his aunt arriving that day, but apparently she's let it be known she doesn't want one of the guest rooms because she doesn't like the idea of sleeping in beds strangers have slept in. So he's decided to give her his room and he'll sleep on the settee. Anyway, I've booked it for you preliminarily, because George could always stay with the major and me in our cottage until Wednesday, as we have a spare room."

"That's very kind of you, Mrs Smith, but it won't be necessary. I shall need a bit of time to sort things out before I leave, anyway, and Ned and Stella must have a few days without me around. So if I leave here on Wednesday, that would suit me fine."

"Splendid," laughed Ned, hugging his bride for having made the suggestion in the first place. "We'll all meet up on Wednesday."

Molly sat down at the table to rest. "You'll see Larry and Des during your stay because Frank just told me they're coming back to Trengillion very soon. He had a call from them yesterday, you see. Apparently, they've discovered all sorts of interesting things about their wreck from old library records and they're desperate to search over it some more. Frank said they'd tried to ring us, but of course we're not home, so they rang the Inn instead to pass on the message. The major's fascinated with their diving activities and the three have become quite good friends."

"I didn't realise that," said Ned, removing his jacket, causing confetti, trapped beneath his collar, to flutter to the floor. "Have they actually been down to see their wreck yet?"

Molly nodded. "Yes, when they visited Trengillion during the Easter holiday. Didn't I tell you?" Ned shook his head. "Oh dear, how did I manage to forget that? After all it caused a tremendous amount of excitement in the village, and a large crowd gathered on the beach to see them off the first time they went to sea. It was quite something, and fascinating to watch. You should see all their new-fangled diving equipment. They have great big bottles of air called aqua thingies or something like that, so they can breathe under water. And they have to wear ridiculous looking suits. It must be really interesting, though, swimming with the fish and seeing all the vegetation. Makes me wish I was a few years younger."

"Wow, is there treasure on the wreck do you think?" asked George, much impressed.

"I don't know. But if there is they'll not be allowed to keep it. They have to notify some officials about everything they find, but they do get a share or something like that. I'm afraid you'll have to consult the major when he comes back from the little boy's room. He knows all about the legal side of things as he's really into it. Whereas, I must admit, much of it goes over my head."

Ned tutted. It appeared marriage to the major had not made his mother any less vague.

A little later, Stella changed from her wedding gown into her going-away-outfit. She and Ned then left the wedding party for the drive to Cornwall in Ned's Morris Minor.

Molly and the major, having driven up from Cornwall the previous day, wanted a break before making the long journey home, and so had a room booked for the night at the hotel where the reception was held.

When most of the wedding guests had departed the celebrations, George, a little inebriated, rang for a taxi and returned to his flat.

After locking the door, he removed his jacket and hung it on the back of a dining chair. From the seat of an armchair he pushed old newspapers onto the floor and sat down to remove his shoes which he tossed, with the laces still done up, beneath the table. With a deep yawn he lay back his head and closed his eyes. Simultaneously, the telephone bell rang.

Cursing, he rose, crossed the room and picked up the receiver.

"Hello," he slurred.

"Good, you're home."

George groaned. "For God's sake, Elsie, what do you want now?"

"Just to know that you're home safe and sound. I trust it went off well, even though you would have enjoyed it all far more if you'd taken me with you."

"No, Elsie, I wouldn't. You and I are finished. It's all over. Done."

"Oh, George! You know you don't really mean it. I'll come round tomorrow, cook you Sunday lunch and then we can make up."

"No," he shouted. "Don't you dare come here ever again. You'd be wasting your time, anyway, because I'm going to Cornwall for a nice long, well-deserved holiday."

"But George..."

He slammed down the phone, staggered unsteadily into his kitchenette, filled the kettle with water and made a mug of sweet, black coffee which he carried into the bedroom and placed on the floor. He then removed his clothes and collapsed into his unmade bed.

"Ruddy women," he cursed, lifting his coffee mug from the floor and taking a sip.

On the top shelf of his bookcase he spotted a picture of Elsie taken the previous Christmas. He scowled and wagged his finger.

"I'm going to enjoy the summer without you, or any other female, for that matter, bossing me about. So you can go and find some other sucker to marry and take to rainy Manchester. I'm a confirmed bachelor and that's the way it's going to stay."

He stood, picked up the picture and dropped it unceremoniously into a drawer. "Take that, Elsie Welsie," he muttered, slamming shut the drawer. "I don't want to be married and I don't need a wife, cos I'm more than capable of looking after myself. So there!"

CHAPTER TWO

A little after midnight, in the light of a bright half-moon, Ned's dove grey Morris Minor pulled up in front of the Ringing Bells Inn, an eighteenth century hostelry situated in the village of Trengillion on the south coast of Cornwall. No lights shone from any of the downstairs windows which did not surprise Ned as it was long past closing time.

Ned parked his car on a wide cobbled area in front of the Inn, jumped out, quietly opened the passenger door and reached for the hand of his bride. Stepping from the car, Stella gazed up at the large, impressive, granite building, overhung from behind with tall trees. She gasped. Through a tangled curtain of leaves, swaying and rustling in the fresh breeze, peeped the silhouette of a dark, church tower.

"It's beautiful," she whispered, as Ned guided her towards a door on the side of the Inn. "Very romantic, although it feels a little creepy with the church so close."

Ned pulled the rope dangling from an old brass bell and almost instantly a tall, bearded man in his late forties opened the door.

"Ned, I didn't expect you for another hour or so yet," he said, eagerly shaking Ned's hand. He then turned his gaze to Stella. "And this must be your lovely wife."

Ned beamed. "Yes, this is Stella, the new Mrs Stanley."

"I'm very pleased to meet you, young lady," said Frank, shaking her hand warmly. "Come inside both of you. Would you like a cuppa tea?"

Stella nodded. "That would be very nice but we don't want to keep you from your bed any longer."

"That's very considerate of you but I'm used to latish nights. I'll show you your room first, and then I'll bring a tray up to you. Where's your luggage?"

Ned turned toward the door. "Still in the car, I'll go and fetch it."

While Ned went to get the suitcases, Stella cast her eyes around the large, dimly lit hallway. In the corner, beneath the coat rack cluttered with outer garments of all shapes, sizes and colours, she spotted a large, black cat. She bent to stroke the animal, inquisitively peeking at the newcomers through its half closed eyes. "Oh, dear puss, you're simply gorgeous." She turned to Frank. "What's he called?"

Frank grinned with delight. "Barley Wine. He was my late wife's pride and joy and he'll be liking your attention as he doesn't get a great deal of fussing nowadays."

Purring with unbridled contentment, Barley Wine lay still as Stella stroked his soft fur and uttered words of admiration. When Ned returned with the suitcases, the smile on his face turned to a scowl. "Humph, I see you're still here, Cat."

Neither Ned nor Barley Wine had the slightest shred of affection for one another. Hence, on hearing Ned's voice, Barley Wine rose to his feet and walked off down the passage, with, if it's possible for a cat to take on such a stance, a look of utter disdain on his small black face.

Frank took the newlyweds up to their lodgings, where much to Ned's delight, he found they were in the room his mother had occupied eighteen months before, on the front of the Inn, facing south.

"We've put you in here because Molly said you liked this room," said Frank. "What's more, your stay here isn't going to cost you a penny. See it as a wedding present from me."

Ned gasped. "But we're staying for four weeks. We can't possibly not to pay any board for that length of time. Especially at the height of the holiday season."

"You can stay for as long as you want," said Frank, obstinately. "But I'll not take a penny from you. I'm doing alright and I'll forever be in debt to your mum and the major for what they did for me after Sylvia's death. You're not just a guest, Ned, you're a friend and so is your lovely wife. Treat the place as your own and we'll say no more about it." He stepped towards the door. "I'll make that tea now, while you get settled in."

Frank left the room quietly so as not to disturb the other guests. Ned pulled Stella towards him and held her tightly. "It was in this

9

very room that Mum first mentioned your name, when she was attempting to tell my fortune. He laughed and then kissed her lovingly. "Whoever would have thought the old girl could have got it so right."

Ned woke the next morning to hear two seagulls screeching outside. He kissed Stella's sleeping head, slipped silently out of bed, crossed to the window and pulled back the lightweight floral curtains. Above, the sun shone brightly from a cloudless sky, the reflection of its rays dancing on the sea causing it to sparkle like jewels on a blue satin cloth. He opened the window, took in a deep breath and looked down below, where his Morris Minor was parked outside the Gents, and Frank was busy sweeping litter from the cobbles.

Ned returned to the bed and looked at his watch lying on top of the bedside table.

"Good grief," he gasped, on seeing the time. "Wake up, Stella. It's half past nine, we'll have missed breakfast."

Stella opened her eyes and yawned. "Who cares? Come here and give me a cuddle."

At half past ten, after the newly-weds had both taken a bath, they went downstairs hopeful of finding someone around. The dining room, however, was empty and laid up for the evening meal, and no-one was present in the kitchen.

"Shall I make us a pot of tea?" Stella asked. "Your Frank did tell us to make ourselves at home."

"Okay, you make the tea and I'll go and see if there's anyone in either of the bars."

Ned walked off down the passage and into the public bar, but no-one was there. He shuddered. The bar seemed so different when empty. So quiet, almost eerie. He glanced around and with lightness of foot, walked slowly across the polished flagstone floor. The sun was shining brightly through the spotlessly clean windows and the strong, evocative smell of beer, stale smoke and tobacco hung in the air. He looked through the open double doors and into the snug bar. The large inglenook fireplace stood empty with a decorative screen concealing the dark area in which logs crackled and hissed noisily in the winter. Above, ticked the old clock, its pendulum still swinging to and fro in its wooden case cracked through the incessant heat of many years. On the ceiling, rows of gleaming plates hung from the crooked beams, and on the sill behind the window seat, stood a bowl of dried, pink and blue hydrangeas.

Ned crossed to the window seat and sat down. The heat from the sun rapidly warmed the back of his head, and thoughts, dominated by past events, quickly flooded into his mind. He smiled. So many memories. Most happy, but some sad.

He jumped. His trip down memory lane was interrupted by the sound of approaching footsteps. Ned stood, left the snug and walked back into the public bar just as Frank emerged from the cellar carrying a crate containing bottles of stout.

"Ah, Ned, I see you're up. I expect you're hungry, because Rose said you'd not been down for breakfast."

Ned frowned. "Rose. What, Rose Briers? Is she working here?"

Frank nodded. "Yes, the poor girl's having a job to make ends meet. She's had a rough time since Reg died, you know."

Feeling utterly ashamed, Ned clumsily sat down. He had been so wrapped up in his own happiness, he had completely forgotten that Reg Briers, the village school's headmaster, had been killed during the winter when a tree had fallen onto his car during a storm.

Stella called from the passage. "Ned, where are you?"

Ned walked with Frank towards the kitchen where they found Stella laying out cups and saucers.

"Tea's made," she said. "Would you like a cup too, Frank?"

Frank nodded and joined them around the table after first showing them around the kitchen cupboards and telling them to help themselves to whatever took their fancy.

"What's happening at the school?" Ned asked, his mind still occupied with the death of Reg Briers. "Has Rose had to leave The School House?"

Frank stirred two spoonsful of sugar into his tea. "She's there for the time being, but the authorities want her out by Christmas. They hope to have a new headmaster start then. Meanwhile, a temporary head comes in each day from Helston."

Ned's face was pale. "Poor Rose. How is she coping? She sounded alright in the letter she sent to me, in response to the sympathy card and letter I sent to her, but that was months ago."

Frank sighed. "She has good days and bad days, but she is slowly coming to terms with Reg's death. I think she likes working here, because, well, she and I have something in common."

Stella and Ned helped themselves to breakfast when Frank left the kitchen, and when finished they washed the dirty dishes.

"What would you like to do today, Mrs Stanley?" Ned asked, slipping his arm around Stella's slender waist as she hung the tea towel on the oven door.

She replied without hesitation. "Sit on the beach and be thoroughly lazy. I still feel tired after all the wedding preparations and the long drive down here, and I simply haven't the energy to do anything other than be idle."

"Good, that would suit me fine too."

Hand in hand the two newly-weds walked down to the beach. Ned was surprised by the number of people taking advantage of the sunny weather, for he had only before ever visited the beach in the winter when often it was often deserted. And although he had visited Cornwall briefly for the marriage of his mother to the major the previous summer, it had been during term time, hence his stay was for just one night and he did not set foot on the beach at all.

"Where shall we sit?" Stella asked, surveying the half-clad bodies of varying shapes and sizes, sprawled across the patches of sand and shingle.

Ned pointed to a formation of rocks creating a small island. "Over there. I used to consider that would be a very good spot for sunbathing when I was here before, but of course I never bothered to try it out because it was winter. We'll have to watch out when the tide comes in though, or we'll get cut off and we're neither of us exactly dressed for swimming, are we? Not that I can swim, anyway."

They climbed onto the rocks where Stella lay back and closed her eyes. Ned chose to remain sitting as he wanted to watch the activities taking place all around them.

Several people were in the sea, swimming or splashing around; others paddled close to the shore: middle aged men with trousers rolled up to their knees and with white knotted handkerchiefs covering their balding heads. Toddlers clutched the hands of their parents as small waves tumbled over their tiny feet. Other children were building sandcastles, looking for miniature crabs in rock pools, or playing catch with a brightly coloured ball.

From rocks which jutted out to sea, an elderly man dived into the splashing waves. As he came up for air, Ned shuddered. Such antics alarmed him. He was unable to swim and had a morbid fear of drowning.

Above the squeals and laughter of holiday makers, came the sound of an engine in the distance. Ned shielded his eyes from the sun with his hand and watched as a small fishing boat emerged around the side of the tall cliffs. As it neared the cove, he realised it was Percy and Peter, two young fishermen he had befriended during his first visit. Ned stood up and waved, glad to see familiar faces. They waved back as the boat slowed to a halt on reaching the water's edge.

Ned was inquisitive and keen to learn of their catch, but Stella was sleeping soundly and he thought it unwise to wake her. For he could not see that she would be very enthusiastic about looking into a boat of smelly fish, crabs or whatever Percy and Peter had caught. Instead he watched from the rocks as the small vessel was expertly winched up the sloping beach.

When Stella finally woke, the water was splashing round the bottom of the rocks, hence the walk towards shore required a wade through the rising waters. Ned neatly rolled up his trouser legs and both removed their footwear. Stella then clutched her full skirt and petticoats tightly together, and they paddled towards dry land, giggling like the children they taught.

Back at the Inn they washed and changed for dinner. Ned was looking forward to seeing the other guests, although he knew no-one would be familiar to him. He was also very eager to see Rose again.

The newly-weds, first to enter the dining room, quickly seated themselves at the table in the window, minutes before the other guests started to arrive. Firstly, an elderly couple in their mid to late seventies, followed by a family, parents with their two sons of junior school age. A middle aged blonde woman appeared next with her teenage daughter, and finally, another young couple.

As the last couple took their seats, Betty appeared from the kitchen with bowls of soup for the first table. Ned felt a huge pang of disappointment. He bore no grudge against Betty, but had been looking forward to seeing Rose. Betty, however, was delighted to see Ned and told him so when she put down his soup.

"It's always really, really nice to see old faces at this time of year," she said, eyes sparkling. "Especially someone like you, Ned, who we all got to know so well."

Ned was touched. "Thank you, Betty, it's really good to be back amongst old friends. May I introduce you to Stella, my wife?" His words were said with pride. "And Stella, this is Betty, you'll remember me telling you about the two girls at the Inn."

Stella smiled sweetly. "Are you the one with twin boys?"

Betty giggled. "Good heavens, no, that's Gertie. I'm not married yet."

"How is Gertie?" Ned asked, as he unfolded his serviette. "Still as chatty as usual?"

"She's fine, and yes, she still has plenty to say for herself, although she's often very tired and so has less bounce. The twins are simply gorgeous, but she's finding them a bit of a handful and she isn't too keen on the sleepless nights. Her mum pops in most days to help, though, so that she can get forty winks and a bit of peace."

"Are they identical?" Stella asked.

Betty wrinkled her nose. "It's a job to say. I think they are, but Gertie says it's easy to tell them apart. But then she usually has them dressed the same, so that's enough to confuse me."

"And are you still working in the factory?" Ned asked.

She shook her head. "No, I'm training to be a hairdresser now and I love it. So if you want your hair done while you're here, you know where to come."

"Jolly good, we'll bear that in mind."

"I'd better go now and let you tuck into your soup or it will be cold. I'll see you later."

"Thanks, Betty. Who does the cooking, by the way? Is it Flo?"

"No," said Betty, retreating across the dining room. "It's Dorothy Treloar."

Ned was dumbfounded. "What! Albert's non-drinking sister?"

"That's right. Only she does have a drink now and again as you'll no doubt find out."

Ned and Stella went into the bar after dinner and Frank greeted them warmly. "When are Molly and the major due back?" he asked, pouring a drink for Stella.

Ned looked at his watch. "Tonight sometime. In fact they might even be back now."

As they spoke, the door of the Inn opened and Molly and the major walked in.

Frank laughed. "Talk of the devil and he's bound to appear."

Molly hugged the newly-weds. "How do you like Cornwall, Stella?"

"I like it very much, although I've seen little other than the beach, where I slept for most of the day, I'm ashamed to say."

Molly reached for a bar stool. "You'll love it. Oh, dear, I must sit down, my feet are killing me."

Ned frowned. "But you've been sitting down all day in the car. How can you possibly have tired feet?"

"Easy, it's from dancing yesterday and in new shoes too. I'll never learn."

She turned to Frank. "So, you've an aunt coming to stay. I hope she's not going to put you about too much. I mean, it's a bit inconsiderate of her to throw you out of your own bed and make you sleep on the settee."

Frank laughed. "Auntie Mabel's very house-proud and ridiculously punctilious when it comes to cleaning. I can see where she's coming from when she says she doesn't want to sleep in a bed where strangers have slept, but the truth is, the guest rooms are a damn sight cleaner than my room. Joyce is very thorough at her job, I'll give her that. I suppose I really ought to ask her to give my room a bit of a clean, but I don't really like to ask. She has enough on her plate this time of the year with doing Bed and Breakfast at her own place, and if the truth be known, I don't really want her to see how messy my bedroom is, anyway."

Molly shook her head. "I'll give it a thorough clean. When is she coming?"

"Wednesday, the same day as Ned's friend."

"Of course. Right, I'll be round in the morning to put you straight."

"Thanks, Molly. You're a good woman. I'll pay you of course."

"You'll do no such thing," she retorted, as the major handed her a gin. "Thanks, Ben. Oh, let's go into the snug and sit down where the seats are nice and comfortable."

As they walked towards the double doors, Dorothy Treloar walked behind the bar and joined Frank. Ned felt a pang of resentment. He did not like to see anyone in Sylvia's place.

"Dorothy seems to be taking over," he hissed. "I hear she's the cook now."

Molly removed her jacket and sat down on the padded window seat. "Ned, don't be so critical. Dot has been a great help to Frank, both mentally and emotionally. You'll find her very amicable when you get to know her. She's a good hard working woman and her cooking is quite superb. I only hope this aunt of Frank's doesn't come and upset her and everyone else when she arrives, as she sounds a bit of a harridan to me."

Ned was not convinced Dorothy was someone whose company he could ever enjoy, even though he had to admit the dinner had been delicious. In reality his bone of contention really was with her brother Albert. Ned had never got to like him, despite the fact Albert had never given Ned reason to justify his animosity.

"By the way, who is Joyce?" Ned asked.

"Joyce?" repeated Molly.

"Yes. Frank referred to a Joyce being the cleaner."

Molly kicked off her shoes beneath the table. "Oh, that Joyce. You know her, Harry Richardson the builder's wife. She's mad about brass and loves polishing and cleaning it. She thinks she's in paradise working here. Still, it takes all sorts I suppose, and I'm baffled as I loathe cleaning brass."

"I hear Rose works here too," said Ned. "But she wasn't on duty tonight."

"No, Sunday is her night off, and Tuesdays too, I think. Poor Rose, I can't believe I ever disliked her. She's a lovely girl now."

"Why was that?" Stella asked, sipping her drink.

"It was the way she used to dress and behave, which with hindsight, I realise was a cry for help. Poor girl, she seems lost without Reg."

"Does she still have Freak?" Ned asked.

Molly nodded. "Oh, yes, but even he doesn't seem so weird now. In fact he's quite a nice little dog."

The major asked Stella about her family and what her father did during the War.

"He was in the Navy, but was fortunate inasmuch as did not see conflict as he worked ashore in the met office."

"Your friend George seems a nice young man," said Molly, not wanting the major to get onto the subject of war and bore Stella.

Ned laughed. "Nice is such a non-descript word, Mother. So mediocre. George is much, much more than just plain nice."

Molly smiled. Ned had taken on the pompous stance of his father again. She gritted her teeth, recalling how she had had to smile sweetly at his new wife, formerly his secretary, at the wedding.

"Hussy," she whispered beneath her breath.

"Pardon, Moll," said the major, only part hearing her mutterings.

"Nothing, dear," she sighed, patting his hand and feeling her cheeks flush. "Nothing."

Several drinks later, Ned began to yawn. "I think I'm ready to turn in," he said, with a twinkle in his eye. "Then perhaps we might even be down in time for breakfast tomorrow."

Stella giggled.

"Off you go," said Molly. "We must be getting back home too, as we've not unpacked the car yet."

Inside their room, Stella drew the curtains across the window and kicked off her shoes beneath the bed.

"Sorry if you were bored tonight, Mrs Stanley," said Ned, hanging his jacket on the back of the chair. I know Mother goes on a bit."

"I wasn't bored one bit, Ned. It was nice to see a couple of familiar faces, even if I did only meet them for the first on Friday night. And how could I ever be bored when you are close by holding my hand?"

"I do love you, Mrs. Stanley," he whispered into her ear.

"And I love you too."

"Promise?"

"Promise."

"Then I'm the luckiest chap in the whole wide world."

CHAPTER THREE

On Wednesday afternoon, George arrived at the Inn by taxi from the branch line railway station in Helston. It had been his intention to drive down to Cornwall, but the previous day his car had made unexplainable noises, thus causing him to decide a train journey might be the more reliable option.

George stepped from the taxi, paid the driver and walked into the bar just as Frank was about to lock the front door.

"Sorry son," said Frank, jingling a bunch of keys. "But I was just about to close."

George grinned. "That's alright, I'm not thirsty anyway, but I believe you have a room for me."

Frank took a deep breath. "Oh, sorry, you must be Mr Clarke. Young Ned's friend."

"Best friend. But please don't call me Mr Clarke, it reminds me of being in the classroom and I'm on holiday now. My name is George."

Frank held out his hand. "Pleased to meet you, George. Are you a teacher, then, like Ned?"

"Yes, that's how we got to know each other. We teach at the same school and so does Stella, Ned's wife."

"Blimey, three teachers at the Inn, I'd best watch my Ps and Qs. I don't want you thinking me a dunce."

George slipped back outside to where he had put down his suitcase by the front door, he then followed Frank upstairs to his room on the back of the Inn.

"Dinner's at seven o'clock Mr Cl...Cl... George, and I hope you'll enjoy your stay here."

"I'm sure I will," George said, absent-mindedly throwing his suitcase onto the bed and casting his eyes around the room. I don't suppose you've any idea where Ned and Stella might be, have you?"

Frank shook his head. "Sorry, but they could be just about anywhere. Gone for a walk. Gone to see Molly and the major, or to visit anyone for that matter. Or they could quite simply be sun-bathing on the beach."

"Hmm, I think I'll go for your last suggestion, and then if they're nowhere to be seen, I can at least sunbathe alone and my venture into the unknown won't be a complete wild goose chase."

"Well, don't you overdo it. The sun's very hot this time of year and we get lots of folks looking more like cooked lobsters than cooked lobsters."

George changed into his bathing trunks, pulled a pair of grey flannel trousers over the top and slipped on a short sleeved shirt and sunglasses. From his suitcase he took out a towel, threw it over his shoulder and wandered down to the beach.

Outside the winch house, he removed his sunglasses and cast his eyes over the long stretch of sand and shingle. When finally convinced Ned and Stella were nowhere to be seen, he spread out his towel, removed his trousers and shirt, sat down and cast a critical eye over the young females enjoying the glorious spell of weather. He sighed deeply. Several of them were quite attractive, one or two very pretty, but none had as perfect a figure as Elsie.

"Still, it doesn't matter," said George to himself, replacing his sunglasses. "I shall be only too glad to have a few weeks without a girl on my arm. It'll be a lot cheaper too."

He laid down in the sun and looked up at the bright blue sky where a flock of seagulls were in flight overhead. He squinted and watched as they squawked off to the right and flew up high above the cliff tops, bringing the spectacle of a large prestigious house into his sight.

He whistled, sat up and removed his sunglasses again. "Just look at that. Now, if that happens to belong to some rich beauty, I might have to review my thoughts about a women-free holiday." He laid back down, closed his eyes, and after fantasising about the house's possible owner, took a nap.

Just before seven o'clock, George heard a knock on his bedroom door and outside in the passage found Ned and Stella. The three friends greeted and hugged each other as though months, not days, had passed since they had last met. Ned told George they were in the room across the corridor, directly opposite.

19

Rose was waitress for the evening meal. She greeted George warmly as he took his seat at the same table as Ned and Stella. His response was to kiss her hand and wink lasciviously, causing her to blush.

Ned scolded him as Rose returned to the kitchen.

"Don't you dare do anything to cause that poor girl any more heartache," he hissed. "She lost her husband just eight months ago and I'll not allow you or anyone else for that matter, to hurt her in any way."

"Steady on, Ned," George spluttered. "I'm not on the brink of seducing her. Don't over react."

"Sorry," said Ned. "But Stella and I had a long chat with her on Monday night and deep down she's really lonely and unhappy. I liked Reg Briers very much and I'll do anything to protect his poor widow."

"Alright, I promise I'll not harm her in any way, mentally or physically. In fact whilst I'm here I shall be a real goody two shoes."

Stella laughed. "Don't be ridiculous, George. We love you the way you are, so don't even think about changing, one jot."

After dinner they sat outside in front of the Inn with a drink. And as they mutually extolled the charms of Cornwall, a car pulled up onto the cobbled area, its driver, a man whom George instantly recognised as the taxi driver who had driven him from the station to the Inn earlier in the day. After turning off the engine, the driver jumped out and swiftly opened the back door of the car. From inside emerged a tall, prim woman in her mid to late seventies. She did not speak, but brushed past with an air of superiority. The taxi driver followed her into the Inn, laden with luggage. Minutes later he returned to his car and drove off.

"Auntie Mabel?" muttered Stella, a note of question in her voice.

Ned nodded. "I would imagine so. She doesn't look as though she'll be the life and soul of the party, does she?"

"Is that the old dear for whom my room was not good enough?" George asked.

"Not so much the room, it was more about the bed, and who can blame her with the likes of you sleeping in it," laughed Ned.

"Ha ha," retorted George. "There's nothing wrong with my personal hygiene. I wonder if she's an old maid or if she's done her poor husband a favour by coming here alone and giving him a few days peace?"

"Neither," said Ned. "She's a widow and she's not here for a few days, either. I think it's for a few weeks. Why, has she taken your fancy?"

"The Cornish air has done nothing to improve your waggish tendencies, has it, Ned?" chortled George. "In fact if anything it's turned you into a right nitwit."

Stella looked heavenwards. "Stop it you two, you're spoiling the peace and quiet of this beautiful evening with your nonsense. And as regards Auntie Mabel, I'm sure she's a perfectly charming lady: after all, she is related to Frank, and a nicer man I could not wish to meet."

"Well, actually she's not a blood relation, she's an in-law. Which reminds me, Frank said on no account should anyone ask her age as she's a bit odd when that subject arises. I must warm Mum."

Stella frowned. "But Frank must know her age, surely."

"Apparently not, and so I can only assume if she doesn't want anyone to know, she's a lot older than she looks."

That night, George had a strange dream. He dreamt he heard a woman's voice calling to him, but for some reason, she referred to him as Harry.

On waking the next morning, he recalled the occurrence and laughed.

"I knew I shouldn't have eaten all that pie for dinner last night. Pastry does not agree with me."

He told Ned and Stella of his dream during breakfast.

Ned laughed. "It was probably that girl on the table in the alcove calling to you from the next room. I noticed last night she couldn't keep her eyes off you."

"What!" spluttered George. "I think you'll find it was you she was giving the once-over."

Stella's eyebrows rose. "She'd better not be or she'll have me to contend with."

Rose found the two young men laughing like unruly children when she brought in the pot of tea. Stella cast a withering look.

"Sorry, Rose. Please, ignore these two, they're each having a juvenile moment."

"George wants to know the name of the girl on the table over there," chuckled Ned, pointing to the table in the alcove. "She's rather taken his fancy."

Rose looked surprised. "Her name is Milly. That's what her mother calls her, anyway."

"Silly Milly," laughed Ned.

"Will you two behave," snapped Stella. "She'll hear you and you sound as though you're drunk."

Ned saw a look in her eyes which he had never before encountered.

"Sorry," he said, sucking his cheeks in an attempt to suppress the desire to laugh further. "It's George's fault. He brings out the worst in me."

"Yes," said Stella, haughtily. "I had noticed."

That evening, Frank threw a surprise party for Ned and Stella. He knew the locals were all keen to see Ned again and meet his new wife, and so he and Molly had put their heads together and invited everyone along. Frank also hoped the party might help welcome his aunt to Trengillion and give her a chance to seek someone with whom she might have something in common. The Ringing Bells Inn, therefore, was packed with inquisitive villagers, holiday makers and residents of the Inn.

Stella proved a huge success with the locals. She was hugged, kissed and had her hand shaken so much she felt quite battered.

"Did you get to see anything of the Coronation?" asked May Dickens. "I've seen lots pictures of the Queen and she looked so lovely. I would dearly loved to have seen her in the flesh."

Ned nodded. "Yes, we were out there amongst the crowds waving our flags in the rain and I must admit we had a really good day because there was a smashing party atmosphere. Shame the weather couldn't have been a bit kinder, though, but then that's a British summer for you. Very unreliable, even for the highest in the land."

Sid Reynolds and his new wife, Meg, daughter of the village vicar, shook hands with Ned and Stella and wished them well.

"Are you still caretaker at the school?" Ned asked Sid.

He shook his head. "No, I only took that job to be near Meg, but now we're married, it's no longer necessary and it didn't give me enough hours, anyway, so I always had to do odd jobs to make ends meet. I've a new job now, working on the local newspaper. It's quite interesting and I really enjoy it."

"Good for you," said Ned. "And are you still teaching at the school, Meg?"

"Yes, but I'm not too keen on the temporary headmaster. He seems very gruff and old-fashioned compared with good hearted Reg. I'll be glad when we get a new headmaster and things settle down again."

"But he may be worse than your temp," laughed Stella.

"Oh God, I hope not. I'm praying for someone relatively young, with lots of ideas who doesn't teach like a robot."

Ned laughed. "But why haven't the authorities found you a permanent headmaster before now? It's eight months since Reg died."

"I know, it's dragging on far too long, I think the temp we have was meant to be the real thing, a touch of nepotism by his brother who sent him to try out the school and see what he thought. I say that, because after he'd been here a while he decided he didn't like the remoteness of the area and so announced he'd only continue until they found someone else."

"I see. So who's caretaker now, anyone I know?"

"Doris Jones," said Sid. "Your mother's next door neighbour."

"What, Jane's Aunt Doris? Mother never told me that. I shall have to have words with her: she's not keeping me properly informed with local news, as there are lots of instances she has failed to acquaint me with."

"Did she tell you about Gertie and Percy's twins?" asked Meg.

"Oh yes. Mum's soppy when it comes to babies, she can't wait to be a grandmother."

As he spoke the door of the Inn opened and Gertie and Percy walked in.

Gertie made a beeline for Ned, flung her arms around his neck and gave him a big kiss on the mouth. "Congratulations. You're just as lovely as ever."

"Congratulations to you too," said Ned, feeling flustered. "On the birth of your twins, that is."

Gertie turned to Stella. "You must be Ned's wife. Gosh, aren't you slim. I've put on tons of weight since I first became pregnant, but then I was hardly a beanpole to start with."

"I'm sure you'll soon lose the excess pounds," said Stella, sympathetically. "Running around after children is very energetic work, as my older sister found out recently. And with two children to care for you should have no problem at all."

"Do you think so?" beamed Gertie, warming to Ned's wife.

Percy put his arm around her waist and gave her a squeeze. "I like you being chubby, you're cuddlier."

Gertie laughed and elbowed him in the ribs. It was obvious they were both very happy together.

George found the youngsters chatting and mockingly scolded Ned and Stella for abandoning him. "I've just been accosted by Silly Milly and her pushy mother. Madge, the mother, made it quite plain to me that they are both here in search of a husband. Apparently, Madge's old man walked out on her years ago and they're both man-hunting."

"So, which one is after you?" asked Stella.

"I don't know. I think they're offering me a choice. But you must remember, I said that I wanted to get away from women, especially ones with marriage in mind. That's the whole purpose of my break."

"Why do you want to get away from women?" asked Gertie, fascinated by Ned's extremely handsome friend.

"Elsie Glazebrook," growled George. "I must go to the Gents." And he was gone.

"Who's Elsie Glazebrook?" asked Meg.

"His girlfriend of eighteen months. They recently split up on George's instigation. He was fed up with her talking about marriage and her longings to return to her native Manchester. George hates the idea of living up there."

"Really. But what's wrong with Manchester?" Gertie asked.

"George reckons it's always raining there," said Ned. "But really he just feels he's not ready for marriage. Not to Elsie, anyway. Personally, I think it's time he settled down or he'll end up a crusty old bachelor. He's thirty three now so hardly in the first flush of youth."

"Well, I think Elsie must have been mad to have driven him away, he's absolutely gorgeous."

"Humph, we'll have less of that, Mrs Collins," said Percy.

"Only teasing," she giggled, slipping her arm through his. "I wouldn't swap you for all the tea in China."

Auntie Mabel, unseen by the residents of the Inn since her arrival the previous day, as she chose to eat her meals in the privacy of Frank's living room, did not put in an appearance until after nine o'clock. Therefore, her presence went unnoticed by most as she crept into the bar and Frank poured her a bitter lemon.

She was dressed in blue with a matching comb in her shock of snowy white hair. Her face was lightly made up. It was not possible to see her eyes behind the ornate spectacles she wore. And although the impression she first exuded had been one of a person haughty and proud, when seen hidden amongst the crowd, she seemed demure and shy.

Molly, by her sheer nature, was the first to welcome the newcomer to the Inn. "Have you been here before?" she asked, after introducing herself.

"Yes, m'duck, but not since the War. My dear late husband, Bert, and I came down several summers running during Frank's early years here. We both liked the countryside, you see, and we enjoyed many walks and rambles together. Seeing this Inn again has brought back lots memories. I don't have many family members of my generation left now. Frank's mother, Edith, was my late husband's sister and she died a few years back. And my only brother, Fred, was killed during the First World War."

"And did you have no sisters?" asked Molly, warming to Mabel's character.

"None that lived to grow up. Infant mortality was still common in those days. Thank God things are better now! And Bert and I never had any children of our own, although we did adopt a couple of nippers, but of course they're grown up now."

"And do you still enjoy walking?" Molly asked, herself a keen walker.

"Oh yes, and that's how I intend to spend much of this little break, walking and reading. I'll not be doing any sunbathing, though. I don't much care for the beach. Sand in everything drives me mad."

"Well, if ever you want company for one of your walks just give me a shout and I'll join you. I live at Rose Cottage, just a stone's throw away and I love a good walk too. I find it perfect for relieving stress and tension."

Mabel smiled. "Thanks, m'duck. I'll bear that in mind."

"Would you like a drink?" asked the major, seeing her glass almost empty.

"Thank you. Just a bitter lemon, please. I'm afraid I'm not a drinker. I have the occasional drop of brandy if I'm feeling a bit under the weather, but apart from that it's just a glass of sherry on Christmas Day. In fact, to tell you the truth I feel most uncomfortable in a pub, even drinking bitter lemon. I don't think it's a place for women, and certainly not one without a man."

Molly gave a little laugh and tried to conceal her brimful glass of gin behind her handbag as she gestured towards the people gathered in the bar.

"Come on, Mabel, I'll introduce you to some of the locals. They're a nice bunch and you may even remember one or two from your previous visits."

"That's very kind of you, m' duck. I'd like that."

As they walked towards the snug, Mabel asked. "Are Godfrey and Amy Johns still living here? Bert and I used to be quite good friends with them but we lost touch during the War. Godfrey was a butcher, he had a shop in town but used to live here in the village. In Amy's last letter she said he was about to retire."

"Godfrey's still here. He lives in a bungalow on the edge of the village which he had built just before war broke out, but sadly he's a widower now. I never knew his wife, she died before I came down here, and I've only ever seen Godfrey once, in the post office I think it was. I'm told he's become a bit of a recluse since the death of his wife."

In all it was a wonderful evening, although tame in comparison with Flo's sixtieth birthday during the winter months the previous year. Being summertime, people had commitments and things they needed, and wanted to do, therefore the evening came to an end at a reasonable time with everyone leaving the Inn relatively sober, except for Albert Treloar, who still drank to excess.

George went to his room feeling content. Trengillion seemed a nice place; the people were friendly and he could see why Ned had extolled its virtues with such enthusiasm. Before going to bed, he sat down in the chair beside the grate, lit a cigarette and reminisced over the day's events.

On the wall hung a picture of an old fisherman. George eyed it with suspicion, feeling the old man could read his thoughts.

"Ridiculous!" he tutted, rising from the chair. "I'm not going to let you bewitch me, old timer, nor am I going to get involved with spooks and people singing in the middle of the night, like Ned did. I'm here for relaxation and pleasure and nothing's going to get in the way of that."

CHAPTER FOUR

George fell asleep as soon as his head hit the pillow and again he dreamt he heard the voice of a woman. This time, however, he could see her also. She was seated in a small boat out at sea which George appeared to be rowing.

She was young and wore a pale green, full length, cotton, gingham dress; a white knitted shawl was draped around her slender shoulders. Her head was part-covered by a green, lightweight bonnet, beneath which flowed long black curls. Around her fingers she repeatedly twisted a lock of hair in a nervous manner, as though to hide her naive shyness, evident each time she threw back her head and laughed at his comical antics.

George woke for no apparent reason, sat up in bed, rubbed his eyes and wondered why he had dreamed of someone from another era. He tried to recollect by what name she had called him. As he punched up his pillows and laid back his head, he remembered the last words she had spoken..."Stop acting the fool, Harry Timmins, or you'll tip us both out."

George sat bolt upright, now fully awake. He climbed out of bed, opened the window and leaned outside. To the east, the sun was rising over the old mine at Penwynton. George took in a deep breath of the clean morning air and sighed. "Who the devil," he muttered, "is Harry Timmins?"

First down to breakfast, George sat alone in the dining room drumming his fingers on the crisp, white table cloth, patiently waiting for Ned and Stella, who finally arrived, ten minutes later, close on the heels of Madge and Milly.

"Have you ever heard of a Harry Timmins?" he asked, before his friends had time even to take their seats.

"Harry Timmins," mused Ned. "I know of a Harry who I used to think was a hit man, but in reality he's a builder. I've no idea whether or not he's a Timmins, though."

"Does he look like me?" blurted George, anxiously.

"What! No of course not. He's short, stout, extremely muscular and must be a good twenty years your senior. And I've just remembered he's a Richardson, anyway. But why on earth do you ask such a silly question?"

"I had a peculiar dream last night. I dreamt I was in a boat with this gorgeous gel who was obviously crazy about me. I've never clapped eyes on her before in my life and there's not much chance of me ever doing so either, as she was dressed in Victorian clothes. It must have been her calling me the previous night as well, but she didn't just call me Harry this time. She called me Harry Timmins."

Stella laughed. "Ugh, how odd. Odd that she should call you by another name, that is."

"Perhaps it's something to do with your room," said Ned, flippantly, lighting a cigarette. "After all, strange things happened to me when I slept in there."

George laughed. "Oh no, she wasn't a ghost if that's what you're implying. I'm not having any of that nonsense. Thank goodness Elsie's not around. She wouldn't be very happy about me taking pretty young women out in boats so soon after our parting, even if it was only a dream. She always got very jealous whenever I spoke to any female under the age of forty, married or single."

"Elsie would have competition for your attention if she was here," grinned Ned. "Silly Milly has her eyes fixed on you again."

"Better her than Madge, I suppose," said George, carelessly. "But I really can't help it if every woman here thinks I'm dashingly handsome."

"Big Head," said Stella.

Rose arrived with their pot of tea. She seemed very subdued and placed the pot on the table without speaking.

"What's wrong, Rose?" Ned asked. "There isn't a sparkle in your eyes this morning."

She sighed deeply. "Nothing, really it's nothing."

"Rose," chided Ned. "You can't fool me. Something's wrong. What is it?"

"I had a letter this morning giving me notice to quit The School House by Christmas. I knew I had to go by then, anyway. But seeing it in writing makes it so official and heartless. I don't know what to

29

do or where to go. My family want me to return to Blackpool, but I don't know. I think I've been away too long now to take up where I left off. And I know I used to say dreadful things about Trengillion but really I like it here and it's where Reg is buried."

Ned reached out and squeezed her hand. "Something will turn up, Rose. Meanwhile, why don't you join us when you finish work tonight and we'll all have a chat and a drink together?"

She smiled. "Thank you. Thank you, I should like that very much indeed."

In the afternoon, Ned, Stella and George went to Rose Cottage to see Molly and the major. Ned told George he did not have to go unless he really wanted to, but he insisted on tagging along.

"Your mum and I were talking about cake at the wedding and she told me she makes a very good coffee cake which just happens to be my favourite. So I shall join you, if that's alright, just on the off-chance she has made one especially for me."

"Of course we don't mind," said Stella. "You're our favourite goosegog."

George didn't quite know how to take Stella's remark, but came to the conclusion it was a compliment.

They found Molly and the major sitting in deckchairs on their front lawn. Ned was surprised by the transformation since he had last seen it briefly a year before.

"You have been busy," he said, eying the weed-less borders ablaze with colour. "It's quite beautiful."

"Well, I have Doris next door and she's a keen gardener. She gave me lots of cuttings and we sowed dozens of seeds in her greenhouse as soon as there was the first hint of spring. Take a sniff at the sweet peas, Ned, they're absolutely gorgeous. I can smell them from the bedroom window in the evening."

Ned was not sure which of the flowers were the sweet peas but followed in the direction of Molly's hand.

"I'll pick you a bunch before you go, to put in your room."

The major rose, offered his chair to Stella and insisted he would make a pot of tea to enable Molly to chat to the guests.

"You have the major well trained, I see," smiled Ned. "I know lots of men who are quite incapable of making tea."

Molly sighed. "I think you'll find in most cases men think it's beneath them to be domesticated. They consider cleaning and so forth to be women's work. The major doesn't do a great deal around the house but he does make the occasional pot of tea and he looks after all the utility bills and so forth. He also cuts the grass and he's beginning to take an interest in the garden, especially the vegetable patch out the back. He does his fair share and is very generous, so I'm not complaining."

On Molly's instruction, Ned fetched a rug from the garden shed, and as he and George sat down on it, the major appeared from the house carrying a full tea tray. George's eyes lit up when he saw a coffee cake.

"I made this for you, George," Molly beamed, rising to cut it into slices. "I remembered our little conversation at the wedding, you see, and guessed you'd be along sometime."

"Mum," said Ned, when all were seated again. "Do you know of a Harry Timmins?"

Molly shook her head. "No, not that I recall. Do you Ben? She asked the major. "The name means nothing to me. The only Harry I know is Harry Richardson, the builder."

"Same here," grunted the major. "Should we know of him?"

"Well, no, not really. It's just that George dreamed of a young woman last night and in the dream she called him Harry Timmins."

The major laughed.

"Really," said Molly. "How spooky."

"Spooky!" said Ned. "That's not the sort of word I'd expect to come from the mouth of a medium-cum-fortune teller."

"Well, it does seem a little odd to dream you're someone else. But often in dreams you get your wires crossed, so it's possible that may be the case with you, George."

"But why Harry Timmins, I wonder?" asked George. "Where did I get that name from?"

"You probably heard that name mentioned by someone yesterday and it stuck in your subconscious without you realising," said the major. "I shouldn't let it bother you, George. Dreams seldom make sense, anyway."

"What did you think of Auntie Mabel?" asked Ned, changing the subject. "I saw you talking to her last night."

31

"She's very nice," replied Molly. "I liked her and I shall do my best to make sure she has an enjoyable stay. Although it annoys me she's so secretive about her age. May Dickens and I tried hard to get her to give us a clue, but she was wise to all our devious questions, so now we're more determined than ever to find out the truth."

"I wonder why some women are so daft about keeping their age a secret?" said George.

Molly agreed. "So do I. God only knows what they think it achieves. I'll be fifty next birthday and don't care who knows it."

Stella laughed. "I'd like to know why Auntie Mabel calls everyone m'duck? I heard her say it to several people."

Molly smiled. "It's a term of endearment in some areas of the Midlands. She's from Kettering in Northamptonshire where to say m'duck is quite common. Much like the Cornish say my 'ansome, or what to me is even more peculiar, my bird."

"Either that or it's easier than trying to remember people's names," added the major. "So many these days have adopted the annoying habit of calling men mate. It really gets my goat."

Stella, having finished her cake, changed the subject again. "May I have a look around your cottage, please? It looks very quaint from the outside."

Molly stood up. "Of course, dear, I'll show you around. Are you coming too, Ned, and George of course. We've decorated since your last visit, Ned."

"Then I must inspect your handiwork," said Ned, also rising.

"It's not my handiwork, nor that of the major. Sid Reynolds did it for us."

"Sid!" said Ned, surprised. "I didn't know he was into decorating."

"Well, he is for family and friends," said Molly. "And the major made it worth his while. He's done a smashing job."

The little cottage was immaculate. They entered through the front door, painted white, which led into a small hallway off which ran the stairs. To the right was the dining room with duel aspect to the front and rear. On the opposite side, to the left, a door from the hall led into the sitting room with a view over the front garden. From it another door opened into a rectangular kitchen which overlooked the back garden, flourishing with vegetables. Upstairs, there were two bedrooms. Originally there had been three, but the major had Harry the builder convert the smallest one into a bathroom shortly after they had first moved in.

That evening as previously planned, Rose joined Ned, Stella and George at the Inn for a drink. She seemed much brighter than at breakfast time and had smiled frequently whilst waiting at the tables during dinner.

They all sat in the snug. Ned and Stella in the window seat, and Rose and George on two chairs round the same table.

Ned bought the first round of drinks, and to relax Rose and put her in a good frame of mind, George repeated his dream and asked her if she knew of a Harry Timmins. Rose was fascinated and racked her brains to see if she could recall hearing the name, past or present.

"If you have the dream again, ask the young woman to give you her name," suggested Stella. "No-one appears to know of a Harry Timmins but they might just know of her. That is of course if she and Harry really exist. Although I suppose if they were from another era, then by now they're probably long dead and gone."

George wrinkled his nose. "But I don't want to get in the habit of talking in my sleep. Someone creeping along the passage in the dead of night might hear me and think I'm crackers."

"Madge or Milly might hear and think you're calling to them," laughed Ned. "Now that could produce quite interesting results."

Rose smiled. "I'm so glad you're all here. I don't really have any close friends. I know it's my own fault and everyone's very good to me now, but knowing people with the ability to make one laugh is very precious and I really appreciate it."

"Well, consider us all your friends. We must meet like this more often, and then I won't feel, and look, like a gooseberry," said George.

"And I should appreciate your company too," added Stella. "Being saddled with these two can get a bit tedious, especially when they revert to childhood."

"Thank you. So, how long are you all here for?

"We've booked for four weeks, but Frank said we can stay as long as we like, so we probably will if the rooms are not needed for anyone else," said Ned.

Rose sighed. "I suppose then you'll all go back to your teaching jobs."

"Yes," said Ned. "But let's not get sorrowful. I don't even want to think about going home just yet. This place is paradise and I shall find leaving it to return to London very difficult, especially this time of the year."

"Have you ever thought about applying for the job as headmaster here?" Rose asked, unexpectedly.

"Me!" gasped Ned. "Well no. No, not at all. Why, do you think I'd be suitable?"

"I think you'd be more than suitable. Ideal in fact. Reg always spoke very highly of you, during the short time he knew you."

"Are you serious?" Stella asked Rose.

"Yes. Think about it, anyway. The advertisement for the position was only advertised for the first time last week. I'll let you have a copy of the local paper, if you like."

"I'd be interested to read the advert, certainly," said Ned.

"Good, then I'll bring the paper to work with me in the morning."

The following morning, Stella woke first. She slipped out of bed, pulled back the curtains, let in the morning sunshine and sniffed the sweet peas taking pride of place on the window sill.

Ned was still asleep, and so she crept from the room and walked along the corridor to the bathroom. When she returned he was sitting up in bed reading the local paper. He laid it on the bedspread as she entered."

"Is that the paper with the advertisement for the job of headmaster? Stella asked.

"Yes. George just dropped it in."

"George! He's up early."

"Yes, he had that dream again and for some reason it woke him up so popped down to the kitchen to see if there was any chance of a cup of tea. He found Rose who had just arrived for work."

Stella sat down on the bed. "I see. And have you read the advert yet?"

"Hmm, yes. It sounds very interesting and I have the necessary qualifications. What do you think, sweetheart. Should I apply for it, or not?"

34

"It's up to you, Ned."

"No, it's not up to me. It's up to both of us and you in particular. If I got the job it would mean you'd not see so much of your family."

Stella moved up beside him and clasped his hands lovingly.

"You're my family now, Ned, and I want you to do what you think best. If you're happy, then I'm happy. Besides, I'm sure my family would like the opportunity to take the occasional holiday in Cornwall."

"But what about your job? I know you're very happy at our school."

"I could get a job down here. In another village primary school, perhaps. Teachers are required everywhere, so I don't see my working as an issue. Besides, if over the next few years we are blessed with the patter of tiny feet, then I'd be giving up work, anyway."

"Then I'll apply. But we'll not tell anyone except George and Rose. Not even Mum. Well, especially not Mum, as she'd never be able to keep quiet. I don't expect I'll get the job, anyway, not being local and having no Cornish connections, but it's worth a try, and even if I did get it offered to me, I wouldn't have to accept it."

"Good, that's settled, then. Now, I think it's time you got up or we'll be late for breakfast."

CHAPTER FIVE

Bright and early the following morning, whilst Stella slept, Ned slipped quietly from the side door of the Inn and walked down the road to the post office, where he posted a letter of application for the job of headmaster. As he passed The School House on his return, he saw Rose opening the garden gate, part hidden between two large privet hedges.

He stopped and waited until she stepped onto the pavement. "Off to work?"

A broad smile caused her eyes to sparkle. "Yes, although it's far too nice a morning to be stuck indoors, even though it's only for a couple of hours."

"Doesn't Freak mind you going off and leaving him?" Ned asked, as they walked along the road together.

"No, I've left him some food and he'll sleep until I get back, and then I'll take him down to the beach. I wouldn't leave him if I thought he'd be miserable. But it's as though he knows, if I don't work, we don't eat. He's a clever little dog, in spite of his odd appearance."

Once inside the Inn, Rose went into the kitchen and Ned returned upstairs to see if his wife had woken.

A little later, during breakfast, the three school teachers sat around the table in the window chatting. George was in a good frame of mind having not dreamed he was Harry Timmins or anyone else for that matter.

"What shall we do today?" Ned asked, as Stella poured the tea. "I thought it might make a change to go horse riding, that's if Frank still has Winston and Brown Ale."

Stella frowned. "But if there are only two horses, one of us will be left behind."

George grinned. "And that'll be me. Rose and I are planning an extremely lazy day, sunbathing, as I have every intention of being

36

nicely tanned when I go home, otherwise no-one will believe I've even been away."

Ned raised his eyebrows. "Sunbathing with Rose, eh? When did you arrange that little rendezvous?"

"A few minutes ago before you two came down. Rose was happily extolling the beautiful weather and so I jumped in quick."

"You never were one to let the grass grow beneath your feet, were you, George? I trust you'll behave."

"Impeccably so. I shall be a perfect gent and chivalrous, as always."

"Good, that's the day settled then. I'll go and see Frank straight after breakfast," said Ned, unable to make up his mind whether the look on George's face was a smirk or a smile.

The conversation with Frank revealed he still owned the horses, but their care had passed into the capable hands of Meg Reynolds who offered to look after them once Gertie found she was expecting twins. Frank told Ned he would find them in the same stables but he must see Meg first to make sure it was alright with her.

Ned and Stella changed into their most suitable clothes on the off chance Meg would have no objections. They then left the Inn and walked along the main road to her home with Sid, in Coronation Terrace, a row of four new houses, the construction of which began shortly before Ned's first encounter with Trengillion, the previous year.

Meg said they could take out the horses as often as they liked, but insisted on this occasion they join her first for a coffee.

"I get a bit bored during the school holidays, especially when Sid is at work all day. And I can't keep popping in to see Gertie or she'll be sick of the sight of me."

"Does she live nearby, then?" asked Ned, taking a seat in Meg's spotlessly clean sitting room.

"Very near, next door at number two."

"That's nice for Gertie to have you nearby," said Ned. "And you'll always be up to date with the latest gossip."

Meg laughed. "Gertie loves to know what's going on, doesn't she? Although, to be fair, she's not been quite so inquisitive since the twins were born, as they take up rather a lot of her time. At the moment though, she, like the rest of us, is eager to see what the two divers will come up with when they're next here. Their wreck is the talk of the village. Everyone is well and truly spellbound."

Ned took a ginger biscuit from the plate offered by Meg and dunked it in his coffee. "I've heard mutterings regarding their popularity, and Mum tells us they're due down this weekend. But where will they stay? The Inn's full at present."

"I expect they'll stay in Cove Cottage. They did when they were down at Easter. In fact, rumour has it, that it now belongs to Larry's father, but I don't know whether or not that's true. It definitely has a new owner, though, because it was put up for sale last autumn and sold fully furnished as a holiday let."

"Cove Cottage, that must be one of the two cottages by the beach," said Ned.

"That's right. The other is called Sea View and I think it would be impossible for anyone to come up with two more unimaginative names."

Nodding, Ned offered cigarettes to Meg and Stella. "By the way, I keep meaning to ask how your mother is these days."

Meg took a cigarette. "Thanks. She's a lot better I'm pleased to say. During the last year she's undergone an awful lot of physiotherapy treatment, but she reckons all the pain and suffering was worthwhile, because now she's able to walk around a little with just a couple of sticks for support. She can stand for a while too, as long as there's something close by to hang on to. Bless her, she made Dad a cake for his birthday recently, I was there to supervise, of course, but she managed it on her own and was so happy to have achieved something. She always loved cooking and has missed it terribly."

"That's good to hear. So, now she doesn't need quite so much care and attention, which is just as well with you having married and left the Vicarage."

"Absolutely, and she's a lot happier for her little bit of independence. It must have been horrible seeing and knowing things needed to be done and not being able to do anything. Poor Mum. She detested being confined to a wheel chair, as she was a very active woman before the accident."

"What happened to Meg's mum?" Stella asked, as she and Ned left Coronation Terrace and headed across the fields to the stables.

"She was knocked off her bike by a car driven by a drunk Albert Treloar. Must be a couple of years ago, now, because I remember being told it had happened during the summer when Jane went missing, which was six months before I discovered this place."

"How dreadful. Poor lady, it must be awful living with a disability."

Ned agreed. "Yes, and sadly due to five years of a relentless war, such ailments are now ubiquitous."

Ned felt a pang of excitement when the stables came into view and the two horses were clearly visible grazing on the lush grass in the paddock. As he and Stella neared the field, the horses trotted over to the gate to greet them both.

"The big one's called Winston," said Ned, affectionately stroking Winston's nose. "And the smaller one is Brown Ale."

"They're beautiful," said Stella, as Ned opened the gate, but she felt her words were falling on deaf ears. "Is that where the tunnel is?" she continued, aware that Ned's eyes were transfixed on the entrance to the stables.

"Hmm," he said, with a shudder. "Sorry, love. I just had a flashback. Yes, the tunnel's in there and I suppose you'd like to take a look."

"Well, of course. After all, I have heard a great deal about it over the past twelve months and more, and it would be foolhardy not to inspect it when in such close proximity."

Ned took her hand. "Then come this way, Mrs Stanley, but I warn you it's not a welcoming sight."

Leaving the horses in the paddock, they walked towards the stable block. The building struck cold as they stepped inside for it had no windows to welcome in the warm sunshine.

Ned let go of Stella's hand and from the straw strewn across the floor, picked up a ladder lying on its side, and leaned it against a back wall.

"Get the torch please, love," he said, pointing to it hanging from a nail beside the saddles.

Stella obliged and passed it to him. Ned then climbed the ladder. At the top he pushed aside a sheet of rusty metal, beneath which lay a wooden trap door. He slid back the heavy metal bolt, opened the door and shone the torch into the dark cavity, revealing a short flight of dark, dingy granite steps. Ned shivered, climbed back down the ladder and handed the torch to Stella. "Your turn, but be careful."

Stella climbed the ladder and her hands felt clammier with each step she took. She did not have a very good head for heights but was reluctant to let Ned see she was afraid. At the top she flashed the torch and peered into the hole.

"Ugh, it smells all damp and musty. How horrible it must have been, trapped down there in the dark, with creepy crawlies running around everywhere."

Ned shuddered. "It was."

Without hesitation, Stella closed the trap door, bolted it, replaced the metal sheet and then descended the ladder. "I don't think anything in the world would entice me down there. Not even if my life depended on it. I feel all itchy after just having taken a glance."

Both were glad to step back outside and into the warm sunshine, each carrying riding kit which they laid on the grass in preparation for their day out. Stella, a keen horsewoman, did the saddling up, for although Ned had seen the horses saddled on numerous occasions, he mistrusted his capability to do everything correctly, and the last thing he wanted was to see his new bride tipped into a ditch.

"Where are we going?" Stella asked, as they led the horses towards the gate.

"I thought it might be nice to go to the old mine. You'll like it there. It's quiet, bright and very beautiful."

As they left the paddock and trotted over the adjoining field, Stella spotted someone walking in their direction through the long grass. "Who's that?"

Ned squinted to see. "It looks a bit like Auntie Mabel. Oh dear, if she's intending to visit the horses then she's out of luck."

"Maybe, but she must be able to see us. So if she is on her way to the stables, she'll, no doubt have the sense to put two and two together."

They left the fields through a wooden gate, and then trotted along a hoof-marked track towards the main road. After crossing the road, they turned into the lane which ran between the school and The School House.

The lane was narrow and winding, each side edged with dry stone walls sprouting shrubs and thick vegetation which hid from view the countryside yonder, even for those on horseback.

Amongst the shrubbery, Stella observed branches of unkempt brambles, each laden with unripe blackberries, dangling, part-hidden between the seed heads of cow parsley and dried foxgloves.

At the bottom of the hill, where a stream ran beneath the road, they dismounted, peered over the granite wall of the bridge, and watched the crystal clear water splashing its way through a path of mud, with glimpses of wild flowers amongst the long grass.

"This stream runs into the sea," said Ned, casting his hand in a southerly direction. "You'll probably remember seeing it trickling down the beach."

"Yes, I do," said Stella, dreamily. She then crossed the road and looked along the valley in the opposite direction of the sea. "Is it possible to explore those woods?" she asked, pointing to a large spread of trees nearby. "I love woods and spinneys. There's a spinney back home, very near to my parents' house and I spent many happy hours there as a child making dens with my friends."

"Yes, apparently it's part of the Penwynton Estate, but locals are welcome to walk there. I'm told in April and May it's full of bluebells, hence, most people call it Bluebell Woods."

"Good, then we must go there one day, ideally when it's too hot to do anything else, as inside it will be nice and cool, especially if the stream runs through it."

"It does. Listen to the birdsong, Stella. Isn't it amazing that such tiny things can make so much noise? I love to hear them singing, especially when accompanied by the soothing sound of gently running water."

Stella agreed. "A bit different to dear old London. No problems with smog here."

They sat for a while on the bridge in silence, enjoying the tranquility and the sweet smells of rural summer. They then remounted the horses and rode on up the hill, past a row of cottages towards a farm as it appeared on the horizon.

"Gertie's parents, Nettie and Cyril Penrose, run that farm, but we're not going any further that way, because the old mine is this way," said Ned, pointing towards the coast.

They left the lane and followed a bridle path across farmland and along the edges of fields where crops awaiting harvest, and alongside meadows ablaze with wild, red poppies and golden yellow buttercups. Beside a five bar gate they dismounted and tied the horses' reins securely to a granite gate post. They then walked hand in hand along a well-worn path towards the old mine.

Stella was enthralled as she craned her neck to look up at the remains of the old mine towering high above their heads beneath the cloudless blue sky.

"We must come here for a picnic one day," she said, enthusiastically. "It's gorgeous."

"You can also get here by walking along the cliff path. If we came that way we'd not have to rely on the availability of the horses and George could come too. Rose also if she wanted."

Stella walked towards the cliff's edge. The sea sparkled a beautiful shade of turquoise blue and, off-shore, rocks and seaweeds were clearly visible beneath the semi-transparent waves.

Ned sat on the grass and leaned back against the mine wall, deep in thought.

"You're very quiet all of a sudden," laughed Stella, returning to him. "Are you tired?"

Ned shook his head. "No, no, I was just thinking about Sylvia. Her ashes are sprinkled here because this was a favourite spot of hers."

Stella sat down. "I think you were infatuated by the old landlady. You always speak of her with such reverence, even though she was a murderer."

Ned leaned forward. "Oh, come on, Stell, please don't call her that. I've told you the story enough times for you to know by now that I think most of her misfortune was brought about by sheer, rotten bad luck."

Stella said nothing but snuggled close by his side. "Anything you say, sweetheart. After all you must be a good judge of character because you married me."

Ned put his arm around her shoulder, hugged her tightly and kissed the curls on the top of her head. "I did have a soft spot for Sylvia," he whispered. "I thought she was very beautiful, but I've never loved anyone as I love you."

A sudden gust of wind swirled around the old mine wall sending seed heads from dandelions and thistles dancing through the air.

Ned smiled. "I think you have Sylvia's approval," he said.

CHAPTER SIX

Ned, Stella and George sat on a bench outside the front of the Ringing Bells Inn after dinner, enjoying a drink in the early evening sunshine before it disappeared in a blaze of colour behind the Inn's roof and the battlements on the old church tower.

Inside the bars, holiday makers mingled with the locals, hearing exaggerated tales of heroic sea adventures and boasts of which fishermen were the most popular with the ladies. Story telling was a challenge for the sea goers as they competed with each other to see who could get the most drinks bought for them in the course of an evening.

When she finished work, Rose joined her three friends outside the Inn, after which they walked down to the beach, taking with them their drinks, after first seeking Frank's permission, for they thought it unwise to be seen absconding with some of his glasses. Once on the beach they sat down and watched as the ebbing tide splashed gently onto the pebbled shore.

"What could be more idyllic than this?" mused Ned, leaning back on his right arm. "It's something people up-country can only dream of."

Rose smiled. "The sea can get a bit tedious after a while. It looks very inviting on a hot summer's day, but everyone knows it's always freezing cold when you actually get in there, and it's hardly entertaining to watch for long."

Ned yawned. "Maybe not, but it's reliable, and its gentle rhythm is very soothing for the troubled brow."

"Your brow doesn't look very troubled to me," said George. "Although I do detect a few tell-tale lines beginning to appear on your ugly mug."

"You're a fine one to talk. Who'll be an old man of forty in less than seven years?" retorted Ned, mockingly counting the few strands of grey hair amidst the dark waves on George's head.

"Shush! What's that, I can hear?" Stella asked, ignoring the men and straining her ears to listen.

Rose looked up. "It will be a boat coming in. One of the fishing boats, I expect."

From around the cliffs appeared Percy and Peter's red and blue crabber, returning home after they had been out hauling their pots. Once the boat was winched ashore, the teachers and Rose, wandered across the beach for a chat.

"You're very late today," said Ned, resting his hand on the gunnels. "The other boats must have been in for ages because I saw most of their owners at the Inn enjoying a pint when we left."

"Yeah, and I'd be with them, but we had engine trouble this morning," said Peter. "Sodding thing! We missed the early tide so didn't manage get out 'til a couple of hours ago."

"If ever you fancy a trip out to sea with us, just give us a nod," said Percy, skilfully rolling a cigarette. "We'd be happy to take you out for the day and show you the ropes. It'd be quite a different experience for you, I reckon, compared with being stuck in a dull classroom all day with lots of noisy kids."

"Wow, thanks," said Ned. "That really would be terrific. We'll definitely take you up on that offer sometime in the next few days."

Percy left soon after to return home to his wife and the twins. While Peter, having no family commitments, called in for a pint at the Inn to try and establish how many crabs other fishermen had had in their pots earlier that day.

"I keep meaning to ask who lives in that house up there on the cliff," said George, pointing to Chy-an-Gwyns, after the two fishermen had departed. "It's rather taken my fancy."

"It belongs to an architect called Willoughby Castor-Hunt," said Ned, sitting down on the shingle. "I've never met him, though, because he lives up-country, but according to the major he's extremely talented and rather rich."

George whistled. "What a waste! If I had a house like that I'd be in it all the time. How many rooms does it have?"

Ned laughed. "More than enough for a crusty old bachelor like you. There are at least five bedrooms and two or three sitting rooms. Apparently, it was pretty near derelict when Willoughby bought it before the War and since then he's spent a fortune bringing it into the twentieth century."

"Oh, Willoughby, eh! So you're on first name terms, then."

"No, of course not. I said I've never met him, remember. It's just such a mouthful to say Mr Castor-Hunt."

Smirking, George lay back on the shingle. "Well, when Mr Castor-Hunt tires of his house on the cliff because it's too small for his wallet, I shall buy it from him and retire down here."

Ned frowned. "Do you know something about teacher's pay that I don't? Because I reckon if you saved every spare penny you earned from now until you retired, you'd still not be able to afford to buy and maintain a place such as that."

"I don't think Mr Castor-Hunt will ever get tired of Chy-an-Gwyns," said Rose, dreamily. "I believe he's very fond of the place and I'm told one of the bedrooms is a shrine to his late wife and it's where he keeps all her belongings, even though she never lived there. But I don't know whether that's true or not."

Ned turned to Rose. "Of course, you must have met him over the years, I hadn't thought of that. What's he like?"

"Beautifully spoken. Gentle but firm. Perfect manners. In fact everything you'd expect someone in his position to be, really. I've only met him on a few occasions when he's been to the Inn for a drink, so I can hardly claim to know him well, and I very much doubt if he even knows my name."

"What happened to his wife?" Stella asked. "I assume from what's being said that she's dead."

Rose nodded. "Yes, she died in childbirth over twenty years ago, along with her baby and he's never remarried. You'd like him, and may probably even get to meet him as he often pops down for a short spell in the summer, and I've not seen him now since Whitsun."

When their glasses were empty they returned to the Inn for the night air was beginning to feel chilly and none were wearing warm clothing.

"What shall we do tomorrow?" Stella asked, as they walked up the road. "I do like to plan things in advance."

"I don't know," said Ned. "I suppose it all depends on the weather. Has anyone heard a forecast today?"

"I had the wireless on this afternoon and they said it would be fine and dry, but of course there's a fifty percent chance that it'll be wrong," said Rose.

"Oh, well, we'll decide in the morning, then," said Stella. "But I think I should like to do something completely different. I've not seen much of Cornwall other than Trengillion and the countryside around it, and so it would be nice to go a little further afield."

As she spoke the sound of a vehicle driving through the village drew their attention and they turned their heads to see what was coming their way. A white van pulling a boat on a trailer passed by. The driver tooted, recognising Rose and Ned, who waved in return.

"Humph, the divers, I assume," said George, a note of envy in his voice.

Ned nodded. "Yes, and they have a new boat. It's even bigger than the one they had last year."

"Someone's got plenty of money, then. Boats with outboard motors don't come cheap and that van must have cost a pretty penny too."

"It's Larry's family with the money," said Rose. "His father is a barrister and his grandfather has his own company. Larry and Des both work for him, the grandfather, that is. He finances their diving activities too because it fascinates him, although their interest in diving actually began with Des' dad, who was a diver with the military or something like that."

"I suppose that's how they get so much time off work, then, if they're employed by Larry's granddad," said George, with much envy. "It's alright for some."

During the night George dreamt he was in the boat again with the attractive young lady who mysteriously called him Harry. This time, however, there was no laughter, no teasing and no frivolity. The young woman was distraught for water was trickling up through a small hole in the bottom of the boat. In panic the two young lovers scooped out water and tipped it over the side. Harry with cupped hands, the young women using her shoes. But their movements made matters worse and water flowed in faster than they were able to dispose of it.

Lifting the hem of her dress, the young woman removed one of her stockings and screwed it up tightly. She then fumbled around on her knees in the boat's bow to locate the hole so that she might use her stocking as a bung. Her plan momentarily worked and slowed down the flow, but within minutes her hosiery bobbed to the water's surface, now rising with increased rapidity. Distraught, she cried with frustration, saying both would drown. Harry said she must resume scooping while he tried to row back to shore. Their efforts, however, were futile. Land, although visible, was too distant and both knew the boat would sink long before the shore was reached.

In despair the couple jumped overboard and turned the boat upside-down to keep it afloat. Clinging to the keel both prayed someone might see their dilemma. But help did not materialise. The cold water gradually numbed their legs; the young woman's arms lost all strength and unable to retain her grip, she slid, screaming Harry's name, into the sea.

Harry quickly followed as she disappeared beneath the waves. His arms splashed vigorously through the deep, cold water, but his efforts were in vain. Visibility was poor. He could not see her, and feeling suffocated, he panicked in desperation. Fighting for life. Fighting for air.

George woke bathed in perspiration and unable to breath with his face buried hard into his pillow. His pleasant dream had turned into a realistic nightmare. He felt sick and drained as he sat up in bed, and breathed deeply to steady his thumping heart.

Looking at his watch he saw the time was half past six. He climbed out of bed and still trembling gazed from his window. The sun was already shining on the corrugated tin roof of the old outbuilding, and birds were singing tunefully in the trees behind the Inn.

Troubled by the dream, he dressed quickly, feeling a desire to walk down to the beach. No-one was about when he descended the stairs and all was quiet in the hallway. Outside, however, on the cobbled area in front of the Inn, Auntie Mabel sat puffing away at a cigarette protruding from the end of her ornate holder.

She smiled. "You're up early m'duck. Couldn't you sleep?"

"I slept fine, but was woken by an unpleasant dream. How about you?"

"I always get up early, even during the dark days of winter. I like to be about when everywhere is quiet and peaceful. Early to bed and early to rise, that's my motto."

"Then I'll not disturb you any longer, and I'll leave you to enjoy the peace."

One or two fishing boats had already gone to sea when George reached the cove, and remaining fishermen were chatting and preparing for a day's work. They nodded to him as he crossed the beach, his destination, Denzil's bench, where he sat and stared blankly into the oncoming waves, pondering over what significance his dream had, or indeed if it had any significance at all. He still felt very shaky and could not get the image of the mysterious girl from his mind. Haunted by the fear in her eyes and her trembling hands, he felt guilty for not saving her life. He then recalled seeing her right foot when she had torn off her stocking. She had only four toes, the smallest was missing and a crooked white scar marked the place where the fifth toe had been. George concluded she must have lost it in an accident at some point in her short life.

A rumbling sound from behind caused him to turn his head. Fishermen were dragging one of the boats down the beach and into the sea. He watched it leave the shore and chug off until it became a small dot in the distance. His eyes then reverted to the shallow, oncoming waves, gently falling, one after another, onto the sand and shingle. And gradually, lulled by the soothing sound of the sea, the horror subsided to be replaced by curiosity.

"It was only a dream," said George, to himself. But one question still occupied his thoughts. He wanted to know if a man called Harry Timmins had ever existed or whether he was a figment of his imagination. And if he had been real, then who was the young woman with the missing toe?

Unable to shed any light on his dream he wandered back towards the Inn. Auntie Mabel had gone inside and there was no-one else around except the milkman in his float parked further along the road. George looked up when two seagulls on the roof of the Inn squawked simultaneously, making him jump. The church tower behind caught his eye and it struck him that if such a person as Harry Timmins had existed and been drowned, then there was the possibility of a grave in the churchyard with a memorial stone to tell of his passing and possibly even that of the young woman too. Delighted with the prospect of finding out more, he ran around to the church full of optimism.

He shivered as he walked beneath the lichgate. The churchyard felt cold and cheerless. The group of tall trees clustered together around the entrance threw long shadows across the graves, shutting out the morning sunshine. Everything was damp with the morning dew, and his feet, on which he wore sandals, soon became wet and squeaked with each step he took. George rubbed his arms to dispel goose pimples and wished he had on his jacket.

Half-heartedly, he walked up and down rows of graves reading the tombstones until his hopes were dashed. For his search revealed the only names at all familiar to him, were Denzil Penhaligon, the drowned fisherman on whose bench he had been sitting, Jane Hunt, the young woman murdered by the Inn's landlady, Sylvia Newton, and Reg Briers, the late husband of Rose.

Dejected and disappointed he left the churchyard and returned to the Inn, none the wiser.

CHAPTER SEVEN

Stella awoke with a strong desire to go shopping, and as she was in need of a pair of flat sandals for the beach, she had a perfectly legitimate reason for a trip into town. She was, however, reluctant to broach the subject with Ned, because the prospect of dragging him along was not one she relished. For although she loved him dearly, she knew he disliked shopping intensely and considered it a tedious pastime more suited to women. Hence, for that reason, back home, she often sought an alternative escort, usually her sister, when the necessity for shopping arose. On this occasion, however, her sister was over three hundred miles away, and so she asked Rose, during breakfast, if she would like to go with her into town to make the necessary purchase. Rose, thrilled at being asked, accepted the offer with enthusiastic gratitude, as she did not get into town very often.

Ned and George, on hearing the plans of the females, realised they could have a men's day out, and both agreed without hesitation, that a trip out to sea with Percy and Peter would be ideal if the two fishermen had no objections to the late arrangement. For the opportunity of being fishermen for the day greatly appealed to the their sense of adventure, hence they ate their breakfast with gusto before running down to the beach to see at what time the two fishermen proposed to take to the water.

Peter was sitting on the sand, smoking, awaiting the arrival of Percy, as the two teachers raced onto the shingle. He told them there was no rush and to take their time, promising the boat would not leave without them, should they wish to return to the Inn and change their clothing.

The girls, meanwhile, planned to leave mid-morning after Rose finished work.

Stella kissed Ned when he hastily returned to change and promised faithfully not to crunch the brakes of his Morris Minor and to drive with care.

George did not mention the drowning of Harry to his friends. He hoped if he ignored the nightmare it might go away and never return. For although it had troubled him deeply for a short time after its occurrence, he could not see that anything could be achieved by boring others with his dreams as often his mother had done to him and his sister when they were young. Besides, the sun was shining brightly, the sea looked calm and inviting and the prospect of being in the water seemed less horrific than during the night.

The fishing boat left the shore just before ten o'clock and headed out to sea in the direction of the Witches Broomstick, which Ned explained to George, was where a sprawled out formation of rocks lay beneath a steep cliff, and access to a small stretch of sand was possible only through what resembled the handle of the broomstick.

Peter stopped the boat by a dahn, a flag and pole attached to a ball which floated on the surface of the water, denoting the spot where a string of pots lay on the sea bed. They then hauled in the pots, one by one, removed any crabs from inside and put rubber bands around their claws.

"Why do you do that?" George asked.

Peter laughed. "If you put your finger inside one of the claws you'll find out. These little beauties are a lot stronger than they look and the bands stop them attacking each other, and us too for that matter."

The teachers, enthralled, declined the offer to test the strength of the claws and continued to watch in awe the two fishermen at work.

"I suppose once in the pots they can't find their way out again," said Ned, tapping the hard shell of a crab walking sideways across the deck of the boat.

"Well, actually they can and they do," said Percy. "Though more by luck, I guess, than good judgment. We don't know how many escape as it's something we don't like to think about too much."

Ned watched the crabs staggering around like drunks and was glad Stella was out shopping, as being a little squeamish, he didn't think she would like the experience at all.

"What happens to them now?" George asked. "Are you going to take them to market?"

Peter shook his head. "No, we'll put them in store pots, which will stay in the sea 'til we're ready to land them another day."

51

The pots were re-baited and returned to the water where they rapidly vanished out of sight. The boat then chugged on to another dahn and the whole process was repeated all over again.

In all, the fishermen had fifty seven crabs that day, but the teachers were instructed by Percy, to say, if asked by any of the other fishermen, it was thirty seven.

Ned frowned. "Why on earth do you underplay the amount you've caught? Surely human nature is to crow about one's achievements and even to exaggerate."

Percy scratched his cheek. "Because we don't want the other buggers fishing on this spot. It's all down to survival. Fishermen never tell the truth about their catches, anyhow, but as you say, unlike us, most exaggerate."

When they arrived back at the cove, they saw Madge and Milly lying on the sand. The two females watched as the boat was winched ashore, they then stood up and strolled over to the vessel.

"Did you catch anything?" Milly coyly asked Peter, attempting to flutter her stubby eyelashes.

"Yeah."

Milly peered into the boat where no sign of sea life could be seen. She scowled. "So where are your fish?"

Peter stepped backwards as she moved closer to him. "In store pots."

Milly, having no idea what Peter was talking about, gave a questioning glance at her mother. Madge, meanwhile, knowing George was a teacher, tried to impress him with her intellect and knowledge of current affairs by suggesting he had a little drink with her some time so that they could discuss the outcome of the Korean War.

Ned tried to hide his amusement but could not resist whispering to Percy, how there were many more benefits to being married than at first meet the eye.

The girls were enjoying their shopping excursion in town. Stella found a pair of comfortable sandals and also bought a pair of walking shoes. Rose, on the other hand, whose income just about kept up with her expenses, admired several things, but said nothing in particular caught her eye and she was not in desperate need of new clothing or footwear, anyway.

Stella sensed the real reason for her frugality and thereafter played down the extravagances of her purchases.

"Would you allow me to treat you to lunch, Rose?" Stella asked, as they walked past Abbott's ladies outfitters. "Please say yes. I want to show my gratitude to you. For if you weren't here I should be a bit lost, or worse still I might have ended up going fishing with the lads. It's nice to have female company, especially as it means Ned can go off doing chap's things without me tagging along."

Rose smiled. "Yes, please. Lunch would be very nice and it will be an experience for me to be waited on instead of being the waitress."

During lunch Rose asked Stella if Ned had sent off his application for the headmaster's job.

"Yes. He posted it early yesterday morning just before he saw you on your way to work. But he's very uncertain whether or not it's what he really wants. He loves Cornwall and now I'm here I can see the attraction, but we both like our school in London too and the people we work with. Ned would also miss George terribly. They get on ever so well together and I often think they're quite inseparable."

"Yes, I had noticed. Does George's ex-girlfriend, Elsie or whatever she's called, teach at the same school too?"

"Elsie Glazebrook. No, she works in a departmental store. George met her just before I became a member of their clique and I believe it was at a party."

"What is she like? I've noticed George frequently mentions her name, although often with scorn. I mean, is she very pretty and do you like her?"

"She is pretty, and yes, I quite liked her because she had a great sense of humour and she and George seemed to bring out the best in each other. But I always got the impression she didn't really like me. She often made remarks like, we can't all be clever, can we? I think the fact she left school with no further education made her feel inferior. God only knows why. I like people for who they are and not for how much knowledge they possess."

Rose smiled. "Good, you won't me mind if I'm a bit of a dumbo, then!"

Rose went straight home after work that evening as she wanted to write home to her parents in Blackpool, something she did, without fail, once a week.

Ned and Stella having spent the day apart decided to take a walk together over the cliff tops to the Witches Broomstick. They wanted George to accompany them, but George, feeling he was spending far too much time in the company of the honeymooners, insisted they go without him, and feigned a feeling of nausea which he attributed to the trip out to sea.

He watched them leave the Inn and heaved a great sigh. The novelty of having no girl on his arm was beginning to wear a bit thin.

He walked back into the Inn and bought a pint of beer, but was undecided whether to drink it inside or out. Seeing Madge waving from a stool at the far end of the bar, settled his dilemma and he promptly went outside and sat on the old wooden bench.

The evening was warm and pleasantly quiet, for as George stepped from the Inn, a family of holiday makers who had been sitting around an outdoor table, finished their drinks and left, thus leaving him completely alone.

From his pocket he pulled out three postcards. Stella had bought a dozen or so whilst in town and had given some to him saying he must drop a line to his family back home to let them know he was at least alive and well. Reluctantly, he wrote one to his parents saying: Having a great time. Weather good. See you in September. The second he sent to his sister and brother-in-law with the same message. But over the third he deliberated to whom it should be addressed. He could not send to just one of his friends and leave out the others, and he certainly could not send it to Elsie either, for she would be sure to misinterpret the message. Hence the third card he put back into the pocket of his jacket, unwritten.

Auntie Mabel emerged from inside the Inn looking very smart wearing a light jacket with a matching skirt and hat. On seeing George alone she tilted her head to one side and tutted. "Oh dear, on your own tonight, young man? A good looking lad like you ought to be inside trying to find a pretty little wife, so that you can settle down like your friend, instead of sitting out here, by yourself, sulking."

"What!" George spluttered. "I wasn't sulking? I was actually thinking about my erstwhile girlfriend."

"There!" Auntie Mabel exclaimed. "See, I was right. You need a wife. Men can't cope on their own. That's why in most cases they die before their wives. The good Lord can't bear to watch them struggling, you see."

George was too flabbergasted to respond.

"Anyway," she continued. "I must be off or I'll be late. And I suggest you get yourself back inside the Inn or ring up your old girlfriend and ask her to have you back before she finds someone else."

"But I don't want her back. It was me who put an end to our relationship, and that was because she kept on about getting married and going to live in miserable Manchester."

"Well, it's your loss," retorted Auntie Mabel. "And there's nothing wrong with Manchester. My father was born there."

George watched as she disappeared round the corner.

"Why is everyone so keen to get me married off?" he asked Barley Wine, busily washing his face beside a large, cracked, uncared for flowerpot containing half dead geraniums and numerous straggly weeds. "The more they go on, the more likely I am to stay a confirmed bachelor."

From the direction of the cove two young men ambled up the hill, deep in conversation. Instinct told George they were the two divers. He watched as they left the road and went into the Inn, each nodding as they passed him by.

With curiosity roused, George finished his pint and stood to return inside for a refill. He would never have admitted it, but he was keen to see the divers in closer proximity and judge for himself whether or not they were worthy of the interest Trengillion had bestowed upon them and their unusual activities. However, as he turned towards the door, he became aware of fast approaching footsteps. Thinking Auntie Mabel was making a speedy return, he headed for the door with haste to escape a further encounter. But as he crossed the threshold, curiosity caused him to look back. To his surprise, Molly emerged around the corner, red in the face and panting.

"George," she said breathlessly, waving to catch his eye. "You're the very person I'm looking for."

Puzzled, George walked back towards her. "Me? Is there anything wrong?"

Molly sat down on the bench. "No, no, not at all. It's just I've a bit of interesting news. If you remember, when you were all round the other day, Ned asked us if we knew of a Harry Timmins."

George felt his heart begin to race. "Yes, yes, I remember."

"Well, Sid Reynolds was round that same evening delivering the Church Messenger. That's a church leaflet, by the way, telling times of services and bits of village news, births, deaths, baptisms, marriages, outings and so forth. Anyway, I asked Sid if he knew of anyone called Harry Timmins, really just for something to say, but like the rest of us, the name meant nothing to him. Well, he's just been round again. And I don't know whether or not you know, but he works on the local newspaper. Anyway, today when he was at work, he was looking up an old story about something or other and whilst doing so he found an article dated September 1900, which was about a chap called Harry Timmins. So you see he did exist. But what's more interesting still, is the article Sid found, was about the fact he was drowned off Polquillick Cove along with his sweetheart, Emily Penberthy. Their bodies apparently, were washed ashore three days after they first went missing. Isn't that simply amazing? I thought you'd like to..."

But George did not hear her last words. His thumping heart drowned out every other sound. Feeling unsteady he lowered himself down and sat on the cobbles before the faintness he was feeling deprived him of consciousness.

CHAPTER EIGHT

During breakfast at the Inn the following morning, a new guest walked into the dining room and seated herself at the table in the corner by the alcove. She was young, had thick auburn hair and an abundance of freckles across her nose and high cheekbones. Rose greeted her warmly, knowing she was unfamiliar with her surroundings, having arrived at the Inn late the previous night. She smiled when she saw the name on the necklace the newcomer wore around her long neck.

"I see you and I have the same name," said Rose, placing a pot of tea on the newcomer's table. "That might cause a bit of confusion."

The newcomer giggled as she touched the silver chain necklace from which hung the letters, R O S E.

"Actually, my name is Rosemary. The only person who calls me Rose is Gran, because it was her mother's name, and it was she who bought me this for my birthday. My Auntie Gloria calls me Mary. But there shouldn't be any confusion if during my stay here, everyone ignores the necklace and calls me Rosemary, like my parents and friends do."

Rose giggled. "I think I'm confused already."

She left Rosemary to pour her tea and went back to the kitchen for a pot for the teachers. When she returned and put it on the table, Ned asked her if she knew anything about Polquillick Cove.

"I depends what you want to know. It's a pretty spot, about a mile on past the Witches Broomstick, if you go by the coastal path, or roughly six miles if you go by road."

"Is there a church there?" George asked.

"A church!" repeated Rose, surprised. "Yes, but why ever do you ask?"

"We'll tell you when you finish work, if you're not in a hurry to get away," said George, aware that Madge was getting agitated by the lack of food in front of her.

Rose joined them later as pre-arranged and found them sitting on Denzil's bench. George then told her about the dreams he had had and Sid's discovery from old newspaper records of the tragedy that had befallen Emily and Harry.

Rose felt goose pimples rise on her arms. "Good heavens! How weird and horrible to have a dream like that. And I suppose you want to know about the church at Polquillick to see if there are any graves for the drowned lovers there."

George was impressed by her quickness of mind. "In a nutshell, yes. We're all intrigued and have decided we really must find out more."

"And we'd like to go today before our curiosity wanes," added Stella. "And if you could come with us to show us around that would be just perfect."

"Oh, yes please. I'd love to go with you, it sounds most exciting. Are you planning to walk or drive?"

"Drive," said George, emphatically, before anyone else could speak. "That's if Ned doesn't mind. I'm far too impatient to waste time walking, even though I should love to take a closer look at Mr Money-bags Castor-Hunt's place."

"Of course I don't mind," said Ned, who agreed his curiosity was also greatly roused.

The drive took half an hour. It would have taken less, but twice they met vehicles on the narrow lanes. Firstly a tractor and secondly a young, female driver, and so in both cases it was Ned who had to reverse into a wider part of the road.

Polquillick, a picturesque fishing village, lay nestled between high cliffs with a harbour wall stretching out across the sea to give protection during the relentless storms of winter. Fishing boats, still numerous in numbers, despite the fact that several had gone to sea, rested on the sandy beach, where holiday makers lay soaking up the sun amidst children building castles with the damp, grey sand, part-hidden beneath seaweed and debris washed up with the last tide.

The church, clearly visible, stood on the hillside amongst houses and thatched cottages overlooking the busy harbour. Ned pointed to it as he parked his car on the side of the road. "It looks very much like the church at Trengillion," he said, turning off the engine and removing the key from the ignition.

Rose nodded. "All churches in the area look the same. I suppose they used the same plans and the same architect. That's if they had architects hundreds of years ago when they were built."

"I suppose they must have," said Ned. "It wouldn't be possible to throw up a church without them, but it's not something I've ever given much thought to. I know they took ages to build, though."

The churchyard, much of which looked time-worn and neglected, was considerably larger than the one at Trengillion and stretched out into an adjoining field.

"I think we ought to split up?" Stella suggested. "It will take ages if we all walk round together and we could well be here all day."

All agreed that was a good idea and went their separate ways.

Ned found himself in an area where the dates on the gravestones emanated from the late 1700s. He knew it was unlikely he would find the graves of Emily and Harry on his patch, but nevertheless he kept on looking, enjoying reading the ancient headstones which conjured up pictures as he tried to visualise the identity of the long deceased.

George's designated area was a shady spot overhung with fully leaved trees, making it feel damp and cool, reminiscent of his wander round the churchyard at Trengillion. His graves were even older than Ned's, around the 1600s, and many had no headstones at all. Those that did stood crooked, tilted by the protruding roots of trees winding through the graves like enormous snakes. Reading the inscriptions was almost impossible due to moss and patches of golden lichen.

Stella was in the newest part of the graveyard, behind a row of old cottages where a new field was being incorporated to cope with the churchyard's overflow. Her heart raced a little when she saw the name Timmins on the headstone of a double grave, but sank when she read that the occupants of the grave were Frederick and his wife, Mabel. Nevertheless she retained the names in her mind fully aware that they may well have been related to the sought after Harry.

It was Rose who finally found the graves, tucked away in a neglected corner, near to a railing, beside a sharp drop overlooking the beach.

She called to the other three after she made her discovery.

The two graves lay side by side. Both were overgrown with long grass, brambles and nettles; neither looked as though it had been tended for years. A metal vase lay dented and rusty beneath Emily's headstone, the flowers which had once adorned it, having long since rotted and been thrown away.

George read out the inscriptions with a quiver in his voice.

Here lies the body of
Harry Timmins
Son of Frederick and Mabel
*
1874 - 1900
Tragically lost at sea.
R.I.P.

Gently sleeping lies Emily Penberthy.
Beloved daughter of Grace and David.
1877 - 1900
Tragically drowned off these shores.
R.I.P.

George shuddered.

"Do you think I'm going crazy?" he asked his friends, feeling rather light headed. "I mean, how can I have dreamed of these people when I'd never set foot in Cornwall until this summer, and why in the dreams was I Harry Timmins?"

"I don't know, but Harry's parents, Frederick and Mabel are buried over there," said Stella, pointing to the area of the graveyard where she had explored.

"I didn't find any stones bearing the name Timmins," said Ned. "But that doesn't matter, anyway, does it? We're not trying to put together Harry's family history, we just want to know something about him."

George shivered. "Let's go. I feel very uneasy, this place is really creepy and we've found what we were looking for."

Rose nodded. "I agree. I feel as though we're being watched by all the people buried in these graves, and they resent our intrusion, which is really stupid, I know."

Ned pulled the car keys from his trouser pocket. "Alright, but there has to be a simple explanation as to why you had those dreams, George. Although for the life of me I can't even begin to imagine what it might be. I think perhaps we ought to visit Mum this afternoon and see if see if she has been able to come up with any bright ideas."

They found Molly in the kitchen of Rose Cottage, headscarf covering her hair and a floral apron tied around her waist as she beat together butter and sugar for the making of a Victoria sandwich. She was delighted to see them all.

"If you'd come a little later this cake would have been ready," she said. "And it should be really delicious too as I intend to fill it with Doris's homemade strawberry jam. She gave me a pot yesterday, which she made last summer from fruit she'd grown herself. Now I can only offer you biscuits as the major finished off the cherry cake last night with his cocoa."

"We didn't come round to eat you out of house and home," said Ned, thinking his mother's life was beginning to centre round the making of cakes. "We're here to see if you can shed any light on the Harry and Emily mystery."

Molly broke two eggs into a basin and fiercely began to beat them. "Now, that is interesting. Put the kettle on please, Stella. So, have you found out anything more?"

Stella filled the kettle while Ned explained the trip to Polquillick and how they had found the two graves in the overgrown corner of the churchyard.

"Well, I'm not surprised that the graves exist," said Molly. "I couldn't see the newspapers getting that wrong, not all of it, anyway. But your finding the graves doesn't help in any way, does it? It only confirms that which you already knew."

"Yes, I agree," said Ned. "But somehow it makes it more real. Do you think it's possible for dreams ever to be true?"

Molly poured the beaten eggs into her large mixing bowl. "Sometimes. And this may sound rather far-fetched, but I wonder if it's possible for George to be the reincarnation of this Harry Timmins chap, and his coming to Cornwall has triggered off a memory from a previous life."

George turned very pale.

"You are joking, aren't you? I mean surely people don't really get reincarnated. Do they?"

Molly shrugged her shoulders. "Who knows for sure? I like to think they do, and it's certainly not something to dismiss without giving it any thought."

"Poppycock," said the major, hearing his wife's comment as he entered the back door to the kitchen, holding a handful of runner beans from the garden. "I'll go along with some of your crazy ideas, Moll, but not reincarnation, and I think it's very irresponsible of you to be putting such ridiculous notions into the heads of these youngsters."

Molly picked up a metal tray from the weighing scales containing flour and spooned it into the cake mixture. "I mention it merely as a possibility. Nothing more and nothing less."

The major shook his head, and muttering beneath his breath, returned to the garden.

"I wonder if there are still any family members at Polquillick, called Timmins," said Stella, pouring boiling water into the teapot. "We know of course that Harry's parents are dead, but if Harry was still alive he'd only be about seventy eight now and so he may well have brothers and sisters of a similar age who are still around. If we could find them and talk to them, maybe we'd be able to find out what Harry was like. You know what I mean, see if he sounds in any way like George; they may even be able to show us pictures of him. Not that a person reincarnated has to be like the person he's a reincarnation of, I suppose."

"Now, that is a good idea," said Ned, hugging his wife. "I certainly think it's an avenue we ought to explore further, although I agree that someone reincarnated would probably bear no resemblance to their previous self, and judging by the sad state of those graves I shouldn't think there are any close family members still around, anyway."

Molly nodded as she slowly folded the flour into the cake mixture. "It might be the case that Stella is right, because even if there is no striking resemblance between George and Harry, other similarities might be apparent. Character for instance, distinguishing birthmarks, skills and so forth."

George shuddered, recalling the dream. "Emily had only four toes on one foot, but I don't have any marks or deformities myself, so apart from a resemblance, I don't think we have much to go on, as I don't have any skills either."

"Are you afraid of water?" asked Rose, suddenly.

George frowned. "Water! What do you mean?"

"I mean, are you afraid of water? Afraid to go near it. I should think someone who had drowned would be very much afraid of water in another life."

George shook his head. "Well, no, I've no problem with water at all, in fact quite the opposite. I love swimming and always have, even though I've never actually swum in the sea. And I don't appear to have a phobia of boats either as I was not at all worried yesterday by our trip out to sea with Percy and Peter."

"I've always had a fear of drowning," mused Ned. "Ever since I can remember. I wonder if it's anything to do with your room, George, and whatever puts dreams into heads has gone to the wrong person."

"Don't" said Stella. "Because that would make you the possible reincarnation of Harry Timmins and the mere thought of it gives me the creeps."

"Do you think it could be anything to do with the fisherman hanging on the wall in my room?" George asked, after a brief reflection. "He could be Harry's dad or something like that. I always feel he can read my thoughts, so perhaps the sight of him before I fall asleep triggers off odd dreams."

Ned laughed. "No, that old boy was called Claude Gilbert and he came from a long line of fishermen and smugglers in this village and I don't think he had any connections with Polquillick. But I know what you mean about him reading your thoughts, because I always felt he laughed at me when I got emotional."

"There's a pub at Polquillick called the Mop and Bucket," said Rose, thoughtfully. "I've never been inside, but it's supposed to be an interesting place, unchanged throughout the ages. It might be a good place to visit and find out if there are still any people named Timmins in the village."

Stella laughed. "The Mop and Bucket. I don't believe it."

"Well, it's not its proper name. It's really the Rose and Crown. But a few years ago they suffered severe flooding when a pipe burst and it took a lot of mopping up because you step down into the bar, so there was nowhere for the water to run away to, if you see what I mean. Then afterwards, some bright spark started to refer to it as the Mop and Bucket, and the name just stuck."

"Definitely worth a visit," grinned George. "If only to say we've been there. Let's go over tonight as soon as we've had dinner."

"You'll be able to come too, won't you, Rose?" asked Stella, as she poured the tea. "Because tonight is your night off."

"I'd love to," she replied.

"How about you, Mum," Ned asked with a grin. "Will you join us?"

"Good heavens, no," said Molly, flattered at being asked. "The major would think I'd gone barmy if I went over to Polquillick looking for evidence to back up my theories about reincarnation. You saw what he was like. Besides, four's company five's a crowd."

"I thought it was two's company and three's a crowd," said Rose, puzzled.

"It is," said Ned. "But Mum likes things to be even and doesn't like people to feel left out. I know what she means, anyway."

Pleased that they might be on the verge of making a little progress, they each took a cup of tea into the front garden.

After removing her apron, Molly followed with a plate of biscuits, having first put the cake into the oven.

CHAPTER NINE

Once again they drove to Polquillick, for although the evening was beautiful and the prospect of a walk, tempting, they did not relish finding their way back over the cliff tops once darkness had fallen, in spite of a clear sky denoting there would be sufficient light to illuminate their way once the almost full moon was shining.

They found the Mop and Bucket in the heart of the village beside the school and a short distance from the cove. The old building was quaint, delightfully picturesque and reminiscent of the cottages so often depicted on postcards and chocolate boxes.

Outside, wooden troughs and tubs full of vividly coloured pelargoniums, broke up the monotony of the rendered, heavily white-washed walls. The door and small window frames were painted black, the roof was thatched and the entrance, through a side door, for which anyone over five foot three would have to duck, led down two steps into the public bar.

Inside, two dimly lit, small rooms were separated by a nicotine stained half glazed door, and each bustled with two very different types of clientele. Through the door marked saloon bar, smartly dressed holiday makers, chatted and laughed. While in the smaller public bar, locals, mostly fishermen, wearing smocks, darned jumpers, shabby trousers and caps part covering heads of uncombed hair, chatted in groups: the only subject on their lips, fishing.

When Ned, Stella, George and Rose emerged through the door and stood at the bottom of the steps taking in their new surroundings, the chat amongst the locals stopped as they looked the newcomers up and down. Ned and George crossed to the bar to buy drinks, leaving Stella and Rose feeling uncomfortable in the company of sea faring men who clearly resented the intrusion of their space.

As they waited the girls cast their eyes around the walls of the bar, where old pictures and paintings of boats, the sea and fishermen hung in profusion.

"Do you think any of these chaps on the wall might be Harry?" Stella whispered to Rose.

"It all depends whether or not Harry was a fisherman. We don't really know anything about him, do we?"

Ned and George returned with the drinks.

"Can't we go in there?" hissed Stella, pointing to the bar where the holiday makers gathered. "Rose and I feel like aliens in here."

"No," said George, firmly, despite the fact he was drawn towards the gaiety emanating from the saloon bar. "Holiday makers won't know if there are any Timmins still living in the village. Like it or not we have to stay in here."

The girls sighed as they sat down on a grubby bench up a corner near to the bar after first rubbing it over with Stella's handkerchief.

"So, who's going to ask this lot about our Harry, then?" whispered Ned, nodding to the locals who were still watching them. "Any volunteers?"

"Not me," said the girls in unison.

"You should have asked the landlord when you bought the drinks," snapped Stella. "He's the most obvious person to approach."

"Well, there's no rush," Ned mumbled, obstinately knowing she was right. "We'll leave it 'til later, there may be a few more folks in by then."

The fishermen, once tired of watching the newcomers, resumed their chat in gruff, muffled tones. George, feeling uncomfortable, cast an eye in their direction looking for any family resemblances.

"I don't look like any of that lot, do I?" he whispered.

"Good heavens, no," said Rose, with honesty.

Ned grinned. "I don't know, between them they have quite a few of your characteristics. The short, plump chap has your cauliflower ear. The tall skinny bloke has your big nose, and the old fellow in the corner has your gnarled, blackened teeth."

"Ha ha," laughed George, mockingly, as he drained his glass. "Very funny, and my round now, I think."

He rose to return to the bar for refills. Ned went with him.

"I'm going to ask the landlord about the name Timmins this time," said Ned to George. "Otherwise I'll have Stella nagging me again."

However, much to the dismay of the two young men, the landlord had been in the pub for less than twelve months. He was new to Cornwall and therefore he was unable to help with the name Timmins.

"It's daft, I must admit," he added, in a light Bristolian accent. "But lots of my locals I know only by their Christian names or nicknames, so there could well be someone called Timmins in tonight. In fact, when I come to think about it, the only chap in here whose surname I do know is old Joe Kernow over there by the fireplace, wearing the red scarf. And I only know that because he bought a car off me last week. I should ask Pilchard when he comes in. That's if he does. But he usually does, but then again sometimes he doesn't. I'll give you a nod if he does, though."

"Thank you, but would any of that lot know, do you think?" Ned asked, nodding in the direction of the fishermen seated alongside the figure of the old man identified as Joe Kernow.

The landlord wrinkled his nose. "Probably. You could always ask, but then they have such strong Cornish accents, you'd most likely as not be able to understand a word they said. And between you and me, they're inclined to put it on even more when speaking to up-country folk. They think it's funny. Weird buggers."

"I see. Thanks, anyway," said Ned. He and George then returned to their seats, where Stella and Rose had their eyes fixed on a picture of Polquillick, viewed from the cliffs, with an exorbitant price ticket boasting the name of a local artist.

"That painting is all out of perspective," tutted Stella, angrily. "The people on the beach are much too small and the houses are standing at a very peculiar angle. I really can't believe that anyone would ever want to buy it. I certainly wouldn't want it on any of our walls."

George grinned. "It must appeal to some or they wouldn't dare ask such a ridiculous amount of money. You could do better than that, anyway, Stella. I've seen some of your work and most of it would knock spots off that poor offering."

"Thank you, George. I think next time I go shopping I shall buy myself a sketch pad and maybe even a few paints. It would be nice to have a few pictures as mementoes of our honeymoon, anyway."

As the evening went on, the chat grew louder. Some of the holiday makers left and a few more arrived.

"I need to go to the Ladies," said Stella, rising to her feet. "Where do you think it is?"

Rose pointed towards the nicotine stained door. "Through there in the other bar. Look there's a sign over the door. And if you're going, I'm going with you."

The girls picked up there handbags, left and returned ten minutes later, perfume renewed, hair brushed, lipstick refreshed and both in fits of giggles.

"What's the matter with you two?" Ned asked. "What's so funny?"

"You'll find out in a minute," Stella replied.

Seconds later, two people emerged from the bar of holiday makers. They were Madge and Milly.

"Well, fancy seeing you here," said a slightly inebriated Madge, unceremoniously seating herself down beside George. "We couldn't believe it when we saw these two nice young ladies and they said you were with them."

George cast an evil eye at the two nice young ladies, as they started to giggle once more.

"Sit down Milly," commanded Madge. "You look awkward standing there, girl."

Rose and Stella moved along on their bench to make room for Milly.

"So, what brings you to this neck of the woods?" Ned asked, feeling he ought to be courteous.

"We just fancied a change of scenery," slurred Madge.

"And someone told us the landlord here doesn't have a wife," Milly innocently added.

Madge glared at her unsubtle daughter and kicked her beneath the table.

"He seems a nice chap," said George, hoping it was for Madge the vacancy of a landlady was being hinted at.

Madge laughed, took a huge swig from her glass, banged it down on the table and burped loudly.

"Err, would you like a refill?" asked Ned, seeing the glass was empty but hoping she would decline his offer and go away.

"How kind. Yes please. Mine's a double house whisky and Milly is drinking sweet cider."

The door opened as Ned waited at the bar to order the cider and whisky.

The landlord, on looking up to see who had arrived, gave Ned the nod.

"That's Pilchard. He's a very amicable chap, I should have a word with him if I were you."

Ned waited until Pilchard approached the bar, he then told how he had been recommended by the landlord, to ask if he knew of any people still living in Polquillick named Timmins.

"Timmins. No, I don't think so, not any more. The only people I ever knew with that name were a couple of old timers called Fred and Mabel and they died some thirty years ago when I were just a boy."

"Fred and Mabel," repeated Ned, recalling the names Stella had seen on the tombstone as Harry's parents. "Did you know them at all?"

Pilchard shook his head. "No, not really. They were pretty poor as I remember and struggled to survive on a farm labourer's wage. They kept themselves to themselves but if I remember correctly they lost a son at the turn of the century, before I was born, of course. It must've aged them a lot, because as I've already said, I remember them as a couple of real old timers, although I don't expect they were any older than sixty at the time. Actually, I've just remembered, they did have some other kids as well. Silly me. They had a couple of girls, but of course I knew them by their married names, not Timmins. I believe both girls eventually moved up-country. One certainly did, because I went to school with one of her kids. Billy he were called, Billy Fletcher. His dad was an up-country chap and that's why they moved away. I think it was Newcastle they went to. His dad certainly had a funny accent, because I never understood a word he said. It broke my poor little heart when he went, though, Billy that is, not his dad. We were great mates. I never saw him again, but I can still remember his cheeky grin. Memories eh? Fancy you bringing them back after all these years. But why do you want to know if there's anyone called Timmins still living here?"

"What? Oh, family connections," Ned lied, his brain addled by Pilchard's digression. "Auntie Flo's trying to put together a family tree and she believes at one time we had folks down here and one of them married a chap called Timmins."

"I see, well it's a common enough name in these parts. Sorry I can't help you anymore."

Ned thanked him then returned to his seat where he was unable to say anything to the others as Madge and Milly were still making a nuisance of themselves and Madge was sitting very close to George.

"I was talking to that Rosemary woman today," said Madge, taking a large swig of whisky. "She's a writer and wants to study Cornish life or some such tosh."

"Really," said Stella, "how interesting. Does she write for a magazine or is she a novelist?"

Madge scowled. "I didn't ask, I thought she seemed a bit hoity-toity. She told me she was a descendant of Charles Dickens and I don't like people who brag."

Rose was quick to speak in Rosemary's defence. "She's always very friendly when I chat to her and she strikes me as being very modest."

"Humph! Well, why's she down here on her own? That's what I'd like to know. It's not normal for a young gel like that to take a holiday alone. She must have some friends. I think she's up to something."

Stella smiled. "But surely if she's here to write she will need to be alone. It's not possible to concentrate with company always chatting and causing distractions."

"Mum only went to talk to her in the first place because she thought she might be down here looking for a husband," added Milly.

Madge giggled, shuffled along the bench even closer to George, put her podgy hand on his leg and scratched his knee with her long, painted red nails.

"I think it's time we headed home," said Ned, feeling sorry for his best friend.

"Do you have room for two more," gushed Madge. "We ought to be leaving too and it'd save us getting a taxi. What's more, we'd be back at the Inn in time for a nightcap."

"Well, it'll be a bit of a squeeze," said Ned, his sympathy now with his car. "But you're welcome to come with us if you don't mind the crush."

George groaned. Milly giggled.

As they rose to leave, Stella bent to retrieve her handbag from beneath the bench and whilst doing so, glanced towards the fishermen, deep in conversation with each other. Joe Kernow, however, was not listening to his younger associates, instead he was staring at George. Stella frowned, for without doubt there was a puzzled look on his lined, weather-beaten face and a hint of sadness in his watery eyes.

She ran to catch up with the others and joined them in the car park where they all squeezed into the Morris Minor. Ned and Stella sat in the front. Rose, George, Madge and Milly sat in the back. And Milly, as instructed by Madge, sat on George's lap. Rose frowned in the darkness. It was where she would have liked to have sat.

CHAPTER TEN

Dorothy Treloar inattentively brushed her thick brown hair, wound it tightly into a small bun on the back of her head and gripped it firmly into place. She sighed deeply. The grey around her ears was getting more conspicuous with every passing day, and still she was an old maid. Her sharp-tongued, critical mother had always stressed she would never find a husband and it looked as though she was right. Dorothy was forty five years old, had never had a gentleman friend in her life, and had no-one to love and care for, except her drunken, but hard working brother, Albert.

She pulled back the skin on her cheeks with the tips of her fingers. So many lines. Lines made worse by exposure to the sun and the harsh weather of winter working on the farm. Still, at least she did not have to do so much of that now. Albert had taken on some extra lads to help with the work, freeing her to work at the Inn, a job she enjoyed. She even had the occasional drink from time to time. Her strict, religious mother would not have approved of that.

She walked downstairs and into the kitchen, put on the kettle and prepared her breakfast. She then washed the dishes, changed from her slippers into her sturdy, serviceable shoes and went into the barn to fetch her bicycle. It was not far to the Inn and usually she walked, but as she was running a little late and had an errand to do before work, she decided cycling would be a more practical option.

The morning was beautiful as she rode down the lane; her tweed skirt flapped in the breeze and the wind whistled in her ears. In the valley a white mist shrouded the fields and from overhanging branches, shading the dusty, winding lane, birds sang to welcome in the new day.

In the basket of her bicycle, a bunch of red and pink roses, picked at first light from the farm gardens and damp with early morning dew, shook as she rode over the bumps in the road, causing wafts of their sweet, delicate perfume to fill the fresh, clean air.

Outside the church, she stopped, wheeled her bicycle along the narrow gravel path and leaned it against the large granite quoins on the corner of the old church tower. She then resumed her walk along the path until she reached a grave, marked with a Cornish cross, denoting the final resting place of Amy Johns. Beside it she veered off to the right and walked across the grass towards a black, polished granite tombstone with matching edges surrounding a well maintained double grave. From a memorial vase she emptied out dead flowers and tossed them onto the rotting compost heap in the corner of the churchyard. She then filled the vase with fresh water, and in it neatly arranged the roses she had carried in her basket. From the black and white granite chippings encased inside the black, polished granite surround, she pulled two dandelion seedlings and a few blades of grass.

"I wish I was pretty, Mum," she sighed, lowering her head, when the chores were done. "And then perhaps I might have proved you wrong and married one day. Now, I fear, it's too late."

She turned away, recovered her bicycle from its resting place, left the churchyard and peddled the few remaining yards round the corner to the Inn, where Barley Wine sat waiting for her on the doorstep.

Frank Newton rolled barrels across the cold, uneven cellar floor of The Ringing Bells Inn to make room for a fresh delivery of beer due later in the day. He had rolled many such barrels in the seventeen months since Sylvia's death. Seventeen months during which not one day had passed without him thinking of the wife he had lost.

"I don't expect I'll ever marry again," he muttered to a mouse as it scuttled across the grubby floor. "Although I think I'd like to. It's lonely these days just having myself to think about and I can't bear the thought of ending my days a sad, lonely old man."

He finished his work, picked up a crate containing bottles of pale ale, climbed the stone steps to the bar, closed the heavy trap door behind him and stretched his arms to relieve his aching back.

"Oh dear, that bleedin' settee's beginning to cripple me. I hope Auntie Mabel doesn't stay too long or I might have to chuck out one of the guests."

73

He unloaded the pale ale from the crate onto a shelf beneath the cash register, after first meticulously dusting each bottle. There was a time when he had put them out all higgledy-piggledy and had not bothered about a bit of dust. But Sylvia had changed all that. She had liked to see them neat, clean and tidy, with the labels facing outwards, so that was the way they had to be now.

As he put the last bottle in place he heard someone humming in the kitchen.

"Is that you, Dot?" he called, pushing the empty crate beneath the bar.

"Yes, Frank. Would you like a cup of tea?"

"I'd love one please, Dot."

Dorothy Treloar took the kettle from the stove and poured boiling water into the old brown earthenware teapot. Then while it brewed, she put rashers of bacon into a frying pan and continued to cook breakfast for the residents of the Inn.

In the garden of Ivy Cottage, Doris Jones watered the plants in her small cedar wood greenhouse and picked a dozen tomatoes from the healthy vines gently brushing against panes of glass in the warm, soft breeze which emanated through the open windows and door. She had picked many pounds of tomatoes already since the end of June and was delighted that she had tried a new variety of seed recommended to her by Jim Hughes. For her abundant crop meant she would have several pounds to spare for the village fete.

Leaving the greenhouse she stepped back into her vegetable garden and walked along the path to the front of her house where in the herbaceous border, brightly coloured flowers covered every patch of earth.

After a brief reflection, she leaned across rows of shocking pink petunias and carefully cut several flower heads from her blue, lace-cap hydrangea. With the flowers lying inside her trug, she then crossed her neatly trimmed lawn and snipped several strands of honeysuckle from the trellis which ran around her front door. Six stems of stock completed the bunch, after which she returned the trug to the shed and with flowers in hand, left her cottage and walked the short distance down the road to the church, without locking or even closing her front door.

Alongside the wall which marked the boundaries of the churchyard, she stopped to examine the crop of green elderberries dripping in large clusters from the strongly scented shrubs. A satisfied smile crossed her face. The berries were many in number and over the years she had found the churchyard bushes a reliable indication as to the quality and quantity she could expect to find from elders growing in and around Trengillion. For Doris Jones was a home-made wine enthusiast, and without fail, for as long as she could remember, had made dandelion wine and occasionally elderflower in the spring, and elderberry in the autumn.

As she emerged from beneath the lichgate she gazed up at the church tower and the Virginia creeper covering the granite walls like a green velvet cloak. She had watched it grow and spread over the many years she had lived in Trengillion and its beauty never ceased to please her, especially in the autumn when the leaves turned to a beautiful shade of red.

In the shadow of a tall mountain ash, she stopped, laid the flowers on the grass, knelt down beside a grave and quietly wept.

"It's two years ago today since I last saw you, Jane. I still miss you, sweetheart, and I think I always will. If you were still alive you'd probably be married by now and perhaps have babies like Gertie. Life's very cruel, love. But then you don't need me to tell you that."

She picked up the vase lying beneath the plain headstone and took it to a tap situated on the wall beside the vestry door. She filled it with clean water and carefully carried it back to the small grass mound beneath which Jane slept. Once the fresh flowers were arranged, she dried her eyes and walked back down the gravel path, lost in thought. She then left the churchyard and wandered up the road to Rose Cottage, where Molly and the major had asked her to join them for elevenses.

After he heard the whistle of the paper-boy and the click of the garden gate, Godfrey Johns walked into his hallway to pick up the daily newspaper lying on the doormat. He then sat down in his armchair to read it, but his concentration was poor due to a line scraped through the dust on the sideboard made by Mabel when she had paid him a surprise visit earlier in the week.

Godfrey threw the unread paper onto the floor, rose from his chair, examined the dust a little closer and felt a sudden, excruciating pang of guilt.

"What would Amy think if she could see how her neat, clean and spotless house had become a filthy, untidy and even a little smelly, pigsty?"

He scratched his chin, wondering how best to deal with the situation, for he felt certain that Mabel, now she knew where he lived, would call again, and that would be nice.

He and Amy had struck up a long lasting friendship going back many years with Mabel and her late husband, Bert. But it was his fault the correspondence had lapsed. For he had not replied to Mabel's last letter, the arrival of which occurred shortly after Amy's sudden death towards the end of the War.

At the time he had been too distraught to write and he hated writing letters, anyway. Then the years just slipped away. And now he had learned that dear old Bert was dead too.

"Poor Bert," muttered Godfrey. "He was a good sort. Kind hearted and generous. Pity he let Mabel bully him though, for it was obvious that she wore the trousers in their house, and that just wasn't right."

He went into the kitchen and opened the cupboard door in which Amy had kept her cleaning clothes, bottles and tins. He picked up a rusting tin of furniture polish and a cloth, wandered into the front room and moved all the dusty ornaments from the sideboard onto the floor. With a great dollop of polish on his cloth, he wiped over the dirty surface, and after using a little elbow grease, the sideboard shone in the bright, morning sunlight.

Godfrey felt a sudden pang of pride. The sideboard looked really nice, like Amy used to keep it. He looked around the room at the rest of the dust and clutter.

"Right, Godfrey Johns," he said to himself. "If you can have the dining room and the sitting room sparkling by teatime, then tomorrow you can go to the village fete and afterwards pop in for a pint at The Ringing Bells Inn. You've not mixed with the village folks for too many years and it's time you did. You've moped around for far too long! Look at Mabel? She's still well presented and sociable too, and she lost Bert far more recently than you lost Amy.

It's time for change, Godfrey Johns. It's time to pull yourself together, pick up the pieces and move on."

Inside number two Coronation Terrace, Gertie Collins, having got the twins off to sleep, was busy in the kitchen with Meg from next door, making cakes for the village fete due to take place the following day. When the cakes were finally in the oven, both young women took a break and sat with their feet up enjoying a cup of coffee and a cigarette.

"Betty's coming round tonight to cut my hair," said Gertie, tucking a stray lock behind her ear. "It's driving me mad resting on my shoulders like this. It always looks so untidy and I don't have time now to spend curling it and suchlike."

"How are you going to have it done?" asked Meg. "I think a bob would suit you. You've the ideal shaped face for a fringe."

"That's what Betty said, so it's probably what I'll go for. I fancied having it dyed too but Percy said no to that. He reckons only old women should be allowed to dye their hair and then only when they need to cover up grey. He hates anything artificial, especially dyed hair and false nails."

Meg laughed. "No fear of him doing a moonlight flit with Madge, then."

"Who's Madge?"

"You know, the peroxide blonde woman staying at the Inn. You must remember her from the party. She was the one chasing Ned's dishy friend, George. She's on a man-hunting holiday with her teenage daughter."

"Oh yes, I do remember. The podgy woman with the tight blonde perm. I wonder why she's come down here looking for husband. I mean, aren't there any blokes where she lives?"

"I don't know, but perhaps she's trying to get away from old memories. I believe she's divorced from her husband and that still bears a stigma with many people, even in these enlightened times."

"Is Frank's old auntie still here? I thought she looked a bit of a harridan, but Mum was talking to her in the post office last week and she said she's really nice."

"I think she's still here. I haven't been to the Inn lately but Sid often pops in for a chat with the lads and he hasn't mentioned her having gone home. But then he probably wouldn't have noticed if she had anyway, as he's completely wrapped up in Des and Larry's progress at present. He's really chuffed cos he's persuaded them to let him write an article about them and their wreck. He reckons it'll be of great interest to people in West Cornwall to learn what's going on in the area. And if the interest shown by Trengillion's population is anything to go by, then I guess he's right."

Gertie nodded. "Whereabouts is the wreck? I asked Percy but he didn't know exactly. That's the trouble with fishermen, they're such fusspots when it comes to locations at sea. Everything has to be precise using landmarks and suchlike so he said he didn't know for sure. I only wanted a rough idea."

"I believe it's over Polquillick way somewhere. It's definitely further on than the Witches Broomstick, anyway."

She leaned forward and flicked ash into the small glass ashtray on the arm of the settee. "Betty seems much happier since she started to train as a hairdresser, doesn't she? I'm glad she found her niche in life. Being artistic, she was wasted in that old factory."

"Yes, but I'm surprised she still bothers to work at the Inn, albeit part-time."

"I think she finds the extra money comes in useful, especially now she's learning to drive. Driving lessons don't come cheap as I well remember when I started."

Gertie sighed. "I wish I could drive. I should have had lessons and taken a test after leaving the farm while tractor driving was still fresh in my mind. Still, perhaps I'll get round to it when the boys are a bit older, and I must admit I miss working at the Inn too. It was such a good source of village gossip. I seldom hear any exciting news from Percy. His stories are all about fishing. He's absolutely hopeless when it comes to passing on female tittle-tattle."

"Talking of tittle-tattle, have you heard about that friend of Ned's weird dreams?" asked Meg, a note of excitement in her voice.

"No, I've not seen anything of them since Frank threw the party. So what's this all about?"

Meg repeated everything she had been told by Sid, about the dreams, Harry Timmins, the drownings and the possibility of George being a reincarnation of Harry.

"Good, God!" exclaimed Gertie, stubbing out her cigarette. "How horrible for poor George to think he might once have been someone else. I'd hate that. But it can't be true, can it?"

"I don't know," said Meg. "But if there is such a thing as reincarnation, it may well explain some of life's mysteries. Like for instance, how Mozart could play the piano and write music at the age of three. Perhaps in a previous life he had been a gifted musician and the talents went with him into another life. It might also explain why some children are brilliant at arithmetic before they can write and why people have phobias."

"Oh, weird. I'm terrified of knives with big blades, so do you think I might have been murdered in a previous life?"

Meg laughed. "Who knows? Sadly, it's something we'll none of us be able to establish until we're gone from this life."

CHAPTER ELEVEN

Saturday morning began with a heavy shower of rain, thus causing the fete organisers to utter words of dismay as they rose from their beds and surveyed the grey clouds looming over the village. The forecast, however, promised sunshine and so with a small dose of optimism, they assembled on the field behind the Inn as planned and set about preparing for the busy day.

Sid Reynolds, with the aid of a tall ladder and his wife Meg, hung bunting from the trees. Percy and Peter carried trestle tables from the village hall and placed them in neat rows on the freshly mown grass ready for the stall holders to place their wares. A tent for tea making was erected in a corner near to the Inn so that water was readily available from the Inn's kitchen. A smaller tent, for the fortune teller, Madame Rowena, was placed in a quiet spot, so those wishing to have their fortunes told could hear the good tidings and words of wisdom without the intrusive noise of laughter, chatter and the high pitched squeals of over excited children.

In the middle of the field, village hall chairs were placed in rows for weary patrons of the fete to rest and listen to the silver band booked to come in from town. And down the side of the field, wooden pegs, each joined with old binder twine, marked a strip of grass along which Brown Ale would provide pony rides under the supervision of Meg, to the village children and anyone else who had tuppence to spare.

Pat Dickens arrived in due course on his tractor with a trailer load of straw bales. These were placed in a shady spot beneath a large sycamore tree for the amusement of the children.

By lunchtime everything was in place ready for the hoped for crowds and Joyce Richardson, donned in straw sunhat and floral dress, took her seat by the gate to welcome patrons with a programme listing the order of events.

Meanwhile, on the field behind, stall holders took their places behind groaning trestle tables laden with colourful wares. Flowering plants, home-grown vegetables, jars of pickled onions, chutneys and homemade jam, covered the plant and produce stall.

Jumble, toys and unwanted household items spilled over onto the grass from the rummage and white elephant stall.

An old bible, paperback novels, magazines and comics stacked in neat piles, filled the book stall.

Mystery gifts, each neatly wrapped in old Christmas paper, were hidden inside the bran tub, which stood on the grass alongside stalls for *Guess the weight of the cake*, *Pin the tail on the donkey*, tombola, raffles and cakes.

The organisers were not disappointed with the response to their labours. The rain clouds had long dispersed, the sun was shining brightly and everyone from the village and outlying areas, it seemed, was making a bee line for the fete in time for the official opening by Doctor Blake at two o' clock.

Ned, Stella and George walked around the field enjoying the atmosphere. Rose was not with them, as she and Annie Stevens were busy in the tea tent serving hot beverages to the thirsty crowds. Molly had also volunteered to help. She and Doris were in charge of the produce and plant stall.

Molly eyed the small tent in the valley where the fortune teller was hidden, and wondered if Madame Rowena, tucked inside, really had talents or if she was someone from the village prepared to predict the first thing that came into her head. She asked Ned to find out when he came to admire her stall. After making several enquiries, Ned eventually discovered from Annie, that Madame Rowena was not local to the village, but a lady who had responded to an advertisement they had inserted in the local newspaper.

"Really," said Molly, on receiving the news. "I must try and get to see what she can tell me then, when things quieten down a bit here. I love having my fortune told. It fascinates me hearing and seeing others in my profession at work."

Ned frowned. "But why aren't you the fortune teller, Mum? Surely it would make sense to have someone from the village and it's right up your street."

"May Dickens did ask me on behalf of the committee, but after I'd thought about it for a while I decided I knew too many people and for that reason alone it wouldn't be fair to me or the public."

Ned frowned. "Oh, but why would you knowing people make any difference?"

"Well, I'd know whether or not they were married, had children and so forth, which would then limit the subjects usually predicted by fairground fortune tellers. People in queues usually get impatient too, so I wouldn't have the time to do a proper job and use my talents to their full potential."

"In that case, Madame Rowena won't have time to be thorough either, and so I still can't see the point of bringing in a stranger."

"But as I've already said, the fact that she is a stranger is to her advantage as she'll be able to make the usual predictions regarding romance, wealth and so forth. After all, that's what most people want to hear, anyway. But let's put an end to interrogation, Ned. It's rather tiresome. Now, where's George? He ought to have his fortune told, just in case Madame Rowena does have a wonderful foresight and might be able to pick up the vibes and say something earth-shattering regarding his dreams."

Ned slapped his thigh. "Now, that is a good idea and it could be a laugh too. I might even have mine done. I'll go and find George. He and Stella are helping Rose and Annie at the moment because they're getting a bit behind washing dirty teacups."

As Ned departed, Frank arrived at the fete having just closed the Inn after lunchtime opening. He stopped by the stall manned by Molly and Doris and admired the quick selling flowers.

"I suppose I ought to buy a few blooms to put in the old cracked pot by the front door of the Inn. It looks so neglected and uncared for, but then that's probably because it is. What would you recommend, ladies?"

Molly smiled. "It's a bit late in the season to be making up pots, Frank, so I'd suggest a fuchsia, as that'll keep on flowering for a month or two yet. What say you, Doris?"

"I'd say the same, and these are all hardy so they'll keep on flowering year after year with a bit of care and regular feeding whilst they're in bloom."

"Feeding?" muttered Frank, alarmed. "What on earth do I feed them with?"

Doris shook her head. "You never did have green fingers, did you, Frank Newton? But don't worry, we'll plant it for you and feed it when necessary. You just make sure you water it daily when the weather's warm or dry."

"Is Mabel not here?" asked Molly, casting her eyes over the field. "I would have thought she'd enjoy something like this."

Frank shook his head. "No, she's gone off to Newquay for the day. She saw a coach trip advertised when she was in town the other day and booked a seat not knowing the fete was on. Although I fail to see how she could have missed all the posters plastered round the village."

Frank selected a large healthy fuchsia and Doris put it beneath the table with a promise to plant it for him later in the afternoon.

Ned met up again with George and Stella as they emerged from the tea tent and both agreed having their fortunes told sounded a novel idea. They crossed to the far side of the field with a modicum of optimism and joined the not inconsiderable queue sitting on the grass beneath a row of elm trees, patiently waiting to hear what the future had in store.

Eventually they reached the front of the queue and it was agreed Stella must be first to go in. She entered the tent apprehensively and was greeted by Madame Rowena wearing a long, loose gown and sitting bolt upright behind a table covered with a thick, red velvet cloth. Stella smothered a smile. On her head the fortune teller wore an elaborate, bright blue turban-like headdress dripping with jewels. It was not possible to establish the shade of her hair as every inch of her head was hidden beneath the voluminous headdress, including the tops of her ears. The lobes, however, were visible and weighed down with huge circular earrings. She was heavily made up, and so the true colour of her skin was impossible to establish, and as she wore a thin veil draped from ear to ear, very little of her face was exposed. But her eyes were clear to see and Stella was bewitched by their vivid violet colour.

Stella, found it difficult not to laugh as she listened to the fortune teller's erroneous prophesy. Nevertheless, she was beguiled by the performance and felt the fee well worth every penny for the entertainment value alone.

She smiled broadly at Ned and George as she emerged from the tent. "I'm sorry to report she's a fraud. She speaks with a foreign accent which I'm sure is not genuine, and although she's impressive to look at, especially her bewitching violet eyes, she's no more capable of predicting the future than I am. I tricked her, you see. Before I went in I popped my wedding ring into my pocket and the first thing she did was look at my left hand. After that she kept going on about a handsome blond chap I'd soon meet. He'll be a doctor apparently, and I'll marry him and have three children."

Ned raised his eyebrows. "Oh, you will, will you Mrs Stanley. Well, we'll have to see about that." Trying to keep a straight face, he then walked towards the tent.

Ten minutes later he too came out grinning.

"She told me the girl I'm dating at present isn't Miss Right, but the person I'll marry will be known to me soon, possibly even as early as this summer and then me and my new love will emigrate to Australia. I must tell Mum. She'll be delighted to know that Madame Rowena is no competition."

George grinned. "Sounds like she's trying to get rid of you. Madame Rowena that is, not your mum."

He pulled back the canvas flap and disappeared inside with a deep feeling of scepticism. Fifteen minutes later he made his exit from the tent and strolled over to Ned and Stella who were sitting on the grass in the sunshine.

"Anything interesting?" asked Stella, seeing a look of amusement on his face.

George sat down beside them. "Not really, but then it all depends how you interpret it. She said I'll soon meet the girl of my dreams and we'll live a long and happy life together."

"But the girl of your dreams at present is Emily Penberthy and she's dead," spluttered Ned.

"Precisely, that's what I mean. But actually Emily Penberthy is the girl *in* my dreams and not *of* my dreams. There's a big difference between the two. You can make it fit if you want, but I think it's all nonsense. Emily's dead and there's no way our paths will ever cross in this life."

"Ah, but what about the next life?" said Stella. "Do you think your paths may cross then?"

"Please, let's not pursue this silly conversation any further. Remember, Madame Rowena was way out with her predictions for both of you, and so there's no reason whatsoever to indicate things should be any different for me."

Later in the afternoon, a huge crowd gathered around a circle of chairs on which sat the silver band. Many danced to the lively Glen Miller tunes, despite uneven grass impeding slickness of steps. When it came to the old wartime favourites, particularly those made famous by the Forces sweetheart, Vera Lynn, almost everyone sang loud and clear. Only children playing on the bales of straw, refrained from taking part in the community sing-song.

George gave a sideways glance towards Ned and Stella as they sang enthusiastically together, swaying in time to the music with arms around each other. They looked blissfully happy, and for a fleeting moment he regretted the termination of his relationship with Elsie. But after more consideration he concluded, he had without doubt, made the right decision, but for all the stress and annoyance she had caused him, he wished her no ill. In fact, his uppermost desire was for her to find happiness with someone willing to jump into wedlock and to whom the notion of living in Manchester appealed greatly.

Percy and Gertie, with the twins and their friends, Peter and Betty, spotted the teachers listening to the band and ambled over to greet them.

"You've had your hair done," said Stella to Gertie. "It looks really nice."

"Thank you. Betty did it last night and Percy didn't even notice when he came in, which is pretty pathetic, don't you think? Especially as he knew I was having it done. Men are so unobservant."

Percy opened his mouth to respond but could think of a no convincing excuse.

Gertie saved his embarrassment by asking George for more information about his dreams. For they had fired up her imagination and occupied many of her thoughts since Meg had first enlightened her about his peculiar visions of a previously, unknown to him, tragedy.

George reiterated the whole story to an amazed Gertie while Stella cooed over the babies.

"But that's really frightening," said Gertie. "Aren't you scared? I mean, how do you ever dare sleep at night knowing you might dream of the drownings again? And as for being someone else, it's too spooky to even think about."

George shrugged his shoulders. "I've sort of got used to the idea now and although it's possible I might have the dream again, I don't believe for a minute that I'm the reincarnation of Harry Timmins or anyone else for that matter. But time will tell what the outcome will be, if indeed there is an outcome. It may well be that nothing further will happen."

"Well, don't bother trying to find out by having your fortune told by that old crone in the little tent. She told me that the person I'm dating at present isn't Mr Right, but the person I'll marry will be known to me soon, possibly even as early as this summer, and then me and my new love will emigrate to Australia. Did you ever hear anything so daft? What she didn't know, of course, was that I stopped wearing my wedding ring when I was pregnant because my fingers were swollen and they're still not back to their normal size, so the ring is hidden on a chain beneath my blouse."

"I told you not to waste your money on all that nonsense, but you wouldn't listen," scoffed Percy.

"But I thought she might say something earth shattering, or at least worthwhile. Anyway, it's a bit of fun and the money isn't wasted because it's all for a good cause."

"I'm going to marry a blond haired doctor," said Betty, with a dejected sigh. "Fat chance of that. The only doctor I know is Doctor Blake and he's married with grandchildren, and his hair is snowy white."

What are the babies called?" asked Stella, ignoring the conversation taking place around her, convinced one of the twins had smiled.

"Tony and John," said Gertie. "And before you ask which is which, Tony is the one sleeping and John's about to cry."

On cue, John wrinkled up his little face and expressed his displeasure with a feeble whimper. Gertie laughed. "I expect he thinks he's hungry, but he'll have to wait. He's a right greedy guts is John."

Gently she rocked the pram in an attempt to get him back off to sleep, at the same time, over the loud speaker Pat Dickens began to call out the prize winning numbers for the raffle, causing patrons of the fete to withdraw from their pockets, purses and wallets, crumpled tickets in colours of pale blue, green and yellow.

The gathered crowds sat and stood in silence as they waited in anticipation to hear their numbers called, thus enabling them to step forward and select from the table at Pat's side, something to their liking from the vast selection of prizes.

As they waited, Milly crept up beside the small assembled group by the pram and waited patiently for them to acknowledge her presence.

"Err, sorry to interrupt," she blurted, when finally she caught Ned's eye, "but I really think I must warn you, while she's in the lav., Mum's just had her fortune told, you see, and she's over the moon, because apparently, her true love is already known to her and she will marry within the year..."

"...Thank God, for that," interrupted George, as a huge grin swept across his face. "Madame Rowena has said something acceptable at last. Tell me, Milly, who is it? Surely not the poor landlord of the Mop and Bucket."

Milly shook her head. "Oh no. No, she should be so lucky. It's much worse than that, for you at least, anyway, because Mum's been told she'll marry a dashingly handsome school teacher called George."

CHAPTER TWELVE

Ned, Stella and George were not very hungry after the fete having eaten several slices of cake and a whole family of gingerbread men made by Flo Hughes. Nevertheless, they put on a brave face and cleared their plates for fear of offending Dorothy Treloar, who had left the fete early in order to prepare and cook the evening meal. Madge on the other hand had no difficulty at all in clearing her plate. She even finished off that which Milly was unable to devour.

"No Rosemary tonight, I see," commented George, as they rose to leave the dining room. "I wonder if she also ate too much."

"Was she at the fete, then?" asked Ned. "I didn't see her."

"Yes, she was walking around with an older women and then I saw her again later helping out with the bran tub. She seemed very much at ease with children and it crossed my mind she'd make a good teacher if she wasn't so shy. After all, she must be brainy if she's a writer."

Ned scowled. "I don't know about that. I've read plenty of drivel in my life and so not all writers are intelligent."

"Well, I suppose not. I'm surprised you didn't see her, though. She was at the bran tub when we were listening to the band and I thought she looked rather pretty. Her hair was in a different style and the colour of the dress she had on really suited her."

Ned raised his eyebrows as they walked into the passage. "Do I detect your desire for the fairer sex returning?"

"No. Well, not for Rosemary, anyway. She's not my type. And what do you mean about my desire for the fairer sex returning? I can assure you Ned it's not been anywhere. I'm just not interested in women who want to drag me to the altar, like Elsie and, God forbid, Madge. And as regards Rosemary I was merely making an observation, but she does have a good pair of legs."

"There's nothing wrong with tying the knot," said Ned. "I'd recommend it to anyone."

88

"Yes, but there's only one Stella and even she has poor taste. To think she chose you when she could have had me!"

The two friends started a mock fight in the hallway. Stella shook her head and cast a pitying look of despair. "Not all teachers are brainy either," she muttered, heading for the stairs to change into her comfortable sandals.

Rose went home after she had waitressed that evening. She'd had a busy day in the tea tent and was feeling in need of an early night. George, not wanting to be a gooseberry, announced he would retire to his room, feigning a desire to begin reading Ian Fleming's Casino Royale, a new book loaned to him by the major. He was also desperate to get as far away from Madge as possible, for she, because of the fortune teller's prediction, had, during dinner, gazed continually at him with a lustful eye. And following the advice of the old adage, 'the way to a man's heart is through his stomach', she let it be known whilst plunging her spoon into an extra-large helping of pudding, that her culinary skills were quite magnificent.

"I don't doubt for a minute that she is a good cook," muttered George, closing the door of his room and flopping down on the bed. "But the last thing I want at present is to be seduced by food."

Ned and Stella went into the public bar, where they found many of the locals continuing the community spirit conjured up by the fete. They had much to celebrate having raised nearly twice as much money as the previous year. Spontaneous singing broke out, and much to the surprise of Ned and Stella, Auntie Mabel, back from her trip to Newquay, warbled her way through the village inhabitants' repertoire with a tuneful voice. And despite the contents of her glass containing nothing stronger than bitter lemon, she succumbed to the magic of infectious laughter with gusto.

Also singing, in a fine tenor voice, was Godfrey Johns, heartily relishing the revival of friendship with his old contemporaries and acquaintances, having successfully cleaned and polished his sitting and dining rooms until his arms ached and the air smelt fresh and clean.

Molly, who never had found time to have her fortune told, discovered, when questioning the females sitting round a table in the snug discussing the day's events, that many had received identical prophesies from Madame Rowena.

May Dickens laughed. "Yes, at least three of us are going to win the football pools and the rest it seems are to inherit substantial amounts of money from distant relatives. The youngsters didn't fare much better it seems. Most were told similar yarns regarding future husbands and wives."

Molly shook her head. "The words cynical and lack of imagination spring to mind, but let's hope she's right with her forecasts of good health and wealth, and is not just a yarn-spinning charlatan."

Rosemary Howard, sitting nearby with the older woman with whom George had seen her at the fete, heard Molly's comments.

"The fortune teller told me that soon I shall have my name in the newspapers," she giggled. "So, like you, Mrs Smith, I dearly hope she is right with some of her predictions."

Stella slept soundly after the day's activities; Ned on the other hand, having eaten too much, found himself drifting in and out of a fitful sleep, for the room on that warm August night, felt stuffy and claustrophobic. He climbed out of bed carefully so as not to disturb Stella, and opened wide the window, hoping the fresh air might enable him to sleep more soundly.

Outside, countless bright stars twinkled from the clear, dark sky and the moon, high over the sea, cast a silver and white glow across the rooftops giving the appearance of a fine sprinkling of snow.

Ned climbed back into bed and optimistically closed his eyes. The distant muffled sound of waves falling onto the seashore relaxed his brain and soothed his mind. An owl hooted from the trees in the churchyard and a gentle breeze blew through the open window causing the pendulous light in the centre of the ceiling to sway gently back and forth.

Ned turned onto his side and snuggled his head into the pillow. Down below something crashed noisily onto the cobbled area beneath his window. He assumed some creature, a cat or a fox, had knocked over the large metal rubbish bin near the entrance to the Inn, but his inquisitiveness was not sufficient to entice him back out of bed to investigate. Again he closed his eyes and attempted to sleep, but found himself even more awake than before.

From across the landing, Ned heard the door of George's room open and he wondered if George was also finding it difficult to sleep; but after brief consideration, he concluded the footsteps he could hear walking down the passage were inevitably George going to the bathroom.

Ned listened, waiting for him to return, but the passage remained silent. He heard no footsteps nor the sound of George's door closing.

Puzzled, Ned sat up, climbed out of bed once more, opened the door and looked along the passage. It was dark and eerily quiet. With a feeling of bewilderment and concerned that George might be ill, he tiptoed along the landing to the bathroom where he was surprised to find no light shining through the half glazed door. Attempting to smother a deep yawn, Ned walked to the top of the stairs. From below he felt a draught. He shivered, sensing something was amiss. Had it been George he had heard walking along the landing or someone else?

Quietly and quickly he retraced his steps, stood outside George's room and listened. He could hear nothing. No breathing. No snoring. Desperate to know whether George had left his room and not returned, Ned carefully opened the door. The room was in darkness, but in the moonlight he could see that George's bed was empty. Ned closed the door quickly, returned to his own room for his slippers and dressing gown and then tip-toed with haste along the landing and down the stairs.

In the hallway, by the coat rack, Ned could see the side door of the Inn was wide open. He went outside and quietly closed the door. As he reached the roadside, he glanced up into the village and down towards the cove. In neither direction was there any sign of George.

Instinct told him to go to the cove. Pulling his dressing gown snugly around his chilled body, he tied the cord and ran down the hill. On the shingle he stopped and glanced back and forth across the beach. It was deserted except for two fishermen standing at the water's edge with fishing rods and lines hovering over the tumbling waves.

From behind Ned thought he heard a noise. He turned quickly and was alarmed to see two headless figures swaying back and forth in the garden of Cove Cottage. With thumping heart he strained his eyes to see more clearly. He laughed out loud; the two dubious characters were Des and Larry's diving suits hanging from the washing line.

Still chuckling, Ned looked to his left. At the foot of the cliff he spotted a figure scrambling up the track leading to the coastal path. Was it George? Possibly, but if so Ned was completely mystified as to why he might be going for a ramble over the cliffs in the middle of the night. Nevertheless, he followed, ducking to hide behind rocks whenever he felt George or the person he was pursuing might turn around. At one point the path was narrow and Ned tore his pyjama trousers on overhanging brambles and tripped on small stones and bare roots not visible in the moonlight. George, or whoever, marched quickly on seemingly unperturbed by the obstacles in his path, while Ned, hot and bothered by his unforeseen bout of exercise, cursed the fact he was unable to gain any distance between himself and the person he was tracking.

Breathlessly, Ned clambered on, stumbling over rocks and passing through dense areas of spiky gorse and flourishing bracken; repeatedly looking over his shoulders, especially so when he passed by the row of eerie, forsaken coastguard cottages which he knew were uninhabited.

Finally, the ruins of the old Penwynton mine came into view. There the mystery person stopped. Ned crept a little closer and to his relief saw that it was George.

Mystified he crouched down behind a boulder and waited, part-hidden, to see what happened next. His ears pricked up when he thought he heard movement on the path along which he had just walked. Nervously, Ned held his breath. Was someone else out taking a late night stroll or had he been followed? Crouching lower still he strained his ears to listen, but not another sound could he hear, other than the sea crashing onto the rocks below. Praying the coast was clear, he slowly rose from his hiding place, but stopped dead when a mysterious rustle emanated from the branches of a lone tree in a nearby field.

Ned turned, gasped and then ducked as a large bird, squawking loudly, swooped down from the tree and into the long grass, searching for prey. It then retreated upwards and flew around the chimney of the old mine. Its enormous wings flapping like pistons: its huge claws empty. Circling overhead it cast shadows in the moonlight; piercing the night air with its blood-curdling cries and squawks. Eventually it left the mine and flew off towards Trengillion.

With heart thumping loudly, Ned raised his head and nervously looked towards the spot where George stood, motionless. Ned was confused. The cry and presence of the bird had not caused George to react, move, or even turn around.

Ned crept a little closer; he gasped, shocked and surprised. George was not properly dressed; he wore only his pyjama trousers and his feet were bare.

Baffled and afraid, Ned left the shadows of the mine wall and crept nearer still to the spot where George stood, his eyes transfixed on the ocean stretching far in front of him. Gently, Ned called to his friend, but George, did not appear to hear. He seemed in a daze, or a trance.

"Good God," said Ned, standing up straight, hand pressed against forehead, as the truth behind his friend's extraordinary night venture became apparent. For without doubt George was fast asleep and had walked to the mine seemingly unaware of what he was doing.

CHAPTER THIRTEEN

Ned stood still, his feet frozen onto a well-worn patch of grass. He tried to think clearly, but his confused, numbed brain seemed incapable of creative thought. Unsure how to react, Ned could only hope that George might suddenly awaken and realise he was in very grave danger. But George, it seemed, was in a world of his own and oblivious of the vulnerable situation he was in.

Ned cursed as the moon momentarily disappeared behind a cloud, plunging the surroundings into darkness. When the cloud passed and he could see once more, he observed that George had stepped further forward towards the cliff's edge. There he seemed to pause, mesmerized by the rugged rocks below, where waves relentlessly crashed, sending foaming spray onto the face of the steep cliff wall.

Ned held his breath, petrified, as adrenalin pumped through his veins. His mouth felt dry and his throat was painfully tight as George advanced yet another hair-raising step.

"No," Ned roared, his voice quivering with fear. He leapt forward and ran towards George, fully aware that it was dangerous to startle or waken a sleepwalker, but reckoning the consequences of not doing so would inevitably result in tragedy. With enormous strides, Ned flew across grass towards the cliff's edge.

"For God's sake, George, stop! You ruddy idiot. Get back. Get away from the edge."

He grabbed George firmly by the shoulders, pushed him forcibly to the ground and slapped him hard across the face.

George shuddered, rubbed his reddening cheek and attempted to sit up but Ned was kneeling on his chest, tears of relief and stress dripping from his eyes.

"Get off, Ned. What the hell do you think you're playing at, and why are you crying, you great pansy?"

"I'm playing at saving your life, you silly sod and I'm not crying. You were going to jump, George. You were going to throw yourself over the ruddy cliff. And why? That's what I'd like to know. Are you crackers?"

George sat up as Ned withdrew from his chest. He rubbed his eyes and looked around. "Where the devil are we, and why is it dark?"

"This is the Penwynton Mine and it's dark because it's the middle of the sodding night," said Ned, wiping his eyes on the sleeve of his dressing gown. "I followed you here after I heard you leave your room and not return."

"But what on earth made me come up here? I've never been to this spot before in my life."

"I don't know?" said Ned. "You tell me."

George scrambled unsteadily to his feet. When he looked down at the sea below, he shivered and rubbed his forehead in a confused manner. "I heard her voice, Ned," he whispered, falling back to the ground, feeling faint. "Her voice. She's got into my head again. Emily Penberthy. She told me to jump. The evil, miserable, crazy old witch: she told me to jump. She said she wanted me to join her. Christ, Ned, if you'd not had the nous to follow me, I'd be dead by now."

He hurriedly crawled away from the cliff's edge. Ned put his arm round the shoulders of his deeply shaken friend and helped him to his feet.

"But you're not dead, George, you're very much alive, thank God. Come on, you're shivering badly and very wobbly, we must get you back indoors."

As they turned towards the cliff path, Ned observed a thick mist far out at sea, rapidly drifting towards the coast.

"Come on, we've no time to lose. We must get back before that mist hits the cliffs or we'll not be able to see a thing."

George looked out to sea. "How odd. The moon and stars are still bright and clear. I've never seen anything like that mist before in my life. It's weird and quite sinister."

"Come on," repeated Ned. "Sea mist is not unusual, but if we don't get back quickly we could well find ourselves lost up here and hanging around until morning. Once it's over our heads it will block out what little light there is from the moon."

George turned and followed Ned already making his way along the coastal path, but stopped abruptly when convinced he heard a rustle in the surrounding shrubbery. He called to Ned in a hushed whisper. Both men kept still to listen for more noise, but only the sound of waves falling onto the rocks below disturbed the silence and stillness of the night.

"I've a horrible feeling someone else is up here tonight," whispered Ned, straining his ears to listen. "I've felt it all along, but I can't think who it might be, or why."

"I expect it's our imagination playing tricks on us. Either that or little nocturnal creatures are out looking for food," said George, in hushed tones. "Come on, I feel a little woozy and not at all in the mood for hunting down spooks."

Ned pulled up the collar of his dressing gown. "I wasn't thinking about spooks. The sounds I heard would more like have been made by humans. By the way, did you not see, or hear anything of that enormous bird of prey out hunting while you were standing on the edge of the cliff? It scared the life out of me."

"What? Well, no, I don't remember hearing any sound other than Emily's voice, and I don't recall seeing anything at all, not even the sea."

With feelings of unease, the two men continued along the path, their senses continually crying out warnings of danger, even though both were confident the worst was over. For nothing in the world would entice George to leap from the cliffs now his faculties were back intact.

George found walking difficult. His feet were both badly scratched, cut and bleeding in places. He cried with pain each time his wounds made contact with something sharp. Ned, unable to bear the knowledge his friend was suffering, offered his slippers to George.

"Don't be silly, Ned. There's no point in us both having lacerated feet. I'll be alright and I'm trying to stick to the grass, but it's difficult to make out sodding brambles in this dim light."

"Alright, but when we get down to the road I insist you put on my slippers. If you get dirt and small stones in your cuts then your feet will take much longer to heal and you'll end up spending the rest of your holiday in a chair with your feet propped up."

George reluctantly agreed. The two of them then steadily made their way back along the rugged path towards the village. But as they reached the end of the track and began to descend the steep cliff path leading into the cove, they both saw, without doubt, a figure walking with haste, in the shadows across the sand on the beach below.

Both stopped and watched as the figure disappeared out of sight.

"Christ, Ned, it looks as though we may have been right about someone up here with us tonight?"

"Yes, but we didn't actually see anyone up there, did we? And the person on the beach may quite simply be dropping off a flask or something like that to the anglers down there." He pointed to the spot where the two fishermen could clearly be seen in the moonlight. Ned was trying to play down his fears, feeling George had already suffered enough. And as no satisfactory conclusion could be reached as to whom the figure might have been, they continued to climb down the remainder of the cliff path. They reached the bottom as the thick mist fell, shrouding the cliff tops before drifting into the village.

George gratefully stepped into Ned's warm slippers when they reached the road. They then hobbled back to the Inn, laughing and swearing amidst frequent cries of ouch and awe, but at the same time nervously glancing over their shoulders, lest anyone else be about taking in the midnight air.

Back at the Inn, they crept into the kitchen and Ned filled a bowl with warm water. George sat down, happy to take the weight from his painful feet. Ned placed the bowl on the floor and George slowly lowered his bleeding feet into the water. Seeing he was shivering Ned took a thick overcoat from the pegs in the hallway and wrapped it around the shoulders of his friend.

George murmured a deep sigh of satisfaction as warmth slowly crept back into his veins, and he watched as Ned put a pan of milk on the stove to heat for cocoa.

"You're a great friend, Ned. No-one could ask for better. I hope you realise just how much I appreciate what you did for me tonight."

Ned felt choked. "Anyone would have done the same had they been in my shoes. A friend in need is a friend indeed." He sat down. "I wish I knew what was going on with you and Emily Penberthy, though. This thing with her and Harry is getting beyond a joke. You certainly do attract some weird women."

George wrinkled his nose. "Couldn't you use your dodgy skills and contact her and ask her what the devil she's playing at."

"Absolutely not," said Ned, flatly. "I leave chatting to the dead to Mum. I only talk to them if they make themselves known to me, like dear Jane did. But do you know? I don't think what's happening to you is influenced by the dead at all. I think it has to be something much more sinister. Telepathy perhaps. Is there anyone you can think of who might want you dead?"

"Elsie might," George jested, "and probably Madge when I ignore her. I can't make out Milly, though, I don't think she really fancies me at all. I think I'm perhaps a touch too old for her."

Ned stood and, laughing, stirred hot milk into two mugs of cocoa paste.

"I don't see how you can be so flippant in view of what's just happened, but then again I suppose it's better to see the funny side than take it too seriously. But I should think the last thing Elsie, and especially Madge, want is you dead, considering they're both desperate to drag you to the altar."

"Ugh!" said George. "What a horrible choice, rainy Manchester or Madge. To be honest, though, I think the most likely cause of tonight's drama was an over indulgence of food. I ate far too much today, or yesterday, should I say? And I believe it has played havoc with my poor old brain."

"Well, luckily it did the same with me, that's why I was awake when you went sleepwalking. Talking of which, have you ever been sleepwalking before?"

"Thanks," said George, as Ned handed him the cocoa. "Yes, but not for many years, although I believe it was a big problem when I was very young, from what my parents used to tell me. Apparently, I used to wander downstairs in the evening and sit with them while they listened to the wireless. Mum would then direct me back to bed whilst still asleep and I'd remember nothing in the morning."

"Oh, I see. That makes the whole episode a lot less worrying then, and perhaps you were just dreaming, after all. I think it's probably best if we forget this evening ever happened."

"I agree. I don't want the good people of Trengillion to think me any crazier than they already do." George yawned. "I say, do you think there might anything to eat? I feel quite peckish now after our midnight stroll, in spite of yesterday's overeating."

"I'll have a look," said Ned, rising to rummage through the cupboards where he eventually found an unopened packet of chocolate biscuits on the top shelf of the kitchen cabinet.

"How about one of these?" he said, holding up the packet for George to see.

"Ideal, but won't they be missed?"

Ned slit open the packet with a knife. "I'll get some more to replace them from the post office in the morning and then no-one will be any the wiser."

After they had finished off their drinks and consumed the whole packet of chocolate digestives, George dabbed his feet dry and Ned put antiseptic cream and sticking plasters over the deepest cuts. They then tidied up the kitchen before making their way back to bed. In the hallway, as they approached the foot of the stairs, a tinkling noise from outside made them both jump.

"What on earth was that?" George asked.

The sound of an electric motor moving away from the Inn promptly followed. Both men heaved a sigh of relief, realising it was the milkman putting bottles on the doorstep.

The sun was beginning to rise as they plodded up the stairs, their eyes prickling through need of sleep.

"I don't think I'll be down for breakfast," said George. "In fact I know I won't. So, I'll see you later in the day."

"Absolutely," agreed Ned. "I shall be asleep as soon as my head hits the pillow. I must leave Stella a note to explain, though, before I crash out, or she'll attempt to wake me."

But a note was not necessary. For when Ned entered the room, Stella was sitting up in bed, wide awake.

"Where the devil have you been, Ned?" she demanded. "I've been worried sick."

CHAPTER FOURTEEN

Ned, Stella and George decided to forget about the midnight stroll affair unless such an incident happened again. For although the notion of an unknown source trying to induce George into taking his own life seemed perfectly feasible during the hours of darkness, in the daytime, when the sun was shining, the idea sounded downright daft. Hence, all chose to believe the incident must have been the result of overeating, and for some mysterious reason it triggered off George's childhood scourge of sleepwalking, which coincided with a realistic nightmare. Nevertheless, as a precaution they decided to lock George's bedroom door each night from the outside, so that he could not get out without the help of his friends who would keep the key. Ned told Frank what they proposed to do, after explaining very briefly, how sleepwalking was the reason behind the fact he and George had been absent from the breakfast table. Frank was amused to learn that George was in the habit of going for a wander in the wee small hours, and to help the situation he produced an old chamber pot, should George need to empty his bladder during the night, after an evening, during which he would inevitably drink several pints of beer.

"I don't suppose you saw anyone creeping about the place when you came in, did you?" asked Frank, as he handed over the cumbersome chamber pot to a clearly embarrassed George.

"No," said Ned. "The only person we were aware of being around was the milkman. Why do you ask?"

"Auntie Mabel," said Frank, looking heavenwards. "She was going about the place this morning like a bear with a sore head. She says someone's stolen her chocolate biscuits and she wants all the guests' rooms searched. Silly woman! She always has a couple with her early morning fag and tea, you see. I expect she'd eaten them all herself. I swear she doesn't know what she's doing half the time."

"Oh, Christ," spluttered Ned. "Sorry Frank, we ate them all. Trust them to have belonged to Auntie Mabel. I'll go to the post office right now and get a replacement packet. I meant to do that anyway, but forgot."

Ned dashed out of the side door. Grinning, Frank turned to George. "Get him to put them back where he got them from, but hide them a bit, and then we can tell moaning Mabel she didn't look properly. What a fuss over nothing."

Frank was of course not told about the possibility of Emily Penberthy's involvement in the sleepwalking occurrence, and neither was anyone else, as it was thought best to keep the theory of her being the source of the excursion, quiet. Ned, however, still felt a little uncomfortable. The whole episode troubled him and he craved the opportunity to talk matters over with his mother. But such a discussion was not possible, for she and the major were away for a few days, having left the village early that morning to visit the major's only brother living, with his wife and family in South Wales.

On Monday morning, as Ned walked into the Inn on his way back from the post office with a newspaper, Frank handed him an envelope with a typewritten address which had been delivered earlier by the postman. Ned was puzzled at first as to whom it might be from, as the post mark indicated it was local. On opening it he found it was a response to his application for the position of headmaster, inviting him along for an interview the following week.

Ned, thrilled at the prospect of a chance to explore further the possibility of a future life in Cornwall, ran up the stairs, two at a time, to relay the good news to Stella.

Later in the day, Ned sat on the beach, watching Stella and George swimming and splashing about in the sea. To begin with Stella had expressed reluctance, saying the water was freezing cold and she could venture no further than ankle deep. But George insisted the temperature felt fine once submerged beneath the water, and had dragged her into the oncoming waves to prove his point.

Ned laughed at their antics but he did not envy them one bit. Instead he lay back on the beach towel and turned his thoughts to his twenty seventh birthday due to fall at the end of the week and contemplated the idea of having a party. He mentioned it to Stella and George as they came out of the sea and dried their shivering

101

bodies on towels warmed by the sun, whilst attempting to control their chattering teeth.

"I think that's a lovely idea," Stella agreed, snuggling up to Ned and warming her cold hands beneath his shirt. "But isn't it a bit too late to send out invitations?"

"Ouch, no, you're hands are freezing. No, because that's not what I would do. I was thinking along the lines of putting a notice in the post office window and another inside the Inn to invite everyone along. I couldn't send out invitations, anyway, because I'd be bound to miss someone out. I'd also mention it to people when I bumped into them whilst out and about, and you both could do the same. But we must emphasise no presents. I don't want people to feel they must shower me with gifts, as that would rather defeat the purpose of a party in the first place. All I want is everyone to come along and have a really good evening. It will be my way of giving something back to the people I consider to be my friends."

"What about food?" asked George, combing his hair, and impressed by Ned's largesse. "You'll have to lay on food of some sort?"

"Of course, but that's no problem. I'm sure Dorothy will be able to come up with a modest buffet. Sylvia did them quite often, although of course she did mix in more sophisticated circles prior to her becoming landlady here. I'm sure it won't be beyond Dorothy's capabilities, and she did lay on a small spread for us and Auntie Mabel when we first arrived, if you remember."

Ned discussed the idea with Frank that evening and Frank rubbed his hands with glee. "Excellent idea, Ned. Parties mean profits and I could do with a new armchair for my living room because the old one is looking a bit shabby. A more comfortable settee wouldn't come amiss either. I'm beginning to hate that bloomin' thing."

"If you'd let us pay for our keep then that'd help towards the cost of new furniture," said Ned, with vehemence. "I feel really guilty staying here for nothing, and you feed us too."

Frank laughed. "I'm only kidding, Ned. "I'm not motivated by money. You see, when I lost Sylvia I realised how unimportant it was. As long as I've enough to pay the bills and keep myself fed and clothed then that's all I care about. I own this place, anyway, lock, stock and barrel, so when I want to retire I should be able to get a pretty good price for it. Enough to buy myself a modest bungalow, anyway. I fancy one like Godfrey Johns had built, but that won't be for a few more years yet."

Dorothy Treloar said she would be happy to put on a buffet. Rose volunteered to help her, and all agreed that Molly could make a birthday cake, if she wished, when she returned home from Wales.

News of the party spread fast. Everyone in the village who had attended the sixtieth birthday party for Flo Hughes, eighteen months before, had visions of such a night being repeated, and those who had missed it, made a note of the date on their calendars to make sure the same thing didn't happen again.

There was also much curiosity to see George. For news had travelled fast and wide about the young man down on honeymoon with Ned and his pretty little wife, who was possibly the reincarnation of a lad from over Polquillick.

Molly in due course returned home and was overjoyed when she heard about the party. She volunteered not only to make the birthday cake but to help out with any other catering, for it looked as though the evening would bring in quite a crowd.

Rose Briers, like everyone else, eagerly looked forward to Saturday, even though she knew for the busiest part of the evening she would have to help Frank, Dot and Betty on the bar. But that did not really matter, because at least she was guaranteed George would be there, as he would never miss his best friend's birthday party.

Secretly, Rose was crazy about George. He was handsome, witty, kind hearted and generous, but she felt unable to tell anyone of her feelings, especially George, and so she kept her emotions hidden and prayed that one day he would sweep her off her feet and they would live happily ever after.

In reality though, she knew her dreams were unlikely to come true. The new school term would be starting in the not too distant future and then he, Ned and Stella would return to London and she would be left alone again, looking for somewhere to live when she had to vacate The School House.

"At least Ned might get the job as headmaster," thought Rose. "And then he'll return to the village and I'll have him and Stella for friends."

The prospect of Ned as headmaster brightened her outlook, especially when she realised, if the Stanleys were back in the area, then George would definitely visit Trengillion from time to time. But would she see him? She might have to leave the area to find affordable accommodation. She might even have to return to Blackpool.

Rose sighed. "I mustn't think about it. I must enjoy the next two weeks and worry about the future after that. Meanwhile, I must find something to wear for the party."

There had been no additions to Rose's wardrobe since Reg's death, and Rose felt there was nothing suitable amongst her modest outfits to catch the eye of a potential suitor. Nothing glamorous or stylish. Most of her clothes were conservative and practical.

Rose felt a sudden pang of shame as she recalled how she had once dressed and behaved. Poor Reg! What a burden to him she must have been. But he never complained and sometimes she even felt he had been amused by her outrageous behaviour, although she could not recall seeing him happier than the day of Jane's funeral when he found her changed.

Rose closed the wardrobe door and sat down on the bed as visions of Reg lying trapped in his battered car came once again to her mind. The incident had happened on the bend by the old Ebenezer Chapel. Young Jimmy Pascoe had run all the way to The School House to tell her. She arrived at the scene of the accident at the same time as the fire brigade and ambulance. He was still conscious at the time and obviously in great pain, but he had uttered not one word of self-pity. His concerns were only for her and what would happen to her when he was gone.

Rose leaned across the bed to retrieve a handkerchief from beneath her pillow to wipe away the tears trickling down her cheeks. Reg had died in that horrid car, clinging onto her hand tightly through the broken window. A young fireman had insisted she stand back so that they might free him from the wreckage, but Reg had clung to her, telling her to be strong and to be happy, for he knew it was too late. That moment was one she would never forget. Seeing him there, crumpled and broken with blood from a head wound soaking into his best suit. The gravity and reality of the situation had not dawned on her then; she had been dazed, everything seemed in slow motion, and it was not until later, when they took away his body in the ambulance, that she realised she would never see him again.

Still sobbing, Rose went downstairs, made a cup of tea, sat at the kitchen table and returned her muddled thoughts to George. Was it too soon after Reg's death for her to seek happiness again? Some would say yes, but she knew it was what Reg would have wanted, and he would have liked George, just as he had liked Ned.

Half confident that she was not behaving badly, she returned her thoughts to an outfit for the party. She pondered over the idea of buying something new, but knew her modest income would not stretch to the sort of outfit she desired. Perhaps she ought to make something? Reg's mother's old sewing machine was in the spare room where it had lay, gathering dust for many years. But Rose had never made a garment in her life and she hardly thought her first effort could be anything spectacular.

Rose sighed. She would take Freak out for a walk, that way she would have time to think. She put on her shoes, left the house and walked down the hill in the direction of Long Acre Farm. Before reaching the farm she stopped and climbed over a gate into one of Cyril Penrose's fields, where sheep grazed lazily on the lush, green grass. She called Freak to her side and put him on his lead as she did not want him worrying the sheep. Not that there was much fear of that. He was quite docile when in the presence of larger animals.

They headed towards the old Penwynton Mine. Once there, they joined the coastal path and headed back towards the village. Several other people were out walking too, making the most of the summer weather and the idyllic settings.

By a patch of grass Rose stopped and sat down to rest. She thought about her future and the possibility of returning to her native Blackpool. She'd had a very happy childhood there and remembered the place with great affection, but a lot of water had passed under the bridge since her youth and she could not imagine herself settling there again. She laughed, recalling George's dislike of Manchester because of the rain.

"What a clown. I'm pretty sure it's no wetter up North than it is in Cornwall, although of course I can't vouch for London and that's the place George would be making comparisons with."

She thought about London, although she had never been there, and tried to imagine herself browsing through the shops and stores with lots of money to spend, attempting to choose a dress for the party. Even in her imagination she was spoiled for choice and could not decide which colour would suit her best.

Her brief day-dream was noisily disturbed, bringing her back to reality, when Freak, leaping up and down on his four, short legs, began to bark at a young boy coming into view with a golden Labrador.

Disappointed that her daydream had been disturbed, she stood up, brushed grass from her dress and continued her walk along the path towards the village. Once back on the beach, Rose removed Freak's lead and paused to survey the sun-worshippers. Many were holiday makers, but a few were locals, mostly young mothers with children busily building sandcastles on the infrequent patches of sand.

Rose sighed, recalling how she and Reg had wanted children, but they had been unlucky.

"It was probably for the best," she whispered, knowing she faced an insecure future. "But it would have been nice to have someone to love, someone close to care for, someone to remember dear, old Reg by."

"Still, I have Freak," she laughed, throwing him a piece of dry seaweed to run after and retrieve. "I gave him a good home and lots of love when no-one else wanted him."

She called Freak to her side and together they walked steadily up the slight incline to the village and home.

As she passed the Inn she thought once again of the party and what to wear. The walk had not helped her in any way at all. She was just as undecided as when she had left.

Further on, she sauntered past Rose Cottage where Molly was deadheading her dahlias in the front garden. Molly looked very elegant, even in her gardening clothes, but then Molly always looked well presented, although the colours she wore now were a little less vivid than when she had first arrived in the area.

"And I believe she makes most of them herself," Rose mused. "Clever lady."

She stopped dead in her tracks; feeling goose pimples run down her arms and back. Would Molly help her? Would it be safe to reveal the feelings which she kept wrapped up? It had to be worth a try, Molly always seemed such an amicable woman and she knew Frank thought very highly of her.

Rose walked towards the little green gate and with thumping heart called over.

"Molly," she squeaked. "I know it's a bit short notice and I know you're a very busy lady, but do you think you might be able to help me, as I have a little problem?"

CHAPTER FIFTEEN

Ned's birthday fell on a Saturday; ideal for a party, bearing in mind many would not have to work the following day. It also happened to be changeover day for several of the Inn's guests and other holiday makers in the vicinity. George was hopeful that Madge and Milly might be amongst the holiday makers packing their bags in order to return to pastures unknown. He was very disappointed, therefore, to hear during breakfast, the two females planning the agenda for their day, including the party, thus realising their departure was not imminent.

"When are Madge and Silly Milly going home?" George whispered to Betty, when she brought in their breakfasts. "They've been here for simply ages."

"Not until September. They're staying for the summer like you lot. Why, are they giving you the run-around?"

"Christ!" he grumbled. "Madge is becoming a right pain in the neck. Milly's no bother, though, I think she's eying up young Peter."

"Oh, is she now?" snapped Betty, haughtily. "Well, we'll have to see about that." And she flounced off back to the kitchen, head held high.

George looked nonplussed. "Did I say something wrong?"

"Probably," said Ned. "I've noticed Peter and Betty in each other's company quite a lot lately. They're the only ones still unmarried in their circle of friends."

Stella and George had strict instructions from Molly to take Ned out for the day on his birthday as she wanted him out of the way so that the bar and dining room could be decorated, even though she knew he didn't want any fuss. They decided to take a picnic lunch up to the old Penwynton Mine, so that Stella could draw the disused relic in a sketch pad Ned had bought in the post office.

Molly also had to put the finishing touches to Rose's dress and stitch a small spray of silk flowers onto the yoke. She had been tickled pink when Rose had nervously asked her to help with a dress. She loved sewing, and knitting too, but knew there was a limit to the amount of clothes one could fit into a modest sized wardrobe.

It was agreed that Rose buy the fabric and pattern under Molly's supervision and Molly would then make the dress. Rose had offered to pay Molly for her time, but Molly insisted it would be payment enough to see the fruits of her labour modelled on a perfect figure. Furthermore, she looked forward to seeing if it would succeed in the object of its making by alluring George Clarke.

On the morning of the party, Molly, Dorothy Treloar and Rose decorated the Inn with balloons, paper chains and streamers, after which Molly and Rose returned to Rose Cottage for the final fitting of the dress, and to finish off Molly's contribution to the buffet, much of which was delivered by Bill Burleigh the baker.

Molly had made as much food as she felt confident with, but there were certain delicacies that really needed the professional touch, such as chocolate éclairs, Danish pastries and vol-au-vents, the last of which Molly crammed with local crab, bound together in a little mayonnaise, a dash of paprika and a squeeze of lemon juice, the inspiration for which she had read in her favourite women's magazine. And to accompany her efforts she filled her largest bowls with salad; spring onions mixed with radish and freshly cut lettuce from her own garden, topped with tomatoes, shaped into water lilies, and thinly sliced cucumber from the greenhouse of her next door neighbour, Doris.

Later in the day, as soon as the Inn's evening meal, which had been brought forward an hour, was over, the tables in the dining room were rearranged ready for the food to be laid out. When the task was accomplished, the ladies returned to their homes quickly to change their outfits for the evening's event.

Dorothy Treloar, who usually wore her hair pulled back tight in a bun, practical for when she had helped on the farm and now practical for working in the kitchen, sat down and looked into the mirror on the dressing table. She groaned. How bored she was with seeing the same old, dull reflection, day in, day out. For two long minutes she glared at the face she had learned to hate. Two long minutes during which she decided it was time to be reckless: time for change. Without a second thought she did the unthinkable and un-gripped her hair to let it hang free and rest upon her shoulders, and where the elastic band had pulled together her thick locks, a pretty wave ran around her head.

Also for working in the kitchen and on the bar, she wore practical clothes. Floral blouses and pleated or tweed skirts were her favourite attire. But Ned's party she conceded was a special occasion, hence she did the unthinkable again and put on the dress she had worn when a bridesmaid to her cousin fifteen years earlier. It was a simple design, dark green satin with a wide sash and bow around the fitted waist, a collared V neck and a hemline just below the knee, but it suited Dorothy; it brought out the greeny brown of her eyes and made her feel feminine.

When she was dressed and her hair combed, she did something even more unthinkable. She brushed a little cake mascara onto her long eyelashes and put on some red lipstick, the same stick as she had used for her cousin's wedding. Pleased with the result, she then clipped a pair of her mother's diamante earrings onto the lobes of her ears; they sparkled through the loose tresses of her free hair.

"Blimey!" said Albert, when he came in from the fields. "Are you feeling alright, Dot?"

She felt embarrassed. "You don't think it's over the top, do you? I mean, I don't look silly or tarty, do I?"

"Dot, you look lovely. Not at all silly or tarty. Just lovely and it's really good to see you looking so. You should dress up more often, you're a handsome woman."

He looked in the mirror and ran his hand over his bristly chin. "I suppose it must run in the family."

Albert drove his sister back to the Inn, he then returned home to the farm to wash and change ready for the party himself.

Rose Briers took a long, hot bath at The School House and tried to relax. She was nervous and very much looking forward to the party, but past experience told her that often things looked forward to, seldom lived up to expectations, whereas events dreaded were often quite the opposite.

Once bathed, she put on her dressing gown, wandered into the bedroom and applied her make-up with extreme care. She lit a cigarette once the task was complete and looked critically at the finished result. Satisfied she looked as good as was possible, she then slipped on her new dress, brushed her hair, dabbed perfume behind her ears and returned to the Inn.

Auntie Mabel looked through her clothes hanging in Frank's wardrobe and finally decided to wear the outfit she had worn for the last party to welcome herself to the Inn along with that nice young couple, Ned and Stella. She knew blue suited her; it always had, although her natural blonde hair was now snowy white, and her blue eyes, once her greatest asset, were hidden behind the thick lenses of her ornate spectacles.

Mabel wore clothes well. Her late mother, a professional dressmaker, had always seen to that, insisting if a garment fitted properly then it would make even the most unsightly figure look good. Not that that was a problem for Mabel. She had always taken great care to make sure she kept her hour glass figure and never left the house without a strong corset beneath her attire. Her late husband, Bert, had been a very handsome man and she did her utmost throughout their long marriage to make sure his eyes never wandered.

With care, she brushed her hair, applied a dash of lipstick to her thin lips and daubed a little face powder over her lightly wrinkled skin. She then clipped on her favourite earrings, hung a string of pearls around her neck and dabbed a drop of lavender eau-de-Cologne behind each ear. With a sigh of immense satisfaction, she then walked through the Inn to the bar where Frank poured her a bitter lemon, after which she took a seat in the snug to await the arrival of everyone else. For Mabel was looking forward to the evening and the opportunity to cast a critical eye over the locals, who she was convinced would be quite incapable of looking anywhere near as well turned out as she considered herself to be.

When the guests arrived for the party many were taken back by the glamour of the three barmaids serving drinks. In fact some did not even recognise Dorothy Treloar. Frank, to use his own expression, was dead chuffed. Betty looked as pretty as a picture with a new hair-do, and Rose in her new dress, looked stunning.

Ned was delighted with the turn out and to his surprise everyone was smartly dressed, determined to show their neighbours they could still rise to the occasion by scrubbing up, even if once youthful looks were long faded and replaced by unwelcome lines and wrinkles which mysteriously increased overnight with every passing year.

Gertie looked pretty dressed in red despite disliking her waistline: several inches more than she felt comfortable with due to the birth of twins. Even Percy, not one for dressing up, had made an effort, although he drew the line at wearing a tie, something he had not done since his wedding day.

Gertie wasted no time and mingled with the crowds seeking out the latest news and gossip, for she seldom had the opportunity to enjoy an evening with old friends and acquaintances. However, she refused to touch any alcoholic drinks knowing if she did she would deeply regret it when the twins woke during the night. Nevertheless, in spite of her outgoing personality, Ned thought she seemed troubled, as though she had something on her mind, and he said so when he enquired after the twin's welfare.

She smiled. "Well, yes, how clever of you to notice, but actually, when I think about it you might even be able to solve my little problem. Would you like to be Tony's godfather? We're having the twins christened on the last Sunday in August. We've got John's godparents sorted, they're Meg, Sid and my cousin, Stephen, but we're one short for Tony and need someone to go with Betty and Peter. That's the trouble with boys, they each need two godfathers, and in my opinion there's always been a shortage of young men in Trengillion. Not that a godfather has to be young, I suppose. I know it's a bit short notice and out of the blue, but please say yes, that's if you'll still be here then. I'd be thrilled to bits if you would."

Ned was taken back. "Well, I don't see why not. In fact I think it would be rather nice. I've never been asked to be anyone's godfather before. You'll have to tell me what to do though, because I've no idea at all."

"Does that mean yes?" Gertie asked, hands clasped together as though in prayer.

Ned nodded. "Yes, I'd be honoured."

Gertie hugged him tightly. "Brilliant! We'll go through the service with you nearer the time when we've talked things over with the vicar. I must go now and tell Percy. He'll be so glad I've got it sorted because he's been getting a bit fed up with me going on about it all the time. You must come too, Stella, and you can bring George if you want. There will be a small tea party afterwards at the farm, so of course you must come along to that as well. We did think of having a little do here but we decided it would be too smoky for the twins. The farm will be nice, anyway, and if the weather is kind we can have tea outside."

Farmer Pat Dickens and his wife May, arrived with their best friends George and Bertha Fillingham. The Fillinghams were fairly new to the village and had only been in their retirement home, Sea Thrift Cottage, for a year. But they had wasted no time settling in and were now regular supporters, and members of, many village groups and organisations.

Molly arrived on the arm of the major, wearing the black dress she had bought eighteen months earlier for Flo's sixtieth birthday party. With the Smiths was their next door neighbour and close friend Doris.

Molly made a bee-line for the dining room as soon after her arrival as she thought decently acceptable, to check that her food was all on display in an orderly manner and nothing had been left out.

During the absence of his wife, the major, with glass of whisky in hand, glanced across the bar to where Harry and Joyce Richardson stood with Joyce's younger sister, Vera, and her German husband, Fritz, a former prisoner of war. Joyce proudly introduced her sister and brother-in-law to the Pascoes from the post office. The major thought Fritz looked a very amicable, quiet and gentle man. But he was a German, and the major could not help but feel he was partly responsible for the death of his late wife and family, even though deep down he knew it was unreasonable to blame him thus and very un-Christian too.

Fritz was meekly standing beside his wife saying very little, for although his English was quite fluent, he had difficulty understanding those who spoke with a Cornish accent. The major's emotions suddenly rose. His face reddened with anger and bitter prejudice as the picture of his murdered family burned hard from inside the breast pocket of his jacket. But gradually the anger subsided, his face cooled and within minutes the resentment had faded away into oblivion. For the major had suddenly recalled a conversation he'd had with Harry earlier in the year, telling how Fritz had spent three years working on a farm in the Midlands whilst a prisoner of war, during which time, his own family had died in the bombing of Dresden.

A lump rose in the major's throat. It was wrong for him to bear a grudge. It was wrong for him not to forgive. He placed his empty glass on a nearby table with a thud, straightened his jacket and crossed the bar, head held high, to the corner where Harry, Joyce, Vera and Fritz stood.

"May I buy you all a drink, please?" he asked, smiling broadly at them all and especially Fritz. "This is after all, my step-son's birthday we're celebrating and I'm delighted you've all come along to join us."

Sid Reynolds, who worked on the local paper, arrived with his wife Meg, his father-in-law the Vicar and, much to everyone's delight, the vicar's crippled wife, Pearl, who put on a brave face by leaving her wheelchair at the Vicarage and walking with the aid of sticks from the car to the seat saved for her in the snug bar.

Flo and Jim Hughes, also put in an appearance, along with Cyril Penrose, on his own because his wife, Nettie, was looking after her grandchildren, the twins. And much to Ned's delight, Police Constable Fred Stevens arrived with his wife, Annie. Ned greeted them warmly, for both had been good friends and a great source of help during his first visit to Cornwall.

Last to arrive were Larry and Des, the divers, their faces tanned a light golden brown, contrasting with their heads of neatly trimmed blond hair, bleached by the sun. The clothing they wore was casual, but chic, their manner polite, although during conversation a hint of the dare-devil manifested itself in the characters of both young men.

The Inn was packed to full capacity, for as well as locals, holiday makers were also there in considerable numbers, although many of them chose to sit outside and enjoy the warmth of the August evening, as they felt slightly intrusive being inside with the party goers. All except Madge and Milly, that is. Those two women had no intention of missing the fun, and as the two objects of their desire, namely Peter and George, were inside, then neither had time to waste mixing with the new arrivals, alfresco.

That was how it appeared to be on the surface. However, in reality, Milly was a shy girl, quite the opposite of her pushy mother and she was more than happy to stand and pretend to watch Peter from a distance. For although Ned and George had nicknamed her Silly Milly, she was far from stupid and quite aware, by their body language, that Betty and Peter seemed very attracted to each other. Hence, for that reason alone she had not the slightest desire to get in the way and make a nuisance of herself. Therefore, when Madge went off in pursuit of George, Milly tucked herself away in the corner of the snug and hoped her mother might not notice her lack of enthusiasm for the mating game.

When the food in the dining room had all been eaten and the candles on the birthday cake lit and blown out, the cake was cut up and distributed amongst the guests, after which the empty serving plates and platters were cleared away and preparations made to create a dance area. Tables were taken outside and stacked neatly in the courtyard at the back of the Inn and Molly's newly acquired Dansette record player, which had been dropped off at the Inn earlier, was then put into position ready for Annie Stevens to put on previously selected records for dancing.

The lively music which emanated from the dining room rang through the walls of the bars, and people sitting outside rhythmically tapped their feet. Some danced, whilst inside, the chat and laughter grew louder to compete with the volume of the music.

Rosemary Howard could not believe her luck. With so many people gathered together under one roof, she felt confident the evening must produce inspiration for characters to fill the blank pages of her book. It might even stimulate her imagination enough to conjure up a plot. She mingled with the party goers, blushed each time Des winked at her, drank lots of port and lemon and felt fame was just around the corner.

Milly, still sitting alone, felt embarrassed and uncomfortable. She was convinced people thought her foolish, devoid of friends and character, and she dearly wished the holiday which her mother had insisted she take, were over and that she could go home. From across the bar she was conscious that Auntie Mabel kept glancing in her direction. Milly felt even more distressed and considered slipping away to her room to avoid the pitying looks of the elderly widow.

But she concluded that in doing so, everyone would notice her get up and know where she was going and why. Milly sat rigidly still, awkwardly fiddling with the strap of her handbag, feeling as though the entire gathering were watching her growing anguish.

From the brightly polished table by her side, she picked up the serviette containing her portion of birthday cake and slowly broke off small pieces in order to make its consumption last as long as possible to pass away some of the time. When it was all gone she dabbed her mouth and hands with the serviette and took a small swig of sweet cider which her mother had left for her.

"You look as lost as I feel," said a voice, as she placed the glass back on the table.

Milly jumped and looked up. A young man stood casually in front of her smiling with his hands tucked inside the pockets of his cardigan. She blushed but did not respond to his comment for she was too shocked to know what to say.

"I'm staying with my Auntie Maude and Uncle Joe," persisted the young man. "Do you know them? They run the post office."

Milly's face broke into a smile. "Yes, I've been in there a few times since we arrived here. They sell very delicious toffees."

"Are you on holiday too, then?" the young man asked.

"Yes, I'm here with my mother and we're staying at this Inn."

He stretched out his hands towards her. "Would you like to dance? Please say yes as I should dearly like your company. I hardly know anyone here and feel a bit of a twit."

Milly felt giddy. A handsome young man was asking her to dance and she had done absolutely nothing at all to attract his attention, other than look lost.

She rose to her feet. "Yes, yes, really I'd like to dance very much."

Hand in hand they then left the bar for the dining room and did not leave each other's company for the rest of the evening.

CHAPTER SIXTEEN

Molly, having danced with the major until her feet ached, stood at the end of the bar and gazed at Dorothy Treloar hard at work. She looked so pretty, her face flushed with the evening's heat; it seemed such a shame that she was not able to join in with everyone else and have some fun. Frank too was working hard. So were Rose and Betty, but at least the girls had something to look forward to later in the evening when things quietened down and they could join their friends.

Molly grabbed the major's arm.

"Come with me, Ben," she commanded. "We're going to do some work."

She dragged the major behind the bar and insisted Frank take Dorothy into the dining room for a waltz around the floor.

Frank chuckled loudly. He had not danced for some time and even then Sylvia always said he had two left feet.

"Would you like to dance, Dot?" he asked.

"I...umm...I...er...umm...don't..."

"That means yes," interrupted Molly, pushing the two of them out of the way. "Be as long as you like. You need to take a break, because all work and no play makes thingy a dull boy."

Dorothy looked like a scared rabbit as Frank whisked her away to the dining room, where to Frankie Laine's number one hit, *I Believe,* deeply embraced couples were shuffling slowly around the dance floor.

"Are you matchmaking, Mrs Smith?" asked the major, as he poured a pint of beer for a holiday maker.

"Maybe," smiled Molly, gleefully reaching to the whisky optic. "Or maybe not."

All in all the evening was a huge success, although it crossed Madge's mind that the quality of George's teaching might be dubious if he was not intelligent enough to recognise the yearning look in her eyes and succumb to her amorous advances. It never even entered her head that he might be repulsed by her podgy arms and double chin, had no desire to put his arms around her cumbersome waist or run his fingers through her heavily lacquered, stiff, peroxide hair. And as for kissing a woman caked in make-up with her lipstick painted high above her top lip, the thought made George feel quite sick. In fact when George looked at Madge, the prospect of living in rainy Manchester seemed like an invitation to Paradise.

Frank and Dorothy had a break lasting forty five minutes, during which time they danced, chatted with friends and associates, and enjoyed a drink. And Dorothy, who had not danced since she had learned how to at school, was happy beyond belief.

Molly and the major insisted on remaining on the bar when Frank and Dorothy finally returned, this was to enable Rose and Betty to take a well-earned break. Betty went straight to Peter's side. Rose thanked Molly with a discreet smile.

"Good luck," Molly whispered.

Rose found Ned, Stella and George outside standing beneath the lamp over the doorway.

"Oh, it's you Rose," said George, as she stepped through the doorway. "I thought for a minute it was Madge."

"Thanks," said Rose, feeling despondent. "Thanks for the compliment."

"No, I didn't mean you're like Madge, or that you look like her. Oh, for Christ's sake, you must know what I mean,"

Ned and Stella both laughed at his discomfort. Stella took Rose by the arm. "Don't be offended, you look simply gorgeous. He's just very edgy tonight and jumps every time anyone comes through door for fear of it being her."

"I'm glad you're here, Rose," said Ned, flicking ash into the old cracked flower pot, now revitalised with Frank's new fuchsia. "If you'll stick close to George, then Madge might leave him alone. I'm getting pretty fed up standing out here. It's beginning to feel quite chilly and I'm sure I just felt a spot of rain."

George took Rose's hand, as the rain spots increased in number. "Good idea. It's about time I had a good looking girl on my arm again anyway. Come on, let's dance and show Madge she's out of luck."

Inside, the smoke filled bars were alive with happy chatter and laughter, and Auntie Mabel, having been persuaded by her old friend and retired butcher, Godfrey Johns, to ditch the bitter lemon for something stronger, was on her third schooner of sweet sherry. It was Rose who noticed the contents and shape of her glass had changed.

"Oh dear, I hope she knows what she's doing. People seem to be under the impression that sherry is an innocuous drink, suitable for old ladies because of its weakness, but really it's quite strong."

Nevertheless, they watched with amusement as straight laced Auntie Mabel teetered to the bar where she insisted it was her turn to buy drinks for Godfrey and herself. It was Molly who served them.

"Don't you think it would be better if you went back to the bitter lemon, dear? You'll be feeling rough enough tomorrow as it is, without drinking more."

"I'm fine, m'duck" Mabel slurred. "I'm used to sherry, anyway, because I always have a glass at Christmas."

With amused reluctance Molly poured another sherry, slid a bottle of pale ale off the shelf for Godfrey, removed its cap and placed both drinks on the bar where Mabel was rummaging through her handbag looking for her purse. Her search was unsuccessful, and annoyed that the purse would not show itself, she tipped the entire contents of her handbag onto the bar.

Frank tutted and shook his head with disapproval. "That must be the last one," he said, part serious, part joking. "I don't want you being sick in my bed."

"I won't be sick," she laughed, opening her purse and dropping half a crown into Molly's outstretched hand. Molly put the money into the till, gave Mabel her change, then helped return her belongings safely back inside the empty handbag. However, amongst the items sprawled over the bar, was an identity card. Molly's eyes became transfixed. She had to take a peep inside, for she knew if it belonged to Mabel then it would reveal her age. With a smug grin, she craftily slid it to one side and then hoping that no-one was looking, she subtly opened it up. What she saw made her laugh out loud.

"You're surname is Thorpe," she said, without thinking. "Mabel Thorpe, what an unfortunate name." She threw back her head and laughed uncontrollably, and as laughter is infectious, within minutes everyone in close proximity was laughing too.

Mabel on the other hand did not think her name was funny. Trembling with rage she dropped the remaining items from the bar into her handbag, fastened it with a loud click, drained the glass of sherry in two swigs, threw back her head and haughtily left the bar without saying a word to anyone, but making sure everyone heard the door slam hard behind her.

"Christ!" said Frank. "She'll sulk for days now. She's never been able to see the funny side of her name and laugh it off. Still that's her problem."

"Oh dear, I feel really bad now," said Molly, trying her utmost to keep a straight face. But she was unsuccessful. For when Molly Smith got the giggles it usually lasted for quite a considerable time.

By midnight most people had gone home. By law they should have done so two hours before, but Frank had little regard for the law if it affected the pleasure his customers and friends were seeking and the amount of money he was able to put through his till. Besides, the law seldom came to the village anyway, as they had a Police Constable in residence, and so come midnight all had gone except those who stayed to help with the clearing up.

Milly, having had a lovely evening with the Pascoes' nephew, Johnny, went to bed feeling thoroughly happy, looking forward to the following day when he had suggested they meet up on the beach.

Madge on the other hand went to bed in a foul mood. George's flaunting his dancing partner Rose, had disgruntled her greatly and she was in no frame of mind to join in with the clearing up.

Dorothy Treloar also left as she wanted to drive Albert, who was teetering badly, home, before he attempted to do so himself. For the sight of poor Pearl Ridge struggling to walk as she left the Inn that evening, brought back the memories of two summers gone, when she had had to come to terms with the fact that her brother's drinking was the sole cause of family life at the Vicarage being destroyed for all time.

George Fillingham and Pat Dickens brought the tables in from outside. Peter dried them with an old tea towel as they were wet due to the earlier shower of rain. May Dickens meanwhile, vacuumed the dining room floor, and Bertha Fillingham emptied the overflowing ashtrays. Molly, Betty, Stella and Rose washed and dried glasses. Frank and the major wiped over the dirty tables. Rosemary, eager to help, went to the kitchen for the broom to sweep the flagstone floors in the bars, but as she headed back along the dimly lit passage, the telephone rang. No-one seemed to have heard above the noise of the vacuum cleaner, and so Rosemary nervously picked up the receiver herself.

"Hello," she timorously said. "This is the Ringing Bells Inn. Do you want to speak to Frank?"

"Who? No, no, I'd like to speak to George, please?" asked a voice on the other end of the line.

"George?" murmured Rosemary, feeling flustered and unable to think who George might be.

"Yes, George Clarke, a good looking, tall chap with dark hair. He's a friend of Ned and Stella Stanley. I assume he's staying there with them. Yes, he must be."

"Oh, oh, I know who you mean, the teacher chap. If you can hang on I'll go and fetch him. We're all tidying up at the moment, you see, because it's Ned's birthday."

She put down the receiver and went in pursuit of George, who she found outside larking around with Ned supposedly looking for glasses in the light of the solitary lamp. George walked briskly into the hallway on hearing of the call, afraid there may be bad news of some kind from home. He was shocked when he realised the caller was Elsie Glazebrook.

"What the devil are you doing calling me this time of night and how did you know I was here?" snapped George, exasperated, although relieved at the same time.

"You told me yourself you were going to Cornwall, so I rang Stella's mum the other day pretending to be an old friend who had just heard about her marriage and said I wanted to send a congratulations card. She gave me the address of the Inn and I crossed my fingers that you'd be staying there too, and I was right. I'd forgotten today is Ned's birthday. Please tell him I send my love..."

"...Elsie, this has gone on for long enough," said George, determined to stop her talking. "It was bad enough you ringing me at

121

home, but to pester me here, at midnight, while on holiday, is no joke, please go..."

"...but darling I had to ring and..." The line suddenly went dead. George slammed down the phone, angry, but flattered, and crept thoughtfully back to the bar where he found the jobs all completed and the place looking respectable again.

"Right, who'd like a nightcap?" Frank asked. "On me of course, you've all earned it."

Everyone took Frank up on his offer. They then made their way into the snug bar and made themselves comfortable.

"Who was that on the phone?" Ned asked, mystified by the smug look on George's face.

"Crazy Elsie," he grinned. "She sends you her love. How ridiculous to phone me here this time of night. I wish she'd leave me alone, though. I was hoping she'd have a found another bloke by now, but it looks as though it's still me she wants."

Ned sighed. "Oh dear, you'll probably find she's on the next train down here now she knows where you are."

George turned pale. "Christ, you don't think so, do you?"

"I doubt it," said Ned. "She'd have nowhere to stay if she did and I can't see her gambling that she'd be able to get you back and share your room."

"God forbid!" sniggered George. "But it might be worth it to see the look on Madge's face."

"Frank, you're bound to see Mabel before me," said Molly. "Please tell her how sorry I am to have laughed so at her name. It was very rude of me and I regret it now, she must have felt so humiliated."

"I'll tell her, but don't you feel bad, Moll. She's silly to let it bother her like it does. She were a Thompson before she married and it never occurred to her when she met my uncle, Bert Thorpe, that if she was to marry him her name would be Mabel Thorpe, and by the time she did it was too late because she was hopelessly in love with him. She tries to keep her name a secret, like here where she insists everyone calls her Mabel and the younger ones, to make it sound more respectful, call her Auntie Mabel. Silly women, she'll get over it eventually, she always does, but of course now she doesn't have poor old Uncle Bert to blame. She always considered her name was

122

his fault, you see. As if he could have done anything about it! The whole thing used to annoy my mother, she liked the family name Thorpe, and I think it was because of that the two women never really got on."

"Oh dear," said Molly, removing her shoes. "So my indelicate outburst may have opened up old wounds."

Frank laughed. "Forget it, Molly, it's the only way."

Rosemary stood close by biting her nails. "Why is Mrs Thorpe's name funny?" She asked.

Molly shook her head. "It's not really funny at all, dear, it's just me being silly. Mablethorpe is a seaside town in Lincolnshire, you see and it just struck me as funny she should be called thus."

"This is like on the night of Flo's sixtieth," said Bertha Fillingham, keen to change the subject in case she started laughing again. "Dark outside and us all snuggled together inside. All we need now is a blazing fire."

"Won't be long 'til I start lighting that again," said Frank, filling his pipe with tobacco. "It's a mucky job but I like to see it and so do my regulars."

"Wasn't that the night Molly here got in touch with William Wagstaffe?" asked George Fillingham.

Molly kicked his ankle. Everyone in the village tried to avoid uttering the name of William Wagstaffe when in the presence of Frank.

"It doesn't matter, Molly," said Frank, aware of the remonstration under the table. "You don't have to protect me from the past. What's done is done."

"How about Molly trying to get in touch with someone on the other side again, then," said May Dickens, eagerly. "That's if you don't mind, Frank?"

He chuckled. "Of course I don't mind, it'd be a bit of fun. Try not to disturb my Sylvia though, she always liked to be in bed by midnight."

Rosemary's eyes shone as though made of glass. She could not believe her ears regarding the conversation she was fortunate enough to be part of. Molly, however, tired from working and dancing, lacked enthusiasm for a séance, but felt she could not ignore the excitement expressed by those around her, so half-heartedly she agreed.

"At least you're sober this time," said Ned, recollecting the state in which his mother and everyone else had been at Flo's party.

They all gathered around two tables pushed together in the snug and on Molly's instruction joined hands. Rosemary made sure she sat next to Molly; she didn't want to miss even the tiniest detail.

Like Flo's party night, the evening was calm. Not a sound could be heard from outside and inside only the ticking of the clock broke the silence. Molly closed her eyes, took in a deep breath and asked if anyone from the *other side* wished to speak to, or had a message for anyone present.

Minutes passed by and nothing happened. Bertha sighed with disappointment.

Molly yawned and then repeated her request. Again there was no response but somewhere in the room she thought she heard the faint sound of female laughter. She opened her eyes and looked at the women sitting around the tables. All had straight faces and appeared deep in concentration. Molly closed her eyes again and once more asked if anyone on the *other side* wished to speak.

A sudden loud crash made everyone jump and Molly yelped as something sharply struck the back of her head. The lights in the snug began to flicker and at the same time a dreadful smell materialised along with a mysterious draught which appeared from nowhere. Everyone opened their eyes and gasped as green smoke slowly pothered from the fireplace; in its midst was the face of a woman cackling.

Rosemary screamed, jumped from her chair and burst into tears. Rose clung on to Frank's arm. The face slowly withered and the smoke dispersed; it then vanished into thin air. The small crowd collectively heaved a huge sigh of relief. Molly, however, sensed more was to come. Standing, she quickly flashed her eyes around the bar. A knock on the window made her jump. Everyone turned. Outside a huge bird, wings flapping, eyes staring, tapped repeatedly on the glass panes with its large yellow beak. Molly stood up swiftly and turned; as she reached out to draw the curtains, the bird circled overhead and then flew off in the direction of the sea. Trembling, Molly returned to her chair. As she sat, something pulled at her hair.

"No," she cried, flinging back her arms. "No, no, get off."

Molly's head was tugged back and forth. The major, white faced, leapt to his feet, at the same time his wife's face was forced down hard against the table and with a forceful blow she was the knocked to the floor.

With the major's help, Molly slowly lifted her head. From his pocket Ned pulled a handkerchief and gently dabbed blood trickling from his mother's nose.

Molly turned towards George. "Emily Penberthy," she whispered, weakly, pushing aside from her face a stray strand of hair. "George, she said we must stop messing around and send Harry back to her, now, before she loses her temper."

CHAPTER SEVENTEEN

Reports of Emily Penberthy's extraordinary behaviour at the Ringing Bells Inn, travelled through the village and outlying areas even faster than the revelation of Mabel Thorpe's name. And the excitement it caused meant people who usually kept themselves to themselves or were quiet by nature, overnight became loquacious as they conveyed the breathtaking details. For although many were familiar with tales of ghosts following the happenings of eighteen months before, when Molly had conjured up a voice making reference to William Wagstaffe, most preferred to believe that ghosts did not exist or were friendly, lost souls not capable of interacting with the living. Consequently, due to the resulting visual manifestation of Emily Penberthy, Molly's name was uttered with the utmost reverence.

Rose Briers hated Emily Penberthy more than she had ever hated anyone or anything before in her life. The fact that this irascible apparition had gatecrashed Ned's party and spoiled a perfect evening, was to her an unforgivable offence and certainly not the sort of behaviour she would expect to witness from a Victorian spirit. For George, because of her meddling interference and bad tempered display, had slumped instantly into a cold and distant mood, thus shattering her dreams, yearnings and humble aspirations. She was also distressed to hear from Stella, that while they had been clearing up at the Inn, George had received a phone call from his old girlfriend, Elsie Glazebrook. And although he claimed to dislike her and have not the slightest desire to see her again, deep down Rose felt the call had boosted his ego and he was actually pleased to have heard her voice.

She walked home from the party alone in the dark, tears in her eyes and a lump in her throat. Once she was safely inside and the front door locked, she went into the kitchen for a glass of water. From inside his basket, Freak woke when she turned on the tap. She apologised for disturbing him and knelt on the floor to stroke his silky coat.

"It's a pity you weren't at Ned's party, my sweetheart," she whispered. "You'd have seen off horrible Emily, wouldn't you?" Freak lifted his paw, rested it on her knee and licked her hand lovingly. With a stifled yawn she kissed his head.

"Goodnight, dear, faithful friend. We'll go for a nice long walkies in the morning, if the weather is fine. Just you and me."

Upstairs in her bedroom, she ripped the new dress from her body and flung it onto the floor, she then put on her nightdress and went into the bathroom to clean her teeth. Above the wash basin she caught sight of her reflection in the mirror. Her face was streaked with tears and mascara. She looked a mess, but she didn't care. She returned to her bedroom with make-up still on her face. She would remove it in the morning when in a better frame of mind.

As she climbed into bed she looked at the picture of Reg. "Never again will I try to win George's affection," she vowed. "Emily and Elsie can keep him, and I shall stay your widow for the rest of my life."

Rose may have been heartened to know that George, likewise, was also unhappy. He was frustrated at being haunted and taunted by something over which he had no control and no idea of how to terminate. He slept badly after the party and lay awake for many hours trying to make sense of the events which had plagued him since his arrival in Cornwall.

The following morning, after breakfast, he visited Rose Cottage with Ned and Stella, as they all wanted to see how Molly was faring, following Emily's outrageous conduct. Molly, still feeling very bruised and shaken, was delighted to see them.

"I was going to pop down to the Inn to see you all. The major has gone to church, he didn't want to leave me alone after I told him didn't feel like going this week, but I insisted I'm alright. If the truth be known, I'm more puzzled than injured. Anyway, would you like a cup of coffee, it's not quite eleven yet, but who cares."

"I'll make it," said Stella, walking towards the kitchen. "You sit down and rest. I know where everything is."

"Thank you, sweetheart," said Molly, as Stella disappeared inside the kitchen. "You'll find a coconut cake in the round tin on the bottom shelf in the pantry."

"So, what do you make of last night's little episode?" Ned asked Molly, when they were seated in the living room. "Stella and I chatted about it for ages after we went to bed but we're none the wiser for it."

Molly shook her head. "I'm baffled too. For a start she's not behaving at all as I would expect the ghost of a young woman pining for her lost love to behave. Believe me, I've spoken to many spirits over the years and this one exhibits more signs of being a poltergeist than a ghost. There's more to this than meets the eye and, damn it, I'm determined to get to the bottom of it."

"Well, the best of luck," sighed George. "Something certainly needs to be done before this grouchy ghost causes a fatality. You and I, Molly have been on the receiving end of her wrath and it alarms me to think just what she may be capable of. Although she looked a picture of innocence when we were out in the boat."

Molly was puzzled by his remark. "Is there something about all this that I've not been told? Because I'm unaware of an incident where she has harmed you, George, other than by causing you sleepless nights and drowning with you in your dreams?"

Ned gasped. "Of course, you don't know about the sleepwalking episode, do you? You and the major went off to South Wales the morning after it happened."

Molly stared, eyes open wide. "Sleepwalking episode! I've no idea what you're talking about. Perhaps you'd better put me in the picture?"

"It happened on the night of the fete. Oh dear, I'll begin at the beginning then you'll know as much as we do."

With the help of George, Ned then proceeded to tell, with renewed enthusiasm, of the fete night's bizarre events. Molly was flabbergasted.

"I cannot believe no-one thought to tell me something of such magnitude," she muttered. "And the bird! I wonder if the appearance of that creature on both occasions is a coincidence or whether it bears any significance. Was it the same bird, do you think?"

Ned shrugged his shoulders. "God only knows. I couldn't possibly say, and of course, George didn't see it. But to be fair, the one on the cliffs behaved perfectly normal. It was just out hunting for food and wasn't crackers like that thing bashing against the windows of the Inn last night."

Molly sighed. "Well, one thing we know for sure is Emily certainly has a bee in her bonnet over something. I wonder if she was as hot-headed in life as she is in death."

George smiled. "Poor old Harry if she was. But I'll tell you what's baffling me, and that's the face we all saw in that stinking green smoke or whatever it was. It certainly wasn't Emily! At least it wasn't the Emily I see in my dreams. The smoke woman was far too old."

Molly frowned. "Hmm, that's certainly food for thought. So who might it have been, then? Perhaps it was a manifestation of what Emily would look like if she was still alive today. Oh, I don't know, I'm only guessing. Really I'm as baffled as everyone else. One thing I do know for certain, though, is I'll not rest until I've made further investigations. Trying to get you to kill yourself, George, and knocking me about is pretty sinister by all accounts, and I shall find out more if it's the last thing I ever do. It's ridiculous as in neither case can we even think of going to the police because they'd think we were both barmy." She laughed. "But then, perhaps we are."

Ned was not at all happy about his mother's talk of getting involved with someone or something which had already caused her injury. "But how on earth do you propose to go about finding out more? There doesn't seem to me to be an obvious place to start searching for clues."

"I don't know," she replied, as Stella entered the room with a full tray. "I shall have to put on my thinking cap and wait for divine intervention or a brainwave, but get to the bottom of it I will for the sake of us all."

Mabel Thorpe stayed in bed for much of the day following the party, insisting the sherry Frank sold was bad thus causing her to feel unwell. And Frank, instead of being offended by her unjust accusations, was just thankful she was out of the way for the day. For he knew if she was up and about, she would inevitably ignore everyone with her tight-lipped scorn, and should a verbal contest arise enquiring whether his support was for her or Molly, there was only one way he could possibly vote. Molly was a good woman, although perhaps a little tactless, but his aunt was an overdramatic, over-sensitive nit-wit. What's more, he was fed up with sleeping on the settee and longed for the comfort of his own bed again.

"Bad sherry indeed! What a cheek! I hope her hangover lasts all day," he chortled, as he swept the cobbles in front of the Inn prior to lunchtime opening.

Rosemary Howard, with a notebook open on her lap, chewed the end of her pen as she sat on the cliff top beside the little wooden gate leading into the garden of Chy-an-Gwyns. She thought it a very romantic spot. The sort of place where murderers and villains might hide away from prying eyes and the law.

Rosemary decided to base her story on the house and the pen chewing was occasioned by deliberation over choosing a suitable name. Finally, after settling on Sea View, she turned her thoughts to choosing a memorable title, and after much reflection opted for Murder at Sea View. Satisfied that her book was off to a good start, she put down her pen, rose from the grass and peered over the garden gate. She knew the house was empty because it was said the owner, Willie something or other, only came down for a few weeks each year. Therefore, she felt certain it would be quite safe to creep into the garden and take a quick look around.

Rosemary opened the garden gate and latched it shut behind her. She then walked between flower borders along the twisting, winding gravel path which made a satisfying crunchy sound with each footstep.

Enchanted by the garden's beauty she wished it were possible to take a look inside the house and admire the views from the upstairs windows. She sat down on the doorstep in the sunshine watching five sparrows bathing in a patch of dry earth beneath a window and thought about the events which had taken place the previous evening. It had been very frightening at the time, but now, in daylight, it seemed much less so.

Rosemary contemplated whether or not she should have a ghost in her story, but decided if they went around beating up old ladies then it was probably not something she ought to dabble with. She wondered if Chy-an-Gwyns was haunted, for in the half-light of evening, when viewed from the cove, its silhouette frequently looked mysterious and eerie.

She stood up and gazed out towards the cliff path. No-one appeared to be around and so she was confident it would be quite safe to take a peep inside the house through the downstairs windows. But to her dismay, when she approached the first huge bay she found curtains pulled across, and even though there was a slight chink in the middle, it was not possible to see what lay beyond.

Disappointed, Rosemary walked round to another window, but once again the curtains were pulled together. Annoyed and puzzled she concluded the drapes were probably to protect the furnishings from strong sunlight and therefore the north facing windows around the back might not be covered over.

She walked around the side where to her delight the curtains were pulled back and she was able to look into a beautifully furnished room, where a large mahogany dining table took pride of place with ten matching chairs orderly tucked beneath. Magnificent pictures hung from the walls. A large ornate mirror dominated the chimney breast above the white marble fireplace, and two crystal chandeliers dangled over the table from the elaborate ceiling above.

Rosemary clasped her hands and gasped in awe. Chy-an-Gwyns was not the sort of house in which to have villains, murderers or ghosts, but somewhere where a beautiful lady in a long frock might live with her husband, and where they would entertain their prestigious friends. Rosemary started to daydream. Her beautiful lady must have a secret lover, a smuggler or poor fisherman perhaps. Thoughts began to flow through her mind, but were abruptly interrupted by a loud cry.

"Hey, what the devil do you think you're doing here?" shouted an irate voice.

Rosemary turned. A small figure with huge shining eyes reflecting the sun was running towards her. It was wearing a large straw hat, a long leather apron, and in its hand, it waved a large gleaming axe. She screamed, took to her heels, fled round the house, down the garden path and back out onto the cliff top. Without stopping to shut the gate, she hurriedly picked up her notebook and pen, ran down the cliff path and did not pause to rest until she was safely back in the cove.

Milly met Johnny on the beach the day after the party, as planned, and while lying in the sun, he told her about himself. He was twenty two years old, had two older brothers and a younger sister. He worked for the electricity board and his hobbies were river fishing and swimming. Milly, an only child, was extremely thrilled by this revelation. She also was a keen swimmer and enjoyed springboard diving too. Furthermore, their chat established they lived just six miles from each other, hence there was no reason why they could not meet again when their holidays were over.

Milly was overjoyed, and for the first time in years felt optimistic about the future and not depressed, as she had previously been, about seeking work on her return home, having recently finished a college course on shorthand/typing.

Madge on the other hand was not at all pleased with the friendship. She had only ever encouraged Milly to look for a boyfriend in order to keep the girl occupied while she went in pursuit of a husband for herself, hence, she was extremely jealous that Milly had achieved that which she had been unable to do.

She considered the relationship between the two youngsters a meaningless holiday romance that would lead nowhere, and told Milly that she was wasting her time because Johnny would not want to see her again once they were back home.

Madge turned from being a burden to George to becoming a burden to everyone. She became aggressive, rude, uncivil, and even threatened to cut short the holiday because she had a very selfish and unappreciative daughter.

CHAPTER EIGHTEEN

On Tuesday morning, the major went out for the day to play golf at his local club, and so Molly, having no lunch to prepare, decided once the housework was done, to take a stroll over the cliff tops to Polquillick so that she might see for herself the graves of Emily and Harry. In case the major may have forgotten something thus causing him to return home early, Molly left a note to say she had gone for a walk, but did not disclose the reason for her outing or her destination, as she was well aware that he was very sceptical when the subject of reincarnation was broached. She thought his early return unlikely, anyway, for the major was a punctilious man, who never left the house without meticulously checking everything needed for his day was about his person, and she would be back, preparing for the evening meal long before his golf was done.

She removed her slippers, put on her sturdy walking shoes and contemplated whether or not to wear a cardigan, for although it was a beautiful day, it felt a little cooler than of late and she considered it may well be chilly once on top of the cliffs where there was no shelter from the wind. A cardigan therefore, she decided, was a must.

Before she left she combed her hair and looked at the bruise which had developed above her right eye following her encounter with Emily Penberthy. Everyone in Trengillion knew the source of her injury, but in Polquillick she would be a stranger, therefore, she slipped her sunglasses into the pocket of her cardigan to wear later, as she did not want strangers to think she might be a battered wife.

Molly left Rose Cottage and walked through the village towards the cove. Outside the Inn she stopped. Should she pop inside and ask Mabel if she would like to accompany her? Molly decided that was not a good idea, for she believed Mabel was still sulking, and it was unlikely, even if she was in a better frame of mind, that she would want to spend time with the person who had made her a laughing stock.

"Besides," reflected Molly, with a sigh. "I can't be doing with having to explain to a newcomer about the Emily and Harry saga, even if Mabel has picked up bits of gossip, here and there, on the subject."

She continued her walk alone down the incline to the beach, where at the foot of the cliff she joined the coastal path and climbed the steep slope, treading carefully on the dry earth, until she reached the top. In front of Chy-an-Gwyns, she stopped to get back her breath and relish the view. A few boats were visible on the clear, turquoise waters below: mostly fishing boats, crabbers from the cove and other villages along the coast. Molly squinted to see if there were any she knew, but was too far away to distinguish one boat from another.

She continued walking along the well-worn, cliff path and into a soft south westerly breeze. She passed by bracken and gorse, happily humming quietly to herself. So beautiful was the morning, so exhilarating was the air, she felt like bursting into song, but thought it unwise as she would feel very silly if she were to meet someone unexpectedly, for it was not always possible to see who or what lay beyond the hills and vales.

After the path went inland a little, she reached a field where Pat Dickens' dairy cows grazed on a patch of grass, still lush and green in a shady spot alongside a hedge. Once she had been afraid of cows, but after having lived for eighteen months in the country, she had learned they were quite harmless if left to their own devices.

Someone was working at the far side of the field repairing a fence. Molly realised it was Jed Dickens, home from university for the summer and helping his parents out on their farm. Molly sighed; she had learned from May that he was their only son, but he had no interest in taking on the farm, hence, it would have to be sold when they decided to retire. This saddened Pat greatly, for the farm had been in the Dickens family for over two hundred years.

"He must be mad to want to leave Trengillion," said Molly, to a cow watching her as she climbed over the stile. "Although I suppose dairy farming is very arduous. Well, I know it is. May has said on many occasions that early morning milking is anti-social. Still, he's a very clever young man, so I am told, and when all's said and done, it's his life."

Eventually, Molly reached the Witches Broomstick where she paused and glanced over the side of the cliff onto the rocks below. She then sat to rest on a huge, flat rock, where she watched a bumble bee buzz from one bloom to another on a clump of pretty pink thrift. When it flew off, she rested her chin on her clasped hand and breathed a huge sigh of satisfaction. For without doubt she was a contented woman and considered she would forever be indebted to Cornwall and her son, for bestowing upon her the gift of happiness. For had Ned not chosen to convalesce in such a beautiful part of the country the previous year, she would never have discovered Trengillion; would never have met the major, and most certainly would still be living, a lonely divorcee, in a rented cottage in Clacton, making the most of her limited talents telling fortunes and dabbling with spiritualism. Yes, life now had made up for the blows she had endured in earlier years, and although she had never fulfilled her wish to have a daughter, she did have a daughter-in-law of whom she was very fond, and it delighted her to see how blissfully happy Stella had made Ned.

Molly rose to continue her journey; after another mile she finally reached her destination and was able to glimpse her first siting of Polquillick. She stopped momentarily to take in the view, charmed and bewitched by its overwhelming quaintness and beauty.

Commencing her walk, she felt over warm, and so removed her cardigan and tied it around her waist; she then braced herself for the steep climb down the cliff path.

Her descent into the village, however, was not as laborious as she had anticipated, for half way down the path, beautifully constructed steps emerged, thus eliminating the necessity to slip and slide on the dry, loose earth. Once safely at the bottom, she walked onto the sandy beach, busy with holiday makers soaking up the sun.

Molly left the cove after first spending a penny in the public toilets by the entrance to the harbour wall. She then headed towards the church, navigated by its turreted tower prominently protruding above a muster of tall trees. On her arrival, she found a funeral taking place and, not wanting to go into the churchyard until it was over, she walked back towards the harbour and went into a small gift shop, next door to an ice cream parlour, to browse through the souvenirs and pass away the time.

She bought nothing from inside the shop but as she was leaving she noticed a rack of postcards; some saucy, but most picturesque scenes of Cornwall. She shuffled through them. All were in colour; many local, and one she liked in particular, was of the cove, taken since the War judging by the dress of the people and the modern cars parked on the harbour wall. Molly viewed it with interest. The picture was brightly coloured with the words, *Greetings from Polquillick* written in red across the top.

She shuffled through the collection of cards to see if there were any variations. All were the same; until she came across the very last one, right at the back. The difference was considerable, for the last card was sepia and taken long ago, around the turn of the century. On it, fishing boats stood in a line across the beach, and beside them people posed for the camera. Fishermen and fishwives: children, some dressed in fine clothes, others in rags. Men with bicycles, one with a horse and cart. Little girls holding dolls, women with prams. All standing amongst crab pots, and fishing nets draped over the sides of wooden boats, within the safety of the harbour wall.

Molly enchanted, felt a pang of excitement. Was it possible that Emily and Harry might be on the postcard? She hurriedly rummaged through the pennies in the pocket of her dress, change from her trip to the post office in Trengillion that morning. She had enough money, and so bought the card and rushed out into the sunshine to view it closely.

Molly could not make out the faces of the people on the postcard and knew also she would not recognise Emily and Harry, anyway. Nevertheless, she was interested to see if any of the men resembled George, but it was impossible for her to say without the aid of her reading glasses. Disappointed that she would have to wait until she was back home to view it more closely, she slipped the picture into the large pocket of her dress and walked back along the street towards the church.

The funeral party was still in the churchyard, and so she sat down on the grass verge opposite and made a daisy chain from the profusion of white flowers growing alongside patches of red clover, until eventually the funeral party left. When Molly felt sure everyone had gone, she crossed the narrow road with the daisy chain hanging around her neck and went into the churchyard through the open gates, looking forward to giving Emily Penberthy a piece of her mind.

At first she could not remember whereabouts in the churchyard Ned had said the graves were situated, and so she walked all around, reading the tombstones, aware of the gravedigger working in the newly incorporated corner of the adjoining field, covering the remains of the person for whom the funeral had just taken place. When he left, Molly ambled over to the fresh grave, curious to know if the name of the deceased would mean anything to her and also to take a closer look at the huge mound of brightly coloured wreaths and bouquets.

She knelt to read the cards after first looking over her shoulder, for she did not want anyone to think she was nosy. The cards were in memory of a woman called Cybil. Molly concluded she must have been elderly, for two of the cards were written by her great, great grandchildren.

Molly sniffed the roses and admired the flowers; mostly chrysanthemums. She said a quick prayer for Cybil and then resumed her search for the graves of Emily and Harry.

After walking the entire length and width of the churchyard, she finally came across the graves tucked up a corner, near to a railing which overlooked the sea. Molly, however, was puzzled as she looked down on the two graves. Ned and Stella had described them as being overgrown, uncared for and rough, but there in front of her, the grass was neatly clipped, the headstones cleared of lichen, and flowers adorned the two grass mounds. For Emily, bright golden marigolds mixed with sky-blue love-in-a-mist, proudly graced a dumpy, glass vase. But as Molly looked closer, she observed that a chipped jam jar, crammed inartistically with stinking tutsan and wilting stinging nettles, interspersed with the leaves of scurvy grass and swine cress, was the offering left on the grave of Harry Timmins.

Molly felt uneasy as she glanced around. The grass could not have been trimmed by a sexton because most of the surrounding graves were still uncared for. Besides, even if a sexton had trimmed the grass he would not have put flowers, or weeds, as in Harry's case, on the graves.

Molly stood and read the inscriptions thoughtfully. Her discovery made little or no sense. If there were no Timmins family members living in the area then who had tended the graves, and why had someone decorated Harry's grave with such disdain? Suddenly, a possible answer flashed into her mind. What about Penberthy? Ned, Stella and George had enquired about Timmins but had not done so regarding that name.

"There must still be Penberthys living around here," whispered Molly. "And it's they who have attended to the graves and for some reason they bear a grudge against Harry or his family."

Her hands felt clammy as she pondered over what next to do. Should she visit the Mop and Bucket and make enquiries there or should she leave it to the youngsters?

Molly was undecided and about to leave for the gate when she heard the snap of a twig from an area where the graves were shrouded from sunlight by a canopy of tall trees. She listened carefully, very much aware that she had seen no-one since the gravedigger had left nor had she heard footsteps approaching along the gravel path, yet without doubt, someone was standing close-by, breathing heavily behind her, for she could feel the draught of breath, warming the back of her bare neck.

With heart thumping, Molly nervously began to turn her head, but before she had a chance to see who or what lay behind, she was struck by a blunt instrument on the back of her head and she fell to the ground, unconscious.

CHAPTER NINETEEN

After an enjoyable day in the company of his friends and a lovely lunch at the clubhouse, the major returned home looking forward to the evening meal, especially as it was Tuesday, which meant dinner would be one of Molly's delicious lamb hotpots. When he reached the house, however, he found the back door was locked. Surprised, he looked beneath a flower pot, removed the key from its hiding place, unlocked the door and stepped inside. The major was baffled. Molly was not in the kitchen, smiling to greet him, pinafore around her waist and a little flustered by the heat of her domestic chores. He glanced around the kitchen. It was clean and tidy, as expected, but devoid of the usual smell of the hotpot cooking on the hob.

The major walked throughout the house calling Molly's name, but received no response. Puzzled he returned to the kitchen where he noticed her note lying on the table beside a vase of sweet peas, saying she had gone for a walk. There was no indication as to what time it was written, so the major could not estimate for how long she had been gone, but he was confused and a little cross. It was not like Molly to go off and not be home in time to cook his dinner; she just was not that kind of woman.

Disappointed the major made a pot of tea and a cheese sandwich, collected the evening paper which was hanging through the letterbox in the hall way, and then sat down to read it whilst he awaited Molly's return.

He read the paper from cover to cover, glancing up repeatedly each time he heard a noise outside. When he finished reading every item of interest, he laid the paper on his lap and looked at the clock on the mantelpiece. It was time for The Archers. The major was bewildered. Surely Molly would not miss her favourite programme without good reason? He switched on the wireless confident at any moment she would come rushing in through the door; but he listened to the broadcast alone. Molly did not return.

As the major rose from his chair to switch off the wireless and return his dirty crockery to the kitchen, there was a knock on the front door. He rushed to answer it and found Doris, wearing hat and coat standing in the little front porch.

"I've come for Molly," she frowned in answer to his puzzled, questioning look. "It's W.I. tonight, Ben. Is she ready?"

"She's not here, Doris," muttered the major. "Come in, and you can read her note."

Doris crossed the threshold and followed the major through the living room and into the kitchen where he handed her the note.

"But this doesn't make sense," whispered Doris. "Where can she have gone? She was really looking forward to this month's meeting. We're going to get a demonstration on basketwork crafts and she was very keen to learn about that."

"I know," said the major, "but I must admit, I'd forgotten. Have you seen her at all today?"

"I saw her in the post office this morning. In fact we walked back home together, but she didn't say anything about going out at all. We just talked about tonight's meeting."

He crossed to the window and looked up at the sky. Only an hour or two of daylight remained and he felt very uneasy.

"Something's wrong, Doris. She must be hurt or in some sort of trouble. I'm going down to the Inn to see if Ned's seen her at all today. Meanwhile, I suggest you go to the meeting as usual and if you find out anything that might be useful, please pop down to the Inn and let us know, won't you?"

"Of course I will, but are you sure you're alright, Ben? You look very pale."

"I'm fine. At least I will be when I get her back."

As Doris left, the major put on his jacket, picked up the note from the table and slipped it into his pocket. He then locked up the house, put the key beneath the flower pot, and made his way quickly down the road to the Inn.

Inside he found Ned with Stella, George and Rose who were alarmed by the look on his face when he asked if they had seen Molly. The major's face dropped when they told him they had not seen her all day. He slumped down onto a bench, pulled the note from his pocket and told how he had returned home from the golf club and found her missing.

Frank, hearing every word, promptly asked Rose, who had the night off, to look after the bar with Dorothy. He then grabbed a torch and suggested they waste no more time talking, but start to search quickly before darkness fell.

They split up into four groups. The first went along the cliffs towards the old mine, the second towards the Witches Broomstick, the third down the lane towards the Penrose farm, and the fourth over the fields to the stables.

Stella meanwhile, as instructed by Ned, went to The Police House to report Molly's disappearance to Fred Stevens. Fred, however, was not in. He had the night off and had gone into town for a game of snooker at the newly refurbished club.

Annie, who was not able to attend the W.I. meeting because Fred was out and so she had to look after the children, took down as many details as Stella was able to give her regarding Molly's last known movements.

"Fred should be home around half past nine, Stella. Needless to say I shall send him straight to the Inn on his return. Meanwhile, I'll try and contact him on the telephone. Although I've a feeling the club's having problems with the G.P.O. line at present, because Fred had to ring one of his friends to see if they were going to be open tonight."

"Thank you. I feel so useless, I can't even make any worthwhile suggestions as to where she may have walked, as we've not done much walking ourselves and I don't really know the area that well. Ned's really upset. I do hope she turns up soon."

"I'm sure she will," said Annie. "Try and keep your spirits up. Molly's a sensible woman and I can't see that she would have got herself into trouble or done anything silly."

Stella smiled. "Thank you, I'd better get back now to see if there's any news."

She walked the short distance to the Inn, praying that the search for her mother-in-law had been successful and a celebration to denote her safe return, be in full swing. When faced with reality, however, she found none of the search parties had returned and the mood at the Inn was still very sombre.

Eventually, dejected men returned. They had not found Molly or encountered anyone having seen her during the day. Hope of finding her was wearing very thin as they had no idea even in which direction she may have walked.

Frank poured himself a large whisky, tossed some coins into the till and stared at Mabel sitting in the corner of the snug deeply engrossed in the chapters of a book. He crossed to her side and sat down.

"Have you by any chance seen Molly today, Auntie?" he asked, abruptly.

She looked up from the pages and attempted to smile. "No, dear. Why, should I have?"

"Well, I don't know. It's just you often go out walking and I hoped somehow your paths might have crossed somewhere or other."

"I didn't go out walking today, I stayed here," she said with a smirk.

"But I saw you go out with your coat on this morning and it was several hours before you returned," said Frank, annoyed by the tone of her voice and the amusement in her eyes.

"I spent much of the day outside reading, sitting on a chair from the shed in your vegetable garden, if you can call a bed of nettles and weeds a vegetable garden. It's a disgrace, Frank Newton. But then you're very much like your mother and she was hopeless at gardening too. Stupid woman! She pulled up some of your father's favourite plants one year trying to help with the weeding, and he never even uttered a word of complaint."

"No, he didn't. He acknowledged anyone can make a mistake, and saw the funny side of it, unlike some folk I know."

Frank angrily rose from the seat, left Auntie Mabel with her book and made a mental note to get the vegetable plot cleared. Not to please his annoying aunt, although he knew she was right, but because it was no tribute to Sylvia to have let her beloved garden become such an eyesore.

George and Ned, who had been in separate search parties, chatted surreptitiously to each other, once reunited, over whether or not there might be a connection between Molly's disappearance and Emily Penberthy's ghost. Bearing in mind Molly had vowed to find out more and both knew how determined she was. They agreed, however, it sounded too far-fetched, and therefore chose to say nothing when Fred arrived at the Inn later, after his trip into town.

Rosemary Howard sat in the corner sipping her port and lemon listening to unfurling events. It occurred to her that if Molly had gone for a ramble then she may well have walked over the cliff tops and perhaps, like her, had been intrigued to see what lay beyond the gate of Chy-an-Gwyns. If that were the case, Molly may have encountered the phenomenon with the axe and big shining eyes, but because of her age, may not have been so lucky when trying to escape. Rosemary felt sick. She knew she ought to say something, but didn't want to admit she was guilty of trespass. Overcome with a feeling of shame, she said nothing and prayed Molly would turn up safe and well before the night was through.

At nine o'clock, after the WI meeting, Doris having first called at Rose Cottage and finding no-one home, arrived at the Inn to enquire if there was any news. When she was told Molly seemed to have vanished into thin air, Doris sat down and wept; partly through worry over the disappearance of her friend, and partly through being reminded of the hours, days, and then weeks when she had waited in vain for news of her beloved niece.

The major, upset by her tears, sat by her side and took her hand. "Come on, Doris, don't upset yourself. Molly's a tough old gel and even if she is in trouble, lost, or whatever, I'm sure she'll manage somehow to get help and be back with us soon."

"But what if she's hurt or injured in a remote spot somewhere? It could be days before she's found."

"She might have fallen down an old mine shaft," Mabel suggested, a hint of amusement in her voice, as she entered the public bar. "I was reading an article in the local paper only the other day saying how many there are in the area. Some of them are very deep and extremely dangerous, you know."

Frank's face darkened to a deep shade of red as he turned to respond to her tactless remark. But Mabel, having succeeded in upsetting everyone, gave a sweet smile and swept out of the bar to her room.

Frank was furious, but the major calmed him down.

"Don't let her get to you, Frank, she's obviously still resentful over Molly's little discovery and sees upsetting us as a way of getting revenge. Rise above it, and at the same time pray to God that she's not right."

As he spoke, Fred Stevens arrived at the Inn, having just returned home from town and eager to see if there had been any further developments. On hearing nothing more had occurred he informed the major they would start searching again at eight o'clock in the morning. Meanwhile, he would report the incident to his superiors in town and phone round to muster up as many local people as possible to help with the search. The major, while disappointed, conceded nothing more could be done that evening and left the Inn. Ned and Stella offered to escort him home and stay with him, but he insisted he would be alright and dawdled home a pitiful sight, arms linked with his close friend and neighbour, Doris, hopeful that Molly would be there waiting on his return, knitting needles clicking as though nothing had happened. But the key was still beneath the flower pot and the house was in darkness. Molly's chair was empty and her knitting lay, as he had last seen it, on the sideboard beside her favourite ornament, a ceramic owl perched on a branch. He did not go to bed, but sat up all night in his armchair reading a book, but not absorbing one word, whilst on the mantelpiece, beside a picture of Molly, the clock repetitiously ticked, as it slowly went through, one long hour after another.

CHAPTER TWENTY

Ned woke early the following morning at first light, having slept very little, worrying over the disappearance of his mother. Stella was still sleeping as he slid quietly out of bed, dressed and then tip-toed from the room.

Once in the passage he unlocked George's door - his first job every morning - and then crept downstairs to the kitchen where he made himself a cup of tea. With cup and saucer in hand, he left the Inn and walked towards the cove.

The fishing boats, having made an early start, were all at sea when he rounded the corner and the beach came into view, but Des and Larry were still ashore, busily cleaning diving equipment in the small front garden of Cove Cottage. They called to Ned when they spotted him to ask if there was any news regarding his mother. When he told them circumstances had not changed, they offered their condolences and told him they were not going to sea, but would be joining the search parties at the given time. With gratitude, Ned thanked them, crossed the beach and sat down on Denzil's bench, where once again he racked his brains and tried to imagine where his mother might have gone for a walk. He knew she was fond of walking, was fit and healthy and quite familiar with all the local footpaths and bridle ways, and he doubted that she would walk in a strange place without good reason. Nevertheless, he could not help but recall Mabel's cruel suggestion that his mother may have fallen down a mine shaft, although he was pretty certain she had no grounds for making such a statement other than pure malice.

His thoughts turned to George, and he wondered if his impetuous mother might have found out something about his dreams and Emily Penberthy. If this was the case, she may even have gone to Polquillick, where Emily and Harry had lived and drowned. Or perhaps she had simply gone to see the graves for herself. Of one thing Ned was sure; his mother was alive. For although he had never attempted to speak to the dead since Jane had moved on, he knew he

145

still had the gift to do so, should he so desire. And if Molly was dead, then she would not hesitate to make contact with him.

Ned finished his tea, rose from the bench and wandered down to the water's edge where the sea was flat calm and crystal clear. He took in a deep breath. The morning air felt fresh and clean, the weather was fine, but he recalled hearing the forecast on the wireless predicting rain later in the day. Ned prayed that wherever his mother was she was not exposed to the elements, for although Molly liked to believe she was tough, she did not like to be wet or cold.

Ned picked up his cup and saucer from Denzil's bench, waved to Larry and Des and sauntered back up the hill where he arrived at the Inn just as Alf Burgess the postman pushed the early morning delivery of mail through the letter box. The two men greeted each other as Alf mounted his red bicycle in preparation to free-wheel down the hill to the houses in the cove.

Inside, Ned picked up the small pile of envelopes and laid them on the table in the hallway, he then returned the cup and saucer to the kitchen and proceeded to climb the stairs. But half way up something told him to check the post. Thinking perhaps there may be a letter for Stella from her parents, he descended the staircase and picked up the bundle of mail. Much of it was for Frank; utility bills in buff coloured envelopes; other forms of correspondence were for guests staying at the Inn. Ned smiled when he noticed an envelope addressed to Mrs M. Thorpe, but his face quickly changed and his heart began to race when he read the name on the envelope beneath Mabel's letter. For in his hand lay a pale blue envelope, strongly scented with lavender and addressed in spidery handwriting to Harry Timmins.

Ned froze. Goose pimples pricked his arms and the back of his neck. In a moment of panic he tossed the post onto the hall table and ran towards the stairs, but he stopped before stepping onto the first tread. He could not leave such an item for all and sundry to see.

He walked back into the hallway and stared at the table on which the post rested. What was he to do with such an unwelcome and bizarre item? Should he hand it to Frank or should he open it himself? Or perhaps he should give it to George? After a brief reflection he decided on the last option, snatched the envelope from the pile and ran up the stairs to George's room.

George was awake and already dressed. Ned handed him the envelope.

"Christ, Ned, where did you get this from?" he asked, handling it as though it was red hot.

"The postman's just delivered it and I thought I'd bring it to you before anyone else saw it. I think perhaps you should open it."

"I don't know that I want to," whispered George, running his fingers over the envelope. "I mean, I'm not Harry Timmins, am I? He's dead. It must be from someone in the village who knows about my dreams and they're doing it for a joke."

"Maybe, and I hope you're right. Certainly lots of people will have heard about your association with Emily Penberthy, by now."

"But what can it be?" George asked, beads of perspiration forming on his forehead. "It feels as though there's something lumpy inside. Oh God, Ned, I really don't think I want to see this. You open it."

"No. Whoever sent it must have intended it for you and I'm sure if Frank had seen it before me, he would have thought the same. Come on, George. Whatever it is it won't kill you, but the suspense is killing me."

George sat down in the chair beside the hearth and nervously slid his finger beneath the gummed down flap. The envelope opened with ease. He peeped inside and pulled out a piece of tissue paper nestled in a corner; carefully he unfolded it on his lap. Both men gasped when a silver necklace slid onto the floor. George picked it up and looked at it closely. It was round, quite heavy and edged with fine filigree

"I think it's a locket. It certainly looks like one, anyway. I can't undo it, though. My hands are too shaky."

He handed the necklace to Ned who carefully unfastened the clasp on the side of the large silver circle. Inside were two head and shoulders pictures of a young woman wearing a high necked Victorian dress with leg of mutton sleeves. Ned shuddered and passed it to George, whose face turned from pale to white when he looked inside.

"This hasn't been sent as a joke, Ned. I must be seeing things. Without doubt, these pictures are of the young woman from the boat, and look she's wearing this locket. I don't believe it! She must be

Emily Penberthy and this necklace must have belonged to her. In which case, who could have had it in their possession and sent it to me? Because, oh God! I know this sounds crazy, Ned. But in retrospect, I'm pretty sure Emily was wearing this very necklace when she drowned?"

Molly recovered consciousness, opened her eyes and surveyed her surroundings; they were unfamiliar. The atmosphere was cold, damp and dim: the only illumination, a faint glimmer of light from a twenty five watt bulb dangling from a large beam, mottled with the tell-tale signs of woodworm.

Molly sat up and touched the back of her aching head. Her hair was stiff with dry blood, but the wound at least appeared to have stopped bleeding.

Confused, she looked at her dismal surroundings. She was in a cellar of some description, for there were no windows on any of the four bare, granite walls. The air felt damp and musty, the floor on which she had been dumped was concrete, and apart from a tray, a chamber pot, a few blankets and a mattress in the corner, the room was devoid of any objects.

Molly pulled the tray towards her. On it stood a glass of water and a tea plate upon which rested a slice of cold toast. Molly picked up the glass. She was very thirsty but questioned whether or not the water was fit to drink. Certainly it looked fresh and the glass was clean. She dipped her finger inside and touched her tongue with water. It tasted alright and so Molly drank down several gulps. She looked at the toast on which butter was spread very thinly. She took a bite, it also tasted good and so she ate it all and then finished off the water.

Feeling slightly better, Molly looked at the door, no doubt the door through which she had been dragged or carried whilst still unconscious. She wondered if it was locked, but felt too weak to check. It was hardly likely, anyway, that someone would go to the trouble of capturing her, dumping her in a cellar and then leave without bothering to lock the door. She sighed deeply and wondered what lay on the other side. Was she in the cellar of someone's home or in a derelict property? Would the people, or person, who had put her there just leave her to rot, or would they ask a ransom of the

148

major? If only she knew what was going on, then the ordeal might not feel quite so bad. But why had she been captured in such a brutal manner? What had she done wrong? Was she just in the wrong place at the wrong time or was her abduction in any way connected to the dreams which had plagued George since he had arrived in Cornwall? Molly had no idea of the answers. She didn't know where she was: whether it was a cellar in Polquillick or Timbuktu. Neither did she know whether it was night or day and for how long she had been unconscious. Her watch said half past six; but half past six when? Was it still Tuesday evening, or early on Wednesday, or even Thursday?

A spider scuttled across the ceiling and disappeared through a gap in a beam. Molly tried to stand, feeling the place was crawling with insects, but her head ached too much and she fell backwards onto the floor. She dragged herself across the cold concrete and onto the mattress. It did not feel too damp, nor did the blankets, and so perhaps they had not been in the cellar for long. In which case perhaps her captor was not in the habit of abducting people and keeping them prisoner, and she was the first, which had her asking again, why?

Molly lay down on the mattress and pulled the coarse blanket around her chilled body. She thought of the major. He would come home from the golf club and find no-one home and no dinner simmering on the hob. She thought of Doris who would be confused as to why her friend and neighbour was not in and ready when she called for her to go to the W.I. meeting, especially as Doris knew how much she had been looking forward to the meeting and had been ever since they had learned about the basketwork demonstration. She thought of Ned and how he had spent a night trapped in the Witches Broomstick, not knowing whether he would ever be found. She thought of the Ringing Bells Inn and her dear, dear friends, of Stella and Rose. Poor Rose, what a disappointment the party must have been to her; she would never succeed in winning George's affection now, as long as Emily Penberthy was around. George Clarke: was he the reason she was locked up? She felt sure he must be, but why was she a victim of his circumstances? She had nothing to do with his dreams, his life, his past. In fact she had known him for only a few weeks. So perhaps the séance was the reason for her imprisonment.

Perhaps she was involved by association and the ghost of Emily Penberthy really was out there yearning for her lover. But a ghost could not have knocked her out, carried her to a cellar and made her toast and filled a glass with water. Molly laughed at the proposition, for if she really had encountered such a multi-talented ghost, then together the two of them could make a fortune if she could get Emily to perform, although she doubted that Emily would co-operate.

She thought long and hard about Harry and Emily; the demands of Emily did not make sense. For if they had both died together, why did Emily think George was Harry's reincarnation? And if people did get reincarnated, why had Emily not been reincarnated too?

Molly snuggled up in a ball and closed her eyes. She felt dirty, scruffy and horribly alone. She wanted to cry, but felt tears of self-pity from a woman nearer fifty than forty, would be a disgrace. But did it matter? There was no-one to see the tears, anyway.

Molly felt in the pocket of her dress for a handkerchief and with it pulled out the postcard which dropped to the floor. She blew her dribbling nose, picked up the postcard and held it close to the light bulb. Sadly though, she was not able to see it any clearer than when outside in the sunshine.

Her aching eyes felt heavy. She lay back down and wanted to sleep. She closed them, and felt herself begin to drift away, but within minutes something woke her abruptly: voices in the distance and footsteps crossing the floor above the spot where she lay.

Molly sat up and tried to hear what the voices were saying. One was very deep and no doubt a man, but it was too muffled to distinguish any of the words or make out to how many people he was speaking. She heard a high pitched laugh and the sound of something scraping across the floor, like a chair being dragged or furniture moved.

Twenty minutes passed by with just voices and the occasional laugh, and then the voices stopped and music rang out from above. Molly realised whoever was overhead was listening to the wireless and the programme which had caused the laughter was now finished.

Above, silence prevailed for five minutes, and then again she heard footsteps crossing the floor. A door in the distance opened and the voice of a woman shouted. Molly froze. It sounded as though someone was walking down stone steps and with each stride the noise grew louder and louder and louder.

CHAPTER TWENTY ONE

Through the door came the unexpected figure of a crabby old woman, slightly bent with grey straw-like hair which she wore in an unflattering bob. Her multi-coloured, floral dress fitted badly, she had holes in the elbows of her cardigan, and her teeth, obviously false, rattled as she spoke.

"So, you're awake then," she snapped. "Good, 'cos you're a damn heavy lump to carry."

Molly, astonished by the unlikely appearance of her captor, was too shocked to speak as the old woman entered the room, crossed to the mattress where she lay and from the pocket of her cardigan pulled out two old stockings and a brightly coloured, red spotted headscarf. Molly gasped, alarmed. Was the old biddy going to strangle her?

"Come and help me," the old woman called, her head tilted towards the open door. "I can't do this on my own."

Squinting in the dim light, Molly nervously watched to see who the accomplice was, but before anyone walked through the doorway, she felt the headscarf being tied firmly around her eyes. Frustrated, she attempted to remove it, but was punished with a severe kick in the thigh.

Molly heard light footsteps as the other person entered the room. She listened hard to see if he or she spoke, but the accomplice remained silent whilst helping the old woman tie Molly's hands behind her back. When the task was complete, Molly was commanded to stand, she was then pushed towards the door and forced to climb up stone steps, where she stumbled, unable to keep her balance, disorientated by her lack of vision.

At the top of the steps they went through another door and into a room which smelt strongly of disinfectant and fish. The floor was solid and uncarpeted. Instinct told Molly they were in a kitchen. Abruptly they stopped. The old woman told her accomplice to make sure the coast was clear. Molly heard a door open and felt a breeze, she was then pushed outside and down two steps.

The air felt chilly. Molly concluded it was either night-time or a dull day, for the breeze was cool and the sun non-existent. Another sharp push forced her to walk along an uneven path and into long grass. She heard squeaking doors open and was forcefully bundled into the back of a vehicle. Molly realised it was a van when she felt the doors slam shut behind her, and heard the two people climb into the front seats. The engine started with a bump and Molly toppled over as the van started to move.

They travelled for what seemed like miles. The driver was reckless. The vehicle sped around corners much too fast. The van's suspension was dreadful. Molly was bounced back and forth, continually hitting her head on the hard sides as they bumped up and down hills and across poorly surfaced roads or tracks. Eventually they stopped. Molly heaved a sigh of relief. She felt sick, light-headed and dizzy. She heard the two people climb out of the front seats and the back doors of the van open.

"Out," commanded the old woman. "Come on, out."

She was dragged from the back of the vehicle and heard the van doors slam shut. Her legs felt like jelly as she tried to stand up straight, and she stumbled as she was forcibly turned around. With each of her arms linked tightly through those of her captors, she was forced to walk along a level surface of earth and grass into a light breeze. Molly cursed that she was unable to see as the two people roughly guided her along. She felt sure the old woman was on her right and the unidentified person on her left. Molly tilted her head to the left to enable her to hear if the second person spoke, but he or she remained silent, listening to the old woman droning on, giving orders and directions. Molly sighed, the only characteristic feature she was able to establish of the accomplice, was he or she was taller than herself, for her arm was stretched upwards a little, in order to be linked.

After going down a very steep slope, the surface changed. They crossed uneven rocks, which increased in size the further down they climbed. Molly's ankles felt strained as she slipped and stumbled over large granite boulders, and when finally they stepped onto a soft light surface, which she instantly recognised as sand, she was very thankful.

The light breeze was now much stronger. Each gust tousled her hair and caused her dress to flap and snap around her legs like a sail on a yacht. She could smell and hear the sea as its waves crashed onto the shore. Negative thoughts rushed through her mind, as she tried to imagine what the outcome of her ordeal might be. Her heart sank. Surely these two people would not force her into the sea to drown.

As they continued to walk the light sand turned solid and wet. Molly gasped as she felt water trickling around her ankles. They veered slightly to the left and after a short distance the sand became dry again. Molly was commanded to stop and sit down. Neither of her captors spoke as one of them tied the second stocking around her ankles. They then left. Molly heard laughter as the voice of the old woman, cackling with derision, wished her a pleasant dip.

Molly sighed, much relieved. She was at least alive and they had not drowned her. Glad to be sitting down, she leaned back against something cold and solid. Was it a rock? Was she on the beach beside a boulder, or at the bottom of a cliff, perhaps? Molly felt her face getting damp. Was it spray from the sea or the first drops of rain? She strained to listen. The sea sounded very close but the voice of the old woman had faded away to nothing. She assumed, optimistically, her captors had gone for good and would not return. But then a dreadful thought crossed her mind. Had they left her on the beach to drown with the incoming tide? Is that what was meant by have a pleasant dip?

Molly began to panic. She had to escape, but first she needed to see where she was. She leaned forward, placed her head between her knees and moved it up and down attempting to force the headscarf away from her eyes. The scarf moved a little, but not enough to see. She stopped and then tried again; this time with success. As she raised her head the scarf fell onto the sand and she saw the dampness on her face was caused by rain, falling from dark clouds looming overhead.

She glanced at her surroundings; the beach appeared to be in a very small cove enclosed by rocks and a steep cliff face. She groaned; there had to be a way out because they had walked there in the first place. The tide, however, was coming in fast and the waves were rapidly smoothing over the three sets of footprints across the stretch of sand over which they had walked.

Molly, very much aware she needed to free herself quickly, cursed that her hands were tied behind her back. Not one to be beaten, she slipped her joined hands beneath her bottom until they were under her knees. She then slipped her feet through her arms, so that her bound hands were in front of her. With relief she attempted to untie the knot in the stocking around her ankles. The knot came undone easily. It was a granny, tied loosely. She concluded her captors were evidently not linked to a fishing family.

With her feet free, she raised herself from the sand and walked to the water's edge. She was definitely in a small uninhabited cove, but its location was unfamiliar to her and could be anywhere along the Cornish coast. She looked up, the drizzle was getting heavier, the tide was coming in rapidly and the light beginning to fade.

Molly, shivered, aware that time was running out. She desperately needed to free her hands. She looked around and to her delight saw a bottle, washed up by the tide. She kicked it hard against some rocks; with a crack, it broke in two. Relieved, she fiercely sliced into the stocking on the jagged edge. It came apart with ease. Molly rubbed her wrists; she was free, but there was no reason yet to be jubilant for the tide was coming in faster and faster. The three sets of footprints were now beneath deep water and before long the remaining sand and shingle would be under water also.

Molly looked at the cliffs behind her, there was no way she could climb them. Her captors had obviously chosen her final destination with care. She looked to the sea knowing the only way out was to swim until she reached safety. Normally Molly would have relished the idea of a challenging swim. She loved the water and was a strong swimmer, but captivity had left her weak, her head ached and she felt anything but energetic. Nevertheless, she realised she had very little choice. It was either swim, or stay and drown.

Molly buttoned up her cardigan and tied her shoe laces tightly as she did not want to lose them in the water. Slowly, she then waded into the sea. But which way should she go? To the right was the direction from which she had walked with her captors. Instinct told her to go to the left. She shivered and her teeth chattered as the water splashed around waist.

She took in a deep breath and clenched her fists. "Here goes. God, please be with me."

With gritted teeth she plunged into oncoming waves. The water was bitterly cold and momentarily her determination to persist began to fade. But then self-will strengthened. She would not be beaten. Her faith in providence and the love of her family and friends, inspired her willingness to survive. She forcefully pushed her arms into the deep, salt water and started to swim, her willpower boosted by sheer tenacity.

After fifteen minutes, Molly observed a stretch of rocks which seemed familiar. She was approaching the Witches Broomstick. Relieved to know she was in known territory and heading in the right direction, Molly veered to her left and clambered onto the rocks as a severe bout of cramp knotted the veins in her right leg. With a cry of agony, she hurriedly sat on the rocks and kneaded her calf to relieve the pain. As it melted away she heaved a thankful sigh and leaned back to rest and restore her breath.

She contemplated whether or not to risk the final swim to Trengillion; acknowledging it might be wiser to seek refuge and rest for the night in Jane's cave. After much thought, however, she decided to carry on. For although she was very cold, she knew the major and Ned would be worried and it was not fair to them, or anyone else who might care, to leave them fretting for a minute longer than was necessary.

"I'm nearly home. If I can keep up my strength and spirits for just a little longer, then I'll be home with the major in our little cottage, enjoying a cup of tea before I know it, and all will be well."

Feeling rejuvenated, she stood up on the rocks, plunged back into the water and swam as though she had an Olympic Gold Medal in her sights.

As Molly approached the cove she saw lights on the cliff tops, shining from the windows of Chy-an-Gwyns, and knew her ordeal was nearly over. And when she saw the beach with its row of fishing boats standing in a line on the shingle, she began to cry. Tears of joy and tears of sorrow streamed down her face and into the salt water. Sobbing and gulping, she swam until the water was too shallow. And then breathing heavily, she limply dragged herself out of the water and crawled up the beach towards the boats. But when she tried to stand, she found she had no strength. Aching and exhausted, she lowered her head onto the shingle and once again drifted into unconsciousness.

And there as darkness fell, stretched out on the cold, rough, shingle, she lay, with raindrops falling heavily onto her sodden, battered back.

CHAPTER TWENTY TWO

At half past nine on Wednesday night, Rose Briers stopped outside the Ringing Bells Inn and glanced through the front window into the public bar. She was feeling very downhearted, for the search to find Molly by the police and dozens of local volunteers during the day, had been to no avail.

Desperate to know if there had been any further developments since she had finished work earlier that evening, she went inside to ask Frank. With her she had Freak, for the two of them were out taking a brief walk around the village before locking up the house for the night.

Frank shook his head. "No, Rose, I wish I could say otherwise. I don't know what else any of us can do. I feel so damn useless. The major's gone back home and Ned, Stella and several others have gone with him. George is still here, though. He's in the snug with the two divers. He said he'd better stay just in case there was any news, then he could run quickly up the road to pass it on. But I think it's unlikely we'll hear anything tonight, now."

Rose glanced to where George sat in the snug bar talking to Larry and Des. She caught his eye and waved. He waved back. She then turned back to face Frank. "I just thought I'd pop in on the off-chance there would be good news, but if not we might as well go home and hope for better things tomorrow."

Frank looked pale. "I pray we find her soon. I can't bear to think of anything horrible happening to dear old Molly. Her disappearance has affected just about everybody in the village. I haven't seen so many glum faces since the worst days of the War."

Back outside Rose pulled her lightweight jacket tightly around her slim body and folded her arms across her chest, for she felt the heavy shower of rain which had sent everyone indoors earlier that evening, had left the night air cooler than of late and decidedly autumnal.

Rose headed for home with Freak loyally trotting by her side, but as they passed the church, Barley Wine ran out from beneath the lichgate and headed towards the beach. Freak, always up for a chase, ran after the cat, barking loudly, and both disappeared out of sight. Rose continued walking up the road towards The School House and home. She felt too weary to join in the chase, but then stopped in her tracks, for she knew if Freak did not return home, as often had happened before, she would have to venture out again later in the evening to find him, and as it felt as though another shower might be imminent, she decided it was foolhardy to continue without him.

She turned around and strolled down towards the cove. When she stepped onto the beach she was annoyed to see there was no sign of Freak or Barley Wine. She strained her eyes. Visibility was poor. The only light shining in the semi-darkness was from a dim lamp glowing above the porch of Cove Cottage, casting eerie shadows through the waving feathery branches of a large tamarisk bush.

Rose whistled and called Freak's name. To her relief she heard him bark and then he whined. She pricked up her ears. Freak's doggy noises were drifting through the night air from the direction of the fishing boats. Rose called to him again. He did not return to her side, but continued to whine, his cries growing louder and more prolonged. Rose felt her heart sink. Was her beloved dog in some kind of trouble, or hurt? Frantically, she ran across the beach screaming his name, wishing she had a torch to light her way. Tripping and stumbling on cobbles, feet sinking in sand, she continued towards the boats and Freak's cries for help.

Eventually she found him, tail wagging, standing beside something lying on the shingle. He licked his find lovingly, betwixt barks and mournful whines. Rose crept a little closer. When she saw Freak's find was a body, she screamed and looked warily over her shoulder. The body was very wet, motionless and slumped face down. Numbed with fear, afraid the perpetrator of the injuries to the unknown person might still be around, she timorously knelt beside it and lit a match to see more clearly. She cried out with surprise and shock when she realised the body was Molly. Shivering with fright, she rolled Molly over, lowered her head and listened for a heartbeat, but the only sound she could hear was her own heart thumping loudly, and whimpers from Freak close by her side.

In desperation, she put her hand over Molly's mouth. Feeling a little warmth, she leapt to her feet with joy and jubilation. Gone was the heavy heart and feelings of sorrow. With a spring in her steps and tears streaming down her face, she ran back to the Inn to proclaim the good news. And as she disappeared out of sight, Freak stood firm by Molly's side, on guard, even though he could see Barley Wine teasingly peeping at him, from the gunnels of Percy and Peter's boat.

Molly came round to find herself tucked up in her own bed with two hot water bottles, one by her feet and the other in her arms. In the room were two men, the major and Doctor Blake. On seeing her wake, the major leapt from his chair and squeezed her hand lovingly.

"Good God, Moll, wherever have you been? We've all been so worried."

Doctor Blake called downstairs for someone to put on the kettle and in due course Stella entered the room with a tea tray, closely followed by Ned.

Molly eagerly took a sip from the cup before attempting to answer the looks of eager curiosity written all over the faces of the room's occupants.

"What day is it?" she asked.

"Wednesday," replied the major. "Where on earth have you been?"

She took another sip of tea and shook her head. "I wish I knew. So, if today is Wednesday then I was in captivity for over twenty four hours. No wonder I'm so hungry and thirsty."

"Captivity!" spluttered Ned. "For Christ's sake, Mother, that's nearly as bad as falling down a mine shaft."

"Falling down a mine shaft," repeated Molly. "I'm not that stupid. There are warning signs near every dangerous mine. I've seen them, and I'd never be inquisitive enough not to heed those warnings. Whatever made you think I might do a silly thing like that?"

The major tutted loudly. "It was a suggestion made by Frank's wretched aunt. We didn't take any notice of her, of course, because she was clearly trying to put the cat among the pigeons by being as unhelpful as possible."

Molly chuckled. "Hmm, it sounds a bit like wishful thinking to me."

158

"Anyway," said Ned, "that's enough about Mabel Thorpe. What's all this about you being in captivity?"

Molly stared blankly at the window. "Well, someone kidnapped me but I've no idea who. In fact, I don't really know much at all, but what I do know I'll tell you and then you can make out of it what you will."

She proceeded then to relay the events which had taken place since she had first set off on her ramble over the cliffs. When she had finished, the major, red in the face, promptly headed for the door.

"I'm going to see if Fred's back from his meeting in town. People can't just go around knocking out women and locking them up in cellars. It's a job for the police."

Doctor Blake, having examined Molly, was confident she had no life threatening ailments. The wound on the back of her head had healed up nicely and he suggested the salt water had probably helped. It had also washed away the dried blood. Nevertheless, he said he would call again in the morning to see how she was doing. Meanwhile, he suggested she get plenty of rest, keep warm and not do any housework for a day or two.

When he had gone, Stella took the tea tray downstairs to wash up and Ned asked his mother the question he had been longing to ask.

"Who hit you on the head, Mum? Was it by any chance the ghost of Emily Penberthy?"

Molly laughed, even though it made her sides ache. "No, definitely not. The blow I received was not from any ghost, of that I am sure. Although we all know Emily is prone to violence, it must have been the old woman, but I find that difficult to believe as well."

"Or her accomplice. Have you really no idea who either of them might be?"

Molly shook her head. "None at all. As far as I know, I've never seen either of them before in my life. But then I didn't see the second one, anyway. The old hag was definitely the boss because the second person didn't say a word as I could hear. I don't even know if it was male or female. I'll tell you what I did discover though, before the attack, which I thought a little odd."

She then proceeded to tell Ned about the graves, how they had been tended and the strange arrangement of weeds and wild flowers on Harry's grave.

159

Ned frowned. "How odd. But then weird things have happened here too. An envelope arrived at the Inn this morning addressed to Harry Timmins, and inside was a silver locket containing two pictures of Emily Penberthy."

"What! But how do you know it's her?"

"Because George recognised her from his dreams. He's very shaken by all this."

Molly sighed deeply. "I'm not surprised. Whatever next! Who on earth could have sent the locket, and why? I shall have to make further investigations tomorrow."

"You'll do no such thing. Doctor Blake said you must rest. Besides, what more can you do?"

"Hmm, I don't know really."

"I wonder if there's a connection between your abduction and George's dreams."

"I've wondered that too. It's feasible of course, but a little unbelievable, don't you think? And if there is a connection, what can it be? I can't see how on earth George's dreams can have got anything to do with me."

"Neither can I," said Ned. "By the way, don't mention the locket to anyone, will you? It's something we're keeping quiet about. At present only you, Stella, George, Rose and me know and we'd like to keep it that way."

"And the person who sent it," said Molly. "He or she knows too."

The door downstairs opened, followed by voices and the sound of footsteps on the stairs. The major entered the room with Fred Stevens, the village policeman, and once again Molly repeated her ordeal.

Rose, still a little shaken, was nevertheless delighted and proud that her beloved Freak had found Molly alive and well, and when George insisted she stay with him at the Inn for a drink to celebrate Molly's safe return, while Ned and Stella waited at Rose Cottage for Molly to regain consciousness, she was even more delighted.

George questioned Rose briefly about her part in the discovery, during which time they were joined again by Larry and Des, who felt involved, having driven Molly home to Rose Cottage in the back of their van after Rose had raised the alarm. Both young men were eager to participate in any discussion regarding her disappearance and astonishing return. Although just what had happened to Molly during the time she had been missing was still a mystery to the patrons of the Inn and would be until they received further news from Ned and Stella on their return at bedtime.

When all was said that could possibly be said regarding Molly, without the conversation becoming repetitious, George regaled the divers with details of his dreams and subsequent events, although as agreed, he omitted reference to the locket, wrapped in tissue paper, back inside the envelope in which it had arrived and tucked inside the top drawer of the chest in his room. The divers, familiar with certain snippets of gossip regarding George since their arrival, were nevertheless fascinated, especially as his yarns involved the sea.

"Our wreck is off the coast near Polquillick," said Larry. "It might help you come to terms with your dreams if you were to visit the area where you may have drowned. It might even bring back memories."

George laughed. "Hang on. I don't believe for one moment that I'm the reincarnation of Harry Timmins, and neither do Ned, Stella, or you either, Rose, do you? We all think there has to be a much more believable explanation, as it's too far-fetched."

"A trip out with us could still help," agreed Des. "You might even be able to recognise the spot where the boat in your dreams went down."

George scowled. "But surely one bit of sea looks much the same as another."

"The sea, yes, but landmarks vary of course. Do you recall seeing the coastline in your dreams?"

"No, I just remember the sea, the boat and of course Emily."

"Oh, well, I still think you ought to come out with us," said Larry. "If you were able to identify the spot, we could then dive down and see if there are any signs of the boat."

"I think the boat was washed ashore a few days after the drownings, if my memory serves me right. On the other hand I'm probably imagining that, because I can't really remember exactly what Sid did tell us regarding the newspaper article. I'm pretty sure the boat's not on the sea bed, though, but I'll go out with you, anyway, because as you say, it could be interesting and I've nothing to lose."

"No," laughed, Des. "Lightning never strikes twice in the same place."

CHAPTER TWENTY THREE

On Thursday morning the police started to make enquiries regarding crabby old women in the area who drove a van, but they were unable to come up with any names. For although plenty of women fitted the description, half of them they were afraid to question in detail, and as none of them owned a van or even possessed a driving licence, there was no reason to suspect their involvement, anyway. Furthermore, Molly's description had focused more on the old women's clothing than her face, so they had very little to go on other than the rattling false teeth, and even then it was conceded she may have more than one set and just preferred to wear old lose ones when in the boundaries of her home for reasons of comfort.

Milly, having heard the story of Molly's ordeal, timorously suggested, during breakfast on Thursday morning, that the old lady's accomplice may have been male, her son perhaps, and the van may well have belonged to him. Ned agreed, and mentioned it to Fred when he and Stella went to call at The Police House later in the day.

"Well, actually we had thought of that," said Fred. "But to look for an unidentified male with an unidentified van in Cornwall is a bit of a tall order, especially when the person in question might not even be male."

Annie, Fred's wife, who was home, nodded. "It's a bit like looking for a needle in a haystack, I suppose. What sort of age does Molly reckon the old woman was?"

"Mum doesn't know for sure. She only saw her very briefly and the light was not good, but she guesses somewhere between fifty and seventy."

Annie smiled. "Oh dear, that encompasses rather a lot of the female population. I think perhaps we ought to forget about looking for this woman and her mysterious side-kick and concentrate instead on trying to find a motive, for as yet I believe there doesn't appear to be one."

Stella laughed. "Unless it's Emily Penberthy. She's the only link we can think of."

"What's the truth about the Emily Penberthy gossip?" asked Annie. "I've heard all sorts of ridiculous rumours, but naturally I've brushed much of it aside as idle chitchat."

"I wish it was," sighed Ned. He turned to Stella. "Shall I tell these good people about George's dreams or will you? Whichever one of us tells it, it will sound ever so daft."

"You tell, after all I wasn't there when you and George were up on the cliffs and often I was making tea when you talked things over with your mum."

"Yes, but you witnessed Emily's attack on Mum during the séance on my birthday and you're so much better at telling stories and retaining facts than I am."

Fred groaned. "Séance! Oh no, not more ghosts, please. I've heard folks nattering about the happenings on your birthday, Ned, after we'd come home, but I've chosen to ignore them."

Laughing, Ned gestured to Stella to regale the story of George's dreams and subsequent events.

Stella spoke fluently, without deviation. Her account was very thorough, although she deliberately left out the detail of the locket.

"Hmm, spooky," grinned Fred, when she had finished. "So, let me get this right. We're actually looking for an unidentified male or female, in an unidentified van, along with a woman aged between fifty and seventy with rattling teeth, the two of whom are probably friends of a drowned ghost called Emily who has a very bad temper. Shouldn't be too difficult to find. I must circulate this description with haste."

"Ignore him," smiled Annie, unable to keep a straight face. "He's just an old sceptic who's fond of trivialising things; although I do sympathise with him. But for all that I wouldn't be surprised if you're not on the right track. As someone once said: Truth is stranger than fiction. Or something like that."

"Mark Twain," said Stella. "It was he who said: Truth is stranger than fiction, but it is because Fiction is obliged to stick to possibilities. Truth isn't."

"Clever girl," said Annie, with a nod. "I'm impressed."

"I teach English," said Stella. "Famous quotes are all in a day's work."

Molly, busy dusting the furniture while the major was away in town on an errand, contemplated whether or not to clean down the shelves in the larder, in spite of Doctor Blake's orders to rest. But on seeing the sun shining brightly outside, she decided to get some fresh air instead and leave the larder for a rainy day. From the front room window she had noticed quite a few weeds showing their heads in the border which ran alongside the lawn, hence she chose to do a spot of weeding instead.

She changed from her slippers into her shoes, put on her sunhat and headed for the back door, but as she reached for the latch, she noticed a bundle of wet clothes piled in the corner beneath the kitchen sink. On taking a closer look, she realised they were the clothes she had worn during her trip to Polquillick. She sighed, knowing if left too long they would soon become smelly and soiled with black spots of mould which would be impossible to remove.

From the shed she fetched her new plastic bucket and filled it with hot soapy water, having made the decision, it would be best to give the clothes a good soaking prior to hand washing the following day, if she felt like it. When the bucket was full she took it outside, went back in to fetch the clothes, and then shook each item to remove any sand and seaweed. Once done she began to drop the clothes, one by one into the suds. As she picked up her dress, she remembered the postcard.

"Oh no," she cried, plunging her hand into the pocket. "Oh no, it'll be ruined."

When retrieved, she carried the limp, sodden postcard back indoors, wiped it gently with a dry tea cloth, and then laid it on the window sill to dry in the sunshine.

"Perhaps we'll still be able to make out a few faces," she sighed, with dismay. "But what a shame. I wish I'd remembered it earlier then it would have been dry by now and probably less damaged."

Annoyed with herself, she returned outside, finished putting the clothes in to soak and then went to the garden shed to fetch the hand fork she used for weeding.

Whilst doing his bread round that same morning, Bill Burleigh the Baker informed Dorothy Treloar, who was busy working in the kitchen at the Inn, that Willoughby Castor-Hunt was back at Chy-an-Gwyns. He knew of this because his office had received a phone call late the previous afternoon to say this was the case and to order a small Hovis loaf and a vanilla slice. Dorothy in turn told Frank, who then told everyone he saw. Hence within a few hours it was common knowledge that the village's most prestigious visitor was back in residence.

Madge received the news with great interest. She was aware that Mr Castor-Hunt was a widower and of the tragic consequences in which his late wife had died. She was also aware that this event had taken place some twenty years before, hence he would be, she guessed, a man in his mid to late forties or perhaps his early fifties. Either way, he was the perfect age for a new husband. He was also rich and had a very nice house.

Milly was surprised to find her mother in a very good frame of mind throughout the day. She did not grumble about George, or Cornwall: did not complain that too much fuss was being made over Molly Smith, and she did not refer to Rose as that skinny trollop. In fact she was quite the opposite and even called Rose dear, when she was waitress that evening. Milly felt her mother was up-to-something, and so did Rose, but neither could fathom out what.

The problem for Madge, was how to bring about a meeting with her intended suitor. She could not bump into him accidentally on purpose for she had no idea what he looked like, and she could hardly go up to his fine house and introduce herself when her only motive for making his acquaintance was to entice him into marriage. No, there was only one possible way, and that was to wait until he came to the Inn for a Pimms, or whatever it was posh blokes liked to drink.

Willoughby Castor-Hunt did not let Madge down. As he walked through the Inn door that same evening she knew him instantly, even before Frank had time to greet him. Madge drooled. He was five foot ten inches to six feet tall; he had dark, impeccably styled hair which showed signs of grey around the ears. Above his top lip sat a neatly trimmed, dark moustache, and the nails on his spotlessly clean hands were perfectly manicured. His dress was casual but smart, his shoes shone like mirrors and he smelled of expensive aftershave.

Frank shook Willoughby Castor-Hunt by the hand and welcomed him back to Trengillion. Willoughby spoke in a soft cultured voice and thanked Frank for his kind greeting.

In the corner of the snug, the major, and Molly, much better having insisted a gin would help speed her recovery, were enjoying a drink with Ned, Stella and George. Rose was not with them; she was still in the kitchen. The major stood to greet the new arrival. The two men had enjoyed many interesting conversations over the years, hence both were genuine in the pleasure they exuded to see one another.

Madge was in the public bar. She seldom sat in the snug for fear of missing something. She lit a cigarette and watched as the smoke it produced wafted in small clouds above her head and out towards the open door. She sighed and contemplated how best to get the attention of the new object of her desire. She drank several glasses of gin and orange, a more lady-like drink she considered than her usual whisky, but was unable to conjure up a workable plan. But then fate stepped in.

Willoughby Castor-Hunt rose to go to the Gents. He left the snug and walked into the public bar. Madge seized her chance, snatched a handkerchief from the sleeve of her dress, dropped it casually onto the floor, crossed her legs, and seductively sipped her drink. Willoughby rose to her bait, bent to pick up the handkerchief, thus revealing a glimpse of the gold cuff link, clipped through the cuff of his crisp, white shirt. He smiled politely as he returned the white cotton square, embroidered in pink, with the initial M in one corner, to its owner. Madge was bewitched. She smiled like the Cheshire cat, grovelled like a sycophantic fool and asked if he would like to join her for a drink.

Willoughby Castor-Hunt thanked her for her kind offer and said perhaps some other time, but at present he was enjoying the company of his friends in the snug.

George observed her actions through the open doors between the two bars with utter disbelief. Madge saw the look on his face and tossed her head in a hoity-toity manner. She had no use for him now. She had found her true love. And as for that fortune teller, she was obviously an incompetent nincompoop who ought to be punished for wasting her precious time.

CHAPTER TWENTY FOUR

The following morning, Ned arose early, took a long hot bath and tried to relax. He felt nervous and very anxious as at eleven o'clock he had an interview to attend in town for the position of headmaster of the village school.

"Try and calm down, Ned," said Stella sympathetically, as they sat down for breakfast. "It's no good getting all het up, especially as you're not even sure whether or not you want the job."

"I know, but it's easier said than done and I want to make a good impression anyway, whatever the outcome, and it's all good practice for the future."

George joined them a few minutes later. In his hand he held an envelope.

"Frank just handed me this. Apparently your mum dropped it in early this morning, Ned. She meant to give it to us last night but forgot to put it in her handbag."

"What is it?" asked Stella. "Have you not opened it, George?"

George took a seat. "No, I've not had a chance."

From inside the envelope he pulled out the postcard which Molly had successfully dried, and although it was crumpled slightly around the edges, miraculously the picture was clear and no-one would ever have guessed it had been submerged in sea water.

"Good God," he said, turning it over to view the back. "It's an old picture postcard of Polquillick."

He passed it to Ned.

"Is there anyone there who resembles me? I can't bear to look but that must be the reason your mother sent it. I wonder where she got it."

Ned quickly cast his eyes over the faces in the picture. "Hmm, I've no idea. I can't see anyone who looks like you, either. But I'm pretty sure one of the women is Emily Penberthy, and I've a feeling I've seen the chap standing next to her somewhere before."

He handed the card to Stella. "What do you think, sweetheart?"

Stella agreed there was a strong similarity between the girl in the locket and the young woman standing by a boat. "I see what you mean about the man next to Emily. But we can't know him, can we? Because this postcard dates back to the turn of the century or before."

George took the card from Stella. "We may have seen a descendant of his without realising. I mean, most of these people will have had offspring, and some of the children on the card are probably still around too. That girl standing next to the unidentified man is definitely Emily, though. I'd recognise her anywhere. I wonder if Harry is there at all. Sadly I don't know what he looks like, as in my dreams of course, I was he."

"I wonder then if this picture is of any significance," mused Stella. "I mean, are there any clues here as to what is going on?"

George sighed. "Sadly, we'll not be able to establish that without identifying some of the other people. Is there anyone we could ask to help us, do you think?"

"I suppose we could go to the Mop and Bucket again," suggested Stella.

Ned agreed. "Okay, but not today, I've quite enough on my plate with this interview."

Ned left the Inn at ten o'clock dressed in the suit in which he had married, and drove into town in his Morris Minor.

Stella, who had thought about going into town with him for moral support, eventually decided to stay at the Inn with George. She knew Ned wanted to prepare himself mentally for the interview and felt her presence in the car may well distract him from the job in hand. Hence, as the weather was glorious and warm, Stella and George opted for a lazy day on the beach with Rose, while Ned was away. With them they took the postcard, just in case they should see anyone who bore the slightest resemblance to any of Polquillick's past residents.

Inside the kitchen of the Inn, Dorothy Treloar dried the breakfast dishes which Rose had washed in the large china sink. She then returned them to the cupboard where they belonged before pouring herself a cup of tea from the pot which Rose had made. With cup in hand she then sat at the table to drink it.

Dorothy had insisted Rose leave early, for it was obvious she was eager to get away and join her friends, George and Stella, and who could blame her! Ned was away for the morning and Rose had confided to her the reason behind his excursion into town, telling her of the interview for the job of headmaster, but swearing her to secrecy, for Ned did not want his application to be common knowledge.

Dorothy finished her tea and washed the cup under the running tap.

"How nice to be young!" It seemed such a long time since she had been footloose and fancy free. She laughed. She was of course still fancy free and she guessed she always would be. No-one was ever likely to take any interest in her now; not at her time of life.

Dorothy walked to the corner cupboard, took out the broom and started to sweep crumbs of toast from the floor.

Frank Newton rolled around the newly delivered barrels in the cellar. Another week had passed by. Another week of his life gone. He thought once more of Sylvia. He missed her company and her laughter. He missed having someone to share his thoughts and problems with. For although he was able to enjoy plenty of chat with people coming and going at the Inn, none was a substitute for a soul-mate. Still, folks had been good to him since her death and he had some very good friends, and as for his staff at the Inn, he could not wish for better.

He thought of Dorothy. Dear Dot, how lovely she had looked at Ned's party. He wondered if she too was lonely. She had never married. What a shame! She was a fine looking woman or would be if she didn't wear her hair in that ridiculous bun and dress in such dowdy clothes. He laughed. What a contrast between her and good old Molly, yet they must be of a similar age.

After clambering up the steps, clutching a bottle of whisky, Frank switched off the cellar light and climbed through the trapdoor into the bar. He felt chilly. It was cold in the cellar. He stood the bottle on the bar, looked at the empty fireplace in the snug and thought about winter and all those long dark days when often the Inn would be quiet, and there was no-one to cuddle up to in the evening. Still, never mind, he had survived the previous winter and it had done him no harm.

He clipped the bottle of whisky into its optic, left the bar and headed towards the kitchen where he found Dorothy emptying the contents of a dustpan into the bin.

"Pop the kettle on please, Dot. I'd love a cup of tea."

Dorothy filled the new electric kettle, switched it on, removed her floral pinafore and hung it on the back of the door.

"Don't go just yet," said Frank, as she reached for her coat. "Stay and have a cup of tea with me, please."

"But I've only just had a cup."

"Go on, Dot. Live dangerously and have another. I'd enjoy the company."

Dorothy hung her coat back and reached for another cup from the cupboard. Frank was laughing. She thought how handsome he looked and how well he had coped with the loss of his wife. And as they looked at each other, both realised simultaneously, that the answer to their problems regarding loneliness lay with them, before their very eyes.

Rosemary Howard was enjoying her stay in Cornwall. She had met all sorts of interesting people which she felt sure, along with the location, would give her sufficient grounds on which to base her book. She was also very excited; for during a brief conversation with Rose the waitress, when she had been the only person remaining in the dining room after breakfast, Rose, after bringing her up to date with the kidnapping of Molly Smith, had told her about a murder in the village two years previous and the existence of a tunnel used to conceal the body. Rosemary, not one to waste any time, decided it would help inspire her writing if she were to find the tunnel and take a look inside, hence, as she sat in her room planning the day's activities, she gave the mission number one priority.

She left the Inn at eleven thirty after deciding not to take her hand bag as it would be in the way for climbing ladders, opening trap doors and all the other exciting things involved with exploring old tunnels. However, she thought it would be nice to buy an ice cream from the post office on her way back, and so she slipped some change into the pocket of her cardigan along with a torch, for she knew the tunnel would be in total darkness.

Opposite the Inn, beneath a lamp post, stood a gypsy woman selling sprigs of lavender. When she saw Rosemary she told her the flowers would bring her good luck. Using her ice cream money, Rosemary eagerly made a purchase, hopeful that its magic might bring about more good fortune than just inspiration for her novel. For there was always the possibility she might come across undiscovered treasure left by smugglers in days gone by.

Rosemary pushed the sprig of lavender into the button hole on the large collar of her green and white spotted dress, and skipped off over the fields to the stables where Rose told her the tunnel's entrance was hidden.

At the gate of the paddock the two horses came to greet her. Rosemary was not used to being in close proximity to such large creatures and stood nervously by the gate hoping if she ignored them they might go away. She smiled when the lavender's luck fulfilled her wish and Winston and Brown Ale, realising she had come neither to feed nor ride them, trotted off back into the centre of the field, to resume grazing where the grass was greenest.

Delighted they had left her way clear, Rosemary quickly climbed the gate and ran into the stables where, just as Rose had described, a ladder lay on its side along a wall. With a squeal of excitement she picked it up, leaned it against the back wall and hurriedly climbed each rung until she reached the top and came face to face with a sheet of rusty metal. With uncontrollable, trembling hands, Rosemary pushed the metal aside. When she saw the trap door she laughed out loud and giggled; a muster of mixed emotions. Using both hands, she fumbled with the bolts and slowly opened up the heavy door. With the tunnel's entrance revealed, Rosemary gazed with awe into a pitch black hole. She could see nothing and the smell emanating from the darkness was damp and unpleasant. But the stale, musty odour did not deter Rosemary in any way. She plunged her hand inside the pocket of her cardigan, pulled out her torch and switched it on. To her delight, five dirty steps became visible in the clear, bright circle of light, Eager to get inside, Rosemary climbed on top of the wall and slowly lowered herself through the open door and onto the top step.

The steps were granite, solid, firm and large. Confident they were safe, she trod on the second unaware that the full skirt of her dress was hooked around the door's bolt. Subsequently, as her foot reached the third step, a large piece of fabric tore away from the hemline leaving an unsightly hole.

"Damn," Rosemary cursed, surveying the damage. "My favourite dress too. Still, serves me right, I should have had more sense and worn slacks."

Determined not to let the unfortunate accident spoil her exploration, she climbed down the remaining steps. At the bottom she flashed her torch quickly around but was very disappointed by what she saw. The passage was smaller than she had imagined with barely sufficient room to stand, even for someone as petite as herself. Furthermore, it was unlikely any sort of treasure could be hidden, for there were no nooks and crannies. At least not where she stood.

She contemplated whether or not to explore further, but decided the atmosphere was too airless and uncomfortable. With a sudden feeling of unease, she craved fresh air and the warmth of sun on her face. With her decision made, Rosemary turned back towards the steps, but as she lifted her foot to climb, a noise from inside the stables caused her to stop. Frozen to the spot she listened. Someone was climbing the ladder. In a moment of panic she leapt forward and ran up the steps. But was too late. The trap door slammed shut in her face and she heard the bolt noisily slip into place. Rosemary banged both her fists hard against the wooden door and screamed at the top of her voice. But no-one responded to her cry, and in her panic the torch slipped from her hands onto the ground below.

Sobbing, Rosemary descended the steps and fumbled around in the dark to find the torch. She sighed, much relieved when it was back in her grasp, but the relief was short lived. For when she attempted to switch it on no beam of light shone onto her grim surroundings. Angrily, she shook it hard, but still the passage remained in darkness.

Rosemary sat down on the bottom step and cried until her throat was hoarse. She was afraid, cold, shocked, confused and had no idea what her next move should be. She sat in the dark and pondered over any options which might aid her escape, but after a while conceded she had very little choice. It was possible that someone might by chance come to the stables, hear her cry and set her free, for she assumed the horses were fed daily and no doubt shut up in the stables at the end of each day. But Rosemary could not bear the wait; she was cold and desperate to return to civilisation without delay.

After discarding the option to wait, she prepared herself mentally for the only other way of setting herself free; by walking along the tunnel until she reached the Witches Broomstick, where Rose said the tunnel began or ended, whichever way you liked to look at it.

Feeling a little more confident she pulled a handkerchief from her pocket, wiped her eyes, blew her nose and stood up to explore her route of escape. Rose had explained in detail how her friend, Ned, had escaped that way in similar circumstances, and so she was confident her destiny was not ill fated.

At first the walk was not too difficult; the ground was fairly flat and she felt her way by running her hands along the wall of the tunnel where loose earth scraped beneath her long nails and her hair was occasionally caught in the tree roots protruding from the roof above her head. But further along, walking became more difficult. The ground turned uneven and began to slope sharply downwards. Panic ensued as she stumbled and tripped over stones, large and small, beneath her feet, until bent almost double, she fell into a pile of large stones, boulders and rubble.

Rosemary picked herself up, recalling Rose telling of a roof fall which had impeded Ned's progress. Nevertheless, he had still found his way through after re-arranging the matter blocking his way. Desperately wishing her torch was working, she fumbled in the dark to find the spot where he had squeezed through, knowing that if it was big enough for him then it would be more than large enough for her. She found it with little difficulty, and eased her way through.

On the other side of the roof fall, Rosemary continued to stumble on along the passage. At one point the roof was so low she had to crawl through on her stomach. Soon after, the tunnel became wider and to her delight she spotted a small glimmer of light in the distance.

Rosemary was now able to walk faster as the ground beneath her feet turned from earth to sand, and the glimmer of light in front grew larger with each step she took. Eventually she found herself outside in the fresh air with the sun on her face and the breeze blowing through her red hair. She felt jubilant, ecstatic and jumped about on the sand with glee. For although freedom was not entirely hers, escape from the gloom and misery of the tunnel was. The lavender had worked its magic for a second time!

Once the jubilation subsided Rosemary contemplated how best to get back to Trengillion. After a short consideration she decided if she could attract the attention of anyone walking the cliff path, they would then, hopefully, come to her aid by sending a boat for her rescue. Meanwhile, she considered herself to be in no danger. The sun was shining brightly; she was warm once again and several hours of light remained before the sun was due to set over the cliff tops denoting the impending fall of darkness.

She climbed up onto the rocks which formed the outline of the broomstick's shape and stumbled along them until she neared the jagged end jutting out to sea. At that point, she could clearly view the top of the cliffs and see the indentation of the coastal path winding its way through gorse and bracken. With optimism, Rosemary cast her eyes along the cliff path. She was in luck, and the magic of the lavender was working again! For along the path a lone figure was visible, walking in the direction of Polquillick. Rosemary shouted and waved her hands to attract the attention of the passer by. The person on the cliff top stopped, gazed down at the spot where Rosemary stood and waved back.

"Get help, please," shouted Rosemary, jumping up and down. "I'm stranded."

She laughed and clapped her hands with joy, relishing the excitement her imminent rescue would bring. She must remain alert, for it was imperative she remember every detail to include in her book. And then Rosemary felt a sudden pang of dejection. A feeling of guilt, and a feeling of unease. The person on the cliff path was not going for help as anticipated, but stood motionless, watching her, making no gestures or showing any sign of support. Rosemary cast her eyes along the cliff tops where the distant roof top of Chy-an-Gwyns gleamed in the sunlight. She shivered, recalling her ordeal in the garden of that house and wondered who or what had chased her from the premises.

Disillusioned, her thoughts returned to the moment someone had closed and locked the trap door above her head at the beginning of the tunnel. Had it been done deliberately or had it been by accident? Common sense told her it could not have been an accident unless the person was stone deaf, for she had shouted and banged on the door with every ounce of strength she possessed. Rosemary felt deflated. Someone wished her harm, but she could not see why unless it was punishment for trespassing in the gardens of Chy-an-Gwyns.

Rosemary sat down on the rocks full of guilt. Perhaps the predicament she found herself in was punishment for her lies. She was not really an authoress, but just a typist on holiday with dreams and aspirations of becoming a novelist. Tears welled up in her eyes. She wished she had gone with her friends to Skegness for a fortnight instead of spending her holiday in Cornwall, alone, insisting she needed time to think and plan; for she had only come up with the idea of writing a book to impress Sam, a young man in the office where she worked, who wrote poetry and songs and of whom she dreamed both day and night. Rosemary's guilt deepened as she recalled telling Madge, boastfully, that she was a descendant of Charles Dickens, for in reality her crowing was nothing less than a blatant lie.

Rosemary looked up. The person on the cliff path was still standing on the same spot and making no attempt to communicate with her or go for help. She scrambled to her feet, waved her arms again and shouted with every fibre in her body, but still the walker did not move or respond.

In desperation, thinking perhaps she could not be heard or seen, Rosemary stepped further back along the rocks until she was confident there was no way her presence was not visible. She waved, jumped up and down and shouted again at the top of her voice. But her exertive efforts caused her loss of balance. With a splash, she fell backwards into the crashing waves, noisily lashing against the rocks on which she had stood.

Rosemary panicked. She could not swim. With heart thumping violently she tried in vain to grasp the slippery rocks. But the more she tried the further away she became, and eventually they were beyond her reach.

Gasping for breath, she splashed and spluttered violently in the cold water, both arms desperately trying to reach safety. But it was no use, the current was too strong.

Rosemary screamed, sobbed and gurgled as salt water splashed into her open mouth and stung her eyes. She was afraid. Angry too, and blamed herself solely for the sorrowful plight which she knew would inevitably deprive her of life. Gradually her arms began to ache and keeping her head above water became an impossible task. She gave one last anxious cry for help, which filled her mouth with foul tasting water. She closed her eyes, sobbing and gulping, until overcome with exhaustion, she succumbed, and disappeared beneath the relentless waves, leaving behind air bubbles from her last pitiful breath.

And as the bubbles dispersed, the lucky sprig of lavender, having detached itself from her green and white spotted dress, rose to the surface of the water and bobbed about on the waves, a solitary act of remembrance, to mourn and lament her untimely demise.

CHAPTER TWENTY FIVE

Frank spent a considerable amount of time during the night thinking about Dorothy Treloar and wondering if she was the answer to his prayers. She did, after all, have all the necessary attributes to make him a good wife. She was the right age, available, hardworking, honest, loyal, and she even liked cats. Barley Wine seemed fond of her too, which had to be a sign of Sylvia's approval. But the problem was he didn't know what she thought of him. Dorothy was a very private woman who kept herself to herself, and so it was impossible to imagine where her feelings for him lay, or indeed if she had any feelings for him at all. The next day, however, fate stepped in.

Frank and Dorothy were working together on the bar as usual, when Albert Treloar came in, and after he had given Frank a précis of his day, he let slip that it was Dorothy's birthday, which did not please her as she liked to keep quiet about her age. Nevertheless, Frank insisted she had a drink whilst working and then later, when they had finished all the tidying up, he insisted she have another. And so after everyone had gone home the two of them sat together and had a long chat, during which time, Frank did something he felt was almost out of his control. Suddenly, out of the blue, he asked Dorothy to marry him. Her response surprised him even more than his impulsive action. For her eyes filled with tears, she grasped his hands and without hesitation said, "Yes, yes, Frank. I'd like nothing more than to be your wife."

The following morning, Molly rang the bell by the side door of the Inn, opened it, popped her head inside and called to see if anyone was around. Rose, drying her hands on her apron, went to see who was about. In the hallway, she found Molly with a bundle of red and white striped fabric in her arms.

"These are the curtains Frank asked me to make for one of your guest rooms. I can't stop though, because the major's waiting for me.

177

We're going down to Penzance for the day, you see. I'm being made a fuss of."

"How lovely. I like Penzance. It always seems so bright and airy down there. These curtains are for Rosemary's room, by the way. The ones in there at present are looking a bit moth eaten. I'll hang them for her later. It'll be a nice surprise then for when she gets back."

"Back?" queried Molly. "Where's she gone?"

Rose shrugged her shoulders. "I've no idea, but she wasn't in for dinner last night or breakfast this morning. I expect she's found something of interest and will be back when she's good and ready. You know what these writers are like!"

"Hmm, it sounds a bit odd to me. Still, I must go. No doubt I shall see you later. By the way, if you see Ned, please tell him we've gone out for the day. He said he might pop in sometime, but of course we'll not be there. Penzance was a spur of the moment decision, you see."

"I'll tell him. He and Stella are out at the moment, though. They've gone horse riding again."

"Oh, good, then they probably wouldn't call, anyway." Waving furiously, she dashed off.

Rose closed the door and laid the new curtains carefully across the chair in the hallway; she then returned to the kitchen to continue with the washing up.

When all her jobs were finished, Rose picked up the curtains and pondered whether or not she ought to hang them without first consulting Frank or Dorothy. To do so, however, was not possible, for neither one was at the Inn, and she was well aware that she probably would not have received a sensible answer from either of them anyway, as they'd both been in a very peculiar mood when they'd gone off together after breakfast, laughing and saying they had something of great importance to buy in town.

Rose walked up the stairs and knocked gently on Rosemary's door. As expected there was no reply. She opened the door and peeped inside. The room was very tidy and the bed was made. She crossed over to the window and took down the old curtains. The bright sunshine had faded them badly over the years causing them to rot along the folds. She hung the new curtains and stood back to admire her handy work. What an improvement! Rosemary would be pleased!

She crossed the room to leave and whilst doing so noticed Rosemary's handbag on the floor beside the bed. Rose was puzzled. Why would Rosemary have left it behind? She put down the old curtains, picked up the bag, and with a feeling of guilt peeped inside. Rosemary's purse was there, so how could she have gone to stay elsewhere without it?

Rose closed the bag, put it back where she had found it and went to look on the dressing table. Rosemary's toiletries were neatly lined along the back and her bag of make-up was in the top drawer. Rose felt something was wrong but conceded it was none of her business. Besides, she should not have pried through Rosemary's belongings. It was totally out of order. She left the room feeling very despondent.

Madge stood by the window of her room and looked out across the rooftops whilst the polish she had just painted onto her nails dried. Milly was out with Johnny, and so she had a little time to pander herself to make sure she looked her best. She turned to leave the window, but stopped when she heard a car coming up the hill from the cove. She glanced down just in time to see Willoughby Castor-Hunt drive by in his gleaming Jaguar. Madge guessed he was going into town; for a trip to the bank perhaps to withdraw some of his lovely money.

Madge looked in the mirror and touched her face. She concluded the sun was beginning to dry out her skin and decided a face pack would not come amiss. She pulled out her bag of toiletries from beneath the dressing table and applied a great dollop of thick, brown paste over her face; she then placed two slices of cucumber, which she had scrounged from Dorothy Treloar the previous evening, over her eyes, and lay back on the bed for twenty minutes so that her beauty products could work wonders.

George, as pre-arranged, joined the divers on the beach for his trip out to sea. It was a fine day, although the wind was a little fresh and the sea slightly choppy.

"Hope you don't get sea sick," said Larry, as they left the cove. "The wind's stronger than the forecast predicted, so we may not stay out too long if it gets any worse."

"I've a cast iron stomach," said George, crossing his fingers behind his back. "So you don't need to worry about me."

The wind, blowing from the east, was behind them as they headed towards Polquillick.

"That's the Witches Broomstick," said Des, pointing towards the rocks. "It was in there that we found the body of Jane Hunt, or should I say the remains. Poor thing!"

George nodded. "Yes, I know. Ned pointed it out to me when we went fishing with Percy and Peter. I didn't realise it was you who found her though. That must have been a pretty horrible experience."

"Well, it would have been a lot worse if the poor girl had still been recognisable," said Larry. "Not that we knew her; as I said we found her remains; she was just a skeleton."

Shortly after the Witches Broomstick disappeared from view, they rounded cliffs and motored into the waters off Polquillick.

George was astounded by their swift arrival. "Good grief, I can't believe we're here already. It's so much quicker by boat than it is by car."

Des brought the boat to a standstill. "That's because we travel more or less as the crow flies. Right, so, where do you think you and Emily abandoned ship? Does anything look at all familiar?"

George glanced around and then shook his head. "No, in fact as regards my dream this is probably a waste of time. I think the best thing is for you to carry on with your work as though I'm not here and let me enjoy watching you."

"Alright, we'll do that then," said Larry. "Not that you'll see much once we're under water. Our wreck is a little further out, just a few minutes from here."

He turned the boat around and they headed out to sea. George sat back and made himself comfortable, looking forward to seeing if the divers made any exciting discoveries whilst he was onboard.

When they stopped, the wind had dropped a little and the sun was shining brightly between formations of patchy grey clouds. Des switched off the engine and the two divers put on their dry suits and aqua-lungs.

George looked around. "How on earth do you know you're in the right place? I mean, you don't have dahns and things to mark the spot like the fishermen do."

Larry laughed. "We don't need one. If you look back at Polquillick, you'll see the flag pole on the church tower is in line with the chimney pot of the thatched cottage below. That's how we know we're more or less in the right spot. They're our landmarks and the fishermen do use them too. Dahns are not just an indication of the location of pots, they're actually attached to the strings. Without them there'd be no way of pulling them up."

"Hmm," mumbled George. "Very clever, and of course landmarks are reliable because they never move."

As the two divers prepared to go into the water, Des told George there was a bag in the wheelhouse containing biscuits and a flask of coffee which he insisted George help himself to, should he feel in need of refreshment. The two divers then disappeared over the side, with Larry saying they wouldn't be gone long as the water looked distinctly murky.

George watched until all traces of the divers had disappeared. He then, determined to enjoy the peace and tranquillity, returned to his seat, closed his eyes and listened to the squawking of gulls and the gentle rhythm of water splashing softly against the side of the boat.

"Bliss! Heavenly bliss. What a way to top up the old suntan."

Sheltered from the wind, deep inside the boat, his thoughts pleasant and his mood complacent, he slowly drifted into a peaceful sleep. His slumbers, however, were very short lived, for a muffled clonk, repeatedly knocking against the bottom of the boat, woke him. Thinking he had slept for a considerable time and the divers were returning, he quickly sat up and glanced over the side, but Larry and Des were nowhere to be seen. Puzzled, he rubbed his bleary eyes and looked again. He blinked, horror-struck, for beneath the cloudy water, drifted the lifeless body of a woman. Her long hair floated away from her pallid face. Her wide open eyes stared up towards the heavens and her twisted mouth appeared frozen with fear.

George attempted to shout, but no sound emerged from his trembling lips. He shivered, confused, light-headed and shaken. Rubbing his eyes he sat back deep inside the boat, too afraid to take a second look. Minutes passed by but no more sounds came from the dark waters. Apprehensively, he stood up and peered back over the side, but the vision had gone: lost without trace. Heaving a sigh of relief, convinced he must have imagined the image, he sat back and waited patiently for the divers to return.

In the public bar of the Ringing Bells Inn, as soon as she had finished her dinner, Madge sat on a stool at the bar as she had done every night since Willoughby Castor-Hunt had arrived in the village. She knew he would speak to her if he put in an appearance because he always did, and on one occasion he had even bought her a drink. He never stayed and talked to her, though, and for that reason she concluded he must be very shy when in the company of ladies and that was why he chose to drink and chat to the men folk instead of her. Still, she was a patient woman and she could wait for a while yet.

Madge was downing her third gin and orange when she heard his voice through the open front door of the Inn. She wondered to whom he was speaking as she straightened her hair and smoothed her skirt. A woman walked in: a beautiful, elegant, slender woman, chatting in a friendly manner to Molly Smith. Close behind them was Willoughby conversing with the major. Madge tossed her hair as they approached the bar. Willoughby took the arm of the woman and looked at Frank.

"I've someone here who I'd like you to meet," he said. "Frank, this is Tabitha, my fiancée. And Tabbs, this charming man is the landlord of this fine hostelry, Frank Newton."

Tabitha and Frank shook hands next to Madge who sat dumfounded with mouth gaping open.

"Fiancée, eh? So are you two lovebirds planning to get married soon?" asked Frank.

"Yes, in December," said Willoughby. "We're planning to wed just before Christmas and then honeymoon in the Bahamas."

"Very nice too. Congratulations to both of you. But you're a dark horse, Willoughby. Keeping this charming young lady a secret."

Willoughby Castor-Hunt laughed. "Tabbs is a physiologist and she couldn't join me at Whitsun because she had business commitments, and likewise she didn't come down with me on

Wednesday because she had a special function to attend. But she's here now, thank goodness."

He blew a kiss to his fiancée who received it with a childlike giggle.

"Did you drive down?" asked Frank,

Tabitha shook her head. "No, I hate driving," she said, in a flute-like voice. "I came by train and Wibby picked me up from the station. Didn't you sweetheart?"

Madge slid off the stool and crept outside into the cool night air without finishing her drink. Tabbs! Wibby! A fizzyollythinging! The Bahamas! She felt sick. Sick and very, very stupid. With a heavy heart she stumbled round to the side entrance of the Inn, sneaked in through the green door and, without anyone knowing or caring, crept up the stairs to her room, where she undressed, climbed into bed and cried herself to sleep.

Shortly after Madge's unnoticed exit, Frank and Dorothy found friends, well-wishers and busy-bodies alike, crossing the threshold of the Inn to celebrate and ratify their engagement. News of the unlikely event had spread like wildfire through the cottages and outlying farms once Albert had been told the news by his sister and showed the ring purchased in town that morning. For like Dot's mother, no-one had ever thought that plain old Dorothy Treloar would ever catch a husband and certainly not one as eligible as Frank Newton. Therefore, many were sceptical about the veracity of the hearsay and the evening was busy with inquisitive drinkers and non-drinkers, who by their sheer numbers and presence brought about a spontaneous party.

Dorothy Treloar, hair lose with bright eyes twinkling, looked ten years younger than anyone recalled her ever looking before. Frank too, looked very smart; his hair and beard had been trimmed and he was wearing his best waistcoat, the one he wore only for special occasions, which the regulars had not seen since Sylvia's thirty eighth birthday, and all agreed they had forgotten just what a handsome man he was.

"This is all a bit sudden, isn't it?" Pat Dickens said. "I didn't even know you two were seeing each other."

"What! We see each other every day, don't we, Dot?" grinned Frank. "I only asked Dot to marry me last night though, and I can't believe you're all here to celebrate before we've even had a chance to announce it."

"Good news travels fast in Trengillion," smiled May. "But what we're all longing to know now is: when the wedding is likely to be."

Frank wrinkled his nose. "Dunno, but sooner rather than later, I hope, eh Dot?"

Dorothy blushed. "Yes, we'd like to be married before winter sets in."

Romance was in the air for others also. Peter, beginning to feel he would soon be the only bachelor left in the village, dragged Betty outside and on impulse asked her to marry him. In response Betty flung her arms around his neck and kissed him so hard he thought he would suffocate.

"I thought you'd never ask," she giggled, when he came up for air.

"I'd have asked you sooner, but I was scared you might say no and then I'd have felt a right idiot."

Betty laughed. "Let's get married next spring when the churchyard is full of daffodils. It always looks so pretty then and the bridesmaids can wear yellow to match."

"Christ, you've got it all worked out already," he said, a look of amazement on his face.

"I've been planning it for ages. Come on. My mum and dad are in the snug, let's go and tell them before they hear from someone else. Are your parents here tonight?"

Peter nodded. "They were outside earlier talking to old Pat Dickens, so I suppose we'd better go and tell them too."

"Brilliant, then we'll run round to Coronation Terrace and tell Gertie and Percy. Oh, Gertie will be so pleased. She always said we'd be good match."

Meg Reynolds went to the paddock to shut the horses up at the end of the day, but as she walked into the stables she was surprised to see the ladder propped up against the back wall. At first Meg was baffled, but then conceded the tunnel was common knowledge so anyone from the village might have been into the stables to take a look beneath the trap door.

As she approached the ladder she wondered for how long it had been there. Sid had shut up the horses the previous night as Betty was round doing her hair and Sid would not have known where the ladder belonged, anyway. It crossed her mind that someone may even still be inside and so, before she put the ladder back in its rightful place she climbed it to take a look, as the last thing she wanted was to leave someone stranded on top of the wall.

Meg climbed up the ladder, found the trap door bolted from the outside and so knew no-one would be in the tunnel. The sheet of rusty metal, however, had not been put back in the right place. Meg tutted. She wished people would put things back where they belonged. She slid the sheet across and on doing so noticed a piece of green and white spotted fabric caught on the edge of the bolt. She picked up the material, examined it, and then put it in the pocket of her jacket. She knew Ned and Stella had looked into the tunnel recently and wondered if Stella had torn her dress whilst doing so. Although on reflection, Meg was pretty certain Stella had been wearing slacks for riding.

Meg climbed down the ladder, put it back where it belonged and went back out into the paddock to call the horses. Once they were safely shut in she climbed over the gate and returned to Coronation Terrace for supper.

Ned, Stella and George were also amongst the jubilant party goers at the Inn, although they had originally planned to visit the Mop and Bucket with the postcard that evening. But as Rose was working and there was an engagement to celebrate, they decided to postpone the trip to Polquillick for a couple of days.

George did not mention the face in the water to his friends, neither had he mentioned it to Larry and Des, even though it had been his intention to tell the divers when first the incident had occurred. But after a brief reflection he decided it must have been his subconscious playing tricks, because he knew, and everyone else knew, that Emily was long dead and there was no way her body was in the sea. She was buried in the churchyard at Polquillick and had been for the past fifty years. And as for it being a ghost, George would not even consider the possibility, hence he pushed it to the back of his mind and set about enjoying the celebrations like everyone else.

It was a very happy evening with much laughter, leg-pulling and catching up with the latest gossip. Molly also found herself the centre of attention, as people asked about her ordeal and details of the mysterious crabby old woman. Likewise, Willoughby Castor-Hunt and the beautiful Tabitha drew around themselves a crowd of admirers, eager to utter words of congratulations, and even though they were unaware of it, the locals spoke in voices they usually reserved for when speaking to strangers on the telephone.

Rose, however, did not feel much like merry-making. She was concerned about Rosemary, for the young author had again not put in an appearance for dinner. At closing time, when the bar staff took a break before commencing with the clearing up, Rose told Ned, Stella and George about her findings in Rosemary's room.

Stella was aghast. "But she can't have gone far without her handbag and purse, or make-up either for that matter, as she was always very well presented."

"Perhaps she has more than one handbag," said George, flippantly. "Elsie had several, all different shapes and sizes."

"At home maybe," said Rose, "but I've only ever seen her with one here, and that's the one in her room. Besides, her purse is in it, and she wouldn't leave that behind even if she did have more than one bag."

"So what are you implying? Ned said. "Surely you don't think she's fallen into the hands of the old woman with the van. I mean, she's not from this area, for a start, and has nothing whatsoever to do with Emily Penberthy and this reincarnation twaddle."

"I'm not implying anything," said Rose. "I just feel something is wrong. Call it female intuition or whatever like, but I often chatted to Rosemary and I just don't think she would have gone off without saying, not for two days, anyway."

"She's most likely staying with a friend," said Ned. "In which case she wouldn't need her purse or war-paint. Remember, you saw her at the fete with an older woman, George, and she was in here with a woman after the fete as well. The stranger was probably her granny, auntie or something like that."

"But if she had a gran or aunt down here why would she have come to stay at the Inn in the first place?" asked Stella.

Ned shook his head. "I don't know, but let's hope she turns up soon. My brain can't handle the possibility of someone else falling into the hands of evil. But if she's still not back this time on Monday then I'll go with you to see Fred Stevens, Rose; just to keep you happy."

Rose smiled. "Thank you, and now I'd better go and help Frank and Dorothy with the clearing up. There's enough of it."

Stella rose also. "I'll come and give you all a hand, otherwise you could well be here all night."

Stella thought Rose seemed a bit down about Rosemary's disappearance and so suggested a shopping trip into town, hoping it might cheer her up. But as the next day was Sunday, they would have to wait until Monday. Rose accepted the offer with gratitude, glad to have something to distract her mind from her worries.

Ned and George on hearing this suggestion gratefully seized the opportunity to plan another day's fishing with Percy and Peter. And as Peter was sitting nearby talking to his new fiancée Betty, the trip was noted and a time agreed.

CHAPTER TWENTY SIX

Madge was fed up. It seemed that romance was in the air for everyone but herself. She felt she was fast becoming forgettable, unloved and invisible. She needed to do something to get herself in the limelight. She needed to become a heroine in some way, for she desperately wanted to be the centre of attention and the name on everyone's lips.

Sitting alone in her room on Sunday evening, while Milly took a bath, she contemplated her options. Perhaps she ought to let it be known she was writing a novel, even if this was not the case. It certainly might impress a few people, just as Rosemary's claims of literary talents had done. Madge thought of Rosemary, she considered it odd that she had paid her board and then gone off elsewhere without saying a word to anyone, but then, on reflection, she supposed writers had money to burn.

Madge's thoughts returned to her own troublesome case. Perhaps she should walk over the cliffs to Polquillick and visit the churchyard there; then if lucky, she too might be hit on the head and captured like Molly Smith. She would certainly be the talk of the village then. Madge's spirits fell, for she had to concede that had she been in Molly's situation she would have drowned, for swimming was one of the many physical activities she had never mastered.

Perhaps then, she should track down the people who had kidnapped Molly. She should go looking for an old woman and a van. Surely it could not be that difficult. The Cornish police were obviously incompetent nincompoops and not up to the job. Madge was thrilled. Detective work! That was the way forward! Everybody would then see that she was a force to be reckoned with. She would become a heroine and her picture would be in all the papers. No-one would ignore her then, cut her dead or dismiss her as a failure. She might even be interviewed on the wireless.

Milly was very surprised during breakfast on Monday morning that her mother insisted she spend the day with Johnny, for usually

Madge made her feel guilty and whined about being abandoned by her own flesh and blood. Milly, however, was wise enough not to question her mother's change of heart, knowing should she do so, it might even cause Madge to change her mind. Hence, with gratitude, she seized her unexpected freedom and dashed off to the post office as soon as breakfast was over.

Madge left the Inn just after ten o'clock and caught the bus to Polquillick. She had, very briefly, considered walking, but decided it would take too long and there was not a minute to lose. Besides, she wanted to look her best, and so could not be seen wearing unflattering walking shoes and practical slacks. Her most flattering dress and a pair of matching high heeled shoes: that was the way to impress the reporters, who would undoubtedly flock to Polquillick to hear her story and photograph her, once her mission was complete.

The bus dropped off its passengers near to the quay at Polquillick. Madge was not sure where she should begin her search so bought an ice cream from the Ice Cream Parlour and sat on a bench to eat it while watching people and traffic go by.

A young man crossed the road who looked very much like George, although he was shorter and his build more stocky. Madge gave a self-satisfied laugh. George would wish he had not rebuffed her advances when she became a heroine, and as for that pompous, Willoughby Castor-Hunt! He and Tabbs could go to the Bahamas, wherever that might be and never come back for all she cared.

Madge finished her ice cream and stood up. She was getting nowhere. Only a few old ladies had passed by and each had looked a picture of innocence. Furthermore, she had seen no vans at all. A little disillusioned, she crossed the road and walked along the path towards the pub. Outside the Mop and Bucket she stopped, having decided its car park might be a good place to look for the vehicle in question. She left the footpath and walked around the dry, uneven surface, but there were no vans and very few cars either.

Madge elected to go into the pub thinking perhaps a large whisky might give her some inspiration, and if it did not, then she could always chat up the landlord. Inside, however, Madge found a woman behind the bar and much to her disgust discovered the landlord had discourteously taken the day off.

As she sat up a corner sipping her drink, she remembered Molly had only been abducted in Polquillick; her captivity had been elsewhere because she'd had a fairly long journey in the back of the van. Madge cursed, she might have to look elsewhere another day. But if Molly had been knocked unconscious in the churchyard at Polquillick, then surely was the place to begin her search.

Madge finished her drink. Should she have another? She decided against it; it was after all wasting precious time.

Madge left the pub and wandered back down the road to the churchyard. She went through the lichgate and cast her eyes over the rows of tombstones sprawled out in all directions. Molly, she recalled, had been looking at a grave when she had been attacked. But which grave? Madge had no idea. Unless it was where that ghost everyone was talking about was buried: Eliza Penlow or something like that. Madge wished she had paid more attention to the local gossip. Her stomach rumbled. Feeling peckish, she wondered what the time was. She paused to look at her watch.

"Damn!" she cursed, realising her watch was still lying on the dressing table in the room she shared with Milly. Convinced it was lunch time, she glanced up at the church tower.

"Humph, how ridiculous," she grumbled, hands on hips. "What's the point in wasting all those bricks building a tower on the church if they're not going to bother putting a clock on it?"

Madge heard a cough. Someone was tending a grave in the corner of the churchyard beneath some railings. Hopeful that the person might be wearing a watch, Madge ambled along the path and asked the time. A crabby old woman stood up to face her. She was slightly bent with grey straw like hair which was cut in an unflattering bob. Her floral dress fitted badly. She had holes in the elbows of her cardigan, and her teeth, obviously false, rattled as she spoke.

"Ten minutes to one, dear," croaked, the old woman.

Madge thanked her profusely, continued along another path and out of the churchyard.

"What a charming old lady," she thought, feeling she had seen her somewhere before.

She walked back up the road and on in the direction of the pub, where once again she browsed around the car park, her mind preoccupied with lunch. Unable to detect the vehicle in question,

Madge was disgruntled and conceded that finding old ladies driving vans was obviously not as easy as she had thought. Therefore, to raise morale she decided another drink might help to give her perspicacity a much needed boost. And so without hesitation, she trundled back into the pub, bought a large whisky and a very large pasty to gratify her insatiable appetite.

Sitting in a corner, Madge consumed every crumb of the pasty and then smoked three cigarettes whilst trying to think of a plan, but in spite of her dedication to the task in hand, no inspiration entered her head and she drank two more large whiskies before eventually leaving the pub and walking off down the road in the opposite direction to the sea.

A few cars passed by, but no vans. Madge sat down on another bench and looked further along the road. Not far away a petrol filling station stood on the opposite side. Madge watched the traffic going in and out, but it was just one car after another. She got up from the bench and continued along the footpath.

After a while her right heel began to hurt. She glanced over the road, where a lane ran off into the open countryside and decided to walk for a little way down the lane to explore. She crossed the road, took off her high heeled shoes and looked at her right foot. The heel was very sore and had rubbed into a blister. She poked it. It felt like jelly and was painful. Madge removed her stockings, pushed them into her pocket and walked on the grass verge, carrying her shoes. The soft grass brought a little relief and soothed her wounded foot.

She continued walking, not knowing where the lane might lead, ambling along around one corner after another. No cars passed by; no-one was out walking; she felt very much alone. Eventually she came across a five bar gate and by it, a large clump of dense grass looked very inviting. Feeling in need of a rest, and a little breathless, she sat wearily down, leaned her head back against the thick, granite gate post and watched the golden corn waving in the field through the bars of the wooden gate.

The sun was warm on her face as she closed her eyes. She thought about her past and laughed sardonically. The early years had in many ways been very cruel to her, especially 1935, when at the age of just eighteen, she had fallen madly in love with a lad in the factory where she worked. Madge sighed: she could still see his fresh young face, hear his voice and smell his breath. Back then, she thought him the most wonderful person in the world, until she realised she was pregnant. She then saw his true side, for when she told him her news, he was angry. The following day he left the factory and the area and she never saw him again. Her parents likewise offered her no support. They disowned her and sent her off to stay with her great aunt in Liverpool, letting it be known, they would not have her back unless she had the baby adopted at birth. Madge had defied them, kept Milly and remained at the home of her great aunt, where together, the two of them brought up the little girl. She never saw her parents again after the day she left. She didn't even know whether or not they were still alive.

Madge sighed; dear Aunt Pru, she had been so kind, so understanding, insisting there would always be a home for herself and Milly for as long as they wished. Madge had taken up the offer with gratitude, and the three of them lived happily together until earlier in the year, when Aunt Pru had died, a grand old lady of eighty six.

Madge thought about Milly. She was determined that her daughter would not suffer the same fate as had befallen her. She wanted to make sure she found someone trustworthy and reliable, someone who would stand by her through thick and thin.

Madge laughed as tears trickled down her rosy checks. "Till death do us part." She'd never had the chance to utter those words. Milly had been brought up to believe that her parents were divorced. Rather that than the stigma of being illegitimate. Milly seldom mentioned her father; she had grown up believing that he did not want to know her, and that at least was true.

Madge thought about Johnny. He seemed a decent lad and that was what she wanted for her daughter. But the thought of Milly leaving to marry filled her with dread, for then she would be all alone in the house that she had inherited from her dear aunt. Alone and unloved.

"If only I could find a husband before it's too late. I'll be forty, in less than four years and no-one will want me then. But then it seems no-one wants me now."

She looked down at the rolls of fat bulging over the belt of her dress. She was aware she needed to lose weight, but ate to make herself feel better. She had curbed her appetite during and after the war years while rationing limited the amount of food she could eat; but since sweet rationing had ended in February, her sweet tooth had returned with a vengeance and, very soon, sugar rationing was to end also.

Madge sighed. "Oh dear! And I'm much too fond of whisky and gin. Still, who cares?"

She snuggled up closer to the gate post and within minutes, snoring noisily, drifted off into a drink induced sleep.

When she awoke, she felt chilled. The sun had moved round and a nearby tree prevented its rays from shining onto her cumbersome body. She stood up, stretched and climbed partway up the gate.

In the distance she could see the sea. There were houses along the cliff tops and farms dotted along the way. In the heart of the village, the Mop and Bucket was visible and, close by, the church tower stood erect beneath the clear blue sky. Alongside the field, into which the gate on which she stood led, she saw a large rambling house standing back from the lane. Its gardens looked untidy and overgrown. Madge wondered if it were derelict or inhabited.

She climbed down from the gate, looked at her foot and considered whether if it might be worth walking on a little further, to call at the house to see if they had a plaster to spare for her heel. She had after all, quite a distance to walk to the bus stop and could not face putting on her shoes and stockings unless the blister was covered.

She noisily blew her nose, straightened her hair and then continued her walk along the grass verge of the pretty lane. Around a bend she came to the house. She stopped. It looked even more desolate close up than it had from a distance, but there were curtains hanging at each window and clean, empty milk bottles standing on the front doorstep. Madge concluded someone must be in residence.

Timorously, she shuffled alongside a straggly cotoneaster hedge on which leaned a broken, wooden gate, detached from its hinges. From its top bar, a weatherworn plaque informed Madge she was entering the boundaries of Laburnum House.

Quickly, she cast her eyes around the jungle in front of her. The driveway was overgrown and uneven; dandelions poked up through every crack and crevice. In the front garden, brambles twisted and tumbled their way through nettles and tall thistles strangled and entwined with convolvulus; each plant was growing spindly in its fight for light beneath a canopy of large trees and shrubs.

Madge felt uneasy. The house looked sinister, and she was undecided whether or not to risk walking further along the overgrown path to approach the front door.

She glanced down at her foot. She had to get back to the Inn, therefore a plaster was essential. Mustering up as much courage as possible, she proceeded along the path towards the house.

Beside the house stood an outbuilding, possibly a garage, part tumbledown and covered with ivy. Madge stopped dead. For behind the building, standing beneath a mountain ash, dripping with orange berries, parked in a higgledy-piggledy manner, stood a dirty, battered old van.

Madge froze. Should she run or should she hide? Fate, however, gave her no choice. From behind she heard a rustle in the bushes, and then footsteps approaching.

"Can I help you?" croaked a voice, low pitched and aggressive. "Are you looking for someone?"

Madge felt her heart skip a beat. Petrified she turned around. On the path stood the crabby old woman she had seen in the churchyard.

CHAPTER TWENTY SEVEN

Around the same time as Madge set off to catch the bus to Polquillick, Ned and George changed into their oldest clothes ready for their second day fishing with Percy and Peter. Stella meanwhile, having bid them both farewell, left the Inn to pick up Rose from The School House, where she had gone after work to feed Freak, prior to the girls' previously planned shopping trip.

The weather was fine when all began their day's activities, and early arrivals on the beach, having secured their favourite patches, were already laying out their belongings in order to soak up the sun and bathe in the sea.

"All some people ever seem to do while on holiday is lie on the beach for hours on end to get a tan," commented Ned, as he and George arrived in the cove. "I can't see the point. They might as well stay at home and lie on their lawns if they're not going to get around and see the sights."

"You're just jealous because you're fair skinned and go bright red instead of brown," quipped George. "And besides, not everyone has a garden let alone a lawn. You don't, and neither do I. What's more, if you fancy a dip in the sea to cool down while sunbathing, then lying on a miserable patch of scorched grass, won't provide the necessary facilities."

"Alright, you win, but I still can't see how people don't get bored just lying in the sun all day."

George stopped dead in his tracks. "Oh God, look at that."

"Look at what?" said Ned, wondering what had affected his friend in such a strange way.

George whistled. "Over there at the foot of the cliffs."

Ned cast his eyes in the direction of George's hand to where Willoughby Castor-Hunt sat on the beach reading a newspaper. Beside him stood Tabitha, wearing only a flattering swimsuit and alluringly rubbing suntan lotion over her long legs.

"She is gorgeous," George drooled. "Now, if I could dispose of your friend Willoughby, perhaps I might wangle it so that I not only get Chy-an-Gwyns, but the beautiful Tabitha as well."

"Dream on," laughed Ned. "She wouldn't give a second glance to the likes of you, even if Willoughby Castor-Hunt didn't exist."

"She might. Who knows? I wish your friend Sylvia was still around, because she'd be able to give me a few tips on bumping off unwanted rivals."

"George!" spluttered, Ned, angrily.

"Sorry, that just sort of slipped out and was totally out of order. I know such comments are strictly forbidden by you and I apologise profusely."

Ned grinned and slapped George on the back. "Only you could get away with it. But for God's sake don't ever make a remark such as that in the presence of Frank. He'd be deeply wounded by your insensitivity and I'd hate to see him hurt."

Among the holiday makers soaking up the sun were Milly and Johnny. Milly, however, lacked the sparkle all had learned to associate her with since she had taken up with the Pascoes' young nephew. For unbeknown to anyone with eyes to notice, she had reason to feel glum. Johnny had told her his aunt and uncle had asked if he would be interested in learning how to run the village post office in order for him to take it over from them when they retired in a few years' time. They had no offspring of their own and were very reluctant to let the business they had built up over many years, go out of the family.

"But I was looking forward to meeting up with you when we were back home," she sighed. "If you stay here I shall probably never ever see you again."

Johnny slipped his arm around her shoulder. "Well, I've not made my mind up yet. They've given me time to think about it. Both of my parents are very keen on the idea, though. I spent half an hour on the phone talking to Dad first thing this morning and I must admit it does seem a very good offer."

"I suppose so and I'm being selfish, aren't I? I know your future's very important. It's just that you're the first person I've come across, since I was a little girl, that I really enjoy being with."

"You could always come and visit me. Tell your mum, that from now on, every summer you must have a holiday at the Ringing Bells Inn."

Milly sighed. "I don't know about that. I think Mum is rapidly going off the idea of Cornwall. She was a right misery all day yesterday and wouldn't even go down for a drink last night. Though strangely enough, she insisted I spend the day with you today, so perhaps she's getting to like you."

Percy and Peter were already by the boat waiting when George and Ned crossed the beach to where the little fishing vessel stood.

"We'll be landing the fish later," said Percy, as they all pushed the boat down the beach and jumped aboard as it plunged it into the gentle waves of a flat calm sea. "So today's catch, along with what's already in the store pots, will be going down to Newlyn."

"Wow," said George, "will there be room for us? I'd love to see the hustle and bustle of a real fish market."

Peter nodded. "Yeah, if you really want to go you're more than welcome, but you'll have to ride in the back of the truck with the fish and it'd be a bit smelly."

"We won't mind that," said Ned, "because surely, it can't be much different to being here in the boat."

They had a poor day's fishing in comparison with the previous one: only thirteen crabs, but nevertheless it was worth going out, and when all the pots had been checked, their contents removed and they had been re-baited, the little boat chugged across the water to the spot where the store pots lay.

"You're really lucky being able to fish for a living and spend each working day in such an idyllic environment," grinned George, as he stretched back in the boat and unbuttoned his shirt to help cool down.

"The weather's not always like this," scoffed Peter. "We often get wet, frequently get cold and we're governed by the weather. What's more, no fish means no money, so it's a very nerve racking existence."

"Yeah, but for all that we wouldn't swap our way of life with anyone else, would we?" said Percy, rolling a cigarette as the gentle breeze tousling his dark curls.

When they reached the spot where the store pots lay, Peter stopped the boat and Percy leaned over the side to pull up the ropes to which the two store pots were attached. Seeing him struggle, Peter went to give him a hand, but still the two of them were unable to pull the pots up and into the boat.

"Bugger, they must have caught on something," cursed Percy. "They shouldn't be this heavy."

"Can we help?" asked Ned, eagerly.

"Alright, but if we can't budge the damn things we'll have to get Larry or Des to dive down to see what the problem is."

The four young men all took hold of a piece of the rope, pulled hard together until slowly they could feel the pots rising upwards.

"Nearly got her," said Peter, standing nearest the gunnels. "One more heave should do it."

They all tugged hard and were relieved when the first store pot came into view beneath the shimmering surface of the sea. But the store pot's outline was not its usual shape.

"Bloody hell," screamed Peter, seeing it first.

All gazed over the side. Tangled in the rope attached to the first store pot, bobbed the bedraggled, broken, body of Rosemary Howard.

The girls, out shopping whilst the lads were at sea, wandered around the town looking at clothes, make-up and shoes. Rose bought a new lipstick after consulting Stella which shade she thought might suit her best, and Stella bought Ned a new pair of sunglasses because he had lost his old pair, or as Ned claimed, someone must have moved them. Stella also bought a tray of water colour paints and a few brushes as she was determined to paint a few pictures of Trengillion and the sea, having been inspired by the pencil sketches she had already done.

As they reached the end of Meneage Street, Stella noticed a signpost pointing to a museum.

"Have you ever been around Helston's museum?" Stella asked Rose. "There might be something inside to do with old Polquillick. Thinking of course of Emily and Harry."

"I went in there once with Reg and most of the things on display were old relics from the town. I don't recall seeing any fishing type exhibits, although there might have been. There were several things to do with mining, I think, not that that's of any help. The museum's only been open for three or four years."

"Shall we go and have a look? We've plenty of time and it might be quite interesting."

"By all means. It should be nice and cool in there and I must confess I'm beginning to overheat; but then that's probably because I'm wearing too many clothes."

The museum was not very big but it was interesting. Stella in particular enjoyed looking at the reconstruction of an early Victorian classroom.

"I should imagine trying to teach trussed up in those straight laced dresses must have been a nightmare," commented Rose. "In fact they must have been impractical for just about anything. Imagine trying to run for the bus with that lot swishing around your ankles, not, of course, that there were any buses."

The next display was a collection of kettles throughout the ages.

"Now that's one of the best inventions ever. The first electric kettle, a must for a tea drinking nation such as ours," laughed Stella.

Rose was amazed. "Good heavens, I didn't realise that electric kettles had been around for so long. Just shows what a dimwit I am."

"You're not a dimwit," Stella scolded. "You've far too active a mind to give yourself such an unjust handle."

The museum sadly did not contain any artefacts which might have helped with the mystery of Emily and Harry, but the girls both conceded it was very educative and worth every penny of the entrance fee.

"I must get Ned to pay this place a visit," said Stella. "That's if he hasn't done so already. Although he hates shopping so much, he'd probably have missed the signpost on any previous visits. He must come though; he teaches history and so it's right up his street."

Stella was pleased that Rose seemed in a happy frame of mind as, for several days she had been trying to establish the reason for her frequent bouts of depression, which she had first noticed long before Rosemary Howard had vanished, hence knew Rosemary's disappearance was not the sole cause of her unhappiness.

As they sat in a small café eating lunch, it suddenly occurred to her what lay behind the moments of sadness. For she observed, whenever George's name was mentioned, Rose perked up considerably, giggled and on one occasion even blushed.

Stella slowly shook her head and metaphorically kicked herself. How could she have been so blind? Rose was obviously besotted with George, but George was so pre-occupied with Emily Penberthy and his dreams, that he, like her, had no doubt been unable to see the obvious. Poor Rose! George would soon be returning to London, and she had to find herself a new home. Little wonder at times she seemed low and dejected. Stella said nothing, but made a mental note that, if possible, something had to be done, and resolved to consult Ned later, during a quiet moment, if one arose, that evening.

After lunch they went to the cinema to watch *The Cruel Sea*. Stella had seen it beforehand in London with Ned, but insisted Rose must see it too. For although she conceded it was really a chap's film, it was a poignant reminder of the great loss of life suffered by naval servicemen during the First World War.

Both girls left the cinema drying their eyes.

"It must be awful to drown," sobbed Rose. "No wonder George's dreams trouble him so. It's bad enough slipping in the sea whilst paddling close to the shore, but to go down, miles and miles away from land knowing you'll never survive, must be one of the most horrible ways to die."

Stella wanted to say that it was only a film based on a fictitious book, and there had not really been a ship called the Compass Rose, but she knew the realities were very near to the truth and it would contradict the reason for her insisting Rose see the film in the first place, if she were to say such a thing.

Stella linked her arm with Rose's. "Come on, let's go for a cup of tea and a piece of cake. Crying has made my throat hoarse and tears cannot bring back those that are gone."

They went into a little tea shop and sat at a table beside the window, where they could readily watch the shoppers passing by.

"This is quite a busy little town, isn't it?" said Stella. "Before I ever came to Cornwall, I imagined shops would be very primitive and it would be almost impossible to buy anything here."

"Well, I suppose it is primitive compared to London, but we're able to get most things we need even if the choice is limited."

Stella glanced out of the window with a contented smile. Two little girls went by holding hands and behind them a small boy attempted to tread on their heels. From the opposite direction, a woman in blue pushed through other shoppers, as though in a hurry. Stella caught a glimpse of her face, gasped and choked on her tea.

"What's wrong?" shouted Rose, jumping up to pat her friend on the back, shocked by the look on Stella's face.

"That woman," gasped Stella, placing her cup back on its saucer. "The one who just walked by. She was the spitting image of Elsie Glazebrook. In fact, I'm sure it was Elsie, even though I know it couldn't have been. Come on, Rose, drink up quickly, and let's follow her, just in case."

"Elsie Glazebrook?" said Rose, knowing the name, but unable at that moment to recall why.

"George's old girlfriend," said Stella, gently blowing her nose. "If it is her, then what on earth is she doing here?"

A look of horror crossed Rose's face as it turned several shades paler. She said nothing, but meekly rose from her chair feeling decidedly unsteady, hoping her legs would not turn to jelly as she followed Stella in pursuit of someone whom she had no desire to meet or see.

The two girls ran along the pavement dodging the shoppers until they caught up with the young woman dressed in blue, standing alone, looking through the contents of her handbag outside the window of a grocer's shop. Holding a list, she went inside. The girls crept a little closer. When she came out, they followed her discreetly across the road and into Wendron Street.

"If it is Elsie," said Stella, as they crouched behind a parked car. "And I'm not convinced because I've not yet had a chance to see her face properly, then she drives a Hillman Minx."

The person in question climbed into a Hillman Minx parked on the side of the road.

"My goodness, it is her," shouted Stella, as Elsie started up the engine. "Quick, let's follow."

They ran further up the street and into Godolphin Road where Ned's Morris Minor was parked, frequently ducking to avoid detection in Elsie's rear view mirror.

Once the doors were unlocked, they leapt inside the car and Stella niftily started the engine, thankful the weather was warm and it started at the first attempt. The Hillman Minx was still visible further up the road. Stella drove fast to catch up, grateful that a couple of other cars were in front, thus hindering Elsie's vision of Ned's car and number plate.

The two vehicles drove out of town, along Clodgey Lane and towards the Lizard road. One of the cars in front turned off at the crossroads, but fortunately a bus, having just picked up passengers, took its place, giving the Morris Minor the perfect vehicle to hide behind.

They drove on for a mile or so and then just beyond RNAS Culdrose, the bus turned off towards Gunwalloe. With the road ahead clear they saw that Elsie was way ahead in the distance.

They kept well back. Stella asked Rose to pass her Ned's new sunglasses. She put them on, in case Elsie might recognise her, although there was still a car between them.

"She's turning off," said Rose, feeling a lump rise in her throat.

The Hillman Minx left the main road and turned into a series of lanes. Stella followed, lagging slowly behind in the bends to keep out of sight.

"Any idea where we are?" Stella asked Rose.

"Not entirely, but I think we must be on the outskirts of Polquillick, that's if my sense of direction is to be relied on."

As they passed a forsaken old house, Rose saw from the passenger's seat, Elsie's car parked in its driveway.

Stella sped quickly by, pulled into the gateway of a field and switched off the Morris Minor's engine.

"Let's go back on foot," she whispered, "and then we can see what she's doing."

The two girls ran down the lane keeping close to the hedgerows. On approaching the house, they saw Elsie Glazebrook standing on an overgrown driveway taking shopping from the back seat of her car.

Overcome with curiosity, they watched as she walked up the overgrown path, shopping basket in hand, and entered the house through a shabby, half glazed, front door. Baffled and intrigued to know why she was in Cornwall, the two girls crept a little closer to the house. Standing behind a flourishing hydrangea, they parted its leaves in order to peer into the large bay window of the room in which Elsie stood facing an elderly woman who appeared to be angry.

Rose scowled. "I'm sure I've seen that old woman before. Something about her seems familiar but I'm not quite sure what."

"Really! I don't know her, but then I'm only a holiday maker."

Elsie approached the table and from her shopping basket removed a brown paper package. With trembling hands, she then untied the string. Inside lay a bundle of candles.

"Looks like they're expecting a power cut," said Rose.

Stella giggled. "Or perhaps the electricity has been cut off because they've not paid the bills."

Elsie picked up the shopping basket and turned to leave the room, but as she passed a sideboard, the corner of the basket knocked against a china figurine. It fell to the floor and broke into several large pieces. The old woman screamed and then slapped Elsie hard across the face. Elsie stumbled backwards and then ran from the room in tears.

Stella and Rose gasped.

The woman suddenly turned and glanced towards the window. The two girls ducked for fear of being seen.

"Do you think she saw us?" Rose gasped, as they crouched behind the hydrangea.

"I don't think so. I'm sure if she had she would have been out by now."

They remained very still, uncomfortable in their hiding place, nervously listening for any sounds, voices, or footsteps. When confident it was safe to move, they crept from the shrubbery, relieved to have escaped detection.

"What shall we do, now?" Rose asked. "I mean, we shouldn't really be here. We're trespassing, aren't we?"

"Yes, I suppose so, and Elsie has as much right as anyone else to be in Cornwall. But it just it doesn't make sense and I really would like to have found out more because Ned and George will ask all sorts of questions, to which we'll have no answers."

Disappointed to have found out very little, both girls turned to leave. Quietly and quickly they crept through the shrubbery and the gateway, and back into the lane.

Feeling safe when on the road, they stood up straight and looked with interest towards the house. Their relief, however, was short lived. For both spotted simultaneously, standing beneath a mountain ash, dripping with orange berries, and parked in a higgledy-piggledy manner, a dirty, dilapidated, old van.

Both girls gasped and ducked again to avoid detection.

"A van, an old woman, and now Elsie Glazebrook," whispered Stella, too afraid to scream. "For God's sake, Rose, let's get out of here."

CHAPTER TWENTY EIGHT

Rose was devastated when she and Stella arrived back in the village and heard from Ned and George of the tragedy that had befallen Rosemary Howard.

"I knew something was wrong," she sobbed, sitting on an old barrel outside the Inn where Stella had parked Ned's car and the lads had greeted them with the distressing news. "If only I'd followed my instincts and gone to see Fred after I found her handbag. Now I feel really bad and partly to blame."

Ned knelt by her side, put his arms around her shoulders and hugged her tightly. "Don't blame yourself, Rose. You were right to feel something was wrong, but if you'd seen the state Rosemary was in, you'd have realised she must have been dead for several days and no doubt had drowned even before she missed her first meal."

"I suppose you're right," she sniffed, releasing herself from Ned's arms to blow her nose, "and crying won't bring her back, I know. You must think me very silly. I'm sorry, it's just that she was always so sweet when I waited on her and she never looked down her nose at me, like some people do. She was always eager to hear stories about the area too. I just wish I'd had the chance to get to know her better."

"Of course we don't think you're silly, snapped George. "We sympathise, and it wasn't a very pleasant experience seeing her come up with that wretched store pot, I can tell you. Poor Pete, he turned as white as a sheet. I think it's an experience we'll none of us ever forget."

George was tetchy, and his voice a little harsh, for he was riddled with guilt and finding it difficult to come to terms with Rosemary's death. Seeing her emerge from the water, brought back the memory of the body he had seen whilst out with Larry and Des, and he knew, without doubt, that it had not been his imagination seeing images of Emily Penberthy beneath the waves. It had been Rosemary Howard, and had he had more courage and sense he could have established her identity there and then instead of cowering in the boat, a pathetic chicken, thinking he had seen a ghost. His only recompense was that to have identified her would not have saved her life. All the same, he felt guilty for not having shared his experience with his friends, and because of his original silence, he knew he would never, ever, be able to tell them the truth, for they would not understand why he had chosen to keep quiet when the incident had first occurred.

"Anyway, what was it you were looking so excited about when you got back?" asked Ned, aware that he had spoken first and not given the girls a chance to say anything about their day.

"Oh, nothing much," whispered Stella. "It doesn't matter. That is, it might be of significance. In fact, I'm sure it is, but I can't think straight at the moment for thinking of Rosemary." She sighed deeply. "The thing is, we saw Elsie in town today, and because we thought it strange, we followed her and she went to Polquillick, that's all."

George turned pale. "What, my Elsie! Surely not! For God's sake! What the hell is she doing down here? This goes from bad to worse."

Rose bit her bottom lip on hearing his reference to *my* Elsie.

"Yes, it was your Elsie, and we've no idea why she's here, but actually there's more to it than that. Oh dear, everything is suddenly so horrible. After we'd followed her car all the way from town to Polquillick and down a narrow lane, she stopped in the driveway of a sinister looking place called Laburnum House, at least that's what it said on the gate. Anyway, in it lives an old woman. Elsie didn't knock on the door, she went straight in so she must know the woman and is probably even staying there. But there's even more to it than that, and this is the most significant thing of all. Parked in the garden is a dirty, battered old van."

"What! Now I'm confused," muttered Ned, leaning on the bonnet of his car. "Whatever can this mean?"

"It doesn't make sense," said George, squirming as a tingling sensation tickled his spine. "If you've found the right old woman. I mean, Molly's so called, crabby old women, the one with the van, and Elsie knows her, then she may well have been the accomplice. But why on earth would she kidnap, and try to drown your mum, Ned? Elsie never ever met her, did she? Besides, Elsie's not prone to violence, she wouldn't hurt a fly. I can't believe it's just a coincidence, though. Oh, there must be a simple explanation."

"And what about Rosemary's death? Do you think it's possible there might be a connection there?" said mused Stella. "I mean, could Rosemary have been kidnapped by the old woman and left in a cove to drown like your mum, Ned?"

"I don't think so," said Ned. "Rosemary had absolutely nothing whatsoever to do with us, so I can't see a possible link at all. Nevertheless, I think we ought to mention it to Fred. In fact, I think we ought to go round there right now and see if he can make any sense of your findings."

Fred and Annie Stevens were sitting together in the Police House, busily tackling the day's chores. Annie was mending a pair of Jamie's trousers, torn whilst he was out playing and climbing trees. And Fred, with glasses perched on the end of his nose, was catching up with his paperwork. Before either had finished their task in hand, a knock on the door made them both jump. Annie put down the mending and went to see who could be rapping on the door with such urgency. She was surprised to find Ned, Stella, Rose and George crammed together in the small front porch, but assumed they had come to enquire if there was any further news regarding the death of Rosemary Howard. She invited them into the sitting room where Fred had already risen to see what all the commotion was about.

They all talked at once, trying to tell of the discovery of the house, the old woman, the van, Elsie Glazebrook and the slight possibility of a link with the death of Rosemary Howard.

Fred and Annie listened with interest, and although they knew roughly where the house was, neither had any idea who lived there or who owned the place. It was not on Fred's patch, but he knew the Polquillick police constable well and said he would phone him when he was sure he had all the facts right. Meanwhile, he suggested they all return to the Inn for dinner and act as though nothing had happened whilst he made further enquiries.

When Ned, Stella and George entered the dining room that evening they found Milly anxiously asking if anyone had seen her mother. She told how Madge had insisted she spend the day with Johnny and in retrospect felt she must have been up to something.

"Not another," Stella whispered, thinking Madge's disappearance sounded ominous. George, however, forced a smile and patted Milly's shoulder with sincere sympathy. "I expect she's found some other poor bloke to focus her attentions on. Don't worry, Milly, she'll be back by the end of the day, and for the sake of all of us, let's hope it's with Mr Right."

Milly frowned, puzzled. "Who's Mr Wright?"

George, exasperated, looked heavenward.

"Oh, I see," Milly giggled, as the penny dropped. "You mean the right person for her. Oh, I do hope so too, but I somehow doubt it. Mum doesn't appear to have much luck with men."

Nevertheless, Milly sat down satisfied with George's theory and speedily ate her dinner, knowing if her mother was out of the way she would be able to spend the evening with Johnny, uninterrupted.

Rose joined Ned, Stella and George when she finished work. The four of them then sat outside the front of the Inn waiting to hear from Fred.

"The nights are drawing in now, aren't they?" commented Stella, buttoning up her cardigan. "Before we know it a new term will have begun and we'll be heading towards Christmas."

Rose laughed. "And I'll be out on the streets. Still, at least I'm alive, so I've nothing to complain about."

They were surprised to find it was Annie who joined them later with an update of developments. "Sorry if you've been waiting for long. Fred sent me to see you because he thought it best as he still doesn't quite know what's going on and who knows what, if you see what I mean. Also, he's waiting to hear if there's any more news about Rosemary. The poor chap's getting quite flustered at present. We seldom get incidents that require the involvement of the force in town and now we've two cases running simultaneously. Although it's assumed Rosemary's death was an accident, so that case should be wound up soon, because we can't see a plausible link between Molly's abduction and the poor girl's drowning."

"What's the latest news then regarding our discovery today?" asked Stella. "Does Fred know who the old woman is?"

"Yes, he's been on the phone to P.C. Dick Remington at Polquillick, who said the old woman is called Daisy Rowe. She's a widow and a bit of a recluse who has lived at the same house for as long as he can remember. He doesn't think she can drive, but her late husband did have a van, although Dick assumes that's not been used for years."

"So, does Fred think that it was this Daisy Rowe behind Mum's abduction?" Ned asked.

"He doesn't know and neither does Dick, but they propose to find out. They're both going to pay her a visit tomorrow morning."

"I wonder where Elsie fits into all this," mused George, now in a much calmer frame of mind. "I mean, why on earth would she be visiting this Daisy woman? It doesn't make sense."

"Well, hopefully we'll know a bit more tomorrow. Fred and Dick are going over around ten o'clock, so they should be able to catch them in. They don't want to go tonight because as I've already said, Fred is waiting for a call about Rosemary Howard. I'll report back to you in the afternoon when I know more."

Ned and Stella went round to see Molly and the major after Annie's departure to put them in the picture. The major was out visiting George Fillingham who had expressed a desire to join the Golf Club. Molly, however, was home, but a little less jovial than usual.

"Oh Ned, I've heard about your dreadful experience today. What a terrible shock it must have been. Poor, poor Rosemary! Such a tragic accident and according to Doris, Jim Hughes is distraught over the fact she's been found dead. Such a dear, sweet girl, and I believe she was only twenty three. Her parents will be heartbroken when they get the news, and I can't help but keep recalling the fact Madame Rowena told her she would have her name in the papers. She was so excited at the time, but little did the poor girl know for what reason her name would be in print."

Ned tried to digest all his mother said. Most of it made sense but he was baffled by the comment regarding Jim Hughes.

"Mum, I'm a bit miffed," he said, as they left the hallway and entered the front room. "Why is Jim distraught over Rosemary's death? I wouldn't have thought they even knew each other."

209

"Well, I suppose they didn't. Although, they might have done by sight. But the reason for his distress is because he frightened her not long ago. He does the garden for Willoughby, you see, when he's away up-country, and when he was up there recently he caught her snooping in one of the downstairs windows. He called to her, but meant her no harm. Anyway, she ran off screaming, because unfortunately he was up there chopping up an old tree root with an axe and had goggles on to protect his eyes. He confessed that he must have looked a terrifying sight and feels he must have scared the living daylights out of her, although at the time he was amused by the incident."

"Oh no, poor Rosemary," sighed Stella. "Thank goodness Rose isn't here as she'd be distraught if she heard that on top of everything else."

Ned sat down heavily on Molly's settee. "I think this has been one of the most harrowing days I've ever been through."

"I can imagine it must be," sympathised Molly. "If only she'd come on holiday with friends instead of by herself, that way she'd still be alive today. It's dangerous getting too near the water, especially if you're not used to the sea."

Ned agreed. "Quite right, but finding Rosemary isn't the only traumatic thing that's happened today. Stella and Rose made a discovery this afternoon which may well be linked to your abduction, and I think will interest you greatly."

Molly grinned and took a chair beside the empty fireplace. "How exciting. Do tell me more. Hopefully you've evidence at last to nail her."

"Nail her," repeated Ned, surprised by his mother's comment. He then proceeded to tell of the girls' trip into town and the subsequent events. As he uttered the last words, Molly's jaw dropped. She was speechless. Her face reddened and then turned white. Ned leapt up from the chair to shake her, thinking she'd had a seizure of some kind.

"I'm alright, Ned," she squeaked, seeing the alarmed look on his face, "but if you go into the pantry you'll find a bottle of Doris's elderberry wine on the top shelf next to the pickled onions. Fetch it in here, please. I need a drink."

Ned did as his mother asked, and Stella, at Molly's behest, fetched three wine glasses from the sideboard cupboard.

"This is marvellous stuff," Molly twittered, filling the glasses to the brim. "1952 was a good year and this reaches parts gin could never touch."

She handed out the wine to her surprised son and daughter-in-law. "What do you think?" she asked. "Is it not pure nectar?"

"It's very good," said Ned, surprised by the impromptu wine tasting and lack of response to his news. "In fact it's quite delicious. But aren't you going to say anything about the old woman and Elsie?"

"I'm trying not to think about it," sighed Molly, laughing feebly. "It makes my brain hurt. Doris's dandelion is very good too, and so is her elderflower, but it's much lighter of course and so doesn't keep for long. Not like the elderberry, of which Doris has a bottle almost five years old."

She emptied her glass. "Pour me another please, Ned and help yourselves to more."

"No thanks," said Ned, firmly. "Surely you're not going to sit here and get drunk."

"Certainly not," said Molly, primly. "Two glasses is my limit. By then I shall feel relaxed and perhaps be able to digest what you've told me, and come up with a sensible comment. For at the moment I'm too shocked to say anything. You see, I was convinced Mabel was involved. The mysterious accomplice, I assumed. And I regret to say I sent her an anonymous letter accusing her thus, which should arrive at the Inn, by post, tomorrow morning."

Sid Reynolds arrived home from work and sat wearily down at the table in number three Coronation Terrace. Meg fetched him his slippers then went into the kitchen to dish up the dinner.

"You've no doubt heard about the body," called Sid, as he slipped off his shoes. "It's caused quite a stir at the office and we've all been rushing like mad to get the story together for tomorrow morning's paper."

"Body!" said Meg, as she walked into the dining room with two plates of steaming food. "Sorry love, but I've no idea what you're talking about."

"Good grief, has Gertie not been in with all the gossip? That's a first! It was after all, Percy and Peter who found her, and I believe Ned and his mate George were with them too."

"I've not seen Gertie all day. I went to the Vicarage this morning and ended up staying for lunch. I've only been back just over an hour, so I've no idea what you are talking about."

"Rosemary Howard," said Sid. "She'd been missing for a couple of days, but everyone had assumed she'd gone to visit someone or something like that. Anyway, they found her body in the sea this morning. It was caught on one of Percy and Peter's store pots. They reckon she must have fallen into the sea somewhere. They don't know when or how, but they're convinced by the state of her that she's been dead for a few days and drowning seems the most likely cause. Although they don't know yet for sure, as they need to do a post mortem. She hasn't been formally identified yet either, although everyone knows it's Rosemary and her parents are coming down tomorrow."

"Oh, no, poor girl. Poor parents," said Meg, laying down her knife and fork. "How horrible. I can't say that I ever got to speak to her, but she couldn't have been much older than me, could she? Such a tragic waste of life."

"She was twenty three. But at least there's nothing suspicious about her death, not like poor Jane. I mean, Rosemary was actually found in the sea and not above the high water mark on a beach, in a wretched cave."

"Had she been swimming and got into trouble then, do you think? I mean, was she wearing a bathing costume?"

Sid shook his head. "No, apparently she was wearing a green and white spotted dress. That's why it's assumed she fell into the water somewhere."

"A green and white spotted dress," choked Meg, turning pale. "Oh no, Sid, then it's not quite as straight forward as you might think."

She rose from the table, left the room and reached for her jacket hanging on the coat rack in the hallway.

"I found this the other day," she said, holding up the piece of fabric for Sid to see. "It was caught on the bolt of the tunnel's trap door in the stables. I knew someone must have been poking around in the tunnel, but thought it was possibly Stella when she and Ned had taken out the horses the other day. It was because the ladder was not put back, that I climbed up to see if the trap door was still open."

"And was it?" Sid asked.

"No, it was closed and bolted but the sheet of metal was not back in place."

Sid took the piece of cloth from Meg's trembling hand. "Then someone deliberately shut her in. I think we ought to pay Fred Stevens a visit as soon as we've finished our dinner."

CHAPTER TWENTY NINE

Ned could not sleep. His mind was a jumble, for he desperately wanted to witness for himself the police's forthcoming encounter with Daisy Rowe and Elsie Glazebrook, and because of his dilemma, he lay awake in the early hours giving the matter considerable thought. But no matter how hard he tried, he was not able think of a plausible reason to go to Polquillick the following morning without confessing his inquisitiveness and sounding down-right nosey. Furthermore, he was afraid to sleep soundly in case he should not wake early, for he knew, if possible, he had to seize the post the minute Alf Burgess delivered it, to withdraw the slanderous, malicious letter his mother had sent to Mabel, before she found it herself. And Ned was well aware that Mabel was an early riser.

Ned was cross with his mother. She had no good reason to suspect Mabel of any wrong doing and had acted purely on a misguided hunch. Her argument being, Mabel wore lavender eau de cologne and the envelope containing the locket had smelt strongly of lavender too. She had also believed Mabel's claims to take long and frequent walks were simply a cover up, and the real reason she was away from Trengillion for hours on end was because she was up to no good in Polquillick.

At half past six Ned got up, had a quick bath and went downstairs to await the arrival of Alf. He was in luck, and had only ten minutes to wait before a bundle of mail dropped through the letter box. Eagerly he shuffled through the envelopes, but to his dismay there was only one addressed to Mabel and the postmark was not Cornwall but Kettering, Northamptonshire. Ned scowled, would it arrive later in the day or had Molly apprehended the postman herself and managed to persuade him to hand over the offensive letter?

The sound of approaching footsteps caused him to turn round quickly. Thinking it would be Frank he smiled in anticipation. It was, however, Mabel who rounded the corner.

"Is there a letter there for me?" she asked, politely, observing the mail in his hands.

"Yes," said Ned, thankful that his mother's epistle had not arrived. "I saw one just now addressed to Mrs Thorpe. Yes, here it is, Mabel." He handed her the envelope with a smile which she mistook for a derogatory grin. She snatched it from his hands and with a cold glare left the hallway.

Ned, flabbergasted by her ungracious manner, began to wonder if his mother might be right. Perhaps Mabel was the mysterious accomplice and Elsie's materialisation was pure coincidence.

During breakfast, Ned expressed his desire to visit Laburnum House.

George rubbed his hands with glee. "Why don't we go, then? There's nothing to stop us. We could get there before the coppers, hide in the bushes and await the consequences."

"What!" spluttered Stella. "Are you both crazy?"

Ned pulled a silly face. "Of course not, isn't that so, George?"

"Absolutely correct. We must eat our breakfast with haste."

Stella began to eat her scrambled eggs. "Well, if you're both going, then I'm going too."

"Oh no, you're not," said Ned, vociferously. "It may well be dangerous and I'm not having you hurt."

"Dangerous," laughed Stella, banging her knife and fork down onto the tablecloth. "What danger can there possibly be in approaching a crabby old woman and Elsie Glazebrook?"

"There may be others in the house," said George, a touch of excitement in his voice. "Something must have caused them to abduct Molly. Perhaps it's the headquarters of an international kidnapping circle."

"Or the occupants are key members of a smuggling ring," said Ned.

"Or perhaps the house is crammed with the reincarnations of long dead thieves, or better still, ladies of ill-repute," chuckled George.

Both men sat in fits of giggles as they continued to think up even more ridiculous motives and theories.

"No-one would ever believe you are both teachers," snapped Stella, indignantly. "You're behaving more like children than children."

She rose from the table, haughtily left the dining room and went to her room to wait for Rose to finish work.

Ned and George drove to Polquillick and found Laburnum House with ease. They parked the Morris Minor in a grass meadow further down the lane, well hidden behind a tall hedge of elder, bramble and rambling ivy. They then crept back along the lane and hid in the front garden amongst the vast amount of overgrown shrubbery and patchy undergrowth, shaded by overhanging trees.

No voices could be heard from inside the house and the only sound in the garden was birdsong drifting from the branches up above, and the chugging of a tractor at work somewhere beyond the back boundaries of the house.

From their hiding place, Elsie's parked car was clearly visible in the driveway, and further along, beneath the mountain ash, stood the much hunted for, dilapidated, battered old van. Just visible on its side was faded lettering, reading, Victor Rowe. General Builder. Polquillick. Beneath was a telephone number.

"Do you think that's the right van?" said Ned, wrinkling his nose. "It looks a bit of a wreck to me and I get the impression it hasn't left that spot for donkey's years."

George agreed. "It does, doesn't it? And we can't see from here whether or not the tyres are flat because the damn grass is too long."

"I've just thought of something else. If this woman and Elsie were responsible for Mum's abduction, then why on earth did they use the van? Surely it would have made more sense to have used Elsie's car. It's far more roadworthy and reliable than that old heap of rust."

"Hmm, good point. Perhaps then, Elsie wasn't the mystery accomplice at all."

"Ouch, you could be right," Ned agreed, rubbing his hand, tingling due to a nettle sting. "Perhaps Elsie had absolutely nothing to do with Mum's abduction and has only just arrived. Either that or they used the van so that Mum couldn't be seen in the back. Are there any dock leaves near you?"

"Dock leaves!" repeated George.

"Yes, they soothe nettle stings and this one damn well hurts."

They successfully found a clump of docks growing near to the spot where they hid. Ned crushed the biggest leaf he could find with his fingers, spat on it and then rubbed it into the large white bumps on the back of his hand.

Suddenly George lowered his head and put his finger to his lips. "Shush, I can hear something."

They listened as the sound of an engine slowly approached and stopped not far away. Two doors slammed shut and the faint murmur of hushed voices and light, quick footsteps ensued. From the lane, two uniformed police officers appeared. They stopped outside the curtilage of the property, subtly viewed the house through the straggly growth of the unkempt cotoneaster hedge, and communicated with each other in low, gruff whispers.

Ned and George crouched lower still amongst the bushes to avoid detection, each finding it difficult to suppress the strong desire to laugh. With hands over mouths they watched Police Constables Fred Stevens and Dick Remington, silently leave the gateway and creep up the garden path towards the front door of the house.

"What would the kids back at school think if they could see us now?" whispered George, mesmerised, as the two police constables approached the front door.

Dick Remington removed his helmet, knocked on the door and straightened his tie whilst waiting for someone to answer. Fred meanwhile, left the doorstep, peeped in through the large bay window and then walked over to the old van and kicked the tyres.

"Who is it?" called a female voice from inside the house.

"The Police," shouted Dick. "Come on, open up, please."

Fred moved quickly as Dick beckoned him to the doorstep. From inside the house, clicking footsteps could be heard running down the hallway. Dick tried the knob, but the door was locked. Without hesitation, he raised his truncheon and smashed the cracked, leaded light panels and pushed his hand through the fragmented glass. With haste, he reached for the key and successfully unlocked the door from inside.

As the two policemen entered the house at the front, Daisy Rowe, pulling Elsie Glazebrook by the hair, escaped through the kitchen door around the back. Cackling, the old woman and Elsie, rushed along the path towards the driveway, past the dilapidated old van and the tumbledown garage. When they reached Elsie's Hillman Minx, the old woman pushed Elsie into the passenger seat and slammed shut the door. She then leapt into the driver's seat, started the car's engine and drove out into the lane with all wheels spinning.

Inside, the police having heard the car engine start up, ran from the house commanding the Hillman Minx to stop. Daisy Rowe, however, had other ideas and the car sped down the lane and out of sight.

The police, annoyed that their suspects had escaped, ran to their own car parked further down the lane and then hurriedly set off in pursuit of the two ladies.

"Christ, Ned," yelled George, as he stood up, amazed by the drama they'd just witnessed. "By the time we've retrieved your car from the field down the road they'll be miles away and we'll have lost them."

"The van," shouted Ned, pointing towards the driveway. "Let's try the van."

They scrambled out of the shrubbery, wasting no time brushing dead leaves and twigs from their clothing, and energetically ran towards the van. The doors were unlocked and the keys were in the ignition.

"Looks like we might be in luck," said Ned, jumping into the driver's seat and attempting to start the engine. The van started first time.

"Wow, brilliant, put your foot down, Ned," George laughed, as the van lurched forwards narrowly missing the gatepost. "We must catch them up before they reach the junction or we won't know which way they've gone."

They sped down the lane towards the main road in Polquillick where Daisy Rowe turned right and headed towards the coast. The two vehicles giving chase followed, causing amazed passersby to stop and stare in disbelief at the spectacle before their eyes. For seldom was the bell of a speeding police car heard in the quiet backwater of Polquillick.

Daisy Rowe fled past the Mop and Bucket, past the church, past the gift shop and past the Ice Cream Parlour. And then, with nowhere else to go, she drove onto the harbour wall, knocking crab pots over the side and sending holiday makers running for their lives.

At the end of the wall the car stopped. Daisy Rowe switched off the engine. Elsie attempted to get out, but the old woman pulled her back and slapped her hard. The police car arrived on the scene as a fight broke out on the front seats of the Hillman Minx. Daisy Rowe pulled Elsie's hair with one hand and repeatedly hit her with the clenched fists of the other. Elsie screamed and writhed to free herself from the old woman's grasp and struggled in vain to open the car door.

The two policemen jumped from their car, waving their truncheons and ordering the women to come out with their hands up. Seconds later, Ned and George pulled up behind the police car in the dilapidated old van. With haste, all four men approached the Hillman Minx, but Daisy Rowe, seeing their advance in the rear view mirror, released the handbrake and chortled with glee. Elsie's car lurched forward with a jerk and plunged over the harbour wall into the sea.

"No, Elsie," George cried, clasping his head between his hands and tearing at his hair with frustration. He clumsily knelt on the side of the harbour wall and repeatedly shouted her name.

The car rocked on the surface of the water as Elsie frantically wound down the car window and resumed her struggle to open the door. Again she failed. The car rapidly began to take in water and within minutes it sank out of sight.

Without hesitation, George tore off his jacket and shoes, leapt from the harbour wall and dived beneath the swirling waves crashing against the granite barrier. Fred Stevens, removed his helmet, jacket, and boots, and then followed by way of the harbour wall steps. Dick Remington attempted to keep back the growing crowd of spectators, all eager to witness the newsworthy event unfurling before their eyes. And Ned, unable to swim, leapt to Dick's aid, thus enabling him to call for assistance on the car radio.

Beneath the water, Elsie, holding her breath, attempted to swim through the open window of her door. George on the outside grabbed her hands and with force pulled her through the small gap. Both then swam to the surface where Ned and Dick reached into the water and pulled Elsie up the rough granite steps. At the top she coughed, choked and spluttered. Tears streamed down her cold, wet cheeks but she insisting there was no need for concern.

Fred Stevens appeared from beneath the water, for breath, and then dived once more, quickly followed by George, once he was satisfied that Elsie's life was not in danger. Minutes later the two men surfaced again, Fred with the body of Daisy Rowe slumped in his arms.

With difficulty, they heaved her helpless body up the harbour wall steps and then attempted to resuscitate her. But it was too late. She was dead.

As the sound of another police car, followed by an ambulance grew louder, Ned looked down onto the face of Daisy Rowe.

"I've seen her before," he said. "I recognise her eyes. She was at the fete. She was the Fortune Teller."

CHAPTER THIRTY

Stella and Rose waited patiently at The School House until the clock on Rose's mantelpiece chimed midday and then, tired of waiting for Ned and George to return, they walked down to The Police House to see if Annie Stevens had any information. They found her outside cleaning the porch windows, and just as anxious as they were for news.

"Come inside and I'll make us a coffee to pass the time. Where are Ned and George? Are they not with you?"

"No," said Stella, embarrassed, with a clear note of anger in her voice. "They went to Polquillick this morning to witness your Fred's arrival at Laburnum House. That's why we're concerned, because something may have happened to them."

Annie tutted and shook her head. "I think your Ned ought to have joined the Police Force, as it seems he has a thirst for solving crimes. And it looks as though George is not much different."

They went indoors and Annie made mugs of coffee which they drank in her sitting room.

"Is there any more news about Rosemary's death?" Rose asked. "I mean, is it possible to say yet when the poor girl drowned?"

Annie placed her mug on the wooden arm of her chair. "I shouldn't really tell you this, although it will be common knowledge soon, anyway. But Meg and Sid were round last night, because when Meg went to shut up the horses the other night she found the ladder propped up against the back wall of the stables, and when she looked further, she found a piece of fabric torn from the dress Rosemary was wearing. It was caught on the bolt of the trap door, and so now it's assumed she went along the old tunnel to the sea, as the door was bolted when Meg found it. This can only mean that someone deliberately shut her in there, as I can't imagine anyone being stupid enough to bolt the door with the ladder up against the wall, because surely that would indicate someone was inside."

The colour dramatically drained from Rose's face. "Oh no, that's terrible. It was me who told her about that tunnel one morning after breakfast. She said she was thinking of using our location as a setting for her book and she might possibly have a murder in it. And so I told her about poor Jane, and said in reality a murder on home ground is really horrible. She was fascinated to hear about the tunnel, even though I painted a pretty gruesome picture of it. I never dreamt she'd want to go down there." Rose burst into tears. "Now I feel really guilty. If only I'd kept my big mouth shut."

"Don't feel bad, dear," said Annie, with kindness. "Had she not found out from you she may well have heard from someone else. Unfortunately the tunnel is very common knowledge these days, and has had lots of visitors in the past eighteen months. Having said that, I don't think anyone since Ned, has walked the whole length of it. Not until Rosemary, that is."

"But who would have shut her in?" said Stella. "Surely not Daisy Rowe or Elsie. That wouldn't make any sense at all."

"Sadly, we've no idea," said Annie. "Unfortunately we know very little about her movements since she's been down here and we know nothing of her friends and so forth back in her hometown. But her parents are on the way down, apparently, so if she had any undesirable associates, we'll soon know. I sincerely hope her death, if suspicious, has nothing to do with local people, though, or this area will soon have a bad reputation. Another of the Inn's guests has disappeared, by the way. Madge Chester has vanished into thin air. Her poor daughter was round to report her missing first thing this morning. She hasn't seen her since yesterday."

They were still discussing Rosemary's plight and the disappearance of Madge when they heard Fred's car pull up outside. As he came into the house he gave a half-hearted smile. He looked very strange, dressed in clothes, not his own, which fitted badly. On his sock-less feet he wore canvas beach shoes.

"Where on earth is your uniform?" asked Annie, as he sat down in his armchair and unbuttoned the jacket he wore, several sizes too large.

"At the station in Helston," he said, wryly. "It got a bit wet."

"Wet!" repeated Annie. "What do you mean by wet? And where are Ned and George?"

"They've gone to the Inn to get changed. Well, George has, because he got a bit wet too. Ned stayed dry though because he can't swim."

Annie stood up and walked over to her husband. "Fred Stevens, have you been drinking? Because you're not making any sense whatsoever. What happened this morning? It's not been raining so why did you and George get wet? Where is Daisy Rowe? Did she abduct Molly? And what has George's girlfriend got to do with all this?"

Fred groaned. "Steady on old girl, one question at a time." He gazed into space a blank expression on his face.

Annie gently touched his face. "Fred, are you alright?"

He nodded. "Yes, love, and to answer your questions. Daisy Rowe did abduct Molly and now she's dead. Daisy that is, not Molly. And Elsie Glazebrook, who appears to be Daisy's great niece, is in custody at the station."

Stella gasped. "Her great niece, and the old woman's dead! But that's terrible. Why is she dead and why did she abduct Molly? I still can't see a connection."

Fred removed the canvas beach shoes and reached for his slippers. "Well, you're not going to believe this, ladies, because it's too daft for words. But apparently, Elsie is here visiting her great aunt, and they have been trying to get George to drown himself because the aunt said he was the reincarnation of her twin sister, Emily Penberthy's lover, Harry Timmins."

"Clear as mud," muttered Annie, returning to her seat. "Try and explain better, Fred."

"Well, from what I can make of it, it goes like this. When George put an end to his relationship with Elsie she was very cross and wanted him back. So she came to Cornwall to spy on him after her mum told her she had a great aunt living down here, who incidentally, she had not seen since she was six or seven. Poor Elsie arrived thinking it would give her the opportunity to follow George, and maybe even, accidentally on purpose, bump into him. But when she got here she found her aunt had gone dotty in her old age. Because when Elsie showed her a picture of George, she insisted he was the reincarnation of Harry Timmins. You'll have to question the lads further if you want a better explanation than that. My poor head's swimming with names and stories which seem pure mumbo jumbo."

"But I still don't see where my mother-in-law comes into this," said Stella, who was trying to digest all she had heard.

"Neither do I, and if you'll excuse me girls I really must take a bath and get into some of my own clothes."

"Yes, of course," said Stella, rising. "We'll not keep you any longer. We'll go and interrogate the boys instead. And thank you, Fred for what you have been able to tell us, even if it doesn't really make any sense."

As they prepared to leave, Rose asked Fred how he got wet.

He took in a deep breath and sighed, thoughtfully. "Because the car the two women were in went over the harbour wall at Polquillick. That's why the old woman's dead. She drowned. God rest her soul. Elsie was saved though because George jumped into the sea and pulled her from the sinking car."

"So George rescued his ex-girlfriend," whispered Rose, tears welling in her eyes. "How chivalrous of him."

As the day unfolded so the truth came to light as George found out that afternoon when he was allowed to visit Elsie at the Police Station. Elsie told him of her distress at their parting and her determination to get him back, and how, after he told her that he was going to Cornwall, her mother had let slip she had a great aunt in Polquillick and so she had followed him down.

"As I told you when I rang the Inn, I phoned Stella's mum after the wedding, pretending I was an old school friend, purely to find out where you were staying..."

"...Where were you when you rang the Inn?" interrupted George. "Were you in Cornwall then?"

"Yes, and I was ringing to warn you about Aunt Daisy, but I had to hang up because I could hear her coming downstairs after her bath..."

"...Bath!" interrupted George, again. "What at midnight?"

"Yes, she liked to take a bath late at night. She said it helped clear her mind and gave her clarity of thought. Would you like me to carry on? And if so, would you please stop interrupting me."

"Sorry, you were saying you'd phoned Stella's mum to find out where I was staying. Please go on from there."

"Right. When I arrived at Laburnum House, Aunt Daisy seemed quite pleased to see me and asked about Mum and Dad and other family things. I told her what I thought might be of interest, and then went on to tell her about you and how you'd jilted me. I think she was only half listening, that was until I showed her your picture. Then she suddenly went crazy, and insisted you were some bloke called Harry Timmins, well, his reincarnation, anyway. And I must admit there is a strong resemblance between you and Harry because Aunt Daisy has a photograph of him and Emily on the sideboard. I told her, her theory was utter nonsense, but she was adamant she was right and said she wanted revenge. She was angry that Harry seemingly was back, you see, but not her beloved Emily. So every night after that she tried to get into your head, George, by telepathy and on the Astral Plane or something like that. It was horrible. She had candles burning all around the room which cast evil, ghostly shadows on the walls. I was frightened. She insisted I gave her something which belonged to you, so I gave her the signet ring you used to wear on your little finger, which you gave to me last Easter. She would then sit and hold the ring while gazing at the photograph which I had of you. She transferred her thoughts regarding the last moments of Emily and Harry's lives into your dreams and then tried to get you to drown yourself."

"But that's ridiculous," said George, feeling very unnerved. "Why on earth should she want me dead for a second time, even if I was this Harry chap?"

"Because she hated you, or rather she hated Harry. She was evil, George, and stark staring mad, and that was because she bore a guilty secret."

Elsie took a sip of water from the glass on the table to ease her throat, hoarse from talking and crying.

"You're not making much sense, love," said George, holding her hands across the table. "I think you ought to start at the beginning and tell me exactly what goes on, or rather went on with Harry and Emily."

"Alright, but first I must thank you for diving into the sea and saving me. I'd be dead if it wasn't for you, and I'll always be

225

grateful, especially as I know when you hear the truth you'll probably hate me forever and who can blame you?"

"I'll never hate you," said George. "For God's sake, Elsie, part of me still loves you, but not enough for me to want to spend the rest of my life with you."

She looked away from his face and in a quiet, gentle voice, little more than a whisper, began to acquaint George with the facts he was desperate to hear.

"Emily and Aunt Daisy were identical twins and devoted to each other, although from what I've gathered they were very different in character. Daisy was bossy, whereas Emily was demure and shy. I think Aunt Daisy also felt she had to protect poor Emily, because when they were children a cart ran over Emily's foot and caused her to lose her little toe. For many years the poor girl had a limp, but eventually she learned to walk properly and by the time she was grown up, no-one would ever have known she had a disability…"

"…Good God, I saw her foot in my dream. Sorry, I've interrupted again, please go on."

Elsie bit her bottom lip. "The twins came from a good family. Their father was a cabinet maker with his own business and was doing very well. Her parents thought she and Harry would be a good match. He was the son of the village rector and planned to go into the church also. Emily went along with their wishes and he became her beau, as Aunt Daisy so old-fashionedly called it, and eventually they got engaged to be married. Emily was happy about the match, because at the time she was infatuated with Harry, he was very handsome you see, but then that goes without saying because he looked like you. Anyway, soon afterwards she met Joe Kernow and everything changed…"

"…Joe Kernow," interrupted George. "Sorry, but I saw him recently in the Mop and Bucket."

"Really, he's still around, then. I wondered if he might be. I expect he's retired now, but back then he was a fisherman; rough, a little dishonest and poor, but a real charmer apparently because Emily fell madly in love with him. But of course she couldn't tell her parents and certainly not Harry because she loved him too. So the only person she had to confide in was her sister, Aunt Daisy, who secretly hatched up a plan to dispose of Harry. She didn't like him, you see, and she knew he didn't like her. He was religious and that conflicted strongly with her leanings towards witchcraft, sorcery and so forth. Anyway, she knew he couldn't swim and so planned to drown him at sea. She made a small hole in the bottom of an old punt in which the family often went for a trip along the coast. She then put a small cork in the hole and waited for Harry to take Emily for a row. When she knew they were going she loosened the cork, knowing the movement of the boat would eventually force it out. Aunt Daisy reckoned that Harry would drown trying to save Emily, and when he had gone, Emily who was a good swimmer, would swim safely ashore, unaware that her sister had freed her from the commitment of marriage to Harry.

Aunt Daisy watched them row out to sea, went home for a while, and then returned to the beach to await the arrival of her sister. She waited for four hours, but Emily did not return. Her body was washed ashore a few days later, and so was Harry's. The boat was never seen again. And the rest, George, as you know, is history."

George sat stunned and silent. He could hear and feel every beat of his heart. His brain felt numb.

"George, please say something," Elsie pleaded. "Please, I've forgotten what it's like to see a friendly face. Oh, please don't look at me like that."

She burst into tears and sobbed for a full five minutes before George spoke.

"When did your aunt tell you all this?"

"Three or four days ago. When first she told me the story she implied it was a tragic accident, but over the past few days, as her anger deepened and everything got more intense, the truth started to come out. Especially after I pleaded with her to stop harassing you. Oh, George, I was utterly disgusted and horrified when I learned she'd been to Trengillion one night with her wretched bird and that she tried to get you to jump from the cliffs. I blame myself for that though, because I stupidly let slip you had been prone to sleepwalking when you were a child. She was delighted when I told her and said it would be a doddle to entice you from your bed if that was the case. I begged her to stop, but she just laughed and said she wasn't finished with you yet. After she told me the truth about Emily and Harry I threatened to go to the police, but she said if I did I'd find myself in much the same situation as Harry had been in."

"So, Ned was right, there was someone up on the cliffs that night and she must have spent the day at Trengillion as before that she posed as a fortune teller," mumbled George, still in a state of shock. "But I can't see why on earth she did that?"

"Well, actually she did dabble a bit in fortune telling when she was much younger, but she soon got tired of it. As I've already said she was into witchcraft too and dabbled with all sorts of dodgy forms of magic. Anyway, the reason Aunt Daisy was at the fete was because she saw an advert in the paper asking for a fortune teller. It was a bit short notice because someone had let them down or something like that. Aunt Daisy was over the moon to get the job, although she said she wasn't going to go to much trouble if she wasn't getting paid, and she only did it because she wanted to see you in the flesh. Oh God, I wish she hadn't, though, because that's when she saw poor Rose."

"Rose!" muttered George. "Now I am confused. Where does Rose fit into this?"

"Aunt Daisy said the spirits told her you were smitten with someone called Rose. So when she saw Rose wearing a necklace with her name on, during her fortune telling, she knew she was the girl in question. Oh dear, this morning, Aunt Daisy told me she went to the village a few days ago selling sprigs of lavender and saw Rose come out of the Inn. She then followed her to some stables and locked her in a tunnel or a passage or something like that. But honestly, George, I didn't know anything about it until today and that was when I found her laughing gleefully as she read the local paper, telling of poor Rose's body being found. She then told me what she had done, and how from the cliff tops she had watched her drown. Just after that the police arrived."

George stunned, felt sick and light headed.

"Oh God! She got the wrong Rose, Elsie. It was poor Rose Briers she must have meant to harm. I never had much to do with Rosemary Howard, the girl who drowned. I thought she was attractive, certainly, but much too shy for the likes of me. This is all going from bad to worse. Poor Rosemary! Poor, poor Rosemary. And what about Molly, Ned's mum? What on earth was the reason for her bad treatment? I can't see where she might fit into your story at all. And what about the locket? It had to be your aunt who sent that too."

"Yes, Aunt Daisy did send the locket. It was to frighten you; make you think you were going mad and to make everyone else think you were crazy too. There were two lockets, you see, both identical and each containing pictures of the twins. They had one each and always wore them, but Emily's must lie at the bottom of the sea now, because when she was found it was not around her neck. The one sent to you belonged to Aunt Daisy. But who is Ned's mum? I mean, why are you asking me about someone I don't know and have never met?"

"The woman your aunt abducted in the churchyard and left to drown, was Ned's mother."

Elsie's face turned very pale. "Oh, no, for God's sake, surely not? That's terrible. Whatever must Ned think of me now? Oh God, George. I never dreamt it was her. But she is alright, isn't she?"

"Yes, she is, but I can assure you Ned will not be very impressed when he hears the truth. Whatever the truth might be. I want an explanation, and it better be good."

A little colour returned to Elsie's cheeks. "The abduction of Ned's mum wasn't planned, it happened quite by chance. It all started, you see, not long after I spoke to you on the phone, on Ned's birthday night. Aunt Daisy was attempting to contact her dead sister, as often was the case since my arrival, although I think most of the time the voices she claimed to hear must have been in her head. Anyway, somehow that night she got her wires crossed with a woman also trying to make contact with the dead, who I now realise was Ned's mum, and she, Aunt Daisy that is, was hopping mad. Oh, George, it was horrible. Aunt Daisy really was a freak. When she went into one of her trances, or whatever they were, she could conjure up offensive smells and thick mists. Her old wrinkled face would contort as she could speak in a voice that would change pitch, tone and accent. Sometimes she spoke in a foreign tongue and often she became violent."

"I know," said George. "I witnessed her bad tempered display that night and it wasn't a pretty sight."

Elsie smiled. "That's a relief, at least you know I'm not lying."

George nodded. "Please carry on."

"Yes, yes, of course. Well, as I've already said, when she encountered Ned's mum in her spirit world, Aunt Daisy was absolutely furious. She started punching, kicking and screaming and lashing out, as you appear to have witnessed. She said the woman she'd encountered was an interfering, meddling old hag who should be taught a lesson. I was very scared at the time. I always dreaded that one day she might take out some of her anger on me, which she did eventually, as you witnessed when she tried to drown us both."

George nodded.

"Anyway, a few days after Ned's birthday, Aunt Daisy came across Ned's mum in the churchyard, quite by accident, I must add. She claimed she recognised her from the evening when she'd knocked her about, and was delighted the opportunity had arisen for her to dispose of her rival once and for all. We were both in the village at the time, you see. We had gone there in my car as I needed to go to the post office and Aunt Daisy wanted to go and view her handy work in the churchyard, as she had spent two hours the previous day tending the graves of Emily and Harry. Although she felt Harry wasn't really worthy of her efforts and only did his grave because she felt it was what Emily would have wanted."

"But she had never bothered to keep them tidy before," interrupted George. "They were in a right old state when we first saw them."

"That's because she'd pushed all the guilt, bitter memories and thoughts of her late sister away over the years. It wasn't until I arrived with your picture that it all came flooding back. Anyway, when I went to pick her up she told me to drive the car as near to the lichgate as possible. I didn't know why, but did as I was told without asking any questions. I then found she had knocked out Ned's mum, and I swear I didn't know who she was. Poor soul, she was lying on the grass, face down with a nasty gash on the back of her head. I was horrified, but fortunately, or unfortunately as the case might be, no-one was around so we were not seen. We took Ned's mum to the beach the following day in Uncle Vic's old van which she kept fettled for collecting chicken food in from a nearby farm, even though she didn't have a licence and never took a test. Aunt Daisy drove and we went the long way round as she didn't want anyone to see the van with Uncle Vic's name on the side. She parked it in an isolated spot where it would not be seen. Oh, thank God, Aunt Daisy's scheming did not go to plan. She was furious when she found her prisoner had escaped from the beach, and I like to think I helped a little by tying her up with granny knots which I deliberately kept loose."

George shook his head in disbelief.

"George, please don't think ill of me. It was all so harmless when I first came down here. I didn't want you or anyone else to be hurt, I just wanted you back. But Aunt Daisy was a formidable character and I was so afraid of her. Also she could read my thoughts. She was crackers and very dangerous as when all is said and done she was guilty of murder. Oh dear, I hope the other poor woman has not suffered too much, as I've no idea who she is, or why Aunt Daisy abducted her."

"Other woman!" puzzled George. "For God's sake Elsie how many were there?"

"Three," she cried, bursting into tears again. "Ned's mum, Rosemary Howard, and some other poor woman who Aunt Daisy had me throw in the cellar simply because she said she was a fool. But the poor soul had only come to the house to see if we might have a plaster for her blistered foot."

CHAPTER THIRTY ONE

Earlier in the day, Albert Treloar had been driving his tractor and potato digger up and down rows of King Edward potatoes in his cousin's field at Polquillick, bringing them to the surface ready for women and children from the village to pick and earn pocket money for their laborious work. The morning was fine and Albert seemed alone in the world, apart from gulls, eagerly following the tractor looking for tasty snacks unearthed by the digger.

As Albert turned his tractor around at the top of the field, the peace was suddenly disturbed by female voices screaming and angry men shouting. Albert abruptly stopped the engine. The location of the commotion appeared to be the ramshackle old house on the edge of the field which Albert knew belonged to Vic Rowe's widow, Daisy. Intrigued, he thoughtfully rubbed his chin. He was after all renowned for always keeping up with the latest gossip, therefore it was his bounden duty to investigate the situation, especially as the boys in blue were involved. For undoubtedly, he had seen the rooftop of a police car giving chase down the lane.

Albert climbed down from the tractor, crossed over the rutted field and walked towards the house where he scrambled over a grass covered, dry stone wall and nimbly dropped down into the large back garden. He glanced around, surprised to find he was in a long forgotten apple orchard, where a dozen or more trees peeped over the tops of rampant brambles, tall magenta coloured thistles, and long grass, gone to seed. Albert looked at the trees, each laden with ripening fruit and muttered to himself about the immorality of good food going to waste; for it was obvious by the state of the orchard, that fruit from those trees had not been harvested for many years.

He walked through the garden where flowering stems of scented mauve lavender peeped through the vast array of weeds and clumps of montbretia, and hens pecking in an area cordoned off with chicken wire. He stopped to admire the hens and then continued to make his way towards the house, but before he reached the building a loud squawk made him jump and caused him to dive in alarm into the long, dry grass. Crouching, he slowly lifted his head. Beside an enormous fuchsia bush, dripping with red and purple flowers, a large falcon flapped its strong, outstretched wings. Albert heaved a sigh of relief when he realised the bird was tethered to the perch on which it stood.

Regaining his stature, he quickly glanced around. When convinced no-one was home, he crept up to the wide-open back door and without hesitation climbed the steps and went inside.

The kitchen was empty and untidy but spotlessly clean. He went into the dining room which was sparsely furnished and looked as though it was seldom used.

He crossed the hallway into the sitting room and glanced around with interest. Like the kitchen it was untidy and cluttered with books and pictures. Albert picked up a photograph of a young couple holding hands. He scratched his chin. The young man in the picture seemed familiar. He grunted with satisfaction on realising whom it resembled; the man was very much like that George chap who was down on honeymoon with Ned, the teacher and his pretty wife.

He put the picture down on the sideboard between the wireless and a tray of half burned candles. He then walked across a faded square carpet, bordered by heavily painted floorboards, badly chipped. After taking a brief glance from the large bay window into the front garden, he left the room and from the foot of the stairs in the hallway, he called to see if anyone was upstairs.

Albert was greatly surprised to hear someone shout in response. But the voice did not come from above; it was muffled and came from below. He retraced his steps into the kitchen, looking for a way to get to a basement or cellar.

In the corner of the room he noticed a small door. He assumed it was the pantry, but on opening it, saw a flight of cold, stone steps. Intrigued, Albert felt around for a light switch and once the stairs were illuminated, he went down.

At the bottom was a door, shabby with peeling green paint, and a key in its lock. Albert turned the key, opened the door and peeped inside. On a mattress in the corner of a dingy, cold room, lay the body of a shivering woman, sobbing. He recognised her as one of the guests staying at the Inn. Albert felt a surge of pity as he crossed to her side and put his arm around her shoulders.

"Now, now, there lady," he whispered, gently. "Don't you cry anymore. Albert's here to look after you now and everything's going to be alright."

When Madge was finally rescued she was very weak. Twenty four hours with a diet of dry toast and tepid water had taken its toll both mentally and physically. As they carried her out on a stretcher into the daylight she was just thankful to be alive.

Gone were the aspirations to be in the limelight. She just wanted to pack her bags and go home, and if that meant spending the rest of her life without a partner, then so be it.

But as Madge discovered later in the day, every cloud has a silver lining. For Albert Treloar, confirmed bachelor and local farmer, was aware that once his sister, Dorothy, left home to marry Frank Newton, he would need someone to look after the house and him. Therefore, the fact that Madge was looking for a husband might prove to be to his advantage. She was after all not a bad looking woman and she did like a drink. And so that evening, Madge had a visitor at the hospital where she was staying overnight for observation. Albert arrived with a bunch of chrysanthemums picked from the farm gardens and, in the course of their conversation, both agreed, that when she was released from hospital the next day, they would meet up in the evening for a drink at the Ringing Bells Inn.

Rosemary Howard's parents formally identified the body of their only daughter soon after their arrival in Cornwall the following day. After which, as planned, they went to the Ringing Bells Inn with Fred to collect her belongings. Frank, who knew beforehand they would be calling, found himself doing unnecessary jobs throughout the day in an attempt to push from his mind the awkwardness of the forthcoming meeting, and for that reason also, he asked Dorothy not to go home to the farm, but to stay with him all day, so that she would be with him for moral support when the Howards arrived.

Fred's car pulled up in the afternoon on the cobbled area in front of the Inn shortly after closing time. Frank, who had just finishing washing the last glass, saw them through the window and quickly called to Dorothy as he went to the front door to greet them.

Rosemary's father, a tall distinguished looking man with auburn hair, shook hands with Frank and introduced himself. "I'm Jack Howard and this is my wife, Ada. I wish our visit could be a happier occasion. We wouldn't have come at all, but Ada, naturally wants Rosemary's things back."

"Of course," said Frank. "I understand. Won't you come in? We took the liberty of packing your daughter's belongings in her suitcase. I hope you don't mind."

"Not at all," said Jack Howard, taking his wife's arm as they crossed the threshold. "I'm glad. It's not a job either of us relished doing."

"Would you like a cup of tea?" asked Dorothy, nervously.

"Or something stronger?" Frank added.

"Tea would be lovely, thank you," said Jack. "Milk but no sugar for both of us."

"And you, Fred?" Dorothy asked.

"Tea, please and just a few grains of sugar."

Dorothy left for the kitchen while Frank led the Howards and Fred into the snug bar where the sun shone brightly on the polished tables and the perfume from a vase of phlox on the window ledge filled the air. Once all were seated an awkward silence prevailed only to be broken by Ada Howard, sobbing.

"Sorry," she said. "I just can't help it. I can't believe she's gone and I'll never see her again." She took a large handkerchief from her sleeve and gently blew her nose.

"If it helps at all to talk about Rosemary, then please do," Frank whispered, the torture of bereavement rekindled in his mind. "She were a lovely girl, we all liked her a great deal and we'd like to know something about her."

Dorothy entered the bar with a tray and handed out cups of tea and pieces of cherry cake.

"Thank you," said Ada. "It's very kind of you to speak well of Rosemary. She liked you all too and thought this village was heaven on earth. I don't know whether or not you know, but she came here because she got this notion into her head that she wanted to be a writer. Goodness knows why, it's not something I'd ever have

235

thought her to be particularly good at, although she did have a vivid imagination, especially when she was very young." Ada smiled. "She used to have an imaginary friend who she talked to day and night. I can't remember what she said she was called, but then it doesn't matter, does it?"

Jack placed his hand lovingly on his wife's hand and squeezed it gently.

"I think she took up with the writing idea as a way to impress that lad in the office where she worked," smiled Jack, trying to put on a brave face, "She was always talking about him. Sam said this, and Sam said that. He wrote poetry and very good it was too. She showed me a piece of his work and I was very impressed."

"One of the many things I find so sad about death," said Dorothy. "Is that when someone's gone then all their memories go with them. All dreams and aspirations, all life experiences, good and bad, because it doesn't matter how many times someone tells others of events in their life, it's impossible for anyone to imagine them accurately, simply because they weren't there. It's such a pity memories can't be passed from one person to another and shared. If they could, we'd all know a little more of life in days gone by."

The telephone rang. Frank rose, asked to be excused and left the bar to answer it. When he returned he found Dorothy looking at a postcard. She handed it to Frank. "This is the last piece of correspondence Ada and Jack received from Rosemary. Read it, it's really quite eerie."

Dear Mum and Dad,
I'm currently in a fishing village called Polquillick as you can see by the picture on the postcard. It's very pretty and very quaint, but I'm curious to know if I've ever been here before. Everything seems familiar. I knew where the school was, and the church, and the vicarage, and the pub. The beach is familiar too. In fact everything is, and I've never had such a feeling of Deja vu in my life. I'll ring you at the weekend.
Love you lots, Rosemary xx

"And had she ever been to Polquillick before?" asked Frank, handing back the card.

Jack shook his head. "No, she'd never even been to Cornwall until this summer, although she did know a little of the county through Ada's friend who retired down here recently with her husband. I believe they met up at some point."

"She was never one for the seaside," added Ada. "She didn't like the sea, partly because she appeared to be afraid of it and partly because she didn't want anyone to see her poor old foot."

"Her foot," repeated Fred.

Ada half smiled. "Yes. The poor girl had only four toes on her right foot, you see. She was born that way. Where the toe would have been was a white scar. The doctors and nurses were mystified when she was born. It didn't affect her walking though, so no-one ever knew there was anything wrong. But Rosemary was very conscious of it. Poor lamb!"

Jack suddenly slapped his thigh. "Daisy! That was the name of Rosemary's imaginary friend. It seemed when she was tiny this friend was a big part of her life. We had to take Daisy everywhere."

That same day, Ned and Stella had cause to celebrate. A letter offering Ned the job of headmaster at the village school, starting in January 1954, arrived with the early morning post.

Ned was thrilled when he opened it, but at the same time was a little hesitant.

"Think long and hard, Stella, before I accept. We must both be absolutely certain this is what we really want."

"I don't need to think long and hard, Ned. I love it here and so do you, in spite of the crazy goings on. There's only one answer to give."

Ned kissed her. "I'm so glad you said that," he whispered, "because deep down, I know it's right."

George was pleased for Ned and congratulated him, but his sincerity lacked lustre, for deep down, on top of everything else, the prospect of losing his best friend was not one he relished.

After breakfast he left the two honeymooners to plan their future together and went for a walk alone over the cliff tops to Polquillick. His visit to Elsie the previous afternoon had left him feeling drained and he had no wish to dampen the spirits of his friends with his misery. He knew also Rosemary's parents were due to visit the Inn and because he felt guilty, he did not want to be around when they called.

The day was dull and it looked like rain when he arrived in Polquillick. The tide was at its lowest and there were very few people on the beach. George made his way to the churchyard, sat on the grass and stared absently at the graves of Emily and Harry.

From along the footpath, he was aware of the shuffling of feet on the loose, dry gravel. When the footsteps stopped he glanced behind to see who was there.

"You're the spitting image of a fella I used to know many years ago," said an old man, gazing down at George.

"Joe?" muttered George, recognising him instantly. "Joe Kernow?"

"You know my name," said Joe, surprised. "How come?"

George gave a sardonic laugh and wondered just how much Joe knew regarding the deaths of Harry and Emily.

"I saw you in the Mop and Bucket, when I was there with friends enquiring about anyone in the village called Timmins. The landlord told us your name then."

Joe scowled. "That must be when I first saw you. It's a Timmins as you remind me of. Young Harry, he were drowned off this shore fifty three years ago and I hear at last the sea has taken that old witch too."

"Daisy Rowe," muttered George. "Is that who you mean?"

"Yeah, she were an evil old woman and a bad influence on poor, sweet Emily. But what do you know of Daisy Rowe, for I take it you're not from these parts?"

"No, I'm a Londoner, but I think you'll find I'm much more familiar with the past than you might ever realise."

Joe sat down on the grass, eager to hear more. George then repeated what Elsie had told him the previous afternoon.

Joe listened intently, nodded throughout. "I did know, at least I guessed it were something like that. I didn't go to either of their the funerals, of course; the likes of me wouldn't have dared show their face, but I saw Daisy here by Emily's grave a few days later when I come up with some flowers. She were in a right old state and kept muttering something about it weren't supposed to have happened like that. I guessed she were involved somehow but didn't want to know any details. I couldn't see the point, and it wouldn't have brought poor Emily back, anyway. Harry's family had a rough time too, his death destroyed the lives of his parents. His father were the vicar here and the loss of his son was the loss of his faith. He left the church a broken man and spent the rest of his days scraping a living on old Ed Bray's farm, and I believe he never set foot in a church again.

Funny thing was, his loss of faith was the beginning of mine. I changed my ways after Emily'd gone. I drank much less, tried to be an honest man and helped others whenever I could. It were my way of letting Emily's influence rub off on me. I never spoke to Daisy again after all that happened. She married Vic Rowe a few years later and I never breathed a word to him or anyone else about what I thought she'd done. She were a silly woman, cos even if dear Emily had survived we would never have got wed. I couldn't have given her the things she were used to, so it wouldn't have been fair to her. And if we had married, she'd have soon got fed of being a poor man's wife. I never took a wife m'self, though, for all that, cos I did love Emily, and now I've nothing to remember her by except fading memories. I don't even have a picture of her."

George slipped his hand inside the pocket of his jacket and pulled out the silver locket.

"Take this, Joe," he said, handing him the locket. "Daisy sent it to me trying to make me think I was going mad. Take it, for it means very little to me."

Joe took the locket and opened it with a bemused laugh. "Well, if you've no objection, I shall have to get rid of Daisy. I can't be doing with having a picture of her about my person."

"Of course, but how can you tell them apart? They look identical to me."

"The eyes, the difference were in the eyes. You can't tell the colours of course in these old pictures. But Emily's eyes were a warm, rich, hazel brown. Daisy's were green and cold. Daisy also carried a bit more weight than Emily. See," he said, holding the locket in front of George. "If you look closer you can see one has a broader face than the other. That's Emily on the right."

From his pocket he took out a penknife and removed the picture on the left.

239

"Do you want this?" he asked, having laid it on the palm of his hand.

"No," said George. "No, definitely not."

"Good," laughed Joe. He tore the picture of Daisy into tiny pieces and threw it over his shoulder, closed the locket, but then sighed deeply. "It's very good of you, but I don't really think I ought to take this. Folks will think I've nicked it or something like that."

"No-one will ever see it," said George. "And if they do then tell them the truth. I feel awful over all this, as though some of it was my fault. You having the locket might be a slight recompense for my involvement, as sometimes I even wonder if I am the reincarnation of Harry Timmins."

Joe laughed. "I don't believe in that sort of stuff m'self, but if you are, then you can congratulate yourself on getting revenge on the woman who caused your death the first time round, and that of Emily too, for that matter. Not many folks can say that. Daisy Rowe would be alive today, so it seems, were it not for the likeness there is between you and Harry. Justice is done at last; that's the way I see it. You've nothing at all to feel guilty about, young man."

Laughing, much amused by Joe's logic, George pulled from his pocket Molly's postcard and handed it to Joe. "Are you able to name anyone on this picture, I wonder?"

Joe glanced at the card with interest. "Where did you get this?" he asked, wiping the lenses of his glasses on the sleeve of his old shirt, before taking a closer look.

"A friend of mine bought it from the gift shop, here in Polquillick, but we're not able to identify anyone on it, other than Emily, that is."

"I've never seen this one before. But that's me there," he said, pointing with a shaky hand. "By my boat and next to Emily. Good God, nearly all the other chaps here are fishermen, or at least they were, most are dead and gone now. Ah, but that fella there, by the little rowing boat with the oars in his hand, that's Emily's father. Good God! That's the very boat she and Harry were drowned in."

"Is Harry on the picture?" asked George, hopefully.

"No, he's not, that's odd. But look Daisy is, there, sitting on a crab pot near to the boat and her father. That horse and cart by Reg Pascoe's boat, belonged to Jim Hendy the coalman. That's Jim o' course standing beside the horse. He were a good friend of mine, we went to school together, but we were both dunces and didn't learn a great deal. And bless me, that chap over there is Vic Rowe, the fella Daisy married, and the young woman next to him is his sister Gabby. She were a real beauty in her day. She's long gone from here, though. She married an up-country bugger and left the area, so I don't know whether or not she's still alive. She might be though, cos she were younger than Vic."

"What happened to Vic Rowe? I know Daisy was a widow, but wonder if he also died in suspicious circumstances."

"No, he died a few years back after a heart attack," said Joe, handing the card back to George. "He were a builder, had his own business and worked too damn hard. He bought Laburnum House for Daisy and himself to live in. It were a magnificent place when he were alive, but I hear it's gone to rack and ruin since his parting. They never had any young 'uns; rumour has it Daisy were barren, but I don't know if that were true or not."

They walked back into the village together, and parted with a handshake at the bottom of the cliff path, after which George, climbed the steep steps and began his walk back to Trengillion. By the Witches Broomstick, he stopped and looked down onto the rocks below. He thought of Rosemary. Even if he should bear no guilt regarding the death of Daisy Rowe, he could not help but feel partly responsible for the death of poor Rosemary Howard. Then there was Elsie, what a rotten time she must have been through, and all of it brought about by his selfishness and not wanting to get married and live in Manchester.

When George arrived back in Trengillion he went looking for Ned and Stella to discuss further their future. For he knew he had shown little enthusiasm over Ned's new job and he felt guilty because of it. He found them, as anticipated, at Rose Cottage, sitting in the kitchen drinking tea with Molly, chewing over the events of the past few days and the latest good news.

"George," said Molly, with a note of excitement in her voice as he peeped around the open back door. "Come in and join us, there's plenty of tea in the pot and it's still quite fresh."

George sat down at the table. "I suppose you're thrilled to know you'll have Ned and Stella living nearby soon," he said to Molly.

"Thrilled! I'm over the moon, and I didn't even know he'd applied for the job. He's a dark horse, just like his father, but then that's hardly surprising, is it?"

"Have you forgiven Dad, at last?" Ned asked, surprised by the lack of vehemence in her voice.

Molly laughed. "I suppose I have. I'm happy, so I've nothing to complain about, and to have you and Stella living close by is more than I could ever have wished for. Forgive and forget, that's what I say."

"And about time too," agreed Ned, emphatically.

"Oh, before I forget to tell you, you'll never guess who was round this morning?" chuckled Molly, quickly glancing at their blank faces. "Mabel, Mabel Thorpe, she came round to confront me over the letter. She said she knew it was from me before she'd finished reading it because she recognised the handwriting. Apparently, Frank has a postcard on the mantelpiece which I sent when I last went up to Clacton to visit Jack and Gwen, and of course being nosey, she'd read it."

"Oh no, what did she say?" grinned Ned, aware that it could not have been too offensive for his mother was smiling.

"Well, she was flattered that I thought her capable of causing such mayhem, although she said, she'd probably not be able to laugh about it if she was still a suspect and the real culprit had not been found. But the ridiculous thing is, at long last she has come to terms with her name and can even see the funny side of it. Although that was brought about by Godfrey Johns. He's asked her to marry him, you see, so she could yet change her name to his."

"Godfrey Johns! But they've only known each other for a few weeks," spluttered Ned. "How can they even think of marriage?"

"I suppose when you're in your seventies every day is precious and you don't have time to dilly-dally around," answered Molly. "They've known each other for longer than that, though. They first met donkey's years ago when she came on holiday with her late husband. She's seventy seven by the way."

"So you've found out her age, too," grinned Stella. "Just goes to prove the old adage right, 'everything comes to he who waits'."

"And is she going to marry Godfrey Johns?" Ned asked.

"She's not made her mind up yet, but she's told him she'll let him know before she returns home next week."

"Are you alright, George?" Stella asked, conscious that he was very quiet. "You look a little pale."

"I'm fine, just a bit drained, that's all. I saw Fred's car parked outside the Inn when I walked by. I suppose he's there now with Rosemary's poor parents. It's silly to say, but I don't feel like I'm me today. It's most odd and I can't explain. I suppose it's just that too much has happened in the last few days and my poor brain can't take it all in."

"Did you go for a walk?" Ned asked, concerned for his friend's lack of vivacity.

"Yes, I went to Polquillick and of all people I bumped into Joe Kernow. He's a nice old boy, we had quite a long chat about the past and he helped me in a way come to terms with some of this summer's events. It has after all been the most peculiar holiday I've ever had in my life. I gave him the locket. He didn't have a picture of Emily, you see, which I thought was very sad. I also showed him the postcard and he was able to identify lots of people including himself, which I'm sure you'll find most interesting."

George, with renewed exuberance, enthusiastically, put his hand inside his pocket, pulled out the card and laid it on the table ready to point out the faces identified by Joe. But the scene on the postcard had changed. The beach was no longer sepia and old, it was brightly coloured, glossy and new, with *Greetings from Polquillick*, printed in red across the top.

CHAPTER THIRTY TWO

Molly, having heard and digested the story of Elsie's part in her abduction, felt she had suffered enough and refused to press charges. Madge, likewise, considered that Elsie was not at all responsible for the treatment she had received and was only following the commands of Daisy Rowe. In fact, she told the police that Elsie had treated her with kindness when the old woman was not in the cellar.

The police were relieved. For Elsie's involvement in Daisy Rowe's attempts to force George to jump from the cliffs and drown himself, via brainwashing on the Astral Plane or with the use of magic and sorcery, was in their opinion, absurd, and it was agreed such a case would never stand up in a court of law. Besides, George, like Molly and Madge, did not want to press charges either.

It was also agreed that foul play regarding the unfortunate death of Rosemary Howard could not be proved. For Elsie swore on the bible that she had not been involved and had known nothing about it until she had found her aunt laughing about the body's discovery when she read about it in the local paper. The verdict therefore would be accidental, and Elsie was free to go.

George, on her release, drove her to the railway station in Ned's car, as her Hillman Minx was a write-off having spent many hours on the sea bed. Rose, on hearing this was distraught. The fact that George had rescued Elsie was hard enough to swallow, even though Rose conceded no considerate person would leave an old girlfriend to drown, whatever the reason for their parting. But for him to take her to the station, she concluded, could mean only one thing. As soon as he returned to London they would get back together and all would be lost.

Rose shuffled into the kitchen and washed the dishes. Her eyes were red from crying and her head ached. The summer was fast coming to an end. Rosemary Howard was dead. George was lost, and she had still to find new accommodation. Could anything else possibly go wrong?

There had, however, been some good news amidst the gloom. She was delighted Ned had been offered the job as headmaster and that he had accepted the position. It would have pleased Reg also to know that someone he had liked and admired, was to teach and help nurture the children of Trengillion, to whom he had been so dedicated.

She washed and dried Freak's bowl, filled it with fresh food, placed it on the kitchen floor, opened the back door and called his name, but he did not respond. Rose sighed, even Freak seemed to have deserted her, for she guessed he had gone down the road to Rose Cottage to see Molly. He was always made a fuss of when he went there and had been ever since he had found Molly lying on the beach in the rain. Molly believed she owed her life to Freak, hence they were the best of friends.

As she tipped away the washing up water there was a knock on the door.

Rose dried her hands, expecting it to be Bill Burleigh the baker as it was time for his delivery. But it was not Bill on the doorstep, smiling with her usual cottage loaf. It was George.

Rose was speechless as she tried to straighten her uncombed hair.

"Well, aren't you going to ask me in?"

"Yes, yes, of course. Sorry, please come in."

He entered the hallway, crossed into the sitting room and sat down on the settee.

"You've been crying. Your eyes are all red."

"No, no, I've not, I had something in my eye. Would you like a coffee or a tea? I'll just go and pop the kettle on."

"No, don't, not just yet. Later perhaps. Come and sit down."

He patted the seat beside him on the settee.

"Well, thank goodness that's all over," he said, taking a cigarette packet from his pocket and offering one to Rose, now seated by his side.

"Thank goodness what's all over?"

George gave her a puzzled look. "Well, Elsie of course. Thank goodness she's gone. Although I do feel dreadfully sorry over what happened to her, poor love. I wanted to take her to the station myself to make sure she got on the damn train. It seemed to me that as long as she was in Cornwall, things would never be able to get back to

245

normal, and so her departure was the best way of ending this nightmare."

A gentle smile of rejuvenated hope crossed Rose's face. "But I thought perhaps you and she might get..." the words faded away.

"What!" he spluttered, lighting the cigarettes. "Me and Elsie again? Good God, no. She was never the right girl for me, although it hurts me to think, she loved me so much that she was prepared to go to any lengths to get me back. Silly Elsie! No, after much deliberation I've come to the conclusion there's only one woman I'm interested in and she's sitting right here on this settee."

Rose, dumbfounded, could neither speak nor move.

"You do like me, don't you, Rose?" he asked, alarmed by her lack of response.

"Like you," gulped Rose, tears prickling the backs of her eyes. "Of course I like you, but..."

"That's great then, because you're coming back to London with me. I'm going home soon, but I can't bear the thought of leaving without you."

"What!" she laughed. "But how, I mean what..."

"Oh, stop babbling and come here," he said, pulling her towards him. "I think you and I have a great future together. I always have ever since the moment we first met, but I had to play it cool because Ned said I wasn't to mess you around, and recent events haven't exactly given me of a chance to pay you much attention. You were always on my mind, though, Rose, and it was thinking of you that helped pull me through the Emily nightmare. And now Daisy Rowe's gone, hopefully I'll be able to pick up the pieces and live a normal life."

"But, if I go with you to London, where would I live and work. I've very little money and..."

George slipped off the settee and knelt at her feet.

"Will you marry me, please, Rose? I don't want to be a crusty old bachelor any more. I want a wife, and not just any old wife, I want you. Oh God! Please say yes or I'll die from a broken heart."

Rose leapt forward, dropped her cigarette in the ashtray and flung her arms around his neck.

"Yes," she choked. "Yes please! George, I love you more than you could ever imagine. This is crazy, just an hour ago my future looked very bleak, but now I have a purpose in life again. I promise I'll make you a good wife. Oh, if only everyone in the world could be as happy as I am at this very minute." She burst into tears. "Poor Rosemary! If she was still alive, then everything would be perfect now. I'll never forget her, though, or think of her without a feeling of guilt."

"I know," sighed George, rising from the floor to sit by Rose's side. "She takes up a lot of my thoughts too, especially after what Frank told us about the meeting with her parents. Do you think she was the reincarnation of Emily Penberthy or are the similarities just a coincidence?"

"We'll never know," whispered Rose, firmly grasping both his hands, "But if Emily and Rosemary were one and the same, then Daisy Rowe drowned her own sister, not once, but twice."

The following Sunday, Ned, Stella, Rose and George put on their best clothes and went to church for the christenings of Tony and John Collins, after which the small group went up to Long Acre Farm for a tea party. As Gertie had hoped the weather was fine, and so tea was served outside on the lawn. Ned was enthralled, the views were spectacular, the sea was clearly visible, and the mine at Penwynton also.

"What a glorious spot," he said to Cyril Penrose, doing the rounds, refilling glasses with cider. "You must love it here."

Cyril nodded. "We do. We've lived here ever since we got married and that's nearly twenty three years now." He placed the cider jug on the grass and sat down beside Ned. "I'm a little worried about the future, though. We don't own the farm, you see. It belongs to the Penwynton Estate and when the old man's gone, goodness only knows what'll happen to us. He's turned seventy now and is not in the best of health"

"I see. I didn't realise you were tenants. So does he have children to inherit the place when he's gone?"

"No, but he has a great nephew living in Canada, of all places, and it's likely it will go to him. I don't expect he'll ever come and live over here, though, which means the whole lot will probably be sold off and even split up. There are a couple of other farms as well as this one, you see. Not to mention acres and acres of land and several cottages. We're all a little worried, I can tell you that."

"And I hear Penwynton House itself is in a poor state of repair," said Ned. "Oh dear! Hopefully the old man will live for a good many more years yet."

"Hear, hear," laughed Cyril. "You're right about the house though. The roof leaks in several places, it's very damp, the grounds are unkempt, and the stable block and most of the out-buildings are starting to tumble down. The old man's losing interest in the place; it's becoming a great burden to him, especially knowing he has no immediate family to leave it to. He never got wed, you see, although he had plenty of lady friends in his younger days, but he never married any of them. He said he didn't want to settle down, but I know he regrets it now. He's a nice old boy. It's a shame he didn't have any kids, but then that's life!"

When Cyril moved on to refill the glass of Pat Dickens, Ned sauntered over to a shady spot beneath a plum tree laden with green fruit yet to ripen, where the twins slept in their pram and the women sat on the grass nearby.

"Come and sit beside me, Ned," insisted Gertie, patting the blanket on which she was sitting, "I've seen very little of you this summer and there are a hundred and one things I want to ask you, although for the life of me I can't think of any of them just now."

Ned did as he was told, although he was conscious Stella may well disapprove. He need not have worried, however, for Stella was deep in conversation with Betty and Rose, both making suggestions as to how she should have her hair styled.

Gertie linked her arm through his. "I win," she said.

"Win what?" asked Ned, puzzled.

"The argument over whether it's best to live in the town or the country. I win, because you're leaving smelly old London for lovely Trengillion, not of course that I blame you for that. I'm really pleased, you'll be able to teach our boys. Their future is in your hands and I think that's wonderful."

She leaned forward and pecked him on the check, "I hope we'll be friends forever, Ned Stanley," she giggled, "because I'll always have a huge soft spot for you."

"Oh God, have you been on the cider?" asked Percy, sitting by her side, "You females are supposed to be on the tea, the booze is for us men. Sorry, Ned, if she's molesting you."

Gertie let go of Ned's arm and put her arms around Percy's neck, "I've not been drinking cider, only tea. See, smell my breath." She breathed in his face and then kissed him. "Cider indeed," she giggled. "And I wasn't molesting Ned either, Percy Collins. I was just telling him how thrilled I am to know he'll be teaching our boys."

Ned, Stella, Rose and George left for London a week later, Rose having informed the local authorities that she was leaving the furniture and fittings in The School House as she had sold them to the next tenants, Mr and Mrs Edward Stanley. She also left behind Freak. For after a great deal of thought and much soul searching, she decided he would have a much better life if he remained in Cornwall. And as Molly was only too thrilled to have him move in with her and the major, it seemed the perfect solution.

Three and a half months later, Ned and Stella arrived back in the village and took up residence in The School House. And two days after that they were joined by newlyweds, George and Rose Clarke.

George had with him a Christmas card from Elsie, in which she had written:

My dear George,

I've just heard on the grapevine that you have married your Rose. Congratulations to you both. You probably know, that following my dreadful experience in Polquillick, I moved back home to Manchester and lumbered myself on Mum and Dad, as I simply had to be as far away from Cornwall as possible. Things have turned out well for me, though, as I had the good fortune to meet up with a childhood sweetheart of mine back in September, and I'm sure you'll be relieved to know, we got married last week, therefore I'll never, ever, pester you again.

Thank you once more for saving my life, I'll never forget you. Please remember me to Ned and Stella. Have a lovely Christmas, all of you, and a wonderful, wonderful New Year.

Lots of love, Elsie and Mike. x.
PS. It's raining today and has been for much of the week, I thought you'd like to know that. Elsie x

Christmas was fast approaching, the days were very short and the weather mild and dry. On Christmas Eve, however, as darkness fell, a few flakes of snow gently fell from the heavens onto the rooftops of Trengillion.

In the evening, Ned, Stella, Rose and George left The School House to walk the short distance to the Inn. In front of the old building they stopped and gazed up at the bright light glowing from the lantern over the Inn's doorway, where snowflakes swirled in the breeze before fluttering to the ground and vanishing without trace. Its simplicity seemed a heart-warming reminder of the star and the true meaning of Christmas.

Inside the Inn, lit only by candlelight, they found the villagers congregated to launch the festivities in the bars. Branches of holly and ivy hung around the fireplace in the snug, and in the public bar, mistletoe dangled sporadically from the old black beams. By the double doors, a Christmas tree, stretched from floor to ceiling, proudly decorated with multi coloured baubles, bells and strands of tinsel. And on the strongest branches, clipped firmly into place, candles burned and flickered in the draughts caused by the movement of people. The pleasant scent of pine filled the air and mingled with the woody smell of burning logs. There was much laughter, much shaking of hands, much hugging and kissing.

Dorothy Newton offered them a warm mince pie as they removed their coats. She looked a very different woman. On her face she wore a little make-up; her hair had been styled by Betty, and she was wearing a beautiful dress of red velvet.

"The candles are enchanting," gasped Stella, charmed. "They're so Christmassy, and the bars look really beautiful too. Well done!"

"It's become a tradition to have the Inn illuminated by candlelight on Christmas Eve," laughed Dorothy. "It started ten years ago during the War, when gale force winds brought the power cables down. Not to be outdone, Frank lit candles and everyone liked it so much he's done it ever since, although there are far more now than there would have been that first Christmas."

Frank, behind the bar, wearing a brightly coloured waistcoat, gave her a loving look as she returned to his side and served Pat Dickens with a round of drinks.

Ned felt a slight pang of guilt for grudging her a place at the Inn when he had first encountered her working there. It was quite apparent that she was good for Frank and good for the Inn too, and it was heart-warming to see that old twinkle back in Frank's eyes.

Sitting at the bar were more newlyweds, Mabel and Godfrey Johns, married in early October, and Madge and Albert Treloar, married in late November. In a dimly lit corner, not caring what went on around them, sat Milly, and Johnny, who had agreed to take on the post office, his decision being swayed by the news that Milly would also be coming to live in the area on Albert's farm.

Betty and Peter, with plans for a spring wedding, mingled with everyone. Frank had insisted that Betty have the evening off work to spend with Peter, for which she was grateful. Nevertheless, every time they were busy on the bar or Frank had to go to the cellar to change a barrel, Betty would rush to their aid by serving and washing a few glasses. Such was her dedication to the Newtons.

Gertie and Percy were not in, they were at home preparing for the twins' first Christmas.

Annie and Fred Stevens, likewise, were at The Police House wrapping gifts ready to surprise and delight their children the following morning.

Ned, Stella, Rose and George went into the snug and sat near to the blazing fire. Seeing it brought a lump to Ned's throat, as he recalled the first encounter he'd had with the Inn almost two years before. So much had happened since then. So many people had come and gone."

In the public bar carol singing began, during which the major and Molly arrived. Molly warmed her hands by the fire while the major insisted on buying the two young couples a drink each. Molly had her usual gin, Ned and George, a pint, and Rose a whisky and dry ginger. But Stella, with a broad smile on her face, asked for an orange juice.

"Orange juice! On Christmas Eve!" spluttered the major.

Ned and Stella, with arms around each other giggled, and then turned to look at Molly who stood in front of the fire with a dropped jaw. Tears welled up in her eyes.

"You don't need to tell me," she squealed. "I know what you're going to say. Heavens above, I'm going to be a granny!"

THE END

Lightning Source UK Ltd.
Milton Keynes UK
UKHW02f0856181117
312887UK00006B/772/P